BRONZE LIG

Lindsay Townsend

ROMANCE

BookStrand
www.BookStrand.com

A SIREN-BOOKSTRAND TITLE

IMPRINT: Romance

BRONZE LIGHTNING

Copyright © 2009 by Lindsay Townsend

ISBN-10: 1-60601-274-6

ISBN-13: 978-1-60601-274-1

First Printing: June 2009

Cover design by Jinger Heaston

All cover art and logo copyright © 2009 by Siren-BookStrand, Inc.

Printed in the U.S.A.

PUBLISHER

www.BookStrand.com

BRONZE LIGHTNING

LINDSAY TOWNSEND

Chapter 1

Krete, c.1562 BC. Summer.

A dusty path rambled from the palace at Phaistos down to the sea, where ships heavy with oil and wine cut the sparkling water between Krete and the rich lands of Pharaoh's Egypt. Down the path ran a youth in a messenger's tunic, sweating in the heat. When he reached a parched field where a bronze-skinned girl with dark tousled hair leaned on a gate watching a piebald bull, he stopped and called out. 'Sarmatia! Hey, Sarmatia?'

The shout broke the fragile alliance. This time, thought Sarmatia, she could make no spirit bond with the beast that would take part in the ceremony. Perhaps the Goddess was angry. Whatever, it would be skill, not trust, that would keep her youngsters alive. If only the herald had not come then.... Knowing her face would show nothing of her mood, she turned.

'Kutatos!' Delight shattered unease: she and Kutatos had been fellow-initiates. 'How are you? Your family? Your wife?'

Kutatos stammered replies, painfully conscious, it seemed, of the gulf between them. Trainer of the Rite of Passage, she would risk her life through not one initiation but many. Only when he came to the message did his voice deepen into the ringing tones of the herald.

'Lord Luktos sends greeting to you and your family...'

'My gratitude is boundless.' Sarmatia gave the expected response, wishing Luktos' messages were not so long-winded.

At last Kutatos came to the point. 'Where may strangers watch the Bull

Rite in safety?'

The answer was 'Nowhere', but she felt too kindly towards Kutatos to give it. Thinking over the Bull Rite, she wondered who Luktos' guests were. Kretans were not eager to witness the Rite of Passage. The courtyard where the bull-riding took place was fenced in by wicker hurdles, yet at any time the bull might charge into the crowd. In the past onlookers had been gored. The death-threat was common to all, binding the people together. Other races had heard of the rite, but few foreigners knew much of the ceremony.

'Who are these strangers, Kutatos?'

'An Egyptian nobleman, Ramose, with his wife and son, and Fearn, the northerner. Ramose and Fearn are tending Minos. I understand that it was Fearn who asked—Luktos sweats to refuse him nothing.'

'I know.' Minos, ruler of Krete, had been ill for over a year and the Kretan healers had despaired of him. They had sent word to the court of Pharaoh in Egypt and to Fearn, the foremost healer of the northern Isle of Stones, begging for help.

Despite her disquiet over Fearn's unusual request, Sarmatia was intrigued. Finally she might meet this man from the edge of the world, who had refused Minos' gold and argued, when the herald first found him, that his own people needed him—he could not leave the many for the sake of one. So matters might have stood had not Minos' herald let slip that the palace healers had begun to desert for fear of contracting the disease. Hearing this, Fearn had decided to set out at once for Krete.

Sarmatia remembered, but hid her curiosity. 'So today,' she remarked dryly, 'I must tell my initiates to perform for Fearn?'

'No, there'll be no impiety,' replied Kutatos, glancing from Sarmatia to the meadow as the bull lifted its head and bellowed. 'Fearn and Ramose know what's fitting.'

'Do they know the risk?'

'They do. My lord Luktos explained it at great length.'

Sarmatia laughed. For Kutatos' sake and their shared initiation, when Kutatos had seen that she kept her feet after tumbling over the bull's horns, she gave her answer.

'Tell Luktos to take his guests to the back of the court, by the pillars. No harm will come to them, I promise.'

Kutatos made his farewells, disappearing behind the long barn of the palace dairy. Sarmatia tried to put the matter from her mind and, wrapping herself in her hooded cloak, she walked back along the side of the meadow to the southern gate of the palace and slipped into the main courtyard.

The heat was so intense it stopped her breath and burned the soles of her bare feet. The sun had been beating down all morning on the stone flags of the court and now the decorated floor—painted with scenes of past bull rites—shimmered, the brightly rendered figures rippling as though alive. Inside the wicker fencing the area was deserted, silent but for the steady pulse of the cicadas.

Here in a few hours' time would be life: the growing of child into adult in those moments that it took to face a charging bull and grasp its horns. The instant the initiate was tossed into the air by the bull he began the Rite of Passage, tumbling through space as through life, without knowledge of the future or his fate. When he landed on earth, it would be away into adult life. Only one such tumble was needed and then the initiate could leave the sacred court. Many, though, elected to stay and help those who were left, sometimes performing the ritual again and 'riding the bull over', as the saying went. Sarmatia had ridden the bull many times but, after six years and rising towards eighteen, she felt herself stiffer than she used to be. Now she was content simply to remain with the initiates and keep an eye on them. Each time the ceremony was performed the bull was a different one.

Sarmatia sighed, thinking again of the piebald bull. He was big and his horns were strong, which was good, yet he was very quick at turning and his mind was closed. She had tried and failed to discover it. Standing in the stuffy bull court, the girl was tempted to join the crowds about the altar and make sacrifice to the gods, but she would almost certainly be recognized. And if word came out that the trainer was worried, how would her youngsters feel? No, the risk of their lives in the rite was sacrifice enough.

She felt suffocated by the cloak and flung it off to carry under her arm. Touching her brow in salutation to the court, Sarmatia turned briskly and went back amongst the people. There were whispers immediately as she was seen for, as was her custom on the day of an initiation, she wore the costume of the Bull Rider. Eyes picked at her linen loincloth, the bronze waist-belt and silver earrings, her naked breasts and scarred sides. All that was missing were the gold ankle bells and the face paint which proclaimed her kin-group. Only a few more steps and the show would be finished. The girl heard a farmer mutter, 'The Passage-Mistress herself, that's a good omen,' and was content.

* * * *

When she next entered the courtyard, Sarmatia was with the initiates and flute players, coming in to music and the greetings of the crowd. Glancing amongst her own family, she noted with relief that her brother Tazaros had kept his promise and stayed away. She always feared that if the bull threatened her, Tazaros would forget he was ten years past the rite and come into the courtyard himself. Breathing more easily, despite the blood heat of the afternoon, she started the seven initiates on their warm-up of somersaults and tumbles, doing a few herself to keep in practice and to ease the slowness out of her spine.

As she tumbled the length of the court, quickening with the music of the flutes, Sarmatia came right side up by the rear of the courtyard. She looked between the pillars and there was the Egyptian, with his wife and son. A child: was it wise to have children here? Sarmatia wondered, though no one else questioned the custom. The boy had his nose pressed against the wicker hurdles, but his father rose above them, straight, like a poplar.

Kutatos had not told her that Ramose was Nubian, dark as a rare pearl. And the man beside him, fully as tall, white as Ramose was black— her breath hissed in her throat when she looked on Fearn for the first time. The healer had red hair, a red-gold beard. He glittered in that fierce Kretan sunlight. A bright stare mirrored hers then Fearn bowed his head.

Sarmatia spun away and was gone, somersaulting over her hands and landing with a soft clash of gold ankle bells. Their meeting of eyes had lasted no more than a breath, yet it kept returning to haunt her as the music shrilled to a climax and the piebald bull was let into the court. Even as the flute players left and the Bull Rite began, her gaze was drawn to the back of the courtyard.

Three of the seven had completed their Passage and two were gone: the fourth initiate should have been ready. As the bull came to a jolting stop at one end of the court, pawed restively and licked the painted flags, Sarmatia motioned to a creamy-skinned, gray-eyed girl. The youngster backed up a step. The bull raised its head, its horn scraping against a pillar. The girl blanched and looked wildly about, ready to run. In three strides Sarmatia made up the space between them and gripped her arm. Unseen by the families, she pressed the flat of her dagger into the initiate's side. Cruel to be kind, she threatened.

'This or the bull if you show your back, Pero!' she whispered, turning the blade for the girl to feel its edge. 'The only way out is through the horns.' Whatever Sarmatia's private disgust and unease, custom and the crowd demanded it. They would not forgive Pero if she failed.

'I can't!' Pero was shaking and near tears. A low murmur ran around the watching crowd like a wind through barley: the mob and the bull would not wait much longer. Pierced by pity, Sarmatia squeezed the girl's thin shoulder. 'Do you want to be a child all your life?' she asked gently.

'Sarmatia, I can't! Those horns, they're like knives, and the bull— Oh, Mother!' Pero's voice cracked. 'It's looking for me!' The bull had trotted out of the shadows at the back of the courtyard.

Sarmatia stepped in front of Pero, shielding the girl. 'Look, it's nothing.' She ran forward, clapping her hands.

The bull halted and its head slewed round towards them, a brown forelock covering one eye. 'To me!' she shouted.

The beast dropped its great horns. She heard the people applaud. With an explosion of dust the bull charged. She felt its hot, closed mind surrounding her. For an instant skill deserted her. She remembered she was too old for the Bull Rite. A blaze of gold spilled from the bull's horns, instinct returned and with it sureness. She caught the horns and let herself rise. Time and the horizon fell back, she could see the blue vault of heaven, the red-mouthed 'O' of the crowd, a flash of red-gold hair as Fearn turned his head, following her descent. Her feet touched the bony rump of the bull, she tucked in her arms and somersaulted off, running forward as she landed.

Behind her the beast gave a sulky grunt, swept this way and that with its horns and lashed its tail. Pero worked her way into its sight, swaying her hips to keep quick and supple. The piebald ambled off in the opposite direction then suddenly spun about and bore down on the girl in another burst of speed. Sarmatia moved to cover Pero's tumble and signalled to the remaining initiates to do the same. She heard the girl seize the bull's horns, with a great smack on each palm, and saw her tossed, arching like a dolphin in mid-air and rising clear of the deadly gilded horns. The time of peril would be when the girl landed. If Pero caught an ankle or winded herself, Sarmatia knew she would have to be in quickly to distract the beast.

There was a shower of dark hair and Pero touched earth to a roar from her family. Sarmatia grabbed her arm and pulled her clear, but was not fast enough: already the bull had skidded round. Too late, Sarmatia realized what the beast had seen. A child had kicked a hole in the fencing and was running out into the turbid afternoon light. No time to draw the bull off— all she could hope for was to reach the boy first.

Sprinting, her insides turning to water, Sarmatia rushed for the child. As her hands closed round his tiny—so tiny!—body and her cheek grazed the stones she thought, with terrible clarity: *I promised they would be safe. I've failed.*

For a second, a dark breathing shadow hung over her. Then came pain, the slow tearing punch of the horn.

* * * *

She came awake suddenly, crying out. Firm hands kept her flat against the stones.

'Peace, Kretan,' said the man crouched beside her, pressing a cloth onto the spurting wound in her side. 'There's nothing to fear.' In the sun his hair framed his broad-featured face like a nimbus, yet there was darkness behind him. The bull was still free in the courtyard.

Sarmatia wet her lips with her tongue. 'The child?'

Fearn jerked his head to one side. 'Ramose has taken his son. He's safe.' The initiates were also gone, the crowd hanging back, uncertain what to do.

They were alone in the court, except for the bull. Fearn pressed on her side again then withdrew the cloth. A dark spiral of blood pooled under Sarmatia's ribs; blood no longer pumped from the wound. She scarcely felt it as he bound the gash with a bandage made from his tunic. 'You must leave, Sir, the bull—'

She broke off, eyes widening, and Fearn whipped round. Ready to gore, the bull was lowering its huge head, its face so close that its breath stirred the bristles of Fearn's beard. Fearn threw up an arm to fend off the horns and drove a fist into the face of the beast. 'Get back!' He hit the creature a second time. 'Learn your lesson!'

The bull snorted and the healer shifted, covering Sarmatia completely with his body. He stamped the stones and shouted at the beast. 'Go on! Go on!'

As Fearn's boot hammered the flags, there came the rumble of a distant storm, like the muffled roar of a lion. The beast started back and with a bellow turned tail and ran.

The man's shoulders shook. 'It always works on the cows at home. If you charge them first -' Fearn started to laugh. He had entered the court, driven the bull off its victim, kept it at bay. In her relief, Sarmatia blacked out.

* * * *

Water trickled in a basin, a cool cloth mopped her face.

'Easy there. You're at home. Your brother's just left your bedside to rest.' Fearn grinned at her. Sarmatia smiled back.

'Good,' said Fearn approvingly. He rose from the edge of her bed and stood, his head touching the rafters of her attic chamber. 'Are you in pain?'

Sarmatia shook her head. There was a nagging ache from her ribs to her hips but she could bear that: it was nothing to trouble the healer with. Fearn gazed at her speculatively through thick-lashed eyes—thinking eyes that she'd seen burn like a warrior's—but accepted her response. Sarmatia wondered how long he had sat by her bed, how long she had been lying there. She watched him walk the length of her room, ducking under the beams, turn and come back. Neither spoke.

Fearn repeated his circuit, stopping by her bed. 'Do you know who I am?'

'You're Fearn. You're here to cure Minos.' With her customary brevity of speech, Sarmatia neglected to tell him her name. She guessed he would know it by now.

Fearn smiled at her again. He was quite young, Sarmatia realized, no more than twenty. 'Ah, yes, Minos. Have you ever seen him?' he asked.

'No.'

'Have you, like me, ever been inside Phaistos palace?'

'No.' Trying to be comfortable, Sarmatia squirmed in her bed. She was hungry, but too shy to mention it. For an instant, although full of questions for this man from the edge of the world, she almost wished her brother Tazaros was with her instead of this tall, bulky stranger, dressed in the long tunic and leggings of a barbarian.

Yet Fearn was comely. His face, with its sturdy features and thick red eyebrows, was pleasing without being handsome and he was taller than most Kretans. There was a big-jointed look about his long limbs, as though he still had some growing out to do. Now he stared at the roof, fingering his beard and chin. Was it possible that he, too, was shy? Gently she touched his arm. 'Will you tell me about the palace?'

Chapter 2

Krete, 1562BC. Summer.

Two weeks later, when she was walking but had not yet resumed her part in the Bull Rite, Sarmatia was summoned by the Snake Priestess in the pillar crypt of the temple.

'Go to the Old West Gate,' the priestess said. 'Fearn is waiting there for you. Guide him to the Grey Mountains, help him to gather the herbs he needs. Take care, for Fearn has Minos' cure in mind. There are two days' rations you'll need to collect. The laundress will provide you with clothes.'

Sarmatia prostrated herself before the Priestess then rose. Before she had climbed the stair leading out of the crypt, the Priestess called her back.

'You must find this a strange order.' It was not usual for men skilled in the art of healing to ask for help.

'Yes, Mistress.' Sarmatia was very still, her eyes tracing the faded pools of blood upon the stone floor. She did not look once at the plump, motherly figure of the Priestess. Pergia could have a sharp tongue when she chose and Sarmatia wanted no probing questions about Fearn. She wanted merely to see him again, to talk to him, to have him talk to her.

Black eyes flicked over her. 'Go in joy, girl. Fearn is a good man. Go.'

Dismissed, Sarmatia darted to the palace stores in a whirlwind of happiness. Snatching two unleavened loaves and a supply of olives and figs, she hurriedly filled a battered sheepskin with water and then rushed to the laundry to collect a made-up parcel of clothing. Despite her aching side and newly-healed wounds, she ran all the way to the Old West Gate, never stopping until she saw the redheaded healer. 'Master Fearn!'

Fearn came through the gateway to meet her. He was dressed for the Kretan summer now, with a short tunic and wide-brimmed hat, though his limbs were still pale as a woman's. 'I always thought Kretans lay in their soft beds till long after dawn,' he teased. 'Are you a rarity then?'

'No, Fearn.'

'And I chose you, thinking you were! Shall we go, before the sun catches us?' He pointed north, where already the summits of the Snow Mountains gleamed in the approaching sun. In a few hours that sun would have ripened to an eye-aching fullness and another summer's day, dusty and still, but the dawn felt pleasant, cool and fragrant with juniper and honeysuckle. Sarmatia paused before starting out, watching the light flow over the countryside and a hawk rising in the clear skies.

The bird stooped, dropping into tall grasses, and she flinched, the spell broken. She turned, but Fearn had already moved off, carrying both bundles of food and clothing. Catching up, she began to walk with him down the street that led away from the palace of Phaistos. They passed workmen laden with tools, pounding up the long slope to the house of Minos, and a handsome farmer with an easy smile, driving his cattle to the palace dairy. Then they left the paved road for the country tracks and twisting grass paths, where they met no other creature for the rest of the day.

* * * *

As they wove their way round the edge of the cornfields, brushing past emmer wheat and blue iris, Fearn told Sarmatia of his own lands on the Isle of Stones. He told her of summers there, when the rowan flamed in the dark woods and the soft hills burned with color. He told of the bleak winters, when no birds flew and men huddled round fires. He sang her a spring song, a careless tune telling of flowers, bees and the new born wild things.

Sarmatia listened, full of delight. Silent, her brother Tazaros called her at home—sulky, said her sister-in-law—but neither would have recognized their Sarmatia as the nimble girl who chattered and laughed with Fearn. When they stopped by a shallow, slow-running river to drink and rest under the cypress trees, Fearn knew that, as with him, Sarmatia's parents were dead: she lived with her elder brother and his wife. For her part, Sarmatia had learned that the healer had no sisters or brothers but that he did have a dog, a half-crossed terrier. 'Called Puddle—you needn't wonder why. Often as a boy I'd slip off to the woods, go roaring through the undergrowth with Puddle always ahead, tail whisking like a flag. When I set out for Krete I'd to leave him behind—he's gray-muzzled, poor fellow.'

'He'll wait for you,' Sarmatia answered at once, aware that Fearn was taking more pains washing his face in the river than he needed. She was rewarded with a quick smile and, seizing the moment, asked about things which had intrigued her ever since she had heard of the Isle of Stones, questions she had shared with no one until now. 'Who made the Great Stone Circle? Was it giants? Why did they make it? Who was it for?'

Fearn wiped the last drops of water from his downy beard and sat back from the river, watching the blue winged butterflies and bullfinches, brilliant against the cypress. A lark began to sing somewhere in the cloudless skies and Sarmatia, waiting, listened to its pulsing music.

Finally he spoke. 'Why do you ask me this, Sarmatia?'

Sarmatia flushed. 'I'm sorry. I didn't mean offence.'

Fearn leaned towards her. This close, Sarmatia saw that his eyes were green, not brown, nor even the rare blue. 'None taken. But you see, I'm curious.'

The healer picked up a handful of pebbles and began tossing them into the water. 'People do question me,' he went on, 'but always on other things. Which crops grow well in my lands, how long are the northern summers, how powerful our kings.' Fearn looked directly at Sarmatia again. 'But somehow you have sensed—'

He stopped, glanced upstream, his mind fired not by stone circles but Sarmatia herself: this little Kretan, who made his heart bang and his thoughts fly the more time they spent together. An active listener, constantly challenging his assumptions, Sarmatia had the quality of sunlight, fertile and hot, illuminating in her pithy questions and thought. And that furry chuckle of hers—he was often tempted to tickle her, simply to hear it, to delight in her laughter. Her skin was taut and sweet-smelling as freshly-baked bread— the same rich color, too: good enough to eat. For the rest, long legs, supple waist, pert breasts, swirling brown hair, charmingly sober mouth, brilliant amber eyes—

'Is it sacred?' persisted Sarmatia, compelled by some spirit to pry, where normally she would have said nothing. 'As the deep cave in the Snow Mountain is to my people?'

Returned to the safely impersonal, Fearn laughed, reminding himself she was still barely eighteen. 'I was right to choose you! Can you keep a secret?'

Trying not to think about the ache in his stiffened groin, Fearn took up another pebble and began to draw in the sand between them. 'Many years ago there was a drought in my lands. All the tribes came together to build the Great Circle, high on a treeless heath where the Sky God would see it, the blue and gray stones painted with the marks for rain.'

The pebble drew the spirals in the sand and Fearn went on, his face quite still. 'The men dug the ditches and the women danced, always in the circle, never breaking step. They set the tallest stones together, working in harness under the dusty sky, like oxen.'

'Did rain fall?'

'It did indeed. When the first stone was raised, the rain began to fall. It poured then till every spring and stream flowed over.'

Sarmatia smiled, though one matter still puzzled her. 'Why must this be secret?'

'Because these things were revealed to me through a vision.' Fearn placed a hand upon his forehead to show that this was sacred. 'Few men, even the shamans, now know the truth of the Circle. To speak of it lightly would be dangerous.' His mouth set hard and his face went grim as he clearly fought his own temper. 'Men have made their own truths now. The place is called the Seat of the Plains-Kings—'

Fearn broke off and Sarmatia dare ask no more. Suddenly she wished she was back at home.

Seeing her disquiet, Fearn strove for the ordinary. 'Look at these, Sarmatia.' He pointed to a clump of tall milky flowers growing near the river's edge. 'What are they called here?'

'Purity, Sir.'

'Yes.' Fearn noted the formal 'Sir' while he bent and examined the blossoms, 'Yes, the white face and faint blush, and its uses...' He snapped a flower off the body of the plant and turned back to Sarmatia. 'I know this one well! It grows freely in my homelands, thrives at every stream's edge in summer. My people call it cleanse-all. I use it for a skin salve, and in love potions.'

Fearn grinned and walked over to Sarmatia. He tucked the bloom stem behind her ear with a steady hand, touching her hair briefly. Picking up their provisions, he started striding over the rough ground, leaving Sarmatia to trail after him as best she could.

They travelled till long after twilight, coming to the foothills of the Grey Mountains. There, just after moonrise, Sarmatia spied out a cave in a tangle of undergrowth, a place where they might rest. When a fire was burning brightly, she hoped that Fearn would speak more of his homelands, and other countries he had visited. She enjoyed traveller's tales.

Nor was she disappointed. For part of his training as healer, Fearn had journeyed for several seasons to learn other peoples' ways of dealing with disease. The memories of those earlier, more carefree days were sweet and he was glad to share them. All that evening, as they ate and drank and tended the fire, Fearn drew a web of enchantment about them, filling the night with strange stories.

'Which place do you care for best?' she asked, as Fearn paused to break up a dry log.

Fearn grimaced. 'There you have me!' He rubbed his beard and face— a gesture Sarmatia recognized as shyness, a further bond between them. Even so she almost missed his quiet answer.

'My homelands have my life, my power. But my heart? It might be here, in Krete.' Fearn rose and clambered swiftly to the entrance of the cave. 'The kindling runs low. I must fetch more.' He turned and was lost to the dark, his footfalls softening with distance.

Sarmatia yawned and settled closer to the fire, oblivious to the smarting wood smoke. She pondered on all she had learned, Fearn's voice running on in her mind. 'Custom in my country makes women the heirs, as well as men.' 'They say a tree grows through earth and heaven.' 'My heart? It might be here, in Krete.' Then she slept, a smile on her lips.

* * * *

She woke, still happy. They had reached the Grey Mountains, survived a night in the wilderness, and her bull-riding wounds had given no trouble. Smiling, Sarmatia rolled onto her stomach, feeling the dry cave floor rasp comfortably against her flesh. She glanced at Fearn who slept, spread-eagled in the center of their small cave, his cloak flung to one side. She watched the bristles of his sparse beard move with every long snoring breath, saw how his nose was scarlet with the sun. Yet these things did not matter.

Absently, Sarmatia plucked the flower Fearn had given her from her hair. Despite a day in the sun its petals were still fresh and its scent sweet. She placed it in their water skin to keep its life a little longer. Then, moving carefully so as not to wake her companion, the girl rolled up her cloak. She padded soundlessly from their resting place up the steep embankment, out of the cave.

Glancing round in the pale sunlight, Sarmatia soon spotted what she was looking for—a wild pear tree, close to a field of cultivated vine, its branches already laden with fruit. Walking along the ancient boundary ridge, Sarmatia made for the tree. After a day of olives and figs, pears would be a welcome change.

'What have you got there, creature-caller?'

Startled, Sarmatia almost dropped the fruit. She glared at Fearn, who had come partway along the ridge to meet her. 'Who told you?'

'No one but you, Sarmatia. Don't look at me like that!'

Sarmatia began to tremble. Her fingers shook as Fearn took a pear from her hands and, crouching down on the path, sank his teeth into the ripe fruit. Finally she could keep silent no longer. 'How do you know?'

'Sit, eat, and I'll tell you.' Fearn spat out a mouthful of seeds. He did not speak again until Sarmatia had done as he'd asked. 'When birds fly over, you see their lives, their feelings, don't you?'

'I see pictures. Empty sky. Strange lands.' Sarmatia knew she was trying to explain a mystery. There were no words for it, this strange state of being, where the lives of animals were one with hers. This kinship had always been with her and was growing, but she wondered how Fearn had recognized it. 'But how—?'

'How do I know? I know because animals are drawn to you. They watch you even now.' Fearn leaned across and caught hold of Sarmatia, pointing over the fields with his free hand. 'Can you not sense them, Sarmatia? Feel their life out there, beyond sight? As a healer I get glimpses of their presence, but you'll know them.'

Alarmed by his knowledge, Sarmatia squirmed from Fearn's grasp. 'We should go, Sir. The sun grows hot.'

Haste betrayed her. She moved too quickly on the ridge and overbalanced, falling heavily on the shaly surface. Before she could rise, arms had wound round her and scooped her up. A long red strand of hair tickled her face as Fearn bent his head.

'Bull-Head! These things aren't to be feared. They're part of you. As you grow, you'll understand, but for now, you'd best pray to your Mother. If you turned your ankle there I'll not be pleased. You're my plant gatherer today.'

Sarmatia giggled at his deliberately contorted face, her fright forgotten. She rested her head in the crook of his arm, secure in the knowledge that this day, like the one before, would be happy.

* * * *

At the end of another month, when Minos was acknowledged as cured and Sarmatia had begun to train again for the Bull Rite, she and Fearn were betrothed.

Chapter 3

Hear me! There was once a royal family who did not love their king. Hear their names. Laerimmer, the Kingmaker, and his sister Kere. Fearn the healer, the strange one. Goar and Gygest, the silver-haired royal twins. Briht the shaman. Anoi and Tanek, sister and half-brother. Chalda, proud and haughty despite miscarrying a bastard. And Waroch, King Waroch, a man like a blown apple, sour and sweet by turns and a smile gone mildewed on his face. Waroch had the blunt, bald head of a newt, the newt's rough, warty skin. Because of him, the royal household was in constant uproar. Harsh words were said and blows exchanged. Some took to living elsewhere. I chose another way—a fire.

It was my right to let Waroch burn: he had failed our people. I shall be a ruler of the Atterians and they will praise my name. One day I will recount to them, as I do to you now, how I set flint against copper, spark against thatch and burned the royal house while Waroch slept.

I started the fire in the roof of the house and watched the pouring gray smoke change to leaping prongs of flame. I saw the insides of the house lit by pools of fire, glowing like the blue flares of marsh gas as sparks kindled the packed-down refuse on the floor. I smelt the pungent, woody scent of burning heather thatch, the sweet scent of oak beams charring. It was so splendid, that fire, so swift-growing, like a living creature.

I'd given Waroch drugged wine that night, to make him sleep the heavier, but soon the rest of the family stirred and raised an outcry. Fat Kere and slim Tanek rushed for the fresh air and were stuck together in the doorway in their haste to escape. The royal twins were yelling and Anoi sobbing. Tanek had even run back inside. Everyone was in panic, assuming that the Long-Haired People were raiding again, while Waroch slept.

Fire singed my hair and clothes, ash blackened my arms and face, but I stayed to the end. I know my duty. Waroch must die and no one must help him. Will you be sorry when I tell you no one tried? Between the heat, the choking smoke, and Briht half-crazed with fear, needing to be dragged out by two strong men, there was no time to save the King. Waroch died as he had lived, in sweetness and harshness, a smile upon his lips as a burning stave fell from the ceiling and pierced his heart.

Tanek, Anoi and Goar were among the last out of the house that night, all royal, all fair, all obsessed. I was the final one to leave that cracking, rolling furnace, and when I turned to watch the whole roof of the house cave in with a crash, fat Kere ran to me and spoiled my quiet celebration. Clutching my arm, her brown eyes starting in her round, sooty face, she cried out to me, 'Where is Fearn? Where is he?'

Where indeed?

Chapter 4

Krete, 1561 BC. Summer.

A sea at sunset. A swimmer cuts through the waves. Water churns under his body and he looks back. Something is there: a seven-headed beast with the body of a snake. It is hunting him.

Sarmatia woke sweating. The dream had been the worst yet. The monster had almost caught Fearn. By habit, her fingers sought and closed over the bronze betrothal ring that he had given her and which she wore about her neck.

Turning over, she sat up in bed. Although she was still eighteen, almost a full year had passed. A year was a long time and even the best of men could be fickle. There was the long journey, too, and her nightmares. Fearn had been right when he had called her a creature-caller: she could charm animals to her side. Yet the elders of her family said that her dream of the sea monster was a sign of her own spirit animal's struggle with her creature-calling.

Sarmatia did not know if that was true or not. Often the two forces seemed to move as one, increasing her power to summon the wildest of creatures. But then her spirit animal was strange, its form unknown even to the oldest of her family. Sometimes it stalked through her sleep, like a lion, yet bigger, and always solitary. A beast without a name.

It was not gentle. In the hunt its predatory greed drove her, warring against her gift of animal kinship, so that she was at once hunter and hunted. Sarmatia had known the anguish of an ibex as dogs' teeth closed about its flanks and throat. Felt terror and frenzy until life itself was extinguished, and then the blood-lust of the hounds, filling her jaws like raw flesh. She never hunted for pleasure. That would have been a betrayal.

Now, ignoring the ever-present ache in her back and legs—the price of my bread, she thought wryly—Sarmatia rose and dressed in her everyday robe. Troubling neither with gems nor cosmetics, she crept from the small room that she shared with house martins and sparrows. Before she sped down the outside stair she caught up her spindle. Where she was heading, idle hands were not approved of, even on a visit.

* * * *

'You couldn't sleep. That's no surprise.' The snake priestess broke off as the spirit which afflicted her closed up her lungs and she battled for breath. She waved aside the goblet Sarmatia proffered. 'No,' she gasped, 'I'd sooner choke.'

'Pergia?' Sarmatia waited anxiously while the older woman's coughing subsided and her plump face took on its normal ruddy hue. 'Pergia, are you well now?'

Pergia leaned forward, black eyes bright. 'Have you tasted that?' She stabbed a finger at the herb tea. 'I'll gag on my own breath before I'll drink that filth.'

'They paid bronze for this potion. Try it.'

The priestess shook her head.

Sarmatia tried to frown but did not succeed. She wouldn't have drunk it either. Resigned, she rose and took up the cup. 'Which this time, Pergia?' she asked, pointing with her free hand at the threshold. 'Lilies or roses?'

'The roses. They were drooping yesterday. Wait, I'll go with you. The air may do me good.'

The women walked through the dark colonnade. It was still night, but the sky was clear and the waxing moon guided them to the center of the small garden. There, half-obscured by briar, was a stone bench. Pergia spread her skirts to sit upon this and, resuming her habit, began to tease out moss from the crazed surface of the stone.

'Your spirit animal's growing,' she remarked, watching the girl share out the goblet's contents between flowers. Sarmatia lifted her head and winked at the priestess. Pergia said this each time they met: it was almost a joke.

'You can see it?' She knew well that to Pergia, like other seers, the spirit world was visible. She had never seen her spirit animal, except in dreams. Not even that first time, when at seven years old Sarmatia had been given her adult name by the elders of the family and her spirit animal had been revealed. It was an old spirit, they had told her, a creature more appropriate for ancient times.

The dark-haired Pergia was also considering this mystery. With her keen sight, she studied her favorite. The Kretan standing in the garden was like a fine Egyptian bronze come to life, save that her brown hair curled down her back and would not be straightened. Her features were gloriously regular and those who encountered the straight, piercing gaze of her amber eyes were always disconcerted.

Sarmatia was beautiful, no doubt of that, and a good part of her beauty came from the power of her spirit animal. It was an intriguing spirit, unnamed and terrible. Pergia was certain that it accounted for some of Sarmatia's uncanny skill with animals, for these could sense her spirit animal's presence and were fascinated by it. In this age, when so many wild things were almost spent, the girl's spirit animal was an oddity. All people had spirit animals, were chosen by one spirit-beast or another, but most could ignore such waning influences. Pergia's own servant had forgotten what beast his spirit animal was, and there were many like him. Such old-fashioned forces were considered private, slightly embarrassing, and were no longer spoken of in even the remotest village.

Suddenly the woman's reverie was interrupted.

'Last night you said Fearn has two spirit animals, the eagle and the salmon. Why has he two and I have one?'

'Because two chose him.' Pergia regretted having spoken of the northern healer's unusual spirits. It was rare to have two, and to have the salmon and the eagle, one subtle and deep, one soaring in flight... The older woman shivered. It was time to bring Sarmatia down to earth.

'I hear that your brother's wife goes daily to the town shrine and makes offerings to win you a Kretan man. I've seen her there myself,' she said, a wicked gleam in her dark eyes.

Noting the none too subtle change of subject, Sarmatia shrugged and emptied the rest of the goblet over the nearest rose-bush. 'Miropa's a dreamer.' She was used to this talk.

'And you're not? Wasting your youth, waiting?'

'Fearn will come. I know.'

The girl's certainty irked Pergia and worried her, though she never let that show. 'I know,' she mimicked. 'What? That Fearn is one of a King's family? That he might have to stay in his homelands? Think, Sarmatia! You're not even one with the moon yet.'

Which is why no Kretan farmer will be interested in me: a body to breed from is all they want. Sarmatia did not reply. She walked farther down the garden, reaching up to inhale a rose's perfume. She and Fearn shared a love of places like these, where a Kretan man would be bored, seeing nothing.

Watching, Pergia could not see her face, though she knew, only too well, the fixed expression she would find there. 'Well?'

'He promised. I wait.'

Pergia sighed, but said nothing. It was an old argument and she was tired. Noting the unusual silence, Sarmatia relented. She set down the goblet and knelt beside the Priestess. She wove her arms around the generous waist, an embrace only permitted in the confines of the garden where no other could see. 'Don't trouble. If I'm here this winter, you'll have your wish. Fearn promised to return in not more than two summers, as soon as he has trained another to take his place as his people's main healer. By then, too, I will have trained my own successor in the Bull Rite.'

Naturally brief, Sarmatia paused after what was a long speech for her. She had spoken without regret or resentment, having accepted this as the reason for Fearn's departure from Krete. If, after curing Minos and herself, he had remained with her without thought for his own tribe, she would have respected him less, not more.

'This is the last summer, for both of us.'

Pergia tweaked a long brown streamer of her hair. 'You always were stubborn.'

'I know.' Sarmatia smiled.

Chapter 5

Isle of Stones, 1562 BC. Winter, six months earlier, five days after a fire which destroyed the royal homestead and its king.

Fearn stood staring out at the winter heath, flexing his arms under a heavy sheepskin cloak. Red-gold hair flickered on his shoulders as he stamped his booted feet. With one hand he scratched at his beard, thicker than the down he'd had on Krete, trimmed to a thumb-width lower than his chin. He was frowning.

That habit of rubbing at beard and chin betrayed Fearn to himself: he was ill at ease and knew it. It was not the thought of death that angered him, nor the foreknowledge of pain. What was pain if not the body's war-cry, telling you when you must fight? And if Briht was right, and the royal family had tricked them and young Tanek into this by a sleight-of-hand with the fate bowl and pebbles, what of it? Someone must be chosen to be king, since Waroch was dead.

A sad thing for Waroch, that he had not been where he should have been that night, tending the royal cattle at Rossfarm. It had rained on the day of the fire and Waroch had stayed at home, in the warm. Fearn recalled how he, Laerimmer and their pert cousin Chalda had walked to Rossfarm, staying on through the night until he had seen the cow drop her calf. The beasts had thrived, yet it was a sorry business which had bred more grief, not only for the King.

Laerimmer. He was the one, thought Fearn. Always the first to mock. As Kingmaker that was his role, yet need the man perform it so readily? One day he would go too far.

That day had come already. In his left hand Fearn carried a stone-headed axe and now he swept and cut with the weapon, parrying the blows of an imaginary opponent. This is what he should do to Laerimmer.

A peasant. A foreigner of no birth or fortune. A southerner with a face like a pig. A girl who'd given herself to a bull. This is what the royal family had said—with Laerimmer leading the chorus—of his betrothed. Of Sarmatia.

Throwing the axe high into the air, Fearn sprinted back and caught it near the head, bringing the wooden shaft closer to check for fractures which in the heat of battle might shatter. He'd not had this axe by him when Laerimmer had puked out his poison, but fists had served almost as well, and he would have finished off the Kingmaker then and there had Kere and the other women not intervened. Fearn could never punch a woman, not even in that red cauldron of anger which rose so swiftly, sizzling in his veins. Often he was sorry when it was spent and he saw the broken teeth and bruises that as a healer he should try to mend, but not then.

Then Laerimmer spat blood onto the ruins of the royal homestead. 'That's about your level, you bastard, striking an unarmed man. You've an evil temper these days.'

'No! Fearn's easy, truly easy.' In her gentle way, Anoi had defended the healer, but none of the other family had spoken up for him. There had been too many mutterings lately about his temper: he could be placid for weeks, calm enough in his healing when he would go days without sleep or food, and then explode over a trifle.

'You wouldn't call him easy if he'd hit you.' Goar had mumbled, sitting on a charred bench, nursing his head. Seeing the healer redden and go for Laerimmer, Goar had caught Fearn's arm, but the healer had cuffed him aside, knocking him onto one of the fallen roof beams of the royal house. Fearn remembered the satisfying smack of Goar's face against the fire-blasted wood. He had been angry with Goar as well, for Goar had said Sarmatia was nothing.

Nothing? His Sarmatia: solemn, quiet, though talkative with him, warm, brave and quick. Like any young thing, all legs. Alive. She had cast herself before the charging bull without thought, concerned only for the child. Now Sarmatia was his to protect, to go back to, beyond the boiling sea.

Fearn stiffened his fingers across the axe blade. He looked again over the cold, treeless land, but there was no one yet.

The family had said he must not leave. 'You're mad,' Kere had said, applying the same mockery as her Kingmaker brother. 'It's not a proper betrothal. Where is the creature's dowry?'

'To make that journey for a girl.' Tanek had scoffed. As easy to teach a blind man the colors of the rainbow as to make his family understand, especially Laerimmer.

'You expect us to believe you'd lose a kingdom for this Kretan, as you call her?' Laerimmer had mocked.

'Watch your mouth, Laerimmer. You can't hide round women forever.'

'Why, would you nurse your anger? That would be new, Fearn, even for you.'

'He's bewitched,' said Chalda, shaking her auburn curls, but her mouth had slipped into an envious pout.

'No, Fearn's a coward.' Laerimmer had said. 'Our healer fears the test. Is that not so, Fearn? Shall I go to the people and tell them?'

The Kingmaker had trapped him then and both of them had known it. If Laerimmer spoke to the Atterians, Fearn knew he could not leave. He could not creep from his homeland with the word 'coward' over his head. Such things went beyond pride or love. It marked you, as a man, for all time.

And so farewell. Sarmatia was his, his sunlight, his way into a larger world —Krete, where the King ruled thousands— and yet he must put such thoughts from him. Here for the moment was his destiny, in this tiny kingdom.

Voices were hailing him and Fearn responded, the burr of his speech filling his throat. Laerimmer, Briht and Tanek appeared on the Sacred Hill, stark against the winter sun. They were wearing beads and feathers, while he was still in his working clothes. Was it carelessness that he had not changed, or a twisted vanity? He was as he was. Sarmatia liked him well enough, though he was not handsome, like Goar and Gygest.

'You're here early, Fearn.' Though it was less carping than usual, Laerimmer's voice still set his teeth on edge. 'Do you hope the goddess of this hill will favor you for that? Take care, Fearn, for the immortals don't always act as we might wish them to.'

'I claim nothing.'

A look of discomfort scurried over the Kingmaker's round face and sharp little eyes. In a slightly raised voice, Laerimmer began to speak of the test.

'The test reveals those who are fit to rule and those who are not. The test shows who is wise and who is not. For every king there is a test, and for each of you now the test will be the same, yet not.'

'What are these riddles?' Tanek tugged at his beaded head-dress. 'Talk sense, Kingmaker!'

'Laerimmer means we'll all undergo the one ordeal, yet draw different lessons from it,' said Fearn evenly. He thought the youth too young for this, forgetting that he was only two years older. He smiled at Tanek, trying to settle the lad, but the slim, blond eighteen-year-old would not look at him.

'What happens if we fail?' Tanek asked the Kingmaker.

'You die.'

Briht blanched. Fearn looked at the shaman and at Tanek and observed, 'There's still time to withdraw.' He stared at the Kingmaker. If Laerimmer spoke now of cowardice and forced Briht or Tanek to continue, the man would pay, and with blood.

'I must go on.' A swarthy, gloomy man, Briht already seemed resigned to hopelessness.

'And I!' exclaimed Tanek, a flame of youthful hopes.

In the boy's kindled features, Fearn saw Tanek's half-sister, Anoi. So many lives warped because Waroch had been too lazy or cowardly to look after his own royal house. Despite the sacred test, Waroch had been a poor king. He would try to be a better one.

What was he thinking? Fearn shook his head and heard Laerimmer telling Briht and Tanek to drink from the goblet of forgetfulness, to eat the leaves of the magic vervain. The cup and gold plate came to him in turn and he drank and ate.

Laerimmer motioned them to a level ridge on the hill and drew three circles on the ground in a mixture of sand and dried blood. 'Step within these. The test is here. If any of you venture outside your circle before I return, his life is finished.' He looked up at the sky. 'I'll be back at sunset.'

The Kingmaker took a step towards Briht. 'It's only a day, Briht, and the gods watch over their own.' He made a sign of protection by the man's head. To Tanek he said, 'Run as you will, boy, but keep within the circle.'

'No advice for me?' asked Fearn sarcastically, seeing the Kingmaker about to depart.

Laerimmer looked back over one shoulder. 'Use that axe. Remember your two spirit animals.' He cleared his throat and spat. 'Earth, air, water, fire: your test is all of these.' He left them.

* * * *

Earth was the beginning. Fearn was starting to feel bored and foolish, standing straight as a stone pillar in his sand circle, axe at the ready. He thrust the axe handle into his belt and rubbed at his beard. A sword-length to his right Briht was rolling his eyes, trying to induce a trance, while Tanek on his left was stifling a yawn. The youth's blond head was tilted back when he started to choke.

Fearn leapt forward to aid the boy, ignoring the taboo that banned his leaving the circle before sunset, but the earth rose and struck at his throat. Knocked back within a solid encircling chimney that stretched far above his head like the tunnel of some giant mole, Fearn heard Briht and Tanek coughing while they scrabbled against the avalanche of earth. He shouted to them to keep moving and launched his body at the soil wall. Dirt buckled under his shoulder but, instead of breaking free, Fearn stove the sand and pebbles inwards and the mass erupted over him in a suffocating black deluge.

Knowing he would drown in that dark flow if he lost his footing, Fearn snatched out, punching his hands against stones and clumps of earth to find something to hold onto as the ground swept around him. It wound a heavy fetter round both legs, squeezed his middle in a massive wrestler's grip. Above a painful drumming in his belly, head and chest came the faint scrape of fingernails against enclosing soil. Briht and Tanek were being buried alive.

'By the goddess, not while I breathe!' Roared aloud, the words gave hope and force. A hard gasp at a time, Fearn pushed his left hand through the surging drifts of mud. The need to let go and lash out was so fierce that his loins ached with it, but that slow, inexorable yielding of the soil, inch by inch, made him wait. At last his straining fingers closed on the axe handle at his belt and he worked the blade slowly upwards from the growing mound of earth. The turgid, creeping muck slithered past his shoulders and reached his chin. Sweating and straining, inhaling dust and spitting dust, Fearn levered an arm from the swamp of soil. He chopped down with the axe-blade at the dark, oily soil-sheath which covered his limbs, heaving gobbets of earth away with the axe-handle. Dirt spattered off his body, finally receding in a slithering rush.

The debris melted into the ground from which it had sprung and, freed from its bone-crushing weight, his body seemed to glow with well-being. Now he could see Tanek and Briht, and it was an immense relief to Fearn that they appeared unharmed, although the boy was still coughing. Dark Briht crouched bemused within his circle, staring at his hands while a neat rampart of earth flowed back down his calves and shinbones into the hillside.

It began to rain. Real rain, thought Fearn with satisfaction, and not the effect of the vervain or the wine. The downpour was cold and refreshing on his forehead, tickling on his beard. Beardless Tanek was washing his face by the shower, but Briht stood and shivered in it. As Fearn opened his mouth to try to encourage Briht, a fish came sliding out of the rain and swam about his waist, scraping a fin against his tunic.

'Greetings,' said the fish, his salmon spirit animal, which Fearn knew through dreams, 'We're pleased with you, Fearn, my brother and I. Here he is now: hold out your fist for him.'

Obediently, as one in a dream, Fearn extended the hand that held the axe. There was a rush of air, feathers beating against his shoulder, and his arm was almost wrenched from its socket as a great golden eagle dropped from the sky to him. Its talons curved over his wrist in an easy snatch and he felt the yellow claws prick against his skin.

'You're at ease with air and water,' said the eagle.

Fearn did not speak but stroked the bird's crop with a forefinger, which his spirit animal permitted. The gleaming feathers, which he had expected would be harsh to the touch, were light and soft. The eagle's gaze was piercing, like the noonday sun of Krete. Fearn could not hold it long.

'Have Briht's and Tanek's animals come?' he asked.

'You can't see them?' said the salmon, breathing rain through its speckled gills. Fearn felt the fish's tail brush along his flanks.

'He's not a shaman,' said the eagle. 'His powers are different.' The bird's head whipped sideways as a low cry issued from Briht. Fearn jerked forward again, but the eagle raised and spread its wings so that he could not see. The fish spat out a body of water through which he could not move.

'You can do nothing for Briht,' said the salmon. 'You must learn to wait.'

'What do I need when I hunt six times in a day, harried by crows, and do not kill?' said the eagle, preening the amber fluff of its legs.

'What is the power that brings me to the spawning river?' said the salmon. In a sudden vivid image Fearn saw the fish leaping a waterfall, driving upwards again and again.

'Draw on this strength, Fearn. You'll need it,' advised the eagle. It fanned out its man-high wingspan and flew off into dark skies. Fearn looked down. The salmon spirit animal had already disappeared.

A crack appeared in the clouds and through it sped a shaft of fire, white, pure white, striking in a zigzag at the Sacred Hill. Smoke poured from the ground as the blaze took hold, a wisp of flame eating its way upwards to the three men. Catching a glimpse of Tanek's round owl-eyes as the youth realized that the fire would reach them, Fearn knew that though Laerimmer had spoken of fire, the Kingmaker had not planned for this, an actual blaze. Here was a test straight from the Sky God.

He was glad of it. Lightning had blasted the hillside yet, when it had lit the heavens a moment before, he knew no panic, only recognition, a premonition soon to be fulfilled. The air was snapping around him, like the red anger, and in the grumble of thunder at the back of the horizon Fearn thought he heard a voice. It seemed to say, *Not yet.*

So what had he to do with storms? He had worshipped light and the sky since childhood, but was there more? He prayed to the Sky God. 'Sky Father, giver of rain, teach me to understand. Why is lightning alive to me?'

He might have said 'a part of me,' for since that flash of searing white he had sensed the crackle of heat through his body. If he could touch Tanek and Briht they would feel it, too.

A scream, more animal than human, sounded from the first circle. Tanek had stamped out the burning grass at his feet, but Briht had done nothing. As the grass by his boots hissed and changed into that orange glare, Briht began to scream. Seeing him paralyzed by fear, Fearn shouted.

'Leave him!' yelled Tanek. 'Who cares if he fails?'

But Briht was one of his people. Fearn stripped off his sheepskin cloak and, leaning at full stretch, battered flames away from the shaman.

'Leave him!' Tanek gestured obscenely with a finger. 'One less!'

Briht's boots had begun to smoke. In his mind's eye, Fearn saw the shaman burning like a wooden beam. To save Briht he must leave the circle.

Fearn stepped straight into the fire's track. Two strides would see him through it, three take him outside the circle, five bring him to Briht. The flame within his nature met the growing flame without. Both burned brighter, the grass fire on the Sacred Hill catching the sleeve of his tunic. Ignoring danger, ignoring even Briht, Fearn dropped the cloak and bunched his fingers into a fist. He felt thunder in his palm. He opened his hand and felt the whiplash of power run up his arm. He was a focus, like the magic-bowl of a shaman, and yet –unlike the bowl—he was aware.

Through the fire torched on his sleeve the Sky God spoke. 'Yours, mortal. See that you harness it right.'

The blaze had reached flesh, scorching the down on his wrist, punching a reminder of fire against his skin. He burned, one with lightning. The pain was rutting in its ferocity.

Fearn closed his eyes, thinking of his eagle spirit animal harried by crows. Briht was still screaming, but Fearn could do nothing, besieged himself by fire. Soon it would be sunset. He and Briht need only wait.

Suddenly part of his tunic fell away and the fire went with it. The rag of his sleeve writhed and charred on the hill, a smoking skeleton of cloth. The mark left on his hand and wrist was like that made by blood-brothers, when they swear an oath. It would fade, but the memory would not.

Fearn took a deep breath and raised his head, starting as the Kingmaker's face loomed into his.

'What have you learned?' hissed Laerimmer.

Fearn thought for a moment. He would not speak of the pact, he decided. That was between him and the Sky God, a promise of future power. 'Patience, Kingmaker. My test was one of patience.'

'Laerimmer clapped him on the shoulder. 'Well done! You and Tanek have both won through.'

'And our shaman?'

Laerimmer pointed to a bulky shadow farther down the hill. 'Briht left the circle. Though I didn't kill him,' he added hastily. 'He died by his own fear. A pity, for his throat must still be cut over the growing crops and now the blood won't be fresh.'

This was ugly, even for the Kingmaker, but Fearn kept his temper. Already, with the test behind him, he was thinking once more of Sarmatia and Krete. He straightened and squared his shoulders, then became aware of

Laerimmer's smirk.

What did the Kingmaker know? What was the final test for Tanek and himself?

Chapter 6

Krete, 1561BC. Summer.

The boy ran slowly and vaulted too soon, lurching forward onto the straw as he landed.

'Do that at your Passage, you'll not live,' said Sarmatia quietly. 'Never leap early, you'll miss the bull.' The boy looked blankly at her through his black hair, but lumbered to his feet to pick straw from his loin cloth and try again.

Remembering her own early failures, Sarmatia stopped him. 'No, it's Twinon this time.' She glanced at a group of whispering initiates standing in the shade of the courtyard. 'Nervous, Twinon?'

A small, wiry boy pushed through the little crowd and moved with insulting slowness to the earth ramp which served as a vaulting point. A born showman, he paused before bursting into action and tumbled well, taking only a step forward for balance at the end.

'Bend your knees more,' said Sarmatia. 'Try again—without the ramp.'

The boy moved off more eagerly this time. Sarmatia knew that what he needed was the shock of the Bull Rite, but the others were still far behind. The girl sighed. Twinon would have to learn to wait, as she had.

'Sarmatia!'

She waited until Twinon had completed his leap and then turned. It was a messenger, a runner.

'You can go,' Sarmatia said quickly to the Initiates. 'Meet here again before dusk. I'll bring Nestor.'

Ignoring the faces panic-stricken at the prospect of facing a real bull, however tame, and Twinon's studied calm, Sarmatia sprinted across the courtyard to the messenger. It was Kutatos. He knew what she was waiting for.

Just in time, Sarmatia remembered her manners. 'Welcome!' She smiled at him and pointed to the shady stair. Kutatos slumped onto the steps and waited as she fetched a cup of water from the pail kept ready for the training sessions. Kutatos drank and gave his news.

'There's a ship in today with a northerner aboard. He gave me something for you.'

Sarmatia felt her heart quicken as much as it did in the Bull Rite. 'You don't know his name?'

'Sorry, Sarmatia, but no.'

'What color hair?' *Please let it be red. Please let it be Fearn.*

Kutatos frowned. Sarmatia dug her fingers into her palms and waited as he visibly strove to remember.

'Brown hair, I think,' replied Kutatos slowly.

'You're certain?'

'Yes.' The answer was definite. 'Brown like yours.'

'Oh!' Disappointment fell on her like a wave, threatening to crush her. She fought to catch her breath, warring with tears. After all her waiting and hopes, it wasn't Fearn. But there was something: Kutatos had brought her it.

'Thanks for telling me.' She took of one of her gold armlets, and held it out. 'Here, a gift for your new-born daughter. I hope it brings her luck.' *Now please give me the "something".*

'I'm sure it will.' Taking the bangle, Kutatos admired its color and delicacy in the sunlight. He rose and – finally! – handed her a fragment of papyrus. 'I think this may be news of Fearn.'

Sarmatia looked at him gravely. 'I hope so.' She touched his arm in gratitude as Kutatos turned and left.

'Sarmatia, forgive me. I can't return. They've made me king. They will not make me marry! Know that I love you. I do not break our vow. Always, I'll remember you. Be happy. Marry wisely. Goodbye, Bull Head.'

Then, scrawled in haste on the bottom of the papyrus:

'Better to be a merchant than a king. The amber trader comes to Krete with this letter. After summer he returns north. If you'd send a message for me, or a thing of yours to keep safe, entrust yourself to him. His name is Loge. His wife travels with him: her name is Ell.'

Loge the amber trader had died in Tartessus, the silver city beyond the Pillars. His wife had handed the letter on for another to deliver. Sarmatia read Fearn's message, wondering how many hands it had passed through. She read aloud, for only the sacred house-snakes could hear her here, in the pillar crypt of the temple of Phaistos. The words jolted from her lips but, even now, she did not cry. It was a strange relief to know that she had not waited for nothing. Fate, not faithlessness, had parted them. A king does not desert his homelands. Whoever heard of Minos leaving Krete?

The papyrus shifted on Sarmatia's knee as a sacred snake wove its way along her thigh and settled in her skirt folds. Sarmatia ignored it, studying the scroll. She noticed how spindly was the script, how poorly drawn its Kretan characters. She smiled at the way the scribe had substituted Egyptian lettering wherever he did not know the Kretan symbol. In these things she sensed Fearn, and the writing on the scroll blurred as she pictured him composing the letter, squatting amongst the ashes of a hut fire and drawing the message on what was probably a last scrap of precious papyrus, found in his baggage. He would have hummed as he worked, his eyes fixed and unblinking.

Comforted by this vivid image, Sarmatia determined what she would do. The letter was proof that Fearn was unchanged: he could have sent no message and waited instead for the second year to elapse, when the vow between them would be finished. *They will not make me marry.* The words were there, stabbed onto the paper in anger. In one place the pen had punctured the papyrus.

Sarmatia stretched out flat in the crypt. Her instincts, which had kept her alive through the rite of the bull and which she had learnt to trust, were edging her forward towards leaving Krete. Fearn had not asked this of her. The journey would be long and might be dangerous. His letter had released her. Yet the message also spoke of the amber trader and his wife as two people Sarmatia could trust—with even herself? The possibility, delicate as a wish, hung about the letter like a thing unsaid. Had the trader not died... Sarmatia clutched the papyrus to her breast in a futile anger.

Know that I love you. 'I love you, Fearn,' she whispered and felt hot tears trickling down her face. She wept for herself, for her family who would never know Fearn now, for their lost life on Krete. She rolled into a ball on the hard floor of the crypt with the snakes coiling about her and cried until her throat was aching and dry.

Finally, she stretched out again and closed her eyes. If the Goddess sent her dream-spirit away, so it would be. She was growing old for the Bull Rite. Her parents were dead— Sarmatia's mother had died in childbirth— and she could not live in her brother's house forever. Yet Kretan men looked only at her hips for child-bearing. They saw nothing more.

Sarmatia's last thought as sleep took hold was of Fearn and the warm embrace he gave her on the day she accepted his bronze ring. Her last feeling was of the cool roughness of the snakes as they crawled over her body.

* * * *

Returning home in the late afternoon next day, she found Miropa waiting. 'So you've finally decided to come back!' said her sister-in-law, as Sarmatia bent under the low entrance of the streetside door. 'What do you have there?'

The girl held out her hand. 'Herbs, for your toothache.'

Miropa peered suspiciously at the freshly-picked plants. Her mouth dipped down at one corner and she flicked the lank, blonde fringe of hair from her brow by an impatient movement of her head. 'That's been easier, since you left. It's my belly now, the curse-cramps, and they've been terrible, keeping me awake at night. Not that you'd know what I mean.'

'I'll make up the brazier fires.' With the older woman's gaze fixed upon her, she was glad of something to do.

Miropa snorted, frustrated by Sarmatia's lack of tears. She lashed out, scratching at any wound. 'Your fancy northerner's given you up, hasn't he? Decided the journey's not worth it.' She paused but, seeing that Sarmatia remained outwardly calm and would not raise her eyes from the kindling fire, Miropa tried again. 'What will you do now? Few men take to another's lees, once the vessel's been dipped in.'

Again I am put in the wrong, Sarmatia thought, clamping her teeth on an unkind answer. The knowledge did nothing to lessen her own grief. 'Let's not quarrel,' she said, stretching out a hand to her surly sister-in-law. 'Saw your brother's son today. Handsome, like all his tribe. How old is he?'

By such persuasion, by admiring her sister-in-law's weaving and by preparing the evening meal, Sarmatia soothed her into a reasonable humor. When the rest of the household returned at twilight, Miropa greeted her husband amiably enough.

'A true welcome!' Tazaros threw off his cap, returned his wife's kiss and pulled her into a rough, affectionate hug. 'A pretty bed-mate, a full table, an obedient sister. What more can a man want? Nothing, eh Sarmatia?'

'Not if he's wise.' Sarmatia smiled at him, her spirits lifting. She cared dearly for Tazaros, dark and compact as a peppercorn. Freed by his presence, Sarmatia became quick and deft. In setting out the platters she paused to throw a scrap to the hunting dog which had crept in with Tazaros, and watched as the farmer played with the hand-reared kid and joked with his wife and the hired shepherd. Doubt gnawed at her. These were her family. To cast them off was unthinkable.

When they had eaten, Tazaros became serious. 'So, Sarmatia, you're back with us after your time in the crypt.' He addressed his younger sister across the ruins of their meal. 'And what did the gods whisper there?'

Sarmatia blushed, aware of Miropa's eye upon her probing for weaknesses. She did not want to tell her dreams to such an audience. Like a bird her spirit had flown to Fearn's homeland on the Isle of Stones, crossing dark seas till it rested on the Great Stone Circle, the holiest shrine of the Island. From there she had turned right around, saluting sun, moon and star.

'Well, sister!' Miropa cried. 'What are you to do?'

'Go.' Sarmatia looked at her brother. 'I learned in a dream that Fearn still lives.' She had seen his face as an old man. 'I must leave.' Her voice was calm, but her hands twisted in her lap like the fading brazier flames.

Tazaros looked at her. 'Let me see Fearn's letter.' He read it slowly, being more familiar with crop tallies. Once or twice he asked the meaning of a written character.

Sarmatia left the table to take the hand-reared kid upon her lap. She dared not guess what Tazaros might say.

Her brother spoke. 'It would seem honest enough.'

'I can go?' Her sense of release was not lessened by Miropa's expression of disgust, but Tazaros checked her.

'Not so reckless, sister. The man Loge, of the letter, where is he? Dead, you say.' Tazaros's face tightened. 'Had he lived, perhaps there might have been a way.' He slammed his knife point-first into the table and glared at

Sarmatia over the hilt. 'You will not go.'

'But you don't doubt Fearn?' Sarmatia started softly, stroking the hand-reared kid.

Tazaros frowned. 'He gave you a ring and you're young, pretty,' he answered, as though to him that explained all. Yet Tazaros was no fool. 'A pretty girl on a ship and a two-month journey. I can't allow it.' His broad hands had found a supper bone to grind on the table. Sarmatia watched the pale bone turning while she caressed the kid.

'Who would touch a Bull Rider?' she asked.

'And we should pay for this?' Miropa interrupted, feeling herself in the right. Sarmatia ignored her. Tazaros, unmoved, gestured for quiet. The battle lay between these two.

'If I had a companion on the ship,' Sarmatia said, 'would that be sufficiently proper for you, brother?'

The man's dark features stormed. 'By all the gods! Your famous luck will not run forever!'

'Pergia the snake priestess should satisfy even you!'

There was an astonished silence. Beside her, Sarmatia heard the hired shepherd mutter a prayer. To him and to many others the snake priestess was such a one of power. In truth, she had not thought of Pergia until then, but at once the thought was good. Need made it so.

'You're very free with Pergia's fellowship,' said Tazaros, approaching her. 'Should you not ask first?'

'So Pergia is a suitable companion?'

'Even Strongylans would not dare abuse our Priestess.' Tazaros ran a hand through his thick, black hair, across his clean-shaven face. 'But you'll never persuade her to leave Krete, Sarmatia.'

'If I do, you must let me go, Tazaros.'

The hired man smiled at Sarmatia's persistence. Tazaros sighed and crouched before her chair. 'How would you travel? It's such a long journey for a girl.'

Sarmatia felt a twist of feeling at the sight of her brother's anxious face. Don't go, habit tugged within her. The bronze ring rocked upon her breastbone. It was too late. She had made her choice.

'Come, Sarmatia. What are these plans of yours?'

'Egypt first, to find Misarios to guide us. Then on to Tartessus and the tin-lands. Fearn's people are the Atterians: the smiths know of them. For gold, a smith will guide me to their homeland.'

'Never mind that. What do you want with Strongylan Misarios? He has an evil reputation.' Tazaros had forgotten that he and Sarmatia were part-Strongylan, through their maternal grandmother. Sarmatia judged it wise not to remind him.

'Misarios knows the safest way through the Pillars.' She nodded to the hired man, who had risen to his feet, bidding goodnight to the family.

The instant the street door closed, Miropa also stood up from the table. 'I can't waste any more time on this foolishness.' She began to clear platters. Tazaros had not spoken, so Sarmatia laid the kid gently in its box by the door to help her sister-in-law. This seemed to stir her brother and he caught her back, his features working with a new thought.

'Egypt! That's the Nubian's homeland.'

Sarmatia nodded. 'But Ramose lives near Memphis. I plan to stay at Buto, with Paser.'

'Kinsman Paser, eh? Well, he's a good host. You'll be safe with him.' Tazaros wagged a finger at her. 'Promise me to keep clear of Ramose. That man got you a goring when you met.'

'I promise.' Did Tazaros know that he had agreed, with that vow, to let her go? Sarmatia looked at her brother, ashamed of her excitement. 'I'll send word from the north, so that you know I'm safe.' Tazaros muttered something. Sarmatia moved closer. 'What, brother?'

Tazaros whipped back his head, his full lips livid where he had bitten them. 'Your dowry will be spent on shipboard places. You do know that?'

'I'll have the gold from the Bull Rite.' From the kitchen below, Sarmatia heard Miropa say that she should beware of filching jewels of hers, but the girl let that pass for the sake of her brother.

'Are we agreed, then, Tazaros?' she asked, under the noise of the domestic chores. 'I don't like us quarrelling.'

Tazaros gave the side of her head a shove. 'You don't like giving in! Nor do I. You leave this house, Sarmatia, and I give my blessing, on one condition. Pergia must agree—and agree freely, sister—to go with you.'

Chapter 7

Krete, 1561BC. Summer.

Pergia had spent a sleepless night. She sat slackly on the stone seat in her garden, hands held loosely in her lap. After a choking wheeze, she spoke. 'You say you've bought a place for me on the Egyptian ship? Why?'

Sarmatia nodded. 'And for myself. Why should you not come with me?' she added quickly. 'What is there for you in Krete?'

Delicately Sarmatia refrained from mentioning that Pergia was nearly thirty years old, with no family and without a dowry. On Krete, for a woman not to marry meant a lonely and poor old age. On ship, Pergia might find new connections. Sarmatia knew she was right to persuade. 'Why deny yourself the chance to travel, to grow?'

Pergia stared at her shawl. 'And the Goddess, Sarmatia? What of her?'

'There are shrines on the Isle of Stones.'

'I have no close family,' Pergia murmured. 'My duties do not bind me to one place. The Mother, as you say, is everywhere. If you desert me, I'll have no one.' In the village only beggars and outcasts had neither family nor friends. The Priestess had even made enemies, some as powerful as herself, through high-mindedness and pride.

Pergia lifted up her head and her black eyes flashed. 'So I must come. See the Nile and the northern temples.' She did not smile. There was a new souring in the affection between them. Sarmatia had failed Tazaros, too, in his wish that Pergia should agree freely to be her travelling companion.

Sarmatia knew this, but justified her actions by reminding herself of the new horizons Pergia would certainly enjoy. She had not really been ruthless, more of a friend. Surely she had done right? Full of guilt, she walked from the garden and ran wildly down to the street to find her brother.

* * * *

Preparations now became hectic. There were clothes to wash and boots to repair, letters of introduction to be sent on to Paser, sacrifices to be made for a safe journey. Sarmatia saw little of her family and, when she was at home, Tazaros was out of doors. Farming was hard on Krete. It was not until the very last evening before her departure that Sarmatia admitted to herself—with a foul-tasting retch—that she was indeed going to leave. Those bundles of possessions standing ready by the door were hers. Yet so far she had spoken no more than a dozen words to her brother, and she would never see him again.

Suddenly afraid, Sarmatia rushed to find him. He was not in the storeroom, nor in the sleeping chambers. In the weaving room there was only Miropa, re-threading her shuttle with bright new wool. Sarmatia called from the threshold: 'Have you seen Tazaros? Do you know where he is?'

Miropa shrugged. 'No.'

'Did he say when he was coming home today?'

Sarmatia's sister-in-law avoided her eyes. 'I don't think he did.' Seating herself comfortably at her loom, Miropa began to work by lamplight, singing softly under her breath.

Her mocking song followed Sarmatia downstairs and out into the street, where there was still no sign of her brother. *Where are you*, thought Sarmatia, as her aching lungs forced her to pause. *Will I go tomorrow, without even a farewell?* Sarmatia knew just how little time she and Tazaros would have together in port, with sailors and cargo jostling round. She'd already experienced that kind of snatched leave-taking with Fearn.

The family shrine. Why had she not thought of it before? Snatching up her long skirts, Sarmatia pelted to the building. With no more than a cursory blink towards the threshold spirits, she tumbled inside.

Tazaros steadied her and began shouting. 'Where've you been? I've waited here for over two oil-wick lengths! Didn't Miropa say where I was?'

'I'm sorry.' Sarmatia was, too. She should have known that Tazaros would come here, where the spirits of their parents would witness their parting. As for Miropa, Sarmatia decided that the best way to deal with the woman was to say nothing of her lies. Miropa should never know the fear and trouble she had caused.

'Got everything then?' demanded Tazaros heartily.

'I have.'

'Are you sure? I saw Pergia in the street today carrying an armload of washing that was just her dresses.'

'Pergia likes clothes.'

'Women usually do.' Tazaros gave his sister a sidelong glance. 'One gown and your ritual costume! I hope you're not going to wear that on ship.'

'Of course not.'

'Can't you stay?'

The question pierced her, but she fought to answer it. 'Tazaros, you know yourself there's no one for me here. You must know too that you and Miropa will be easier—it will be better—when I'm gone.'

Tazaros took a long, heavy breath. 'I agree with you on that, but I still don't understand. Why do you want to leave?'

'Why not? A promise has been made.' Sarmatia felt herself grow hot. 'If I were a man, no one would wonder at my going.'

That reply, although true, did not satisfy Tazaros. He scratched at his scalp, a habit when puzzled. 'Why Fearn? Is it because he was a stranger, and different? Or because he saved your life? And how long did you know him? One month, perhaps two?'

'That's longer than you knew Miropa before you married her.'

Tazaros sighed, reaching across and grasping Fearn's ring in his fist. He tugged on the cord on which she wore the ring about her throat. 'Do you know this man at all? This foreigner?'

'He knew me! He understood—' Sarmatia stopped. She wanted to go on and say that Fearn had recognized how she was different, how animals were not wild and strange to her but a part of her, rounding out her life. Without the bird's song or the cat's sinewy grace, what kind of half-awake existence would there be for her? But she could not say this to Tazaros. He'd think her mad. 'I talked to him,' she finished awkwardly.

'That's enough, is it?'

But Sarmatia could see that already Tazaros knew it was enough. They embraced silently, each willing the other not to weep. Sarmatia knew that the hurt she was feeling was still the tip of the pain. The full shaft would take months to work its way in and years to heal. She wrapped her arms even tighter around her brother, feeling her backbone crack.

Finally she had to let go as Tazaros roughly pulled away, pacing up and down the family shrine. 'Go on then! We're not enough for you, Bull Rider. You must have a king!'

Ignoring the tears which rose in Sarmatia's eyes then, Tazaros burst from the building, running out into the darkness. For better or worse, her farewells were finished, her choices made. Now she could only leave.

Chapter 8

Egypt, 1561 BC. Summer.

The scribe, Paser, sends this letter to his father. A ship from Keftiu has come and brought the child of our brother. Sarmatia is the name of the maiden. She is a girl taller than your son Paser, a priestess of Apis, the glorious ox-god. She has a face as bright as a star. The bustling Priestess of the Snake, Pergia, neat even to her braided black hair, is her companion. Write to me. Fare well!

The scribe, Paser, sends this letter to his father. I have written letters for Sarmatia concerning the seaman Misarios. Misarios lived once in Busiris and I wrote to the scribe there, saying, 'Send me word of this man,' but the scribe answered that Misarios was no longer known in Busiris. Now Sarmatia and my servants wander through the streets of our city, seeking news. There is no one in Buto who has heard of Misarios. Father, have you word of him? If you know where he is, write to me.

Today a herald of Akenptah, the High Priest, came to my house! I am to sail to Mazghuna, to be presented at the palace of the priest! Concerning my family and guests, who have also been invited, I have advised each as to how they should behave.

I shall write soon, father. There is much haste in my house. My wife has instructed the servants to wash all our clothes.

Chapter 9

Isle of Stones, 1562 BC. Winter, five months earlier.

Fearn chopped wood because he was still learning patience. In the midwinter after the great fire that had destroyed his royal family's home he needed something against which to pit his strength. Time was moving on. He should be making ready for a long sea journey. Two years he'd asked Sarmatia to wait, and already five seasons had passed and he no nearer to going south.

The first testing, and Briht's death, now a week ago, had not been enough. The royal family wanted more blood, and he and Tanek were the ones to supply it. Fearn's axe smashed into the wood on the block and two log halves, each as long and wide as a man's foot, flew steeply off the wood block in opposing directions.

'Were you hoping that was our Kingmaker's head?' came a voice.

Fearn grunted and hauled another timber onto the block. 'Stunted wit,' he muttered, swinging the axe and feeling the blade bite into the tender wood. He kicked the split log into the pile and wiped shavings from his brow.

'Have you taken root, man?' He glared at his visitor. Fearn always found Goar's languid manner irritating. 'What is it? If it's Chalda and Laerimmer's latest quarrel, I'll have heard it before in another guise.' Without waiting for a reply, Fearn cast his eyes over the sagging roof of the royal house. 'Someone must work here.'

'And if it were left to such as me, we'd starve with cold or hunger? You must be right, Fearn: you're usually right.' Goar smiled, the dimples in his cheeks and chin belying any malice in his words. The iciest girl had been known to melt at that smile, and even Fearn discovered he was not immune. He relaxed and extended his free hand.

'I've a bear's temper today. Say what's on your mind, Goar.'

Goar, as easy in this as in all things, shook hands and said in his light voice, 'You don't really want to fight Tanek.'

It seemed unlike Goar to be so perceptive, yet the man was right. Healing was Fearn's trade, not killing. Two years older than Tanek, Fearn knew he would have the advantage in the fight, whereas he and the twins were of an age and height.

'Don't go wishing you could fight me or Gygest. It's against our natures, too.'

Goar startled him a second time, making Fearn wonder if he had been hasty in his judgment of the man. He shook his head. 'Fighting you or your brother might be more of a match. Trying to make me nervous, Goar?'

Fearn meant the question as a jest and was surprised by the cold answer. 'I'd hoped to change your mind about food. Tanek and Anoi have left for the battlefield and I thought you might wish to break bread with us. We are your family, healer.'

There was a further, hidden, barb in this reply, touching on his personal affairs, and Fearn reddened. 'A family which forces its children to murder. Oh yes, we're a nice breed.' He gripped the axe again in both hands.

'Go on,' he said, through gritted teeth. 'Let me be. Tell Laerimmer to make Tanek king!' he yelled after his cousin's retreating back, but such an act was against custom and both of them knew it.

Walking into the woodlands, Fearn found his mood darkening as the sun flickered out between the trees, a bronze mirror sinking into the black lake of night. He did not want this kingdom, or this fight. Let Tanek have the crown. The boy was already obsessed by it.

Fearn ducked under the last boughs of ash and hazel into a twilit forest clearing filled with people. In their midst was a young warrior, tall yet lightly made, dressed in boots and short tunic. Tanek carried a spear and a round, leather-covered shield. His long fair hair was coiled and plaited with beads and feathers. Fearn closed on the youth, the crowd giving way to let him through.

As he approached, Laerimmer pushed his way through the crush and tossed two strange crowns onto the ground. These were of leather and bone, the sharp yearling antlers of a stag. With sinking heart, Fearn plucked them from the mud. He, unlike Tanek, had never been a follower of the Horned

God, a cruel deity thirsting for the sacrifice of slain men. These earth gods were not for him: rather the wonders of sunlight and sky. Fearn knew that the Horned God would not fight for him. Grimly, he bound one of the crowns about his temples. When he had done, it seemed that the horns of a stag grew out of his red-gold hair. He held out the second crown to the young warrior and spoke.

'It seems strange not to greet you today, Tanek, and I'm sorry for it.'

The beardless youth's face showed no expression. He snatched at the crown and stabbed downwards with his spear, driving the point into the dead grass between them. 'Here's what I'll do to your guts, Fearn!'

Fearn's shoulders dipped. No one heard him sigh. While Tanek fixed the antler crown on his head, Fearn stripped off his sheepskin cloak, revealing a much-patched, sleeveless tunic. He looked round at the mass of people, sickened by the blood-lust shining in their eyes. Then, out at the mob's back, his sweeping gaze found Orm, his father's brother. Lame Orm had taken Anoi, Tanek's half-sister, into an embrace and was speaking to her.

The scene gave Fearn a strange comfort. A cluster of memories of his stocky Uncle Orm fell through his mind. To no one but his grandmother and Orm had he been able to show grief when his parents had died in that summer plague. Here at least, in Orm and Anoi, were two who did not revel in killing.

'Get back,' he commanded the rest. 'No one should die today who needn't.'

The crowd fell back, merging into the trees, and he and Tanek were alone in the clearing. A fire had been lit at its flattest point and they would fight by the garish flames.

It was sundown, midwinter, and freezing. Their breaths hung in great clouds before them. Fearn could feel his tightened scrotum, his body hairs stiff with the cold. An owl hooted and he spun into the path of the sound.

'You look afraid,' mocked Tanek. 'Your face is as white as a woman's.'

Fearn gazed at the boy, trying to look beyond the maze of muscle and bone to the man beneath. This was the same impulsive youth he had wrestled and chased round the royal homestead only eight days ago. By ill-chance they were enemies, and it seemed that Tanek was pleased that they should be so.

Fearn approached the young warrior, firelight playing over his strong profile and silhouetting the eerie horn crown. 'All men should be afraid to face death, or to give it.'

'Coward!' Tanek rushed at him.

Tanek was quick and deadly, yet Fearn was almost as fast and taller, with a longer reach. They fought around the blood-red fire like two stags locking horns amidst the flaming colors of a winter forest, and each time they joined, Fearn's heart hammered his breastbone. Out of a great stillness round his head and torso the bronze spear thrust in and his axe knocked it aside, metal blocked on stone.

Tanek leapt back and the axe shaft bounced harmlessly on his shield. He struck, aiming for the bowel. Fearn jerked sideways and shot his arm into the black space left by his opponent. The axe cut a huge divot from the top of the wooden shield and Tanek toppled forward from the force of the blow. Fearn knew he could strike now and finish it, but a boy?

Tanek regained his feet, slashing out with both spear and shield. He was becoming possessed by the Horned God, frenzy glowing in his face. Fearn parried blow after blow, his own attacks increasingly awkward and weary. The Earth God was winning, and where was the Sky God that should be in him?

Suddenly Tanek cut for the heart and struck flesh, his spear ripping through sinew and muscle. Fearn yelled, the cold pain sparking in his mind. Now he felt his god, blasting the lightning-bolt into his injured right arm. He had been dreaming, listening to the soft counsels of despair. Now he was awake.

'Sarmatia!' The paean ripped from his lungs, echoing round the clearing as he swept up a rock the size of a man's head and whipped it at his enemy, smashing a second gaping hole in Tanek's shield. There was a rush of light, cool and shade, a jolting crash, and Fearn's shoulder barged into Tanek, snapping the man's shield-arm and knocking him down. Again the axe swung and fell and Tanek's crown shattered, fragments of horn hurtling into the fire. Fearn heard the shriek as the Horned God fled, deserting Tanek as he writhed and died.

Fearn sank to his knees beside the corpse and tore the crown of the deceiving Horned God from his own bloodstained hair. Battle-hot and burning, he started to lay out Tanek, clumsily hacking at the boy's tunic to bind and hide his head. Some inner voice was telling him to hurry, so that

Anoi would not see Tanek with half his jaw gone, an ear and temple smashed. Part of the horn crown had embedded itself in the soft mess of the lad's brains and Fearn was attempting to remove that when the first of the crowd reached him.

They were laughing and congratulating him on a good fight, not mourning as he expected. Men seized and shook his hands and women grabbed at him, several dabbing his bloody arm while making bawdy comments on his battle-prowess. A few pressed against him in blatant invitation.

Fearn was still youthful enough to be shocked, particularly when Anoi forced her way through this admiring tide of flesh and came face to face with her brother. Staring blue eye met staring blue eye. Anoi uttered a low moan. Her pale, narrow face, translucent in the firelight as the slender moon above them, searched for and found his. He flinched against a look of loathing, a raised fist or a curse and yet there was none, only a clear, tear-bright gaze and gentle, accepting grief. Alone and unaided, she completed the grim business of laying out the corpse. Anoi made the women's attentions towards him, the living victor, vulgar.

Bile rose in Fearn's throat. He swallowed the bitter mouthful, conscious of a throbbing in his arm. He made his right hand into a fist and the ache worsened, yet he could tell there was no lasting damage. He would have a scar for life—a truer reminder of Tanek than an urn of bones in the burial ground.

And it was surely time that arrangements were made for the boy's interment. Where were Laerimmer and the other heads of households? Trying to ignore the patting, twittering women, Fearn got off his knees. All the Atterians seemed to be in the clearing, even children and babes in arms. In the semi-darkness Fearn caught glimpses of faces, row after row of white discs raised up to his as he passed. Fire and moonlight glinted on copper brooches and daggers. People were waiting for him to speak. They seemed to lean in towards him, to lean on him.

For an instant they seemed heavy, till a thought sped through his mind like a lightning track. Gathered close around, in their holiday clothes and mood, these people shone like the beads of a necklace. The people were a king's ornament.

His thought grew brighter: he would bring Sarmatia here. She would be the Kretan wife of an Atterian king.

First there was Tanek, and Anoi. Fearn walked quickly through the crowds. Well away from the fire and the main crush of people he spotted the Kingmaker speaking in close whispers to his own healer apprentice, Jart. He did not wait for them to finish, but strode up and grasped Laerimmer's shoulder.

'I want a grave-mound raised for Tanek,' he said, ready to answer the Kingmaker's objections to such an ancient funeral rite, but the reply was not Laerimmer's.

'By the Great Bear, put down that axe!' It was Kere, the Kingmaker's sister, who spoke. She, the women and most of the crowd had followed him. As Fearn stood amazed at men and girls he'd known all his life craning and straining for a better look at him, Kere was smearing some fearful-smelling unguent on his wound. He turned thankfully to a familiar craft.

'That ointment won't be needed.'

'I say it is, Fearn. You're our healer no longer.' Kere waved a hand at his apprentice, who had the grace to look surprised although, after Laerimmer's whispers, Jart must have guessed. Fearn blew out a long steam-cloud, his features settling into harsh lines. He held up a fist to kill the rustle of chatter and pitched his voice above the sputtering wind.

'Since when is a king not a healer?' He pointed to the kneeling Anoi, her long hair trailing on the ground while she tended her dead brother. 'I take Anoi into my care. There'll be three days' mourning for Tanek.' He paused a moment to think. He must say this next thing right. 'The Kingmaker shall crown me when I return from Krete.'

The wind was rising, flapping cloaks and tunics, blowing Fearn's hair into his eyes and mouth. It carried Laerimmer's answer to him in a discordant echo: 'You cannot leave. You are bound to the land.'

Everywhere, the wind seemed to be laughing. Laerimmer's face, dim but distinct in the dusk, bore a broad smile. Behind him the crowd, slower to understand, began to protest.

'You can't leave us!'

'You're our king!'

'Hail the King!' Laerimmer dropped to one knee, and the people answered, 'Hail the King!'

Their chant was a sword in Fearn's heart, killing his hopes. Warriors and headmen gave the royal salute and the closer masses pawed him with their hands, hungry for leadership. If he failed these Atterians now, they would kill him, as Laerimmer must have known, when he shouted.

A void opened in Fearn's mind as he realized how he had been trapped, and into the gap came Chalda.

'Is it so bad that you must stay with us, Fearn?' Her fingers slid down his arm to the hand still gripping the axe. 'Tell me, Fearn, do you have no use for your other weapons?'

Her hand seemed to slip then from the axe across his loins. By the nearest onlookers it might easily be missed, or seen as an accident, but Fearn knew it was deliberate. Had he not seen Chalda act in the same way with his own apprentice? The two should have been betrothed, except that Waroch had not allowed it, saying that Chalda should not marry a commoner. She had tried to force his hand by becoming pregnant, but miscarried the child. Lately it seemed that her sights were set higher. Why seduce Jart when a new young king was there for the taking?

Laerimmer, whose eyes missed nothing, mentioned a royal marriage. Around him, whistling like the wind, Fearn could hear the crude jokes. But the family would not trap him a second time. Releasing the axe and catching Chalda's wrist in a grip which would pain the girl but keep her silent, Fearn spoke to the people. He told them to return quietly to their homes, for it was winter and dark and would soon be very cold.

'Those of you with children must think of these things. There's nothing more for you to see. The royal family will take up Tanek's body and we'll hold a watch for him tonight.' He saw the disappointed looks and promised them a feast when he was crowned. After that, the Atterians were content enough to call their families and leave. Yet another hour passed before Fearn had said farewell to the last stragglers and well-wishers. A king, he was finding, is rarely alone.

He returned to the clearing, to where his own family squatted near the embering fire, warming winter-frozen fingers and feet. He had hoped Gygest or Goar would have had the sense to use the axe he had left to cut down timber for a bier, yet neither he nor the others had even chopped firewood. Kere and Chalda were both shivering, though they at least had retrieved his sheepskin and draped it on top of their cloaks as an extra layer. Cursing under his breath, Fearn walked towards them, boots and leggings creaking with frost. The twins darted up to meet him, Goar punching him on the back and calling him lucky. Laerimmer spoke to him, but Fearn's eyes, always good, had seen a cramped, lonely figure at the poor side of the fire.

Ignoring the Kingmaker's congratulations, Fearn walked round to where Anoi was seated by her dead brother, hugging her knees and rocking herself. She had laid her cloak over the boy and a sudden wood-flare shone on her face, showing it bleached with cold. She had been Tanek's only living close-kin. Even in looks they were alike, both slender and fair, although Anoi was tiny and fragile while Tanek had been tall and wiry. The pity of it wrenched water into Fearn's eyes. She was too young to have to bear such grief. Eighteen years old. Sarmatia's age.

'Anoi.' He forced himself to speak to her. The rocking stopped, though her eyes would not meet his. What could he say? At the end of the fight, it had been Tanek or himself. Would she blame him for living? 'I'm sorry.' The words seemed nothing, worse than nothing, an insult. He could not bear her huddled silence. Slamming his fist into the frost-splintered ground to stop his own tears, Fearn whipped round, leapt to his feet and tore the cloaks from the twins' backs.

'Have you no shame? This child is half-dead through grief and cold, and you sit at ease and talk and do nothing?' Crouching, he wrapped Anoi's stiff form in the two cloaks and almost gave way when a white hand crept from between the cloak folds to clasp his and a clear voice whispered, 'One day I shall give you a cloak, Fearn. I promise.'

He hushed her quickly, then rose and sprang forward. He seized Kere and Chalda by the scruffs of their necks, hauling them upright. 'Look after your cousin, little idlers!' he snapped, sending Kere off with a push and Chalda with a slap. Rubbing their affected parts, the women hurried to Anoi and Fearn moved on to the twins and Laerimmer.

'Where's Jart?' he demanded.

'I told him to go home with his family.' Keeping himself tightly muffled against the cold, Laerimmer tried to sound unconcerned. 'He's no longer wanted here.'

'By you and Chalda, no doubt. But he's my man, not yours.' Out in the shadows from the fire Fearn heard Anoi beginning to weep. Though that was a healing sign, it heated his already quickened temper. He must keep a tight rein on himself. 'I'm the King.'

Instantly all were agreeing: Laerimmer smooth, Gygest solemn, Goar enthusiastic. Not one grieved over Tanek. It was as though the youth had never existed. Unfairly, perhaps, Fearn felt his anger blister into rage. He hung on grimly.

'Wait a moment.' His voice choked off theirs. 'If I'm King, then I must rule. And I will rule.' His eyes flashed. 'As king I cannot leave. But I swear this: I'll choose my own mate, and in my own time.' There had to be a way. If he could but find it.

'Forget the southerner. What we need is a union within the royal family.' Laerimmer had spotted the softening in his face. 'The people must come before pleasure.'

'Oh, I don't know,' drawled Goar. 'Our cousin's not unattractive.' With both hands he described Chalda's generous curves. 'And no doubt your girl will find consolation, Fearn.'

It was enough: the fight, the injury, a kingdom he did not want, his shiftless, selfish family and Goar's foolish speech. Fearn's hold on his patience snapped and the gale began.

'You speak like this to me, your own King? By the Mother, you're even more lacking in sense than I thought! I've kept silent before, but now I shall speak and you will listen. Goar, delighter of women! Where was your woman-love today, with Anoi stretched like a pining dog beside her dead brother? Gygest, the stronger of the twins! Why have you not used those arms to rebuild the royal house, fit for a king? Laerimmer, subtle and sly. You see all things and nothing!'

The wind howled in his ears, blocking their replies. Out of the black night came hail, scoring against flesh. Fearn took a deep breath. The rage was dark within him, a storm gathering.

'I'll never sleep in the royal house again unless Sarmatia is at my side. I shall live in the house of my father, Orm's house, and you'll seek me there for my judgments.'

The power was growing, drawing in his body like a strong fire. The Sky God was in him, throwing a deeper burr in his voice. 'It's time you learned what kind of king you have.'

'O, Mother,' whispered Laerimmer, his features grayer than the sleet, 'he's a storm bringer. That's his kingly power.' He sank to his knees and covered his face.

Fearn watched Laerimmer dispassionately. His sight was altered and he saw the clearing and those within it through a flowing river of symbols: spirals and running lines, such as are carved on the standing stones by shamans. Then he floated above the forest, looking down on the trees, on his own body.

'You've not forgotten our pact?' asked the Sky God at his back and, though the cost of speech was a tearing of his vitals, liver and heart ripped as though by an eagle's beak, Fearn kept himself and his anger whole.

'I remember,' he answered, his voice no more than a rasp.

'You'll summon me best by standing stones. Your forefathers understood such matters.' Heat that might have been breath fell like a brand upon Fearn's neck, but he remained silent. After an age or an instant the god said, 'Your spirit animals chose you for your strength. For their sakes, mortal—for they are aspects of myself—I grant you power. Call me where you will.'

Lightning struck the stone axe by his feet, flinging it high into the air. Jolted back into his own body, Fearn saw the axe falling to earth. He ran and caught it by the smoldering wooden handle as the second thunderbolt blew into the stone head.

The force of the blast passed through stone to wood to bone: shoulder blade, hip-bone, ankle. He was illuminated in a starburst, tossed back off his feet like a doll. Over and over he tumbled in a narrow passageway of light: sunlight, snow-light, moonlight, distilled into a single point striking into the cores of his eyes.

'The vision of a god. See what I see, hear what I hear.' The passageway itself spoke. Impaled by the eye of the Sky God, Fearn saw the world through an immortal's gaze. Mountains, trees and lakes were before him. He skimmed over seas, riding the knife of light, using anger to resist pain, channelling all into a tight beam. A country, village, street, crowd, face—

'Sarmatia?' He saw her walking in moonlight. Her hair was longer and glossier than he had remembered and he drank in the changing lines of her body. He could hear her calling to her brother. The Kretan street in which she moved was dusty. There had been little winter rain.

The scene blurred, the eye too hot for Fearn to hold. The bright passage closed about him.

Whenever you wish, this joining is here,' said the light. 'Use it as you will. You need not raise a storm. Speech, sight and touch are in my gift for you, and for the woman.'

'No, not for Sarmatia,' whispered Fearn, the last shred of his anger burning away. 'I beg you, withhold your gaze from her.' Set against his injured arm, the sight of the Sky God was worse to bear.

But a link had been made. Before he returned from the trance to calm and order his family, Fearn sought once more the burning eye and re-entered that pitiless light. He could not endure it long, yet he knew that he would use the god's eye again to find Sarmatia. To stretch out his mind to her, his hand...

For now he was content to know she was safe. Still the link was there and he would visit her through it. If he could, and the god allowed it, he would speak to her.

Over the following months, as winter gave way to spring and summer, he sought Sarmatia out. At times he could not make the link: the god did not allow it. Those times he could, he spoke to her, but she did not hear him.

Not yet, but she will, Fearn vowed. Each time he entered the burning eye of the Sky God he was determined that one day she would hear his voice.

Chapter 10

Egypt, 1561 BC. Summer.

When Paser, his family and guests entered the Palace of Akenptah, Sarmatia was detained by the Steward. The others were led away while she remained in the antechamber.

'You must come with me.' The Steward opened a door in the wall.

Sarmatia looked into a long sunlit gallery and hung back.

'Do not fear,' said the blue-wigged Steward, his voice hissing in the quiet. 'The Priest Akenptah is famed for his hospitality. Go to the end of the gallery. My lord awaits ahead in the Great Hall.' He bowed stiffly and left her.

The gallery was deserted. Sarmatia walked forward, desert sand pricking her toes. The quiet and the heavy scent of figs steadied her. Her companions would be safe. Akenptah was noted for his guest-gifts. Perhaps she should ask him to find Misarios.

Sarmatia grinned. She ran down the stair where the gallery joined the Great Hall. The barrel vault of the hall rose over her head. As she stood, hesitating, she felt something tug at her hair, then a burning cold. Over the din of her heart came a voice, *This man is a friend, Sarmatia.*

She turned her head slowly. Behind her the stairway was empty. 'Fearn?' From unease she was suddenly exhilarated. Fearn was not here, yet he had spoken. 'Fearn?'

There was no answer. The presence within and about her head eased, their moment of joining slipping away. Sarmatia moved to keep with it and stepped down the last step, the brightness within herself stretching to a single thread. It showed her a path to the dais then faded.

Sarmatia sped past the frescos of the Great Hall and dropped to her knees beside the dais throne. The figure seated there, its face hidden by the shadow of a column, turned towards her. There was a low laugh as the Nubian leaned forward.

'Welcome,' Ramose said softly. 'I see we remember each other. My son, you will be pleased to hear, is well.'

Sarmatia held his gaze, though her scalp was tight. She had been betrayed. It was not Fearn who had caught her by the hair. Like the fated warrior of ancient tales, she had been led by an evil spirit. 'My kinsman and the others?' she demanded, concern for their safety overriding her fear.

Ramose straightened, features impassive as he curved his hands over the lion-head carvings of the throne arms. 'They are being cared for by my wife. You, no doubt, have questions.'

'How can you be Ramose and Akenptah?'

'Listen to the word. "Aken-Ptah", "Pleasing to Ptah." I am his priest.' He touched the golden ornament of the god on his breast. 'Yet I am also Ramose.' The hand came down again onto the carved lion-head.

'I heard that Ramose lived in Memphis.'

'I have many estates.'

Sarmatia thought of the power concealed in that quiet, dignified response. She swallowed.

'But you're thirsty and I've offered you nothing.'

'No,' answered Sarmatia, glancing at the guards posted close to the dais steps. 'It's passed.' It would not be right for her to eat in the house of Ramose, whose son should never have been allowed near the bull, a man who might still be her enemy.

'Still, some wine might be pleasant,' said Ramose. 'Or have you tasted the waters of my country?' He rose from his chair and stepped from the dais, walking to the darkest part of the hall. In a series of precise movements the tall black priest removed a jar from its wooden tripod and poured water into two goblets.

Sarmatia took a sip of the Nile. It was warm, though kept in shade, and tasted faintly sweet. Gratefully, she drained it off.

'Come.' Ramose led her to the sunlit side of the hall. There on the wall, between the narrow windows, was a painting of a bull, the golden disc of godhead shining between its horns. Ramose halted beside the painting.

'Here is Apis, the bull whom you hold sacred through the rites of initiation.' Ramose touched a painted hoof in reverence. 'In this land, the

God Apis dwells in the temple of Ptah at Memphis. Oh yes,' he added muted laughter to Sarmatia's gasp, 'there is more to bind us together than you know. You have served Apis. Apis lives on earth as a bull, and that bull is under the protection of Ptah. I am priest of Ptah.'

Sarmatia gazed upon the painting, an arm clamped to her side where she had once been gored.

'Were you very sick then?'

Sarmatia brought her hands up to her mouth. A vision of the Bull Rite flashed before her eyes. 'I walked within a month,' she answered shyly through her fingers.

'Did you receive the letter and jewels?'

The question took Sarmatia by surprise. 'I knew of no letter,' she began, but Ramose's reaction overtook hers.

'At last, the light of Ptah brings understanding.' The Nubian breathed a great sigh. 'You feared that I might blame you for drawing my family into danger, yes?

'I thought you'd be angry. It was through my error that your son was put at risk.'

'You were the one gored.' Ramose touched a side of his body through the flowing white robes. 'Would every leader have taken such pains?'

Sarmatia thought of Twinon, the boy she had trained as her successor in the Bull Rite. Twinon would have kept his skin safe. Once in the courtyard, by custom man, woman or child was fair game for the bull. 'I can't speak for them.' No one had died while she was trainer.

'You were a fast runner, to reach my son before the bull. Faster than me.' Ramose halted in his account, his handsome face still. After a moment he went on. 'It's time that we complete this matter.' He clapped his hands. I know whom you're seeking and will supply you with ship, cargo and crew. 'I'll help you find Misarios. Does this please you?'

'Very much! Thank you.' For a moment, Sarmatia felt she had almost too much to think of: this unexpected generosity, the play of the spirit world upon her life, Fearn's voice.

Ramose bent his head and set the kiss of welcome upon her forehead. 'I'm pleased that you're here,' he said softly. 'And I know Fearn the healer. You need not fear his spirit-voice. Heed what it tells you.'

He turned on his heel and walked towards the stairway, a nobleman sure of his power. When he reached the stair he looked back at Sarmatia. 'Come. In my house you have nothing to fear.' He smiled and held out his hands. 'Let us join the others.'

* * * *

Three nights later, Ramose gave a banquet for his guests and the nobles of Memphis in the west wing of the Palace. It was a sultry evening and Sarmatia was glad of the sheer robe that she had been given to wear. When sure no one was watching, she wiped her face—remembering her eye make-up too late—and cast an envious glance at her companion.

Pergia, dressed as she was and with a beaded wig covering her black hair, looked cool and comfortable, chatting animatedly with Neith, wife of Ramose. Sensing Sarmatia's gaze, Pergia lifted her head, looking across the low tables set with food and wine, and smiled, but then frowned and looked away. Egypt was a pleasure. She had even lost her breathing problems in this dry, comfortable heat, yet why should she forgive Sarmatia for bringing her here? Pergia gave her attention to her dish of spiced meat, wiping her hands on her napkin, snapping her fingers at the servants for more wine.

Sarmatia returned the smile, but something in her ached like a bruise. She picked up her bronze cup and drank. From his couch by her right side, Ramose gently clasped her arm.

'Is the banquet to your liking?'

'Indeed, my lord.' Sarmatia did not understand why she could eat so little. Perhaps the servants, the nobles in their linens and jewels, the imposing design of the west wing, open to the sky, its four huge pillars of cedar wood, the vines from which guests plucked their own grapes, intimidated her more than she cared to admit.

Ramose leaned towards the girl and fed her a delicacy from his own dish, running a finger along her bottom lip. 'You're as beautiful tonight as Queen Karomama.'

The brief caress disturbed Sarmatia. Strange feelings had lately been stirring in her. She knew that sensitivity of skin and smell through the animals in their times of season, yet it was queer to feel such heat herself. And it was more intense, and not to be easily put aside as so often in the past, when she had instinctively withdrawn from animal-kinship with any beast that was in heat. Her life she would share with the wilderness, but not that.

Now, it seemed, she was changed. She was no longer a child, putting something aside as being too old for her. She had matured since leaving Krete. Her breasts ached now, which was something new, and there was that uncanny fluttering in the pit of her stomach whenever she looked at Ramose. What was happening to her? What was happening to her animal spirit? Pergia had spoken no more than the truth. Somehow it was growing inside her and was part of these strange new feelings. Sarmatia glanced across at the priest, imposing in his black ceremonial beard-wig and jewels, the damp evening heat molding the linen robes and head-dress to his body, and at once her animal spirit moved within her, sending a tingling prickle between her breasts, a prick of invisible claws.

A hand clasped on her arm brought Sarmatia back from these thoughts. Ramose smiled at her again. 'Yes, as rare as your animal spirit.' He kissed her forehead and breathed against her hair, 'Take care it doesn't master you, your animal spirit. Take care.' Then he drew back.

While Sarmatia was still shaken by the warning, still more by the unexpectedly tender and sensual touch of the priest, the door leading to the garden crashed open. Ramose swept Sarmatia from her couch and pulled her and Neith behind him, yet it was not an armed attack. One of his own servants burst into the hall.

'Crocodile, Master!' the woman screamed, raking her fingernails down her face in a frenzy of terror and grief. 'My daughter has fallen in the river!'

Her cry brought every man in the room to his feet. Ramose shouting, 'Bring spears and torches. We'll save her yet!'

But Sarmatia was ahead of them. Scattering dishes of food and wine, losing a sandal and leaving it lying, she sprinted through the open door. Paying no heed to the priest's pounding run after her or to his shouted warnings, she leapt down the steps of the terraced garden and rushed for the water. Snatching a torch from a servant, Ramose was in time to see Sarmatia dive into the muddy river as the huge body of the Nile crocodile closed on the screaming child.

Chapter 11

Did you think that Fearn had killed me in the fight for the kingship?

But then I would have missed those amusing little scenes between Chalda and our new king, between Chalda and Jart, our new healer. That silly youth is pining for her, although Chalda is venomous to him. She wants to become Fearn's wife, and primps and poses beside one of the house beams, in the hope that one day he'll notice. Myself, I can't see that happening. Fearn lives away from the royal homestead now. 'Anoi shall come with me, and live with her mother, in a kindlier house,' he said on the day he left. So Chalda has little of the King these days, although she usually works in a kiss when they meet, and Jart glowers and sulks for the day. A ridiculous pair, and well-matched.

Fearn is not the only man who is scarcely to be found in the royal house. With summer coming on, Goar is charming the unmarried girls. Young and tender is how he likes them, and he woos each one with an intensity of a madman. He has his reasons.

Life is hope. My hope is the fruition of my plans, my children to rule after me. I do not think anyone can stop me: not Fearn, not Goar, not the southern woman who waits. She'll get nothing.

Everything is perfect.

Chapter 12

Egypt, 1561BC. Summer.

While Ramose dispatched officials to scour the country in search of Misarios, he insisted that Sarmatia and Pergia leave Paser's house and stay with him.

'Stay for as long as you wish,' Ramose told Sarmatia. 'If this place tires you, we'll go elsewhere.' His lips curved into what, in a less dignified man, would have been a grin. 'I have many estates.'

He wished to impress Sarmatia. Daily, he re-lived the evening of the banquet, examining their every word. She would not give up her journey easily, yet she must sense the sympathy between them. Their attraction seemed good to the priest, quickening his senses, yet it was a flawed thing.

She was unruly and, yes, Ramose acknowledged reluctantly to himself, she loved the creatures of the wilderness too well. Still, she had saved his servant's child from the crocodile. No one else could have done that.

The events of that evening were branded on his mind. Swimming strongly, a blur of gray in her clinging gown, Sarmatia had reached the child, clutching the little girl tightly to herself as the crocodile converged on them.

What happened next had been incredible. The huge reptile had circled round Sarmatia and the weakly struggling child, ponderously flexing its ribbed tail. Overcome by fright, the child hooked under Sarmatia's arm had threshed no more but had frozen, falling silent as the grieving crowd.

As with his own son in the Bull Rite, he had been too late. Reluctant to see the inevitable, Ramose had been tempted to return to the palace, but others were watching so he must, too.

The silence, the lack of screams, had surprised him. Intrigued, Ramose had peered more intently across the oily water. Without releasing her grip on the child, perfectly calm and still, Sarmatia had watched the crocodile as the great beast continued to wind its long way round her. Peacefully, it had passed into the river's darkness, vanishing into the night.

There were many hands to help Sarmatia as she had waded from the river, but Ramose had been first. Returning the little girl unharmed to her mother, he had embraced Sarmatia and praised her for her courage.

'I was in no danger.' The blunt answer had nothing to do with modesty. Rubbing water from her eyes, the girl had given him a disconcerting stare. Meeting those relentless amber eyes, Ramose had felt a sudden chill.

Sarmatia was too wild...

* * * *

Life in Ramose's palace was luxurious. Pergia settled to the lazy days of picnics on the Nile and the evenings of splendid entertainments. Her health improved as the spirit plaguing her lungs disappeared. Pergia became, if not slim, then trimmer, with a fresher complexion.

Glad for her friend, Sarmatia tried to be like Pergia and be content, yet found that she was not. She missed Tazaros, even Miropa, with a sharpness she had not expected.

Ramose meanwhile heaped riches upon her. Witnessing her rescue of the child from the river, he gave Sarmatia a solid golden torc in the shape of a curving crocodile. It had eyes of ruby and jaws of opal.

'It's beautiful!'

'But not so beautiful as the creatures themselves?' said Ramose, caught between admiration and censure. Certainly, he did not invite Sarmatia hunting more than once. She had struck a nobleman for shooting a nesting heron, and had broken his bow.

Time slipped by, and Ramose summoned his guests to an audience in the Great Hall. 'We've found Misarios,' he told Sarmatia. 'But wait.' He cut short Pergia's exclamation. 'There's a problem.'

'Is he unable to travel?' asked Sarmatia.

Ramose sighed. 'Unwilling is nearer to the mark.'

Misarios had killed a man at Memphis in a brawl. With the aid of a bribe, he'd escaped with his life but had been enslaved. Purchased by a rich widow, he had remained in her household and was now apparently content.

'Was he told everything?' asked Sarmatia. 'How the ship would be his, he his own master, after one voyage?'

'He didn't seem interested.'

'What a fool!' cried Pergia. 'Is he a slave by nature? Can't he be persuaded by other means?' She glanced at Sarmatia.

Sarmatia blushed. 'That wouldn't be right, or wise,' she said, trying to placate the older woman. 'At sea we'd be in this man's hands.'

'Another mariner might be better for you,' said Ramose.

'I'd prefer Misarios,' said Sarmatia. Misarios, she knew, would bring them safely through to Tartessus.

* * * *

So Marye, the widow, and her slave Misarios were summoned. They came, the woman bitterly protesting.

'Why does she complain?' Pergia asked when she saw them. 'He's a poor answer to a widow's prayer.'

The Strongylan had surprised everyone. Small, fair and wiry—Pergia thought him puny—he seemed like a child until he spoke. His voice was deeper than Ramose's.

'Sounds like a god,' said Pergia with grudging admiration. 'Let's hope for your sake that it's not fate we're hearing.'

Sarmatia nodded, ignoring the barb. The blond mariner said little and when he did it was always to say that he was content. She stepped out of the alcove, from where Ramose had told them they could watch without being seen, and crossed the Great Hall. She walked softly. Only the priest knew she was there. At their agreed signal he broke off discussion and rose from his chair, coming down from the dais.

'Sarmatia!' He embraced her in front of the startled Marye. 'What rich robes are these?'

'They're Strongylan, my lord. My grandmother was Strongylan.' Sarmatia turned, pretending she did so for Ramose. The stiff linen skirts and high bodice moved as though part of her. Well aware of Misarios's dropped jaw, Sarmatia glanced at the priest, who bent and kissed her again.

'A hit.' Straightening, Ramose said formally, 'Your grandmother's spirit is beautiful in you. But come! You must meet a fellow islander. The gods have brought you together.'

Marye grabbed hold of Misarios's arm. He glared and flushed as she whispered. The widow's possessiveness plainly irked him.

Sarmatia forced herself to speak. 'Misarios, son of Tychios. What brings you so far from Strongyle?'

The mariner shuffled, disliking these reminders of his country. His reply was reserved. 'Fate has brought me here.'

There was silence. Sarmatia longed to speak freely, but the widow's eyes froze her. She turned to Ramose. 'May we withdraw to the garden?' Alone there, perhaps Misarios would be more forthcoming.

'You have my permission.'

Sarmatia led Misarios out into the sunlight, walking past willow and fig trees. 'How long will your looks last in this desert?' she asked.

The mariner scowled, cupping a pink oleander bloom in a bony hand. The petals came away in his fingers.

'Will she keep you when your good teeth and fair hair have fallen out?' goaded Sarmatia.

'She's promised me my freedom. And my own lands. That's a better future than the one you're offering. The sea's cruel, another slavery.'

'I know.' Sarmatia's voice softened. 'I lost my father to it. But he died alive,' she added roughly, catching herself, ' not half a man!'

Again there was silence. Misarios tipped back his narrow head and stared at the red sands beyond the garden. Sarmatia gazed at a sickly rose, remembering her father. He had been a fisherman, drowned in the seas off Krete. She was glad now that Fearn had remained in his homeland. On Strongyle half the women were widows twice over.

'I won't do it.' His voice was firm, but Misarios' pale eyes were unconvinced. Sarmatia decided to attack.

'What's one voyage to you? Has Egypt turned you jackal-hearted?'

'No-one calls me a coward!'

'Then sail with us.'

Misarios gave a bark of laughter. 'You're a persistent one!' This time he spoke without rancor.

'We'd be sailing to Tartessus, the richest city in the world.'

'And Marye?' Misarios tossed the question at her, his lips moving while he calculated the wealth to be gained from such a venture.

'Take her with you,' replied Sarmatia blandly.

'It will be late in the sailing season. That should mean good prices for the cargo.... Mine?'

Sarmatia nodded, not trusting herself to speak.

'I don't know.' The Strongylan looked Sarmatia up and down with his watery blue eyes. 'You're a pretty maid, but you should smile more. Was your mother's family truly Strongylan?'

'Yes.'

'And if I still say no, what then? Will that black, Ramose, send me boating on the Nile with a crocodile as steersman?'

A servant must have told him. Sarmatia looked away, suddenly ashamed. She should not be trying to force the man like this. 'I offer freedom,' she answered and, recalling the bitter glances of Pergia, added, 'Freedom to refuse. I'll ask Ramose to buy you from the widow and let you go.'

Misarios grinned. 'You should have said that first. I'll come as a free man, and gladly. It's time I was on the move.' He tapped her wrist with his fingers. 'Perhaps I wanted to be asked.'

* * * *

Once free, Misarios showed his mettle. In less than a week he returned to Mazghuna with several sailors. Before Misarios found a ship, however, Ramose received a message from Pharaoh. He had been summoned to Court.

'I doubt if I'll be gone for more than a day,' the priest told Sarmatia on the evening before his departure. 'These affairs are often mere squalls, over in a moment.'

'I hope so, my lord.' Sarmatia guessed it was unlikely that they would meet again, with inundation so close, but she clung to that small hope.

She and Ramose were walking in the garden, watching the twilight gild the pool and burnish the papyrus flowers. They moved silently. Their parting had robbed them of words. Two close strangers, Sarmatia thought, as she glanced at the noble profile of the Nubian. It crushed her that she would never know more of him.

Ramose sensed this. Thoughts he had been attempting to suppress since the evening of the banquet blazed into him. The girl was young, fresh and beautiful. He was a fool to let other considerations sway him.

He guided Sarmatia to the loggia where they had sat many times and drew her down onto the marbled bench. 'You are sorry that we must part?' Let her but admit that.

Sarmatia was remembering an oak tree which she and Fearn had once seen on Krete. One side had been blasted by lightning, the other grew green and flowered. As it had been with the tree, so it was with her: one half alive, the other dark. Haltingly, shy of speaking, she told Ramose.

She is torn, mused the priest, and he knew that it was the first time in Sarmatia's life that she had been so greatly divided. That he was the cause was gratifying, yet the image of the ruined oak could not be ignored. From the corner of his eye, Ramose noticed a small dust-devil making its whirlwind track in the desert beyond his palace. The god of storms was out there, outside the bounds of civilized society, and Fearn had been granted part of that destructive power. He must go carefully.

'All change brings fear and anxiety. The memory shows your heart. It means nothing more.' To soften his words, Ramose clasped her hand.

Sarmatia smiled sadly. 'It's hard. You've been more than father. More than brother.' She stopped, amazed at her words. Did she really feel like that?

Ramose laughed, the triumph sweet to him. The girl's breasts rose and fell in a sigh. He put an arm about her shoulders and hugged her. 'You're young, and life seems stark. But when you're married and have sons, then you'll wonder at the child you were in Egypt.' Perhaps it was a risk, mentioning marriage, but this quiet way was best for the moment, Ramose decided.

Sarmatia's fingers crept beneath her golden torc and settled on Fearn's ring. She was ashamed of her grief, of her doubts.

Ramose watched her face. As priest he could see the animal spirit within her, its power casting a glamour over her skin. 'You're strange,' he said at last. 'Yet I'm sorry our fates do not run closer. If you find the north cold, then return here. You'll find a welcome.'

He said nothing more, but it was enough. Sarmatia kissed his hand. 'Thank you, my lord. I'll not forget.'

Seductive, musky scent rose from her. Previous uncertainties were swept aside in a rush. Lifting the girl's head, Ramose kissed her on the lips.

Part of her wanted this, thought Sarmatia. There was relief in succumbing, in not thinking or choosing but having the choice made for her. She closed her eyes and opened her mouth, feeling his tongue inside her, feeling his body against hers. Almost hairless, Ramose was smooth and sinewy to the touch, the muscles of his back and shoulders firming in response to her hands. She brought her hands to his throat to remove the gold necklace and smelt the desert on his burnished skin. His fingers were caressing her breasts and as they moved to her flanks Sarmatia heard the dim roll of thunder, matching her own blood pulse, a reminder of the inundation to come.

That brought her slightly to her senses. 'No,' she mumbled, attempting to draw back. She was betrothed to Fearn and he had spoken to her, here, in Egypt. What was she doing? Ramose was not for her. This was a foolish, dangerous infatuation. 'No,' she said again.

Twisting back from the kiss, Sarmatia resisted the soft words, yet could not break free. Gentle and persistent, Ramose lifted the hem of her gown to run a hand under her robe and her protest strangled itself in a gasp. Now another, louder thunderclap sounded as he withdrew his teasing fingers and pushed her slightly away onto the cold marble.

'Come away from the sky,' he commanded, his voice strong with desire. The girl was so deliciously responsive. 'Give yourself to me, inside.' He pulled her from the seat. 'We shall see the Pharaoh together.' His first love-lie, for a man does not take a minor courtesan to court. 'Come, my love.' He added the endearment to enmesh her further, brushed a finger along Sarmatia's shoulder and, growing impatient, hurried ahead, shouting for wine.

Lagging behind, torn between the dazzle of infatuation and true feeling, Sarmatia came to the end of the garden pool. She knelt and splashed water over her flushed face, then rearranged her gown with trembling fingers. She could not go back into the palace and meet the haughty Steward or Ramose's wife Neith with such a wild, staring look. Yet what should she do?

'Goddess, help me!' she whispered, listening for another voice. The evening sky was heavy about her, carrying the slightest sound—the rustle of a breeze on the river, the patter of footsteps.

Ramose's wife walked down the steps to the pool and Sarmatia hid her face, worrying at her lower lip with her teeth. She decided to withdraw, but Neith stopped her. 'Stay here, Kretan. Leave my husband to me.'

Sarmatia snapped her head up and locked eyes with the Egyptian. The hand on her shoulder fell away.

'I've seen others, before you. A serving wench or two. Ramose thinks I'm jealous, and yet why should I be? He's a lion of a man, not easily filled.'

Walking through her garden, snapping off dead flower heads, Neith was content, complacent. 'Soon, I'll send a girl in to him. Tomorrow, he will be gone and you and your people free to leave.'

She paused, glancing at Sarmatia's face. 'My dear, are you so beguiled by him? Do you really believe he loves you?' She gave a little smile and turned back to her gardening. 'Tell me, has Ramose promised you anything? He keeps his word.'

When Sarmatia did not answer Neith went on, in a kindlier way, 'Let me not be cruel. After all, you saved my son on Krete and you are my guest, as well as my husband's. You must believe me, when I say I bear you no ill-will.'

Crushing a nectar-stealing moth between her fingers, Neith continued, 'If you stay, I'll not treat you badly, although it would be better if you go.'

Neith stepped into the loggia and beckoned Sarmatia.

'Now you must decide,' she said.

Chapter 13

Egypt, summer, 1561BC

Without the aid of a spirit-voice or Neith's advice, Sarmatia chose to continue her journey. Ramose had her respect: he had showered her with gifts, inflamed her senses, and yet the thing she felt always closest to her heart was a simple bronze ring. Fearn had given her the promise of companionship. For that she would go without Egypt and its comforts.

Pergia came too, although this time Sarmatia had not pressed her. Under the guise of friendship Pergia had good reasons for leaving Egypt. She fancied a Tartessian husband, and thought the she would do well on the ship, with sailors to charm and Sarmatia to torment. Her capricious treatment of the girl had become a habit, justified by her promise. She had sworn to travel and so she would, and Sarmatia would pay.

Their ship was a Strongylan merchantman. It was a good boat, undecked amidships, with a single mast and sail and a cargo hold by the stern. The sternpost curved over the steering platform in the shape of a viper. In the center were the rowing benches and rowlocks where the lead-weighted oars could be used to guide the ship into port or add more speed with sail on the open sea. *Viper* was the ship Sarmatia asked for in the harbor, on the day the omens allowed them to leave.

* * * *

In flood the Nile becomes Egypt, covering plains and valleys so that only the towns rise above the shining blanket of water. On ship the crew sun-bathed, allowing the current to do the work. Sometimes they passed the sickle-shaped *baris*, filled with revelers, for in a good inundation there are many festivals. There was much cheerful passing of wine and food from the laughing, feasting Egyptians to the crew of *Viper.*

At the last town before the sea they took on fresh food. Still in darkness, the crew rowed *Viper* out of port to catch the morning breeze, oars whipping clouds of phosphorescence out of the calm black water.

Wind came at day-break, rippling the surface of the sea, and the square sail was hoisted. Rigging groaned and the sail bellied out. Sarmatia, standing by the bows, felt the boat tip sideways. She made a grab for the stempost. *Viper* rolled and the ram plowed the dark blue sea, rising to burst through the wave in a snort of spray. Sarmatia glanced back at the flat delta of Egypt and then forward, thinking not of Ramose, but only that she should have braided her whipping hair. The last lingering doubt was extinguished then, forever, in her mind.

Viper ran before the wind, and aboard ship, crew and passengers became easier with each other. Pergia especially grew close to the men. She had discovered a blood-tie with their youngest member, Kerewos, a bond which had quickly matured into affection, while to the other sailors the priestess became a kind of talisman.

Even Misarios caught this new mood of friendship and he and Pergia mellowed towards each other. Soon the small, plump Kretan priestess was praising Misarios for things which she had earlier condemned, and one evening, when the ship was beached to take on fresh water, she and Misarios wandered off, their hands scarcely a breath apart as they walked side by side through yellow sea-poppies and silver cotton-weed. When they returned, long after twilight, their arms were linked and Misarios shouted to his men that there would be a wedding soon and where was the best wine?

Yet before any weddings, *Viper* had to reach Tartessus. The summer was drawing to a close, and everyone knew that if they were to sail north that season the Pillar Straits would have to be cleared soon, before winter. A rough wind could dash the ship to splinters in that narrow channel. There was an easy ten days' sail for *Viper* to the Pillars, but then the ship was stopped, and not by poor weather.

It began with Kerewos. On only his second voyage, he was homesick and despite—or maybe even because of—the presence of Pergia, he felt anxious for his widowed mother. He looked at the tall cliffs of the Pillars and heard the great ocean thundering on the other side and he shook his head. He said nothing, but he did no work. Others followed, and Misarios found his commands ignored.

Never one to delay, even if wise to do so, Misarios revealed his thoughts as soon as the men gathered and sat down. If there was a mutiny, he knew who was to blame, right enough, the ship's cook, Oineus, a balding, limping older man who had turned out to be a grumbler.

'So, Oineus, you want my place.' He spat on the deck between them. 'That's all you'll get from me.'

A dagger flashed from a man's fist. Pergia screamed as Misarios lurched backwards. Oineus closed in, but Misarios leapt to his feet, lunging with his own dagger. The cook cried out, shielding his head with his arms, but the blade did not touch him and the crew jeered, pleased at the sport. Sarmatia frowned and was silent, sickened by this quarreling. She took Pergia into her arms and found her trembling. 'It'll be all right,' she whispered, praying it was so. 'They will not come to blows.'

Oineus glanced about, seeing Misarios move towards him. The flesh hooks and knives of his trade were stowed under a rowing bench. His gaze fell on Pergia, huddled in Sarmatia's arms by the bow. Sarmatia glared at him, warning him to keep away.

He dropped to his knees. 'No, Misarios,' he whined, edging back toward the women. 'Spare me. I was wrong. I swear to be faithful.' The sailor put out his hands and sighed as his fingers grasped one of the spears of *Viper*'s tiny battle-hoard. He yanked the shaft free and stood.

Misarios paled, yet never paused in his approach. The crew drew back, out of the path of the spear.

Horrified, Sarmatia thrust Pergia out of harm's way. She ran between the two men, desperate to stop this.

'Are you mad? Has a spirit mazed your wits? Oineus, lay down that spear. Settle scores later, on land.' She turned to Misarios. 'This way solves nothing. V*iper*'s yours, we know, as Oineus will witness.' Sarmatia prodded the older man, and Oineus sulkily nodded his head.

To her relief, the men relaxed: the crisis was over. Kerewos took the spear from Oineus's unresisting fingers and returned it to its place. Misarios found the sailor's dagger and carefully handed it to Agakles, his second-in-command.

Agakles remained standing. 'Oineus spoke of wrong. And that's why we're here, gathered about the rowing benches.'

Kerewos murmured agreement, content now that Agakles had chosen to speak.

'It's this sea,' Agakles went on, pointing towards the Straits.

'Tell him, Agakles,' called Kerewos.

'Yes, tell me.' Misarios grabbed his second in command.

'We can't go through the Pillars.'

Misarios bellowed incoherently. He pushed Agakles back onto the gunwale, where the man's long hair trailed into the sea. 'I decide!' He tightened his grip.

'You're choking him!'

'Keep back!'

Oineus and Kerewos pulled Misarios off Agakles. Instantly he turned on them. 'Women with beards, that's what you are!' He paced over the ribs of the ship, dangerous as a cornered animal. 'Twice I've passed those Pillars. Twice!'

'It's the world's edge!' cried Kerewos.

'The Underworld!' roared Oineus. They were all shouting.

'I've been there, I tell you!' Misarios slapped his hand on the mast. 'It's a huge sea. And there's Tartessus beyond those Pillars, a city richer than Knossos and Thebes together.'

Kerewos shook his head. The lure of gold meant little to him. 'Hear that thundering?' He appealed to the crew. 'That's the water falling off the world.'

'So, am I a liar?' spat Misarios.

Agakles grabbed him and held him back. 'Winter's coming,' he said, trying for calm. 'All seas are bad then.'

'And Tartessus a safe port,' replied Misarios. 'But, I see, you'd desert me.' He threw down his dagger hilt-first upon the hull, in the gesture of betrayed fellowship. The men stared at him, round-eyed.

Misarios spoke, voice breaking. 'Would I ever keep anything back from you? Take the lion's share of the spoil and leave you jackal pickings? No, once I get into port I'll deal straight, because I'm an honest man.'

'That's right,' muttered the crew uncertainly.

Misarios smiled. Things were moving his way again. 'We'll vote. That's fair, yes?'

The men agreed. This was indeed fair.

'Good! ....And the women vote, too, as they sail with us.' Misarios turned to the bows and beckoned. 'Those who are with me, come beside me. The rest, stand off.'

Pergia immediately clasped Misarios, who gathered her into a silent embrace. Agakles was next, somewhat shamefacedly, Sarmatia thought, as if he knew that Kerewos and Oineus had hoped he would lead them in revolt. Those two shuffled away, their choice made.

Sarmatia was left. If she chose to support Kerewos and Oineus, it would be a tied vote. Hers was the deciding cast.

'Which is it, Sarmatia?' asked Kerewos eagerly.

She hesitated, knowing that if they waited a season their journey would be easier. They could turn the ship back and run it onto a beach where there was fresh water, plant rather than sell the cargo of wheat and harvest it in late spring. The coast was rich in game and fish. They would not starve while waiting for the crop. Afterwards *Viper* could sail on to Tartessus, then northwards, in fine summer weather.

But no - life was too short for such uncertainties. Pergia had found a husband and it was time she herself had a mate. It was a small risk and they would take care.

With no more than a glance at Kerewos, Sarmatia stepped beside Pergia as Misarios said quietly, 'We go through.'

* * * *

They passed the opening of the Pillars, riding the tidal race like a feather. Soon Kerewos was singing and the others chanting the chorus, although Misarios said not a word. Manning the helm was effort enough. The sea shone hard as glass and sweeping tides curled together as breakers over rocks. Only he knew how close they came to the spurs that could sink them.

Even so, when *Viper* lost the wind and rode at anchor an hour or more, Misarios devoured every scrap of food left from the previous night. He enjoyed living on the edge. And it was in this cheerful mood that he spoke to the others, telling them what lay ahead.

'Only two more stretches to go, then it's on to Tartessus. There we'll trade a part of the cargo and divide the profits.'

The crew cheered and Misarios smiled. 'Perhaps we'll settle other debts there, too.' His gaze fixed on Oineus. 'But first here's the narrowest part of the straits.'

Misarios jumped down lightly from the helm onto the benches, squatting between his men. 'It'll be dangerous. The winds and sea change quickly. The tides can pull a ship onto the rocks.' He paused to allow his words to sink in. 'We'll wait for a steady breeze, then go. Once we sail there's no turning back. We pass through, or die.'

The crew nodded silently. Oineus even crossed his arms in prayer. Watching their faces, Misarios was satisfied. They would obey him instantly from now on, no argument. 'Wait for my signal,' he told them as they settled to the grim task of waiting. 'May our gods keep us whole.'

* * * *

'Hold that sail-rope steady, man!'

Agakles tried to keep a grip, but could not. The wind, keen and gusting, wrung the rope from his fingers.

Sarmatia, knowing the *Viper* to be close to a wrecking surf line, dashed up from her bench.

'Leave it, you. That's for the men!'

Sarmatia ignored Misarios' bellowed command, grasped the rope before another crewman scrambled from the benches and pulled, ducking instinctively as the great square sail above her head cracked and filled.

Viper shot forward, turning from the white water of the rocks. It cleared a low, surf-curdled spur and sped on, rolling almost from oar lock to oar lock. Sarmatia could hear the whisper of breakers as they passed by with only a beam's-width to spare, but had no time to feel relief. Already the tide was sucking them back. Passing Agakles the sail-rope, she slid into her place, hearing the hoarse orders of Misarios.

'Port side, row harder!'

'Get that starboard rope hauled in!'

'Put your backs into it, come on!'

Beating time with his foot, Misarios was scarlet with effort, his hands covered in red welts from the steering oars. Again, he bullied the crew to find that final, spine-grinding burst.

'Seven strokes, then rest. Count!'

'Seven, six, five,' chanted the crew.

'Two—one,' gasped Pergia. She slumped clumsily onto the ship's side, too spent to drag her heavy oar from the ocean. The spirit that had afflicted her in Krete had returned with a vengeance. Her breath came in rattling squalls.

One bench in front, Kerewos spewed out his wine on the deck. The ship was a wheezing lung, pitching in a steep-sided bay.

'Anyone hurt?' cried Misarios, when he had caught his breath. 'Kerewos?'

The youth shook his head, smiling wanly.

'Pergia?' Her ragged sobbing was alarming, and she'd been flung backwards by *Viper*'s last surge, almost losing her oar.

Pergia forced herself to suck in a full mouthful of air. 'Nothing broken.'

Misarios, his matted blond hair darkened by sweat and spray, allowed his hands to slip from the steering oars. 'Let out the anchor stones, and then rest,' he said warmly. 'You've done well. We're through the Pillars.'

* * * *

The following day began well. Misarios roused the crew before dawn and they heaved up the anchors for the last leg of the voyage before Tartessus, wind and tide running in their favor.

Leaving Pergia to sleep after her rigors of the previous day, Sarmatia clambered up to the bows. Here was her favorite place, at the apex of the bows where the ship locked together. From here she could watch the ram snuffle through the waves and turn back the water. She could feel the surge and pitch of their progress and taste the salt on the wind. Better yet, she was the first to see where they were heading. Riding the tip of where the unknown became the known, the unexplored the familiar. This would be something she could tell Fearn.

That morning, as the sun rose in swarms of shade and color and *Viper* ploughed her north-west course across the mouth of the straits, Sarmatia knew that she could see farther and hear more from the watch-place than ever before.

'Look there!' she cried to Agakles, pointing to a huge shoal of tunny feeding in the shallows. But already *Viper* had glided past and Sarmatia laughed, pleased now that only she had seen the fish and known them. She turned back to the sea, shading her eyes against the tawny sun. Moments later she cried out again. 'Water! Fresh Water!'

'Where?' Misarios dashed up, scowling across at the steep, russet-colored cliffs. Tartessus was less than a day's sail away, but Misarios's experience would have taught him never to pass by a watering-place, however close to port.

Sarmatia guided him. 'See the tree-studded point? Beside that is a sandy cove. There is the spring.'

Finally seeing the water, Misarios roared out commands and the ship swung shoreward, going quickly on the current. Soon, *Viper* was safe in the cove at the southern side of the Pillars and Sarmatia was shaking Pergia awake.

'We've stopped,' she told her, as Misarios came to embrace Pergia. 'We can wade ashore. The crew is going to refill the water barrels.'

The Priestess grunted and shook out her hair, shoulders cracking. 'What pleases you?' Her pink, round face was set in an ugly grimace.

'Just the day.'

'Easy for you, isn't it? Where you wish, we go. Like fools!'

Sarmatia stared, wondering how the morning had turned so quickly. Others, she realized, were staring too.

'We chose together,' she said, hoping that this would calm Pergia's strange anger, but the priestess caught hold of her.

'I had a dream last night—a true prophecy.' Suddenly Pergia shook Sarmatia. 'Silly bitch! Chasing a fantasy!' Quick as an adder, she brought her hand up and struck Sarmatia on the cheek. 'And what of Agakles?'

'What is this?' cried Sarmatia, a shadow passing across her heart. Her face smarted, but she felt cold, her skin clammy. 'What can I do?'

'Nothing. You're days too late.' Pergia turned aside and lurched past the bewildered Misarios, standing uncertainly beside the mast. 'Kerewos, help me down.' Her breathing came unevenly again—sign of the evil spirit fighting within her small, bustling frame.

Silently the youth jumped from the boat into the knee-deep water. *Viper* had not yet been beached.

'Wait. Don't go!' cried Sarmatia.

Pergia ignored her, leaning down over the bows. Kerewos reached up to help her, bracing himself against the ship.

It was his last act. There came a shout, a war-cry, and Kerewos pitched forward into the sea, an arrow piercing his back. Pergia wheezed, 'No! It wasn't you in my dream!' But the young man was dead.

'Set seaward!' Misarios knocked Pergia into the hull, away from the deadly arrows, and strained to lift the heaviest anchor.

Six men and two women, armed with spears and bows, broke cover, rushing for the beach. They were slender and quick, painted for battle. They dropped on one knee to aim their light, curved bows and were searingly accurate. Agakles screamed as a dart passed through his hand when he reached for the last anchor.

The boat was shuddering beneath Sarmatia's feet. It floundered out into the sea, rowed desperately by the crew, and the warriors broke into a sprint in a final attempt to stop the sailing. As they came closer, Sarmatia realized that the men's leather waistbands were decorated with shrunken heads.

Horror took hold of her. She edged closer to Pergia, who knelt in the bows, stiff and silent as Kerewos himself. 'You beasts eat men,' she whispered. 'May the Mother blast you for it!'

At her words Pergia gave a whooping cry, scrabbling at the stempost as though she might somehow bury Kerewos there. She rounded on Sarmatia. 'This is your doing!' she shrieked, finally catching a full breath.

'No!' Sarmatia shrank back against the ribs of the ship. She was still appalled by what had happened, numb with shock and despair. Kerewos, as young as she was, now dead. How could this be? She felt sick, and ashamed for still being alive.

Pergia rose and shook her fist in Sarmatia's face. 'He's dead, the last man of my family, because of you! You were always jealous of him. I should have known you'd somehow do him ill. By the Mother, if only the gods had granted me better foresight! I'd have slain you myself, before the Pillars!'

'Wait!' Sarmatia shuddered, as the crew closed in. 'We all chose—' Her cry was lost amidst the scream of sea-birds, as hands took hold of her.

Chapter 14

Isle of Stones, 1561 BC. Late Summer.

Satisfied, Fearn threw the adze down into the roof, shearing off the loose tufts of heather precisely at its apex, and straightened to look out across his kingdom.

It was summer. The hay had been gathered in, the uplands were filled with the cries of growing lambs. The forest burst with game. In the hazel and coppice woods, trees were loaded with swelling berries and nuts.

He had been king for three seasons. The trappings of kingship, the golden diadem, the tall colored throne, had become familiar. Used as he was to respect as a healer, Fearn had been ready for the greater respect due to him as a king. Waroch had known respect without affection. Fearn had won both. 'Woodman,' people called him, for his way of sitting in council, knife in hand, carving handles, rakes and hooks while he listened to their complaints. Laerimmer and the highborn said he should no longer heal, and protested against his work as thatcher and forester. Waroch, who had been idle, had made sufficient business out of ruling to attempt nothing else.

Down in the yard someone was whistling a tune about a girl with nut-brown hair. Several new verses had been added, touching on imagined attributes of the king's betrothed. Oh, the people knew of his Kretan but they did not know it all. Only one man in the kingdom knew that he had written to Sarmatia.

The idea of a letter had come to Fearn in the spring when two strangers, Loge and Ell, had sought him out at his father's house.

These two were traders, carrying amber and spices on their backs. Finding they had travelled widely, Fearn contrived to speak with Ell in private. Tempted by fresh bread and that marvelous Atterian butter, the trader's wife had willingly sat apart from her husband and the rest of Fearn's family and had soon begun to talk freely.

Despite her outlandish costume and heavily accented speech, Ell had been worth listening to. She surprised him by saying that there were many women travellers—some who journeyed with their husbands, like herself, and many more who travelled alone. The roads and sea-ways were safer each year, as rulers grew more powerful, and women could always claim special protection from the Mother Goddess. Ell prayed to her in the form of the Moon Elder, and said she was a useful deity to have at your back. 'With her help I sailed to Krete by myself, before I was married.'

He had questioned her closely and her every answer had given him hope. At the end of the evening he had given her a gold armlet and said he might have some trading-work for her, for which he would pay handsomely. After a night of thought without sleep, Fearn had done what he could with a letter, then sent for Loge and Ell to carry it south.

Ell had been persuaded first, and a promise that salt, beer, butter and furs would be waiting when he returned to Fearn's kingdom had also won Loge. They had sworn to bring Sarmatia back with them, if she was willing. They had left for Krete five months ago, one month after Fearn was crowned.

Now Fearn retrieved the adze, covering the hole in the roof with hides and stones. As the youth below burst into the song's bawdy refrain, he scrambled sure-footedly across the thatch along the line of the shiny roof-timbers and swung himself one-handed down from the crossbeam of the doorway. The first the lad knew that he had finished thatching for the day was when his arm clamped about him.

'Good-day, Dill,' said Fearn. 'I'm an enemy.'

Dill kicked his heel against his shin, drove an elbow into his heavily-muscled torso and smashed his head back. Fearn jumped and let him go. After Dill had catapulted forward and fumbled his knife from its sheath, Fearn stood still, feeling along his jaw.

'Good! You'd have pulped the nose of a smaller man with that head move, although it's best not to need the move at all. Remember, I'd still have had time to cut your throat.'

Harsh words, but as Dill felt his overall approval, the lad raised his own knife and hollered.

Fearn smiled. 'Have the others come? Then tell them I'm on my way. Go on, you young fool.'

Dill flew across the yard of Rossfarm, vaulting the fence. His shouts faded as he ran into the tree-lined fields.

Fearn watched the fair hair and tan-colored clothes blending in with the tall nodding heads of wheat. He understood and shared the youth's excitement, yet what they were about to do was forbidden. It was against recent custom for the king to keep a bodyguard or standing army. Fearn did not miss the bodyguard, yet it seemed folly to have no young men trained to arms. Since his early youth, when he had travelled to learn the ways and means of other races' healing, Fearn had also seen war. To him it was not enough to say, 'The Atterians dwell in peaceful lands.' Times alter, neighbors change.

Against that day Fearn was secretly gathering a war band. A score of youths, not one up to his full strength yet but each recklessly daring and free still of the bone and muscle ache that had already begun to affect him. They met whenever they could, slipping away from their work to join the young king. Fearn had selected the cropped hay meadow of Rossfarm as one such meeting place. The message had been sent. The boys should have collected their weapons from the hiding place and be waiting for him at the field.

Fearn left the thatching tools where they were, but tucked the stone-headed axe into his waistband. Setting out across the fields, he brushed his fingers over the down-curved heads of wheat, taking off the flowers and seed pods of poppy, marigold, blue cornflower and the purple corn cockle and stuffing these into his work tunic. Coming to the end of the wheat, he loosened his belt and emptied the weeds near a broken plough which had been left to rot in the field.

Ahead were water-like shimmers of movement, young voices, laughter. The troop had set up their spear and arrow targets, the wooden stumps and torn old hides, and were roughing about. As they saw Fearn, they stopped their knockabout fights and rushed forward in a stampede of flying limbs. The oldest was scarcely nineteen. They all thought they would live forever.

Though the twenty were there, he called out their names, and their answering settled them enough to begin the day's lesson.

'Bring me the tanged throwing spear and the leather-bound spear.' These were the only ones whose points were made of bronze. The rest were copies, chipped out in flint or stone. As two youths gave them up, Fearn checked along the weapons' edges. 'Aren, this spear is blunt again. If you can't take better care of it, it'll be given to someone who can.'

Several hands offered to take the spear. Metal weapons were prized. In the kingdom there were only three bronze daggers, two bronze spears, a dozen arrowheads and a single copper axe—the hoard of some Atterian smith working before Fearn's grandparents were born, when each farm had been a law unto itself. Since that time, the sword had come into its own as a new weapon. They must do the best with what they had.

Fearn showed the troop how to hold and throw the spear, how to carry it through undergrowth, how to make certain that it did not move or break from its wooden shaft. He set them crawling belly-first over the hay stubble, then running and throwing at a man-sized target. Each had a turn with every spear, so they would learn to adapt to the different weights and the subtle way each weapon behaved.

'You should take a spear, Fearn,' said Aren at one point.

'And spear take on axe!' called out a youth. It was known that Fearn preferred the axe as a weapon. At the beginning he'd been clumsier than the boys in handling the narrow-shafted javelins and had practiced relentlessly to improve and keep ahead. Yet the troop had not been easy enough with him, or sure enough of themselves, to challenge him before now.

Peeling down his tunic and tying the sleeves about his waist, Fearn scraped a line with his heel in the meadow. 'Aren, your spear.'

The boy tossed it and Fearn caught the shaft, grounded the spear and leaned against it. 'Pass my mark. If you dare.'

It was not a formal challenge and they did not answer, merely stepped over the line: two shock-haired youths who did everything together and, pushing his way from the back, the biggest boy there, still only seventeen. Fearn tossed him the axe from his belt. 'Use it well.'

Sowter was a great mass of bone and muscle, a freckle-faced, slow-witted lad, but solid and steady on his feet. His gray eyes brightened at the sight of the axe and the sandy stubble on his cheeks trembled as he struggled to express thanks. The other two lads grinned at each other, aware of the boy's stammer, and Fearn tapped them briskly with the spear.

'Come then, three to one. You should manage it.'

'Nnno...I'm with Fff...' Sowter clearly thought it unfair to fight three against one. Deciding that actions were easier than words in expressing his allegiance, he swung at the youths. In his hands, the axe became a horn. He slashed with it, bellowing like a bull. Fear prodded the two out of Sowter's reach with the spear, tripping one headfirst into a molehill. The other fell back, clutching his knee. 'We'd not armed!' he croaked.

'Yet you passed my mark.' Fearn grabbed the boy's tunic and hauled him upright. 'Sowter, dust him off and see to his friend.' Leaving them, Fearn beckoned the other young men. 'The first lesson of attack—surprise!' He swung an open palm, and the boy not quick enough to duck was caught. 'The next lesson—know your friends.'

He moved to take Sowter's hand and praise him then hesitated. Something was different about the field. Perhaps it was no more than a passing cloud, or a change in the wind.

'Drop your weapons within reach and make as though you're searching in the grass. Someone's coming!'

A scent of roses drifted into the meadow. Dropping his own spear, Fearn struggled to untie his tunic sleeves and not appear bare-waisted before the girl stepping lightly from the tree-shade. Roses and a rose complexion—it would be Anoi. Chalda could not wear perfume. It stank on her like hemlock.

Chalda and Jart, the new healer, were married at last. The girl seemed content, apart from the odd biting word or glance, but such was the zest of Chalda's nature.

Anoi was different, softer. She troubled him, even as her dependence touched him. Gei, her mother, was old and older yet in her mind, so the girl had no one. Perhaps that was why she sought him out. Certainly she must never guess that he liked her rose perfume. That and her long blonde hair. And her tender little hands. And her sweetness.

Fearn frowned and collected his thoughts. He was betrothed, an act as binding as marriage. Anoi was too gentle for him, too simple. It was better that he be as a brother to her.

Leaving the boys and the weapons, Fearn jogged down the slope. 'Good day to you, Anoi. Are you seeking mushrooms, too?'

Anoi laughed. 'Oh, Fearn! Don't tease. I know why you're here.' She tucked a strand of golden hair behind her ear and stood before him. 'I want to join you. See, I've brought a dagger.' The long slim sheath swung from her cloth belt. She showed him the blade. It was of an antique style, green with age, but had been newly honed and sharpened.

'If warriors attack,' she said, blue eyes growing darker, 'then women too should know how to fight.'

Her clear voice carried and the troop behind Fearn smirked, secure in their young manhood. Sowter shook the axe at her. 'You think you can carry this, little girl?'

He stammered and the other youths laughed at him. Fearn let them go on, reflecting that Sowter deserved it. By waving the battleaxe, the lad had given the game away. What he should do about Anoi he was less sure.

'Anoi, what if a stray blow on the practice field should scar you?'

'Would that matter, Fearn?' The lock of hair had come free again, and drifted across her face. He caught it then loosed it quickly when he saw her face. In their youthful hero-worship, Anoi and the troop were much alike.

'You're in my care,' he answered, hating the way he sounded, so pompous, but saying it anyway. 'I'd be lacking in my duty if I brought you harm.'

As though he had said nothing, Anoi calmly removed her belt and stepped out of her long robe. Underneath she wore a short brown skirt of simple woolen cords. It was not an Atterian garment. Fearn had seen only one of its like before, worn by the wife of the Northern amber trader, the woman Ell.

Tightening the drawstring at her waist, Anoi slipped past him. Fearn closed his eyes and heard the gasps and one long whistle. He was astonished himself. Yet Anoi was a modest girl. She wore the costume artlessly.

He finished breathing in and caught up with her. 'You may stay with us,' he began then made the mistake of looking down when her dagger sheath hit his leg. The blood surged in his ears at the glimpse, through the cords, of the round white thighs topped by the mound of golden fuzz. He forgot to ask how she knew of their meeting.

So Anoi joined the group. She made a sprightly, quick little warrior, with a good eye. Fearn was glad of her presence to spur on the youths. Once the first impact of her costume had passed, he found it easier each time to treat with her. She was Anoi, his little cousin, not Sarmatia.

It was not in Fearn's nature to change allegiance. He had written to Sarmatia rather than lose her utterly and now, through the gift of the Sky God, he had spoken to her in the palace of Ramose and knew that she had left her homeland. The young king had seen no more than their first meeting, but he remembered Ramose from Krete and had not been anxious for Sarmatia's safety. The priest, he knew, would help her.

It did not matter that she was not with Loge or his wife. Sarmatia was coming.

Then came the voyage. For five days Fearn endured the Sky God's sight, shadowing her movements on the quiet sea journey to the Pillars, and when he thought her safe Fearn set to his own work like a madman. People said he looked haggard and was driving himself too hard.

It was wheat time. By the fields of Rossfarm, where the Atterians grew their corn, Fearn sacrificed one of his cows to the earth. As the beast sank onto its side, felled by a blow from his axe, an eagle screamed and dipped out of the sun. He took heart from the sign, and from his own clean killing. Later, working amongst the harvesters, he passed word around that the war band should meet in the first gleaned field at sunset.

They came as arranged, but so did the Kingmaker. Laerimmer was fingering one of the bronze spearheads, and to his left and right were the members of the Council, each holding a weapon. The other arms were stacked beside the troop, who sat together, sullen as prisoners. Only Anoi and Sowter raised their heads as he approached. Fearn could not believe that any of them had betrayed their secret gatherings.

Knowing that the Council were waiting for him to sit before they settled themselves, Fearn kept them standing.

* * * *

He's angry for us, thought Sowter, watching the king sweep along the line of the Council with his long, powerful stride, and he hugged that knowledge to himself. Fearn, he was sure, was not sorry for deceiving the elders, not a bit, though in the midst of a speech he had glanced once at Anoi and his gaze had softened. Sowter did not care for Anoi in that he agreed with the Council, who called her war-training unseemly though he forgot the girl when Fearn winked at him.

The argument droned on, mostly to do with the king's rights and those of custom.

'You pursue me like a boy,' Fearn was saying. 'You question these youngsters, perhaps trick them into revealing our meetings. Why have you not treated straight with me?'

Fearn paced about. 'The weapons you hold were made by our people. They were needed then and I say they're needed still. It's stupid to stay in a kingdom as rich as this and wait for the wolves to raid our homes. We must keep them out! And one day, who knows? Our people may wish to go beyond our borders. I myself have traveled far as a healer, and have considered journeying again, to the Great Stone Circle, after harvest. It's the place most pleasing to the Sky God.'

He did not add that the shrine was far to the south, on the road to the tin-lands and the Great Sea.

Several of the Council looked wary but said nothing. They knew the Sky God was the King's chosen deity. Fearn touched the stone axe at his belt in a gesture they would see.

Laerimmer blew his nose on his sleeve and raised his dark moon-face. 'Perhaps we should touch on such matters in private council. We appear very far from agreement.'

You are not winning, you mean, thought Sowter.

* * * *

Fearn bowed his head. Anything less than an outright refusal was good. He had planted the seeds for change in men's minds, and as king had learned when to wait. 'Is there more?' He could see that Laerimmer was keeping something back.

'A brawl over a dowry,' replied Laerimmer. 'The bride's father demands the Sky Rite, to settle the issue.'

'The Sky Rite, for such a matter?' Fearn had done the rite before, for similar reasons: it seemed a fashion with his people. He must try to explain again that the summoning of the god was not a conjuring trick. Would the people listen? They seemed dazzled by the lightning, the spectacle of the rite.

'The Atterians are already gathered for harvest,' added Laerimmer. 'It could be resolved tonight.' He was as bad as the rest, although he knew something of the dangers of possession.

'We must return to Rossfarm,' said Fearn. He'd better get the ritual over.

If dispute went on too long, he would need the war band to put down wolves within his own kingdom.

* * * *

It was a four-field walk to the farmstead, and Laerimmer trotted beside him, glancing up now and then as if trying to read his face. For two fields Fearn kept a steady countenance then lengthened his stride until they were well ahead of Council and war band. He had a shrewd notion of what Laerimmer was working up to say, and decided to speak first.

'I must look out a gift for Chalda and her husband. Their marriage pleases me greatly.' He saw Laerimmer's black snake-eyes widen and added, 'When I come to breed, I want to be sure no other seed's been planted in the furrow.'

Laerimmer reddened, for he could not deny that Chalda was well along in pregnancy. She had been with child when she accepted the new healer's token.

'There is Anoi,' he said after a moment.

'I think not. Anoi isn't for me.'

'By the Mother, Fearn, why not? I've seen you look at her.'

Fearn blushed. 'I'm a man, with a man's desires.'

'So marry her. As King you need to marry.' Laerimmer lowered his voice still further. 'You must, Fearn. The royal kindred withers within itself.'

'You were never so keen on Waroch marrying.'

'Waroch was over thirty years old. I was never sure that he could mate. Now you and Anoi—it would keep the kingship within the family.'

They were closing on Rossfarm, and the Kingmaker felt safe enough in the sight of people to say more. 'A true king puts the needs of his land first.'

Power, dynasty and state—the bright mass Laerimmer saw. And yet where were the people in the Kingmaker's thinking, Fearn asked himself, the man, woman or child he had cared for as healer? In a larger kingdom he might have become a creature of policy, but his homeland was small. Seventeen families, three rivers, eight wheat fields, four barley, three flax, two woods and upland pasture: to rule here, he needed everyone's name.

So he remembered Sarmatia and the vow he had made to her.

* * * *

Before he invoked the Sky God, Fearn tried to reason with the battling father and son-in-law, but they would not be reconciled. The lightning came without rain. He gave judgment in favor of the father.

Weary after the rite, the King did not notice Chalda. When they collided, Fearn gave the greater start. His arms came up, to enfold and protect her gently bulging form, but Chalda pushed him away.

'Am I a whore, to be manhandled?' Her voice was cruel, because his kindness meant nothing.

'Chalda, don't.' Fearn thought of his earlier words to Laerimmer and was ashamed. She gripped his hair, to pull herself up on tiptoe.

'I hope she's dead,' she breathed by his ear, and jerked back. The evil-wish hung between them, then Fearn broke the cord, taking her red mouth under his.

'Isn't this what you want, bitch?' he hissed, feeling her freeze.

About them, crowds surged like water stirred in a crock. It was harvest, everybody drank, bawdy scenes were common. The King might be rougher than some, but he'd never left a young girl in trouble. Mostly he kept himself to himself, a wise precaution, with other royal kin sowing wild oats. Yet it was all young fun.

One of Fearn's war band was not so sure. Once, for a bet, Aren had spied on Goar and his latest girl, watching the whole procedure. He thought Fearn and Chalda looked wrong. She wasn't squirming or giggling. The red-haired man hung over her like a tightened bow. Another youth he might have grabbed, but this was the King.

'Fearn!' Aren used the name, fearing nothing else would reach him.

Fearn gave no sign of hearing. Laerimmer moved towards the pair, gathering Chalda's husband from the crowd. More of the war band, recognizing Aren's voice, darted in to see what was wrong.

'Leave hold there!' cried Jart, never in awe of his former teacher.

'Take her then.' Fearn thrust Chalda back. 'I don't need her, or any of her kind. I'm going south.'

'No,' said Laerimmer.

'I'll go alone.'

Several of the crowd sniggered. A few bold sparks added farmyard jests and the whole mass erupted. They knew about the King's southern woman. Their laughter battering his ears, Fearn strode out of the yard.

That, too, was part of being king of a small country.

Chapter 15

Isle of Stones, 1561 BC. Late Summer.

Orm knew the moment Fearn entered the homestead that something was wrong. One touch, and he looked likely to explode. Laerimmer must have been goading him.

'You'll not have eaten, by the look of you.' Orm fetched beer and bread, and Fearn stood at the table to eat. His boots and leggings were torn and water-logged. He had run most of the way, fording a river and risking a short cut through the forest in the bright moonlight.

'Going out tomorrow?' asked Orm, refilling Fearn's cup.

Fearn nodded. He had his father's mouth, thought Orm, although in height and breadth he was unlike either of his parents. An oddity, like himself. 'Do you want to talk? I'd rather hear it from you than the garbled tale I'll get elsewhere.'

'Soon I'll tell you.' His uncle Orm had been read the letter he had sent to Sarmatia and knew more than anyone else. He would decide later what to leave out of his account.

Orm sensed that the young man needed to think. 'One of your cattle is lost in the forest. I heard her bawling.'

'I'll take the pony tomorrow and find her,' said Fearn, grateful that his uncle knew when to hold back.

* * * *

Next morning he was off before dawn. Saying goodbye to no one, he collected fodder and food and led the stiff-maned pony softly through the gate. Outside the palisade he mounted, turned the pony's head south-west, away from the forest, and kicked the beast to a canter.

A half-day to reach the border and to find the ridgeway, what harm would it do? When the time came to go south, it would mean he would be even quicker. Just after sunrise he reached the narrow saddle of land that marked the southern tip of his kingdom. Resting the pony, Fearn continued on foot, leading his mount over the heather.

He took care not to be spotted, but the score of warriors waiting on the border had not. Drawing closer, he saw Kingmaker and Council blocking the way and, behind them, the fathers of the young men he was training in the war band.

More old men, thought Fearn in disgust. To fight his way through them would be dishonorable. The spur was the only southern path through his kingdom. To reach it, Laerimmer and the men must have marched through the night. In every way, from planning to execution, the Kingmaker had out-maneuvered him. To go south was merely to invite humiliation.

Sarmatia had not yet reached the Isle of Stones. In another three days there would be the flax harvest, and he would be needed. Until then, he had a pony, food, fodder and other lands to explore.

To the north were the blue-haired tribes, but they were too far away. To the west, a hunter people, where he would need a guide. The east it must be—into the kingdom of the Cattle Men, who bred the long-horned cows.

Stories from his grandfather's day, of the great raiding parties between the Cattle Men and the Atterians, were coming back to Fearn. Though each Kingmaker had frowned on it, the cattle raid was the proper sport of kings.

Because of him Sarmatia was in danger. As yet, it was impossible for him to help her, but he had been taking life too easy for a man. He would raid the eastern lands, defy Laerimmer and his Council, and bring home cattle, more than that single cow, missing in the forest.

Stealthily, Fearn urged the pony back from the southern pass and, after several false starts, found the switchback track going east. He mounted, and leaned forward into the wind as they jogged along the path.

Pressing ahead to the eastern limit of his kingdom, Fearn swam the Big River with the pony and slipped into the Cattle Men's homeland. At this side of the river every step through the yellow globe flowers took him farther into hostile territory.

Marking the way he should return, Fearn guided the pony through clumps of hemlock and sweet cicely, trying to disguise their tracks and scent. Dappled by sun, they came to a clearing and a small pond. He looked back at the broken undergrowth. A boar might have done the same, rushing down to drink.

So far, all was well. To go on, he should skirt the pond, keeping trees between himself and the pond clearing. But was there need? Woodland animals would come here only at day-break, and few hunters would lie in wait from noon until the next dawn.

Listening for the alarm cry of the blackbird, Fearn started for the pond. While it was quiet, he would water the horse. On the raid itself they might be running for their lives.

Sinking its nose into the green water, the pony pricked its ears. Fearn slapped its rump as it reared from the bulrushes, brown eyes staring, and flung himself across its back. The three half-clad youths and the girl they had been sharing broke cover as horse and rider headed deeper into the forest.

In his own country he would have got away, but the landmarks were strange. The shouting grew louder, strange faces loomed between the oaks, a javelin whirred.

It was like smashing into a tree. The reins slashed through his hands and were gone, the pony a black panic, careering away. The javelin head burst through his belt, blood pouring over his hands, and the ground met him with darkness.

Chapter 16

Tartessus, 1561 BC. Late Summer.

The journey into Tartessus was grim. When *Viper* anchored in the fine, stone-built harbor, its crew did not cheer. Had they landed on a hostile shore, they could not have been more solemn.

The fat harbor master, though perplexed, treated them well. 'You're the first new ship for a month,' he told Misarios, heaving himself aboard to check for plague. 'It's late in the season for boats through the Pillars.' He winked. 'That'll give you a good price for your cargo. Have you perfume there? I'll pay well. It's for my mistress.'

Misarios reached into one of the cargo barrels strapped in its new place against the mast step. 'Take this as a gift.'

The harbor master blinked. His check of the crew was thorough, yet they were clean of plague. The harbor master shook his head. 'You can go ashore,' he said, expecting the customary rush. Each man quietly left his place and filed one by one from the ship. The harbor master gawped. A crew like dumb oxen, and with a handsome woman aboard!

Something moved in the dark hold. The harbor master blundered across the keel and whipped back its wooden cover. He rounded on Misarios. 'You said I'd seen the crew, but who's that?'

'It was a passenger.'

Pergia came beside Misarios. 'The bitch isn't going anywhere.' She caught the Tartessian's arm. 'It's blood-cursed, and one of our men is dead. Do you want to be next?'

Hastily, the harbor master withdrew his hand. 'You'll bolt the hold?'

'Locked and weighted.'

'My men will guard your ship,' said the harbor master, baking away. 'I'll take you to a house of refreshment.'

* * * *

Deep in the hold, Sarmatia heard Pergia's words and bowed her head. It was true. She accepted the judgment, as she accepted her lack of water or food. She had deserted Kerewos, left his body in the hands of cannibals, without burial rites. His soul might wander forever, because of her.

Now there would be no northern journey. When the cargo had been sold in Tartessus, the ship was to return to Krete. If she survived, she was to be given to Kerewos' village for judgment.

Some time after there was a scrabbling, a wrenching back of the hold cover, and then light. Sarmatia flinched and turned away. Hands took hold of her head. Fresh water lapped her cracked lips. She clenched her teeth.

'Drink!' The cup was jammed between her jaws and Sarmatia spluttered as water gushed over her. She drank instinctively and that first draught was enough. 'Slow!' The cup was drawn aside and Sarmatia groped for it. 'No more now. You come ashore.'

Strong hands grasped her arms and legs. She was borne up into the daylight, set upon a sheet, her bundle of possessions lain beside her, and lifted from the boat.

* * * *

Sarmatia knew she was dreaming, but she was still angry. She faced Fearn across the river which divided them and cursed him. 'Why don't you speak? Help me!'

The figure of the healer said nothing. It grew smaller, without moving back from the edge of the roaring water. 'Answer me!' Sarmatia beat her fists upon her thighs in fury. 'What should I do?'

Still silence. Sarmatia tried to leap into the river, but some unseen force prevented her. Her thoughts were eloquent. 'Five months I've traveled now. I've left my home, family, country for you. Must I go on, beyond all I've known, without a word from you?' Sarmatia stretched out her hands. 'You've not been silent. Not while I was in Egypt. Tell me then, it's not for nothing!'

This must be your choice, Sarmatia.'

'Why? Why now?'

You have chosen before. You found it easy over Kerewos. Why is this time so different?

Sarmatia shuddered, tasting the bitterness of conscience. Tears poured from her eyes. 'Curse you,' she whispered.

* * * *

When she woke fully it was light. She was lying in a hammock, suspended from the beams of a house. A palace, she thought, noting the rich wall hangings. A serving girl dozed by the carved wooden door. Sarmatia spoke. 'What is this place?'

The serving girl started and raised her head, looking at Sarmatia with the brittle eyes of fear. Gently Sarmatia repeated the question. The girl put a hand to her lips and shook her head. 'Where am I?' This time, Sarmatia spoke in Egyptian.

'You'll get no answer from her. She's a mute.'

The spiteful voice echoed through the chamber. Sarmatia spun out of the hammock and crashed onto the floor. 'Still trying to find your feet?' mocked Pergia behind the carved door. 'In a way you have. Prince Pepi Akauhos has plans for you. You're his supplicant.' Fully restored—after her relapse following Kerewos' death—Pergia's comfortable breathing filled the space between them. There was a rustle of rich skirts as she turned.

'Oh, Misarios sends congratulations at your good fortune.'

At the sound of footsteps going away, Sarmatia jumped to her feet, lunged past the mute girl—who had made no move to help her when she fell—and pounded on the locked door. 'Don't leave!' It made no difference.

Sarmatia waited, listening for the slightest sound beyond the door. The day waned and the small chamber was plunged into darkness. The serving girl slept in her niche beside the threshold. Sarmatia raised her arms to the rafters and prayed to the Mother Goddess.

I am alone. Whatever well-wishes had been sent, the friendship between her and the others from *Viper* had been shattered. Sarmatia could not forget how they had left her in the hold. It must have been the Prince, this Pepi Akauhos, who had ordered that she be brought here, and the others, too. Yet why were they here? She was a supplicant. Pergia said that the Prince had plans for her. *Stop thinking of Pergia.* Sarmatia rocked in the hammock, swaying back and forth.

In the morning she heard bolts being drawn back from the door and positioned herself in the center of the chamber, ready for a confrontation with Pergia or a meeting with Pepi Akauhos. The door swung inwards, admitting two guards and a servant. The servant gave the mute a tray of food then turned about. Sarmatia tried to reach the open door but the guards blocked her. They withdrew backwards, facing her with their shields. Again the door was shut.

A second, silent day passed and a night, and in the morning the guards and servant came with another tray of food. They appeared to understand neither Kretan nor Egyptian, and though they took care not to touch her in any way, Sarmatia could not leave. There was a bucket in the chamber for her water and waste. She tried through signs to communicate with the mute girl, who would only shrink back and flinch.

Sarmatia knew she was a prisoner, a special one, who could not be bruised through rough handling by the guards or sullied by the hands of a servant. Half-knowledge nagged at her.

Now, whenever the mute girl slept, she would scour the chamber for a possible means of escape. The single window in the room was barred by a heavy wooden grill, but she tapped the wood, and the paneling on the walls and roof, hoping to find a rotten timber that she might punch through. One night she tried to prize a flagstone from the floor, but her eating dagger would not take the weight and she could not budge the heavy paving.

Fear and panic ate at her but she fought them down and prayed again to the Goddess. It seemed her prayers were answered, for on the fourth morning of her strange captivity, Sarmatia realized how she might escape. That morning, when the guards drew back the bolts, she stayed within the hammock. As they filed into her chamber she clutched at her stomach and began to writhe and moan. The servant dropped the tray and rushed to her, uncertainly touching her forehead. Sarmatia cried out, as though delirious. One guard was dispatched to fetch help, the other dropped spear and shield when Sarmatia stiffened and her harsh breathing stopped. He leant over her, cursing both serving women, and Sarmatia seized the horsehair plume of his helmet, dragging it down over his eyes. She gulped in air, grabbed her bundle of possessions in one hand, lashed at the guard with the other and leapt off the hammock for the door.

Swift as the mute was to try and close it, Sarmatia barged through, slammed and bolted the door behind her and heard the guard within hammering and shouting as she ran away.

She was lucky. Her chamber was not in the main complex of palace buildings. Hitching her skirts, she dashed to the end of the long corridor which connected her cell to other rooms and, hearing the steady tramp of approaching soldiers, darted into the first open doorway she found. It was the royal nursery, full of toys and cribs, but no children, only a plump nurse and two midwives, who screamed when they saw Sarmatia and tried to hide themselves behind a clay bathtub. Sarmatia ignored their shrieks. She had seen the window. Rushing to it, she flung open the shutters and vaulted onto the sill. Behind her came a shout as the soldiers reached the nursery and she pushed herself from the window ledge, not caring how far she fell. Hands grabbed for her hair but were too late. She dropped six feet, landed and ran, zigzagging as she had in the Bull Rite to avoid pursuit. Without looking back she pelted across a yard, leapt a drainage ditch and ran along the course of the mud brick walls which surrounded the palace. A great hue and cry was coming from the palace but she was out and Tartessus was before her.

* * * *

First, Sarmatia found a quiet alley and disguised herself. She plaited her hair like a boy's and smeared dirt on her face. Using her dagger, she cut her robe so that it hung about her knees like the ill-fitting woolens of a peasant. Hoping she would meet no one from *Viper,* she set out for the port.

Compelled by obstinacy to finish what she had begun, Sarmatia had decided to continue her northern journey. It seemed the wisest course. She did not know what this Pepi Akauhos had in mind for her and there was no going back to Krete, but in the end, stubbornness, too, made her go on.

In this, Sarmatia was helped by the happy chance that Kretan was the tongue of sailors. Here in the city, the speech of her homelands was everywhere, a pleasing thing after the uncanny silence of the palace.

Yet when Sarmatia asked along the waterfront for sailors who made the trip north, she was told: 'Ask in the place of the metalworkers. It's the smiths who travel to the northern tin-lands, no fishermen go there.'

So Sarmatia turned about and left the brightly-hued boats and hauls of cod fluttering on the cobbles of the fish-market. She did not go willingly. The smell of the port put her in mind of her father and her childhood. Soon she was lingering, held back by the drama of a catch being landed. Such beauty and knowledge of the sea, to wither in the sun—

Struggling for breath in the heat, Sarmatia could not hope to avoid the collision. The tall figure dashed into her side, knocking her forward. She found herself brutally steadied by her hair and heard the muttered, 'Gods! These peasants!' before the stranger was gone, striding up to the boats to harangue a disembarking shipmaster.

She was a striking figure. At six feet, the woman stood out in any crowd. Her storm-dark hair was scraped back into a thick, black pigtail and tied by a strip of linen edged with gold. Despite the heat she wore soft leather boots, branded on their sides with a crossed hammer and file, the mark of her smithying trade. But it was the huge strawberry birthmark which made the woman unique. Stretched like a hand up the left side of her face, it was a sign of unquenchable fire.

By now the stranger had a mob about her and Sarmatia found herself standing on tiptoe to watch. She wished she knew Tartessian, although the woman's gestures were entertainment enough. Despite a fleeting pity for the shipmaster, Sarmatia could not help smiling as the stranger shook fists at his boat, raising eyes to heaven, and she laughed with everyone else when the fisherman offered the woman the pick of the catch before she ripped her cloak and so set the curse that had rung out from her lips.

The woman snatched up her fish and disappeared down an alley. The crowd sighed and turned once more to their everyday concerns, disappointed the argument had not gone further. Sarmatia did not move. Men and women jostled round her. She was intrigued by this ugly female, who in her haughty way was much like Pergia—as Pergia had been, when they were friends. Perhaps, the thought rose in Sarmatia's mind, she should discover more about the metal smith.

There were many eager to tell. The woman's name was Bride. She was an adventurer, turning her hand to anything so long as there was gold and trouble. But what set Sarmatia hurrying after Bride was her conversation with an old woman, who had beckoned to her through a crack in a door.

'You're wanting to hear about Bride,' hissed the woman in Kretan. She looked at Sarmatia with bright, malicious eyes, without opening her door farther.

'Yes, mistress.' Sarmatia was not surprised the woman knew. Gossip spread like plague in towns. 'What do you know?'

The woman giggled, shielding her face from the sun with a dirt-encrusted hand. 'You saw her this morning, bullying the fisherman? It was over an eel he'd sold her. She said it was rotten, though she'd eaten it, mind! That's how Bride is, she wants her rights.'

'All that for an eel?' Sarmatia was impressed. 'Is she good-hearted? Is her word enough?'

'It's said she'll see friends through fire.'

Sarmatia dropped her gaze. Her face must give nothing away, reveal nothing of her spiraling excitement. 'Does she travel far? The north, say? Does she know the ways?'

The old woman nodded. 'She goes to the wilds every winter, looking for gold.' She lowered her voice. 'Is there a feud between you?'

Sarmatia met the gloating eyes. 'No, mistress. I'm seeking passage north.'

She felt revolted by her own prying. She should be meeting Bride face to face, exchanging names and gifts, not creeping about the houses asking questions like a beggar. She pressed a few copper coins into the woman's palm and left, running down the street in the direction Bride had taken.

* * * *

It was noon. The city should have been asleep. Sarmatia squatted in the shade of a wooden stall to cool off and looked back along the alley where she had crossed from the port of the fishermen to the second harbor of Tartessus. The street was empty as far as the stone pillar marking the boundary between the two halves of the city, but from the start of the port of the silversmiths, the sloping street exploded into life. Clothiers draped in rare silk, potters with basket-loads of goods, cooks with braziers, kebabbing in the middle of the road where sparks would not fire the houses, were as numerous as dust. They silted up the passage through the street to a slow trickle. There were fortune tellers, gamblers and slavers, even an ox-cart which kept jamming between the low roof eaves and had to be maneuvered free.

Sarmatia took in the colors and shape and movement with an unwearying eye but, sensing the owner of the nearby stall becoming ill at ease, she rose to her feet and battered through the crowds until she found one of the street cooks. Such men wandered all over the city.

Sitting on the ground beside him, she brought out her gold ankle bells, taking care they did not catch the light. She hated parting with any of the sacred gems of the Bull Rite but had no choice. She needed to find a friend in this strange city. 'Yours. If you say where Bride can be found.'

The cook never glanced at her face but prodded the dust with a wooden spit. Sarmatia dropped the gold into the hollow; the man covered it with his foot. 'Go to Great Street. Look for goldsmiths.'

The cook held out a freshly-done spit of mutton. It smelt delicious and Sarmatia, who rarely ate meat, took it. Today, with her spirit animal quickened by the sights and smells of the city, she craved meat. Sinking her teeth into the succulent roast, she spoke again between mouthfuls. 'See those children, staring? When I go, feed them.' She sucked and finished her own spit, plunged it into the dirt, and stood. Suddenly her eyes narrowed. 'I'll watch, so keep faith. I know the curse that can make a man a leper.'

The cook hastily set more kebabs upon the fire as Sarmatia moved on. The lie had served her well, she thought. She need not stay. On Krete famine had touched no one for four generations. In Tartessus, children fought pigs for scraps. 'Tartessus bright with gold, fairer than Knossos,' so the city was known to the world. Something must be wrong with men's eyes.

* * * *

Great Street was flagged and clean, without middens. It could have passed for a sacred way. The quiet was intense beside the din of other streets. Men whispered, pacing slowly. No gold was seen—that was bargained for in private, inside the old mud-brick houses, but there was plenty of silver. Sarmatia would not have been surprised had the road been covered in it. Even children playing outside tossed silver dice from hand to hand.

She passed down the street. Merchants peering from doorways ignored her, thinking her a simple provincial. For her part, Sarmatia tried not to betray amazement at their lavish wealth.

'Men speak truly when they say Kretans are eager. The gannet's less grasping!'

Sarmatia's head came up. She knew the speaker. Bride was there in the street, clearly pleased with herself. 'A bird told me that a handsome Kretan boy was looking for me,' she went on in Sarmatia's tongue, showing her first words meant no harm. 'Are you the Kretan?'

It was a beginning, but Sarmatia's pride smarted after that public joke. Merchants had stopped bargaining to look out into the road and how could she say her name or reveal she was a girl in their hearing? She felt the meeting should be more formal. 'You're mistaken, Mistress.'

Bride frowned. 'I've been an hour searching. You're not the one?' She was fidgeting with the fastenings on her man's tunic, as if unsure what to do.

Sarmatia was ready then to admit that she was, but before she could answer, a silver-merchant's child began to laugh, flapping her arms like the wings of a gannet. Feeling slighted, Sarmatia's stubbornness would not let matters go. 'I was looking for a famous metal smith,' she answered, making a joke at Bride's expense, tit for tat.

Bride started forward. 'Bold pup! I've not spent an hour in the day's heat for you to mock!' Tossing her hair plait behind herself with an impatient movement, the woman advanced. Her fingers were knotted into fists.

Too late, Sarmatia realized what she had done. Here was a fighter, whose ring-studded hands looked as murderous as a boxer's, and whose anger she had woken for the sake of the last joke. She herself had neither the spur of anger nor of right, although she moved towards the metal smith, so that bystanders could not think she was afraid.

There was a scuffle behind her and a Tartessian smith, still black from the forge, tossed a pair of knuckle-dusters into the dirt between her and Bride. 'They're up for grabs, plough-boy, to even the fight!' he yelled, and the growing crowd laughed and moved closer.

Sarmatia dived for the strips of bronze yet even with the sun in her eyes Bride was faster. She snatched the bands up and waved them, the sun sparkling over their raised surface. They were the kind of knuckle-dusters that were illegal at the games, with spikes of metal clustered over the top edges.

Sarmatia stepped back and looked round but there was no way out. The crowd had closed up behind and was already laying bets. Bride slowed: no need to hurry. Her features seemed set, yet the left side of her face, with its ugly scarlet birthmark, looked susceptible to gentleness. Too late now, Sarmatia thought.

'The plough-boy doesn't want to fight.' chanted the crowd, as Bride closed in and Sarmatia slowly put up her fists.

'So let's change the rules!' Bride pulled back and dropped off the knuckle-dusters. Before any could protest, she had plucked a dagger from the waistband of a soldier. The mob stiffened, sensing that some of the threat had shifted onto them. Sarmatia wondered what was coming, although she sensed that she might trust the woman. Bride's words confirmed this.

'I'll tell you what we'll do, plough-boy. I'll cut you just to prove you're my ox, and we'll let the thing rest there.' *Trust me*, her eyes seemed to say. *It's only to stop a riot and the scratches won't show in a week.*

There was a blur of movement and the woman's fingers raked along her side. Sarmatia gasped as spindle-sharp nails drug into her flesh and ripped the seams of her robe, leaving her exposed to the waist. The mob closed in, eyes gleaming.

'Back! All of you!' That was Bride, voice pitched over the muttering of the crowd. They fell away and Sarmatia was alone. Bride strode up and took her by the shoulders as Sarmatia swiftly covered herself with her arms. 'What's your name, girl?' Her tone was brisk but she had dropped the knife.

'Sarmatia.'

Bride's hands tightened briefly. 'Gods! The famous Bull Rider! I thought you a common farm-hand!'

The anger which had been absent before flooded into Sarmatia at that indignant cry. 'Bull Rider, peasant, it's all one. My father was a fisherman. Yours must have been a boar trapper, who ate his catch raw!'

This time Bride laughed. 'Very good!' She gave Sarmatia a shake. 'We're going to be friends.'

Sarmatia stared. This was what she had hoped for, but now events were moving so swiftly she scarce knew what to feel. 'You're strange.'

'My forge is at the end of the street. We'll go there, away from these clods.' Bride waved a finger at the crowd. 'I want to know you better.' She released Sarmatia and moved away, then glanced back. 'Are you coming?'

That note of uncertainty proved Sarmatia's undoing. It was as though a forest bear had suddenly left off threats and rolled on its back to be tickled. 'Yes,' she admitted, 'I am.'

Chapter 17

Isle of Stones, 1561 BC. Late Summer.

What dreams he had then Fearn never knew but he woke to evil. The javelin that had felled him from his pony had passed through his left side. A bloody bulge of flesh and cloth hung over his belt. As the body was injured, so was the spirit. The tie between himself and Sarmatia had perished and would not return in this alien kingdom.

Fearn was close to death, too, never more than in his first waking moments. The four he had disturbed—the youths and the girl—knew that the girl's javelin had hit and were searching the undergrowth for him. Clutching his side, Fearn crawled away from them. The closely-growing trees shielded him but he could not stop gore dripping across hazel and woodrush. Sinking onto his stomach, Fearn wormed his way under the low branches of a holly and in its prickly heart waited his fate.

As the group came nearer to the trail of blood, their high voices called to each other as they ran in a line a sword's-length apart. Their tongue was like the common speech of the Isle of Stones. Fearn understood most of what was said. One of the boys was suggesting they should stop the chase to return to their settlement for more men.

'This raider's dead meat, but there might be others.'

'Shut it and search! He's not got far.'

'That's fine for you, but these thistles prick.'

'Should have put your leggings on.'

'Hey! We're not complaining.'

The youngsters paused, arguing, and Fearn used the cover of their shouts to roll from the holly into denser, sharper brambles. Under an arch of thorns he lay flat on his stomach, pushing the side of his stone axe against the javelin wound to slow the blood welling from his body. He hoped the brambles with their ruddy foliage would disguise his track and deter the youths from any careful search.

They were almost on him. Two lads skirted the holly, shaking and parting branches—he'd been wise to move when he did. One scampered towards his hiding place and Fearn prayed that the muck he'd smeared over face and hair would be sufficient for him to blend in with his wretched den. Like any wounded animal, he lowered his head and eyes.

The brambles rocked, buffeted by a spear. Fearn heard a yelp as the long thorns sprung back, then the bush swayed again, more savagely. A stick thrashed into the undergrowth, cracking down across Fearn's shoulder. Another jabbed at his head. So the end begins, he thought, and neither cried nor flinched at the blows. Something warm and sticky fell on the back of his neck. Another drop pattered onto his hand.

'Cows' tits! Another nosebleed!' The youth was trying all the wrong things to staunch the flow and the others crashed through the wood to advise. By the time they had found his leggings to hold to his nose and cleaned him up with their own tunics, they had lost enthusiasm for the hunt. Grumbling at their comrade, the four set off back to their village. When they saw bloodstains on the grass, they thought it was the boy's nose bleeding.

The wood became still. Fearn was tempted to stay put. He knew that as soon as he moved the wound would gape. Yet it wasn't safe to stay in one place for long. Pressing the stone axe deeper into his wound, muttering a charm against evil entering his body, Fearn dragged himself out of the brambles. Slowly he returned to the pool, sliding down the shallow bank into its chilly water. Almost at once the pool changed color. Sitting at the bottom, Fearn loosened his belt then eased the tunic away from his body to reveal the damage.

A clean entry where the cast had gone in and a jagged tear where it had twisted out. Any higher and it would have hit a rib. Lower or deeper and it could have pierced his guts. The main thing was to stop the bleeding.

There was bistort growing by the pool which Fearn cut, chewing on the dark roots then spitting them over the wound. As healer he had stopped cuts with powdered bistort root and even with a large gash the magic of the plant still worked. Cobwebs taken from between the stems of the bulrush were next and then it was time for the mud. Fearn smeared mud from the pond edge over his side until bistort and cobwebs were sealed in.

Afraid to eat while hurt, he threw away his food, but swilled out his mouth and refilled his water skin from the pond. Stripping off his leggings, he used one long piece as wadding and the second as binding round his middle. Wrapping his cloak around the whole, Fearn backed out of the pool.

His mistake was sleeping. He was weary, in pain, and sleep, the greatest healer, but he dozed too long stretched out beside the pond. Another dawn showed when he stirred and felt at his side. There had been no more bleeding and he blundered to his feet. Stumbling barefoot along a deer-run in the dawn chill, Fearn thought gratefully of his own house and hot soup, laced with Maewe's scoldings. His Uncle's wife could say what she liked once he was home.

The morning was windless and Fearn aware of every sound and his own slow heartbeats. The cry of a wolf pack, hunting somewhere in the same forest. He checked the rising sun's position to be sure he was on the right track. By a tree stump he paused to take a sip of water. The wolves howled, turning his way.

Ignoring the jarring stab it gave him, Fearn twisted back. Through the trees he heard the rumble of horses. Horses and hounds.

He drained off his water skin and flung it far into the woods, hoping the dogs would scent it and change pursuit. Keeping to the deer-run, Fearn quickened his pace to a steady jog. He would never outrun hounds. He must outwit them, and their masters.

Fearn threaded and re-crossed streams, laid false trails, doubled back, kept always to dense woodland to slow and fool those following. Finally he had to rest and, setting his back against a spreading beech, looked round.

The tree hid him but he could see the Cattle Men, four squarely-built warriors on horseback. In the woodland and glimmering dawn he could not see their faces. A pale ray of sun flashed over their jet cloak fastenings and sharp bronze. He counted three stabbing spears and a couple of those new long swords—few hunting weapons here.

Counting on their not expecting it and anxious to put more distance between them, Fearn slipped between the trees without doubling back. Catching his scent on the deer path, the hounds behind bayed and quickened their loping run.

Then, wading through the saplings came another enemy. It burst onto Fearn, iron-hard claws tearing for his throat. He slipped and that saved him.

The bear's jaws gaped. One bite and it would have his head off. He shouted, kicking out his feet. The frenzied mass descended, blood and fur blinded his eyes.

The four warriors did not hurry to remove the body of the black bear from the man. They waited till the spear stopped twitching. Only when the dogs began tearing at its flanks did they heave it away.

'It's the raider, alright,' said one. 'He's still alive.'

The others laughed. Fearn's eyes flickered. 'Water.' He spoke in his own tongue and was answered in the same.

'Here's my water bag.' The one who spoke seemed to be the leader. He watched Fearn struggle to lift his head, then, before he could drink, knocked the skin aside. 'No more till you've answered my questions. How many of your sort crossed the river?' He shook the water bag by Fearn's ear.

'What's your name?' said another, prodding his spear butt into Fearn's side.

'Seems familiar to me.' The leader leaned right over Fearn, breathing his foul breath into his face. Fearn saw something smooth and white wriggling in the man's grimy nostrils.

'Purge yourself for worms. Eat a spray of bracken and be warned, it works fast.' They were going to kill him and Fearn wanted them to remember him just as much as if they had fought.

'That's it! The healer!' The leader grinned, drawing back for the other warriors to stare at their captive. 'What are you doing so far from home?'

'No business of yours, unless you're a king.' A sword hovered between his eyes and Fearn looked along its point into the snub-nosed, bearded face. 'Are you?'

'There are four here. Take your choice.'

Fearn breathed in slowly. If this was to be his last breath, he'd make it a deep one. 'Then you'll understand when I say I was on a cattle raid, alone. Unless the kings of the Cattle Men have forgotten the old ways?'

Snub-nose's grin broadened. 'You're right there, speaking of the old ways.' He slipped the sword into its leather sheath and turned to the others. 'Let's get the dogs off the bear: I've a fancy for a footstool. Pity her cub got away.'

'What about him, Narr?' asked the warrior with the spear.

'Patch him up.' Narr raised a hairy fist to quieten the protests. 'The old ways, yes. Patch him up then take him to the Killing Tree.'

Chapter 18

Tartessus, 1561 BC. Late Summer.

'What you need is food.' Bride ducked out of the street into her shuttered forge. Bull Rider or not, the girl was green and her teeth were chattering.

Sarmatia sat down amongst the ashes with her head on her arms. Resting like that, brown spirals of hair spilling from its single plait, she was again the boy Bride had fancied in the city. Thwarted, the metal smith slammed the door behind them.

Flushed in the day's heat, mouth aching as two wisdom teeth bored their way up through her gum, Bride had been looking for some distraction. Finding Sarmatia near her own forge, she had taken in the sweeping black brows and lashes, the faint copper-rose stain to the high cheekbones and strong chin, the glowing, eager gaze, and decided that the town-talk was right. Here was a very handsome boy. Even the surly manners were a challenge.

Desire had died with the revelation of the girl's sex. It wasn't that she disliked women—she'd loved her mother—but a strong man, a pretty boy, was what Bride wanted for her bed.

'Sit still. You're cold. I'll build up the forge fire, after I've found that waste of a serving girl.' She straightened and squeezed through a narrow opening at the back of the forge. There was a loud slap and a shriek. She came back with wine.

'Lazy thing was asleep. Let the fire go out. Only keep her because she's a good cook.' Bride had won the creature in a raid off Kerinthos, but was growing tired of her grudging service. She poured two cups to overflowing and pushed one at Sarmatia. 'Take off that tunic. My servant will stitch it.'

Sarmatia nodded and moved to obey, but Bride noted how she drained off her wine. Youth touched her and she liked the way the girl handled herself.

'It can slow you down like that when you've had a near meeting with death.' It had happened to her once in battle and she had never forgotten.

'You didn't cut me, either.'

Gratitude was there, but Bride, who would have received the humblest of thanks as no more than her due, whistled. 'Gods! Are you always this blunt? Do you really think I carve my guests up?' Irritated, Bride tossed her cup aside and moved to the forge. 'I admit that at first I thought you were a fool.' If the girl could be forthright, so could she.

Sarmatia said nothing, kept her face still, but her eyes gave her away just like a boy, and Bride laughed. 'That seems unfair? Well, remember that your tongue's no great peace-lover! Still, that's past.' The moment of bad temper dismissed, Bride picked up a broom to sweep out her forge before lighting it. 'How old are you?'

'Eighteen.'

Bride was amazed. 'It's those scars on your body.' Sarmatia's left side looked to have been cut over a dozen times. 'I was certain you were two years older.' Even then, the girl was nowhere near as old as herself. At twenty-six Bride was rapidly approaching middle age. 'Let me look at you.'

She tried to catch the girl's head with one hand, but Sarmatia drew back. 'Hold still!' The speed of her reaction reminded Bride of what her guest had been. 'You Bull Riders are all alike.' Snatches of tavern song had spoken of the girl's looks, but not her height. Sarmatia was tall for someone who had ridden bulls for six years. 'How did it feel, to ride for the gods?' Curious, Bride saw nothing wrong with the question.

The glowing eyes were turned on her. 'It's sacred.' The words emerged in a growl. Sarmatia looked as stubborn as she had on the street.

'What's the harm? You're a long way from Krete.' Bride was not one for worrying over religious niceties. The world she inhabited was firm, practical. Expecting laughter, which she might have got from a youth, Bride was disconcerted when Sarmatia gritted her teeth.

'Don't ask me that,' the girl shot back. 'In fellowship.'

Bride's fingers tightened angrily round the broom handle, but she forced herself to relax. It occurred to her that for all her lovers she had never known a female friend. 'I'll go see what's keeping our dinner,' she said.

* * * *

They had a good meal: baked fish with almonds, steaming wheat pancake, hot and cold vegetables, raisins and olives. Wine flowed as Bride talked and watched her guest. There was a warm stillness in Sarmatia that invited secrets. You could tell by the way she breathed that she listened. Her eyes, the color of warmed copper, rarely strayed from Bride's.

At length Bride stirred the fire to light up her own features. She was easy enough with her birthmark but curious as to how others viewed it. Bride wondered if Sarmatia was shocked or repelled by her appearance. She had met both. Often, especially since her maturity and the rounding out of her big woman's body, there was admiration at the way she carried off the disfigurement, even, in some rare cases, acceptance. Sarmatia, Bride suspected, was one of those few. She decided to test her. 'You were looking at my mark?' She jabbed a finger at her scarlet cheek.

'Yes. I thought the firelight would make it redder, but it seems darker, like a spray of hyacinths.' Sarmatia cleared her throat. 'Tazaros, my brother, wears those for luck.' It was the first time she had mentioned her family.

Bride grinned. 'You're saying I've a flower up my face?'

'If you like.' Shy, Sarmatia frowned. Words like striking, handsome, vivid, did not come easily to her.

Pursing her lips, Bride decided Sarmatia wasn't being funny. She was perfectly serious. Such youthful fancy wasn't much to her taste but it amused her and, Bride reflected, it might be interesting to find out what the guild would make of her guest.

Lately, the metalworking guild and her place within it had been on Bride's mind. Two days ago, coming out of a side street, she had encountered Ytho, the guild treasurer. He had detained her, tugging on her tunic. 'You've heard the latest, I take it? The Prince is settling two Hyksos smiths near the palace. Do you know what that means?'

Bride thought that even with the new beard Ytho still looked like something you would scrape off your shoe. 'You can work that out for yourself,' she said. 'Given time, of course.'

In his indignation, Ytho let her go, allowing Bride to walk smoothly away. His shouts followed like a bad smell. 'You've got to share! If the guild goes down, we'll make sure you go with it!' She had turned at that, but the crowds hid him. A slippery customer, Ytho.

On her return home, Bride regretted that she had not let Ytho hang round longer. For once, he might have had more than stale news. Everything depended on whether the Hyksos could smelt iron. If they had that secret, her own tricks with bronze would be worthless.

Striding back to her forge, Bride forgot Ytho and the Hyksos smiths. They were no direct threat to her survival. Men like Dares and Periphas were.

Bride knew their sort from other cities, the kind that picks over garbage with a knife and sleeps out in the street. You could not tell the shade of their skin or hair, it was all drink and filth. A colorless, dangerous pair.

These two had raided her forge the night before last. When she had heard bodies thudding against the wall thatch, she had thought they were revelers in the city returning home and rolled over on her pallet to sleep. A muffled scratching near the forge door, a series of crashes, bitten off laughter, brought her fully awake. The serving girl had let a man in.

Her house was on two levels: forge, kitchen and maid's corner below, her own room above. Bride dressed quickly and strapped on her sword. The long blade tapped on the ladder struts as she descended.

The forge had been ransacked. Everything worth stealing was gone, the rest smashed. She wondered how she had heard nothing then recalled that the wine her maid had brought that evening had tasted off. She had poured most of it away in a libation.

They were in the kitchen now, the lovebirds, no doubt pleased with their haul. The door was ajar and Bride peeped through, expecting anything but what she saw.

Not one man but two. The gangling one was poking fingers into bread and meat, unstopping amphorae, sucking off a mouthful, spitting into each vessel and then levering them forward. As she set her eye right up to the crack he overturned another and lentils spilled across the floor.

The other, thicker-set man had the maid pushed over the bench and was kneeling up to her. In the darkness Bride could not be sure if he had a knife laid to the girl's breast or not. The man thrust and grunted and Bride hastily stepped back. She knew the men by their stink.

The second man had finished and the tall Tartessian was rolling up his tunic to take his place when the girl made a break for the door. If she had drugged her mistress and let them in for a little money, she regretted it now. Bride let her pass through to the forge then stepped into the doorway between girl and men. 'Greetings, Dares, Periphas.' She inclined her head to both. 'I'll have my metal and tools back. They're there, behind Periphas.'

She stared at the gray men in her kitchen, Dares fumbling with his clothes, Periphas his dagger. Having been assured by Ytho that the tough old bag would definitely be sleeping and they should be able to lift every scrap of ore and metal in the place, her appearance had caught them off-guard. They watched each other, clearly waiting for a chance to rush her, neither wanting to try first. Periphas' hand tightened on his knife and Bride's sword leapt, a ripple of darkness, for his guts.

'The privy door's behind you. Go through it and get out.'

The privy door banged twice and at the sound of running footsteps Bride sent the girl to bolt it while she started picking through the mess.

Setting the forge to rights, buying new stores, took most of the night and next day and gave her time to think. Dares and Periphas were thieves yet they would also work for hire. It seemed to Bride by their wrecking and looting, even to the foodstuffs in the kitchen, that they had been looking for something. Had Ytho sent them? Bride shivered in the cold dawn. Her metalworking secret was secure, but for how long? Dares and Periphas were the kind who would come back with more men.

Bride flicked her hair plait over one shoulder. It seemed she would be trekking early to the wilds this year, but she did not want Ytho to think he had succeeded in driving her out of Tartessus. She had still been mulling over what she should do when she had met Sarmatia.

'What are you doing so far from Krete?' she asked, as they ate.

Sarmatia did not say much. There was a journey she must make to the Isle of Stones. There was a man. She showed Bride a ring, a plain thing that she wore on a cord round her neck. About the man she said nothing, only his name.

'How did you come to Tartessus?' Bride asked, but Sarmatia shook her head and said that did not matter. Strangely, in spite of this reticence, Bride believed her brief account. Sarmatia did not look like a hardened traveler, and though there was a haunted air about her, she was surely as she appeared, a girl on a once in a lifetime journey. Bride envied Sarmatia her certainty. No man she knew was worth it.

Still, there was this to be said for Sarmatia, she kept her vows. And she was here in Tartessus, so she had a sensible head on her shoulders. Bride cracked a few jokes. The girl delighted her by laughing out loud. By the end of the second wine jug, she had decided. 'Well, child of the bull. What would you say to traveling with me?'

'I'd say yes. I want to go north.'

Bride reached across and gave Sarmatia a push. 'You're close,' she said, blue eyes sparking. 'Aren't you going to tell me how you came here?' Without waiting for an answer, Bride rose and shook herself. 'How are you with horses? Do they unnerve you?'

Sarmatia shook her head. She had never seen a horse but she knew she would not fear one. No animal terrified her. That was part of her power. 'I don't think a horse would hurt me.'

'Good! Because soon' —*maybe very soon, if Dares and Periphas came calling*— 'I'm riding out through the wilds to the shores of the Tin Seas.' Bride grunted as she picked up a log and flung it into the center of the fire. 'I'm going to the Isle of Stones for gold and there's a place for you on the journey. I'd welcome your company,' she added, surprising herself.

Sarmatia thought of how she liked to be by herself but then recalled with a shiver her time in the ship's hold. She knew now what it was to be lonely and had grown less proud of her independence. 'Then I will go with you,' she answered, walking gravely across the dirt floor of the forge to embrace Bride as custom demanded.

Chapter 19

Tartessus, 1561 BC. Late Summer.

Two days passed. Bride provided Sarmatia with boots and clothes for their journey and Sarmatia helped her in the forge. The work was to her as dangerous and glamorous as the Bull Rite and it quickly drew her and Bride into a close alliance. Sure that the girl would not talk, Bride showed Sarmatia the secret of adding lead to molten bronze, a trick she had learned in the East and which she jealously guarded, despite pressure from her guild. This made the metal far easier to work.. For the moment Bride contented herself with repairing her own weapons and equipping Sarmatia with a slim sword.

'I'll teach you how to use it sometime on our journey.' She tossed the blade across, laughing as Sarmatia's jaw dropped. 'Careful when you hold it. Gods, put it away! Here, wrap it in this sheepskin. We're moving.'

Sarmatia glanced up from the thick fleece which strangely would not move beneath her fingers. Bride watched with something of a smile and nodded. 'Yes,' you've guessed. You've seen my skills, now I want to see yours. I'm taking you to the horses.'

* * * *

Sarmatia came upon the horse-herd by the stream where warriors watered their hunting dogs, though she had known of their presence on the wide, grassy plain before then. The stallion's pride rose to her from the ground itself, like thunder in her head. *I am King, I am King!*

She did not doubt it. Even the bulls had not lashed up her blood like these horses that burst over the earth like a winter flood. Her limbs ached to run with them, and the dried grass tops scratched her legs as the rasping tongue of a mare quickens her foal into life. Her first sight of the herd, drinking by the stream, brought Sarmatia to a sudden stop. They were so beautiful, these huge, glossy bodies, shining in the morning like polished bronze. And the brown eyes, widening not in fear but in warning. She was stilled, awed, waiting for a sign, the sun covering her head with an amber mane of light.

Then the horses moved, crushing the slim thread of birdsong beneath trampling hooves. The ground flexed like a drum as they rushed out of the water, blond tails spilling behind. Sarmatia, still waiting, understood the sultry pleasure of spring, the chill terror of the wolf. She laid aside her sheepskin and sword and filled her hands with grass, coaxing the horses to her.

The stallion came first, rushing forward and lunging to a stop as Sarmatia held her ground. She spoke softly and soon the leader bent his head and nuzzled her fingers empty, chewing the grass, learning the scent of friendship. It was he who called the rest of the herd and gave them leave to rub their flanks over Sarmatia's hands.

Later, Bride dared not believe what she saw. Sarmatia stood a moment amongst the circling horses and then moved through the middle of the herd, darting casually by the deadly hooves of the stallion. Seeing her like this, with creatures she had never seen before, Bride began to feel uneasy.

Still sprinting, Sarmatia shook her long brown hair out of its plait, laughing when a colt started back from her. She mopped her sweating face and pointed to the stream. The stallion wheeled round and headed for the water, Sarmatia keeping pace with his easy canter. One by one, they lost the other members of the herd to the lush grazing of the stream meadows, but they themselves drew closer, the horse's long mane and Sarmatia's hair mingling on the breeze in a weave of shades and textures. As they ran the sun poured golden from them both, like spray from sporting dolphins.

They entered the water, clattering over the pebbles of the stream bed. The leader dipped his head into the coolness and Sarmatia sprawled full length in the tingling embrace of the river. Only their throats moved as they drank.

Soon after, as if obeying some agreed signal, the chestnut horse moved to the bank, nostrils flaring as he sniffed the air. Sarmatia followed, dripping, hair and clothes clinging to her body. She glided alongside the stallion and traced her fingers down his neck, then, in a fluid motion, vaulted onto the horse's back. She dug her heels into the chestnut's side and they moved, the horse skimming over the field. They cleared the scrub and galloped over the grassland, earth spurting beneath the stallion's tread. As they reached the slight rise where Bride was standing, Sarmatia checked the horse with her knees. They approached at a slow canter, Sarmatia drawing her body upright. 'Here is the leader.'

Bride shrank back. Sarmatia gazed down, her face impassive, eyes burnished in the fierce fires of the trance. She spoke again, her tongue thrusting the words out. 'His name is Gorri. Remember it!'

Turning her head, Sarmatia flicked Gorri gently with her foot. The chestnut surged forward and, turning, Bride had a view of the girl's straight back, her whirling hair, before distance lost the pair and they were gone.

* * * *

Sarmatia awakened slowly and reluctantly. She was flying on wings of bronze. She was not Sarmatia alone but Sarmatia-and-Gorri, guardian of the herd. Twined lives...

She blinked and was one again, sighing involuntarily as the keen edge of consciousness returned. She was lying on a straw pallet, a woolen blanket covering her. Half-suspecting where she was, Sarmatia turned to be sure.

The slight rustle brought Bride from the shadows. She bent close, face dark with concern. 'Sarmatia?'

'I'm here.'

A sigh of relief escaped Bride. 'Do you know how long you've been out? A full day! I've missed a day's trade thanks to you. There you were, slumped on my doorstep like some wild thing, after I'd given you up for lost on the cattle plains. We're to go out in two hours' time.'

'Go out? To the wilds?'

'Of course!'

Sarmatia started up. 'I must—'

'Eat.' Bride pushed her back onto the straw. 'You've had nothing since the morning before last.' Bride rose and headed for the kitchen.

Sarmatia grinned when she heard Bride clumsily sorting through cooking pots, cursing as she swung the cauldron off the fire and burnt her fingers. Ever since waking, Sarmatia had felt her energy returning. Her hunger was another sign that all was well. She had been like this before, at the end of the Bull Rite. Gratefully receiving a steaming bowl of stew from Bride, Sarmatia inwardly thanked the gods for keeping her safe then turned her attention to the food.

'I said you were hungry!' Bride exclaimed approvingly, when Sarmatia finished her second bowlful of the hot, spicy stew. 'Want something to wash it down? Good. I'll join you.'

Bride brought flagon and cups and took the empty bowl from Sarmatia, tossing it into the middle of the floor. 'The girl can clear that,' she said, sucking spilled wine from her hand. 'When we leave, I'm giving her to the smith at the end of the street, but until then she can earn her keep.' She handed Sarmatia a brimming goblet and seated herself beside the Kretan. 'I want you to listen.' She first took a long swallow of the wine.

'There'll only be two of us on this trip and it will be hard. I hope you hobbled Gorri on the cattle plains. We don't want to spend the first day chasing wild horses. Or do you just whistle and he comes racing like a boarhound?'

Sarmatia laughed at the thought. 'I'd like to see that! Gorri comes and goes as he pleases.'

'And if he leaves, you walk?'

'Why not?' Sarmatia's eyes twinkled. 'I'd have the pack-beasts for company.'

Bride gave a bark of laughter. Thank the gods the girl had a sense of humor. 'You would, too! If only we could ride from the city, what a triumph! Just to see their faces.'

Sarmatia suddenly felt rather guilty. She'd told Bride nothing of how she had come to be in Tartessus, nor of her escape from the palace. So far her disguise had seemingly paid off, but she would not feel easy until they had left the city. 'How long will the journey take?'

'Through the wilds? Thirty to forty days. Longer if the weather catches us. Snowfalls are rare on the mountains this time of year— What was that?' Bride drained her cup and strode to the door. The knock came again.

'Open on command of Prince Pepi Akauhos!'

'Don't!' whispered Sarmatia. She had understood nothing but the name, but knew that if the soldiers found her she would be taken back to the palace. And what would happen to Bride? 'Don't open it!' She motioned that she would run out through the back. She didn't really expect to escape but this was less about fleeing than about saving Bride from suspicion.

Bride grabbed Sarmatia as she turned and pointed to the pit where ash was emptied from the forge. She twisted back to the door and made great play of fumbling the locks.

'Wait a moment!' she called, while Sarmatia buried herself in the ash. She dropped a piece of sacking over the girl's head so she could breathe and opened the door. 'Yes?' Bride spoke in Egyptian so that Sarmatia could understand.

'Your pardon, Lady,' said the guard. 'We are seeking a Kretan girl, a captive who escaped from the palace four days ago. It was said she has been seen hereabouts.'

'A Kretan slave? You'd do better to look in the port, amongst the foreigners.'

'We've been there already. You met with her, it's said.'

'Not by any of my guild.'

'So if we may search?'

Bride snorted. 'Search my house? For a runaway slave?'

The guard was making excuses. 'Forgive me, Lady, but we seek no slave. This girl is free.' He lowered his voice. 'She is sacred. If we do not find her, things will go bad in Tartessus. This is the supplicant the Prince has waited for, these many years.'

'Enter then.' Bride stood back from the door.

Under her covering of ash Sarmatia stiffened, dreading the moment when her sacking head cloth was torn away by the smith. But Bride merely leaned against the edge of the pit and waited as the men searched. 'What's the other news from the palace?' She casually stirred the ashes with her broom.

The guard sighed. 'Not good. The Prince has guests, but these have fallen out amongst themselves. One is dead and has been left out on the midden.'

Sarmatia clenched her teeth to stop the cry that rose in her throat. She heard the soldiers leave and felt a sick relief that Bride had not betrayed her. She coughed, ash suddenly irritating her lungs, and Bride reached into the pit and dragged her out.

'How are you, Pepi Akauhos' supplicant?'

Without mentioning Kerewos, Sarmatia said that she'd been locked in *Viper's* hold and brought from there to the palace. 'I must go back,' she finished. 'I must know what's happening.'

Bride brought wine and made her drink it. 'If you value your life, don't go back.'

'I'll climb the palace walls and look from there. I needn't go inside.' Sarmatia was determined to do last rites this time, as she had not been able to do for Kerewos.

Bride shook her head. 'All that tale about your being sacred, you were still a prisoner. There's some prophecy surrounding Pepi Akauhos and a supplicant. No one but the Prince knows what it is, but I can't think it will be good for you.'

'I'll take care.'

Bride laid a hand upon her shoulder. 'If you're set on this, wait till dark. Any corpse will keep till then. We'll put off our journey for today.'

* * * *

After sunset, Sarmatia left Bride's forge and ran through the empty streets. There was a full moon and she flattened herself to the shadows and crept past the main palace gateway. The chained watch-dog barked, but quietened after her silent command. She scaled the mud wall and slithered along its wide, flat top. Below was the yard she had crossed. The reek of the midden grew stronger. With a glance round for any guards, Sarmatia let herself down on the other side of the wall.

'Help me! Please!'

Sarmatia stiffened. The voice had spoken in Kretan. 'Where are you?'

A sigh, light as dust, was her only guide. Sarmatia scrambled along the sides of the foul midden, oblivious now to the piles of rotting refuse and rank, flyblown remains. A few paces on, she found a body prone amidst the mud.

'Oineus!' Sarmatia heaved the man onto his back, cradling his head on her thighs. Horrified, her eyes ran across his bloodied face and body, fixing on the bronze dagger bulging from his gut. She knew instantly that the soldier had been right: Oineus was beyond help. She also knew who had done this.

'Misarios,' gasped the sailor, confirming her thought. 'He struck and the others watched. Ach!' Oineus arched his back, biting his lip. 'Help me!'

'Here!' Sarmatia caught the sailor's clawing hands and wiped his sweating face with her clothes. Yet what was the use? The man was dying. She gathered Oineus closer, rocking him in her arms. Misarios' ominous words, *We'll settle other debts there*, hung heavy in her memory. Misarios must have bribed the guards and dumped Oineus here, in revenge for what had happened on *Viper*, she thought, sickened. What was the murder of a cook to a Tartessian Prince or his men?

'It was my last trip.' Oineus said in a reedy whisper. 'Then home to the grandchildren. Have things for them, in my pouch.'

'Lie still!' Sarmatia desperately mopped his face again. There was only one thing she knew that would stop Oineus' pain, but it would mean his life. How could she?

'Sarmatia!' Oineus pierced her anguish of remorse and uncertainty with new urgency. 'The dagger! Pull it, for pity's sake.' He began struggling with the next breath.

She had to do it. Unable to watch his suffering, Sarmatia wrenched the blade from Oineus' body. He sighed and his head lolled on Sarmatia's knees.

She kept his body there for a while, seeking to comfort Oineus' ghost. Finally, sprinkling the spirit-freeing earth over the man and kissing his stilled lips, Sarmatia eased the corpse from her lap and rose wearily to her feet.

She looked about. There was nothing for her here. Pergia had known of this killing yet had allowed Oineus to die alone, slowly and in pain, on a midden heap. Sarmatia turned on her heel to go back over the wall. Moonlight flared at the corner of her eye. She spun about, Misarios' dagger at the ready, but there were no guards. The moon had caught the edge of a marble pavement, farther on from the midden and wall. Intrigued, Sarmatia ran to the pavement and looked along its length. It led from the main building of the palace to a great marble slab of an altar. Sarmatia began walking towards it. Pergia's harsh voice ran in her mind: *Misarios sends congratulations at your good fortune*. Then Bride's final words when she had set out that night: *Pepi Akauhos is desperate for a son. He would do anything to get an heir*.

Her limbs moved slowly, as though underwater, but her reaching hands found cold marble and she could see the altar had been prepared. Wine and corn were here, in two basins, and leather straps to fix the beast of sacrifice were tied in readiness. Yet these narrow bindings were not for an ox.

Sarmatia placed her wrist beside a thong. The thought of the empty palace nursery tumbled through her mind. She was to have been sacrificed. Pergia and the others had known this. *They would have let me die, my throat cut like a beast's.* Her spirit-voice had said nothing. Fearn had given no warning!

It was too much. Sarmatia reeled. The bronze ring was cold on her skin and she snatched at it to hurl it away. Her fingers closed round the metal.

But the familiar gesture of comfort revived. In spite of everything, she laughed. She had not needed a warning. She had saved herself.

I'm alive, she thought, and her fingers found their strength again as they grasped the dry mud-brick and brought her safely out of the palace grounds.

Chapter 20

Isle of Stones, 1561 BC. Late Summer.

Fearn learned to his cost that the Killing Tree of the Cattle Men was a single ash in a wood of oak. It grew in the middle of a circular glade and ravens rested in its outer branches. The base of the tree was so broad that three men, with outstretched arms, could scarcely encircle it. The top of the tree swirled in a wind no other tree could reach. Its leaves were as long as daggers, its roots broke up through the earth and were dark with blood. Up and down the ash ran a squirrel, a red tail-blur, pattering between twigs as deftly as rain. Cattle Men called the tree the rod of the earth bull. To Fearn it was a terrible horse, rearing and dark.

He swung from the tree, baited on its branches like a falcon as it tossed in a midnight storm. The Cattle Men had bound his wound and given him water to keep him from dying too quickly, and the ravens waited for his eyes. The sun was on his back in the morning and on his face in the evening and what he suffered only dead men knew.

The four kings put him on the tree with another man, a lame man, who wept as they bound and hung him by his wrists from a high branch. Fearn they hung above him, and his feet swung past the man's arms and brushed at the crown of his head. Later, as the ropes sagged with Fearn's weight, his feet pressed hard against the man's skull. By then the lame man was dead so it did not matter. Fearn stood on his toes on the dead man's forehead and rested his arms and rope-burned wrists. A raven pecked at one heel, found that it kicked and left him.

Next day, the four kings came to the glade with three old hags. They cut the lame man down and buried him between the ash tree roots. Finding Fearn alive, one old woman climbed the ladder they were using for a closer look. She prodded his chest. 'You the Atterian king?'

That needed no answer. Fearn cleared his throat. The woman was not as old as she looked, though she was pallid and had hobbled up to his grim perch. He thought: Should I care? Then, Have these people no healer?

'You, alternate days, eat fat-hen, chew on dandelion leaves.' The first would give strength, the second ease the ache of her joints. At his voice, harsh through dryness and pain, the woman slipped on the ladder, her head jerking. She scurried down two steps, changed her mind and came up closer. Her breath, like that of Narr, the eldest Cattle King, was fetid.

'My man has the toothache.' She mentioned cousins, each with cramps and pains, the same afflictions as amongst Fearn's people. He said nothing. Scolding, the old woman went away.

At midday she returned with her family. They cut him down and fed him, giving him strong beer for the pain. Fearn lay in the shade of the ash and men and women squatted beside him, showing off the abscesses in their mouths, their swollen joints and bent backs. He told them of this and that plant, how to use it, what spirits needed to be told and why. Some cures would work fast and others would be of little use, but by then he'd be dead. As with Narr in the forest, Fearn wanted these Cattle People to have something by which they'd remember him.

One man had brought a cow stricken with maggots. When Fearn told him how to save it, he and the rest were so grateful that they cut strips off their leather cloaks to bind round his wrists so the ropes would not cut when they strung him up at sunset.

Another long night followed. By day-break, the four kings and two of the three old women were astonished to find him breathing. Narr spotted the leather hanging from Fearn's wrists and shouted, 'Who did that?'

'Don't know. I was asleep.'

Narr laughed. He and the others sat down to watch him dying. 'You're a sharp one!'

Ignoring that, Fearn used the slack in the leather bindings to swing himself and wrap his long legs about the branch he was tied to, resting his shoulders and aching chest. Yelling, one of the four kings leapt to his feet, but the others wrested his bow from him and sent the king off to wherever the Cattle People lived. While he was gone, Narr climbed the ladder.

'We could have done with you last summer.' He rubbed absently along his forearm. 'Our healer died after an accident. We burned the plough, but it made no difference. My old woman knows some things, but the skill's not in her blood. You, now, your mother was a healer.'

'I can't cure your arm. It's in the bone.'

Narr chuckled at his impatience. 'We'll see what you can do. Me, I trust you. Had a man worm-purged like you said, then tried it myself. Excellent!' His hand slapped the ladder. 'The others are more wary. Ivak says we should practice on you first, but I want you to provide the cure.' His brown eyes twinkled then darkened. He stared at Fearn but made no move yet to break his leg-hold on the tree. 'There'll be time for that if my son dies.'

'Ivak talks too much.'

Narr grinned but the ladder trembled slightly on the tree. By rights, this red-haired Atterian should be dead. Since it seemed he could work against nature, Narr hoped Fearn would find a way to preserve the life of his heir.

The litter bearing the sickly child was already being carried into the glade. Lying slackly on its furs was Narr's son. Narr fixed him with a desperate eye. Since his fever began the boy had been growing weaker. His mother now walked beside the litter, clutching his hand and hiding her tears. Behind her came the Cattle People in their leather cloaks trimmed with jet buttons, their weather-hewn features resigned.

Fearn from the ash saw a ten-year-old invaded by spirits. The evil was in the child's head, pushing out his skull until it was almost as round as a sheep's paunch. His body, starved by the spirits' greed, showed wrinkles in the skin where there had once been flesh and muscle. Peeping out between the limbs of a leather toy, the dark eyes were listless in the ruined face. In spite of his father, Fearn pitied the boy.

Waiting for the right moment, he watched as the litter was set down under the tree and Narr jumped down from the ladder to fuss with his son's bedding. Concentrating on the large bulge at the front of the child's skull, Fearn let go his feet and hung in the sky. 'Spirits, can you find no better place that you must eat into this boy's head?'

At his ringing voice, Narr's face was an upturned dish of amazement. The spirits moaned in the child. Fearn threw down a challenge to them. 'Come, let me free you!'

In his mouth Fearn could taste their fear and hope. He spat and spoke to Narr. 'Fetch the sharpest knives in your kingdom, the strongest drink. Fetch fire and water.' He coughed, his lungs drowning as his body swayed on the ash. 'Return my axe to me.' Fearn closed his eyes, praying to the Sky God. His fate now rested on the life of the child.

For the second time he was released from the tree, given water and food. Narr himself brought his axe and when Fearn saw it he walked unsteadily to Narr to take it. Touching the blade for luck and tucking it into his waistband—even though it must be on the wrong side because of his sticky wound— made Fearn feel more himself. Confident, he knelt beside the litter.

The child was trusting, probably too weak to be fretful or afraid, and his skin was cool and free of fever. To keep him so, Fearn made a potion of beer and herbs, gathered from the woodlands by the Cattle People's children. He had the lad drink deeply then stroked the boy's forehead, humming softly to quieten the spirits, until the child slept. After he had washed his hands and passed the knife blades through the fire, Fearn laid his knuckles on the boy's skull and pressed gently.

Between the crown of the child's head and his temples, where his skull was swelling like an over-ripe apple, Fearn caught the ripple of a spirit. He pressed again, sensing an answer through his fingers. They would leave the boy alone, if he could release them.

Shifting the bedding, Fearn raised the child's feet. His head was down, to assist the free flow of blood that would carry the spirits out of his skull. Working quickly, Fearn began to cut those forces a way out. The flint knife grew bloody. He threw it aside before it was blunted and reached for another, scoring the same circle, again and again.

To his relief, the child was thin-boned. At the fourth knife, the piece of skull broke and Fearn eased it gently away. From out of the circular hollow in the boy's skull came a rush of blood, almost as thin as water. Fearn let it drain a moment and then pulled out the wadding from beneath the child's hips so the boy would lie level. The ten-year-old expelled a long shuddering sigh and whimpered. Fearn put a dressing over the wound. The child's dark eyes flickered. 'I'm thirsty,' he whispered, in his own tongue.

Narr thrust Fearn aside. 'My son!' He kissed the boy repeatedly. His wife, bending down to the litter, glanced at Fearn. 'It's all right,' he told her. 'The spirits have gone.'

Ivak, standing with the people, did not believe that. He had seen a trephination done before. 'There were no screams. He has no magic ox-bones. The demons gave no clear sign of leaving!' His protests were loud and certain. Ivak strutted to the litter and would have poked under the boy's head-dressing, had Fearn not stood in his way.

'You should sacrifice to your gods,' Fearn said quietly.

'I want to look.' Ivak moved forward.

Fearn stopped him. 'The child needs rest.' He smiled. 'He'll live.'

'You'll never know,' snapped Ivak. At his command, six warriors came out of the crowd.

'Is this how the Cattle Men repay debts, Narr?' Fearn shouted, struggling with the warriors.

Snub-nosed Narr shrugged his wide shoulders. Ivak was his brother king. 'What can I do? You must be our sacrifice.' His words were a distorted echo of Fearn's earlier thought. Absorbed in the world of his family, Narr wiped a trickle of blood from the forehead of his sleepy child.

* * * *

Ivak hung Fearn low on the tree by his feet. For an evening Fearn endured the taunts of the men, the sly strokings of the women as they passed him to pay their respects to Narr's son. Afraid to move his child, Narr remained in the glade and his brother-kings and their families stayed with him. When the child stirred fully and asked for food, the makeshift camp came alive in celebration. While he ate, they drank the rest of the strong beer and danced round the ash tree in the orange sunset.

A third night started and still there were no Atterians to rescue Fearn. Did they think themselves well rid of him? he wondered. Were they searching other countries? Coaxed by his voice, a dog came and licked Fearn's face, then urinated on him, an act which caused a storm of jokes amongst the Cattle People. Fearn ignored that, thinking of the old dog that had been his boyhood companion, the one he had told Sarmatia about. Since Puddle, he had sworn to have no more. Setir the shepherd kept the dogs.

He fell asleep. Waking with his head dipped in darkness, ankles numb, Fearn realized that the rest of the camp were snoring in the moonlight.

The Cattle Kings had made a mistake in leaving his hands free. He reached for the axe still at his waist and flexed his arms. Two-handed, not caring how he fell, Fearn chopped up at the ropes around his feet.

Lindsay Townsend

He dropped hard onto his backside, but was quicker than those in the camp at finding his feet. Casting about the ground for his sword, Narr found himself with Fearn's arm about his throat and his voice in his ear.

'Single combat, one to one. If I win, you let me go.'

Fearn's strength after what he had been through was uncanny. And how had they forgotten to strip him again of his axe? The gods must love him. Narr swallowed, motioned his men back. 'No need, you're free!' he croaked. 'Next time, we'll come to your lands. It can be single combat there.'

The arm around Narr's throat tightened. 'Do your brothers agree?'

Narr gave a sign, and was relieved when his younger brothers nodded.

Fearn let him go and limped away. Walking at this speed, he would be lucky to cross the Big River at midday. Thinking of the likely reception he would get from his family and worrying that now lost, the Sky God's eye would be forever closed to him, Fearn was already full of disquiet.

'Wait!' called all four brothers. Fearn looked back at them, green eyes feral and dangerous.

'You owe us your life,' said Narr. 'Does that warrant no thanks?'

Fearn folded his arms across his chest. 'I'll not kill you when you come for my cattle.' He turned again and trudged into the moonlight.

'And we won't kill you, healer,' came a voice behind him. 'Only your best cows!' Fearn gave no answer but limped on.

The four kings followed at a distance. After they had seen him safely across the Big River and into his homeland, Ivak cleared his throat and said, 'I'm sorry, now he's gone.'

Back in his own kingdom, Fearn walked a lonely road, seeing no sign he had been missed. 'Sarmatia, Sarmatia,' he called out once, 'What kind of land are you coming to, where a king has no friends but his enemies?'

Chapter 21

Isle of Stones, 1561 BC. Early Fall.

Sarmatia stretched, drawing close to the fire. She warmed her numbed hands, tossed back her cloak and moved away from the blaze. Hers would be the final watch through to sunset. She'd need her wits sharp.

Walking past Gorri, Sarmatia went to the river. She knelt and drank, tasting the resin from the pines. Here in this country was where she liked to be.

In thirty days of hard travel, land and sea, she and Bride had come to the Isle of Stones, Fearn's homeland. How many days then before she would meet him?

Sarmatia closed her eyes, remembering the healer she had known on Krete, calling his name in her mind. How was he living and what was he doing? Her thoughts reached out but found nothing. She could go no higher than the animals, it seemed, in joining her spirit with another's.

A breath of movement was her only warning. Even as she turned the figure was on her, pushing her underwater. Sarmatia coughed and kicked, tearing wildly with her hands. 'And if I were an enemy, Bull Rider, you'd be dead!'

Bride let her up and dragged her from the river. 'What should have been with you?'

'My sword.'

'Then why wasn't it?'

Sarmatia shook her head. Somehow her shame was freezing into anger and she did not deserve to be angry. Her stilled face told its own story. Bride left off taunting. 'Here,' she said, with a sigh. 'I did say that this camp was safe. Let's forget this and begin again. After we've eaten, I'll show you something of my battle-trade, as I promised I would, that time in Tartessus. I only hope you keep yourself alive long enough to profit by it!'

* * * *

The following morning, Sarmatia woke to an odd gray dusk. It was not fog. She could see Gorri as he browsed the tough grass. Yet the light... She stared at the milky sky.

'That sickly pallor is a typical northern dawn,' said Bride, kicking out their fire. 'If we're lucky, we might be blessed with the sun.'

'Poor sun,' murmured Sarmatia. 'Where do we go today?'

'Towards the northern ridgeway. Once on any ridgeway, the going's easy.'

'They're roads?' Sarmatia looked across the wide moorland running away from the river. 'Who made them?'

No one knew, Bride answered, as they began their day's journey on foot, walking to allow Gorri's hooves to harden after the sea crossing. The pack animals had been exchanged for gold, but Gorri had chosen to go with Sarmatia. Talking as they walked, Bride guessed that the ridges were older than most of the tribes, seeing that they cut across kingdoms. They had probably been built at the same time as the big mortuary houses, whose gleaming, chalk-covered mounds were often sited at crossroads.

'Wait till you see them,' Bride said. 'They're as big as your Kretan houses and still used. Men go to them to be healed as well as buried, and women eat the chalk to ease childbirth. The ridgeways are always busy.' Bride paused. 'That's why we must travel the northern ridgeway at night. It will be quieter.'

Sarmatia threw Bride a narrow look. Bride grinned. 'Yes, I do have other reasons.'

'Care to share them?'

'Later. Give me three days, Sarmatia.'

Concerned by Bride's almost pleading tone, Sarmatia nodded. 'If you're sure.' She smiled. 'You know I'm a good listener.'

'That's what I'm counting on, in three days. Do you know how many days then?' she asked with false cheerfulness.

It grieved Sarmatia to see Bride so, but for the sake of friendship she entered the spirit of this uneasy game. 'To the Atterians?'

'Not forgetting your man Fearn! Less than a week.'

* * * *

Their first two nights on the ridgeway were peaceful. The weather was mellow, the road easy. Bride taught Sarmatia some of the common language of the Isle of Stones. Sarmatia repaired their clothes and kept a sharp eye out for trouble.

Around her, the land changed from high moor to groves of wind-gnarled oak, bare of foliage except for the mosses that tickled her face as they rested in the day. Sometimes the road tipped off the ridge and drove along valley floors. Then Sarmatia could see the distant homes of men, their fires sparkling in the darkness like drifts of pollen. It was a beautiful country.

But food was running out, as was fodder for Gorri. The ridgeway had been picked clean by masses of sheep and cattle. Spotting a gray-white burial mound as the next ridge marker, Bride was particularly excited.

'That's the crossing of the Lead Road!' She leaned so far forward on Gorri that Sarmatia grabbed her cloak to stop her tumbling off. 'We've almost made it!'

'Care to tell me now what we've made, Bride?'

'Eh? Oh, never mind that, just an old warrior talking. It's good to see the Lead Way.' Bride continued to brag about the deals she had struck on the Lead Way. In between, Sarmatia learned that they would travel the Lead Road for a final night then take the Copper Way into the lands of the Otawe, and finally the Atterians.

First they needed provisions, and for those Bride insisted that they could do no better than leave the ridgeway at the crossroads and go down to the nearby village. 'It's a place used to traders,' she added, when Sarmatia asked about this possible trouble they had so far been avoiding. 'We'll have no strife here!'

* * * *

They reached the place at midnight, after less than an hour's journey. The village was a large settlement of forty houses, secure behind a palisade of timber and rubble. The huge gates of the palisade were open, and through them Sarmatia could make out a crush of people standing round fires, casting thankful glances at the strong walls of the village. They were mortally afraid of wolves in this land, though she had yet to see one.

Past the village ran a meandering stream and Sarmatia slid from Gorri's back to lead the stallion gently to the ford. One step after another, hearing alders creak over her head, she coaxed the horse into the chill water until they had reached midstream. There she stopped, jerking her eyes up to the stars of the Great Bear as her body stiffened against the shock.

Sarmatia! Don't go through the gate!

Fearn's voice was so urgent that she was convinced Bride must have heard, too. Sarmatia put a hand up to her head, trying to prolong their spirit-joining, but the moment had passed, leaving a wash of conflicting feelings: joy, gratitude, alarm. She stumbled, splashing blindly in the dim light.

Instantly, Bride was off Gorri's back, hauling her to her feet. 'Get on! What's wrong with you?'

Sarmatia stiffened again, resisting attempts to push her forward. 'We mustn't!' She gripped Bride's arm with cold fingers. 'Not in there!'

'Come on, we haven't all night.'

'No, Bride, listen—'

Now there was light: a glare of torches, a maze of men. Sarmatia tried to defend Bride, but found herself thrust face-down in the water. Then she felt a sharp blow to her skull and saw only darkness.

* * * *

'Yes, you'll be rewarded well for Bride. Six years I've waited ... Throw a bucket on that.'

The cold water brought Sarmatia round, stopped her swaying on her feet between the guards. The harsh, blurred voice continued: 'What's she called? What's your name?'

'Where's Bride? What have you done with her?'

The squeal of laughter made her blink. Focusing, Sarmatia looked about. She was in a circular hut, well lit by many torches. Part of the building was behind a thick wool hanging, with a backed chair in front of it, covered by bear pelts. Bride was nowhere to be seen. Abruptly, her questioner stopped laughing and lounged back upon the pelts, rubbing the fur the wrong way. 'You know Bride?'

'She's my friend.' She fixed her eyes on the man in the chair. A brown-haired man of middle height, perhaps of middle age. Skin gray as whale blubber, dark eyes seemingly without pupils or lashes, hands dimpled and clumsy with gold rings. He glided forward on the chair and Sarmatia silently willed him not to touch her. 'If you hurt Bride, I'll kill you.'

'A proud one, you've got me a proud one!' For a moment the dead voice was animated and there was color in the gray face. 'But we'll see. You'll shriek like the rest. Take her out!'

And Sarmatia was dragged into the early dawn, where she was sick in the fresh, cold air.

Chapter 22

Isle of Stones, 1561 BC. Early Fall.

At that moment in the Atterian kingdom, people were anxiously waiting for Fearn to wake up. Orm had found him in the fields late last night, slumped over a wall. The young king's face had been gray with pain, and beneath his knotted eyebrows he showed the whites of his eyes. For a terrible moment Orm had thought he was dead then Fearn drew in a faint breath. Now he lay by the fire in his house, covered by every blanket Maewe possessed. Orm held his hand—it was deathly cold. Fearn was deathly still. Last midnight, soon after being brought indoors, it had taken four men to hold him down when he had shouted in a trance.

He was breathing faster, a muscle in the side of his face twitched. Suddenly he jerked and gasped like a new-born drawing its first breath. His eyes rolled back and refocused.

'He has her!' His hand burned and his fingers clenched round Orm's. Hearing him, the family lunged forward. Maewe pushed them back with a rake that she grabbed from the wall.

'Get back!' She beat about them with the rake. 'He's alive. He needs quiet.' Maewe bundled the onlookers outside, with the look of a woman glad that Orm had sent no message and that none of the royal family were there to fuss and look down their haughty noses. She left her husband and Fearn alone.

Before the Sky God's sight darkened, Fearn was talking. Orm could make no sense of it. 'Who is it?'

'The King across the Winter Born, in the plains. King— Ach! It's fading!' Fearn clapped his hands to the forehead, trying to wring out the trance. 'No, it's no use, I can't see.' He closed and rubbed his eyes. His body went slack and he did not resist as Orm lifted his head to give him water.

'You're getting a bit big for this.' Orm refilled the cup from the ready pitcher. He saw Fearn drink nearly half the bucketful. 'Better?'

'Yes, the burning's going.' Though too proud to admit it, Fearn was glad of Orm's cradling arm. 'What should I do?' he said to himself. 'Sarmatia's been taken.' Try as he might, Fearn could not recall the Plains-King's name, or picture more than that one searing glimpse of his kingdom. The flashing heart of the vision was gone, leaving him blind. He sighed and looked at his uncle.

Fearn had looked at him like that, thought Orm, when he'd told the twelve-year-old lad his parents were dead. The advice he'd given then must do now. 'Wait. Time will help you.'

Stifling a curse, Fearn had to give way for now. Orm felt the young king stiffen then grudgingly relax against him and knew that soon he would sleep. Fearn's own body would compel him to sleep. Orm lowered his nephew's head, tucked the bedding round him and shuffled away from the fire.

Maewe was waiting in the doorway, still clutching the rake. 'What's happened?'

Orm snatched the rake from her and flung it down. 'What do you think? His girl's just come to the end of her journey.' The brief anger gone, resignation replaced it. It was sad. It was life. Orm hoped he was wrong, but felt certain that he and his wife would never see Sarmatia.

Chapter 23

Isle of Stones, 1561 BC. Early Fall.

Two weeks after her capture found Sarmatia put to the lowest kind of work. Just then she was scouring cauldrons in the shallow waters of the Winter Born. Carvin's men had killed a red deer and there was to be a feast.

Sarmatia yawned and wearily dunked the encrusted pot into the river. It was still over an hour to dawn. No one in the village had stirred when she passed except Bride, a slave like herself. Bride had tried to speak, straining forward on her chain, but Carvin's man had beaten her back and shoved Sarmatia past the tiny lean-to forge.

Sarmatia rubbed harder on the brightening metal with her greasy rag, imagining the grime she was loosening off was the skin of Carvin's face. She watched the debris drift into darkness. Across the river a fox barked to her, then turned its yellow gaze and disappeared. Sarmatia smirked when her guard started, but it was a brief pleasure. Her back ached from the beating of the previous night.

Sarmatia rinsed the last pot, gathering them into a rough cloth that she slung round her back. She gripped the two cauldrons by their handles, one in each hand, and began the long stagger back up the slippery track to Carvin's hill fort. Every few steps she had to stop and swap round her burdens, while the guard prodded her forward before her breath was halfway steady. At the edge of the village, seeing a girl he fancied emerge from a hut, he told her to go on alone.

Sarmatia seized the chance to see Bride, whose forge was set on a natural terrace looking over the thatched roofs of the village. Bride was hammering the edges back onto knives and tools, panting great clouds of steam into the dawn. Unlike Sarmatia, she had no guard over her: instead a heavy bronze chain attached the metal smith to a massive boulder. Sarmatia wondered that Bride could even move. 'How long?' she whispered in Kretan. Carvin's men were everywhere.

Bride glanced at a series of grooves scratched into her boulder. 'Fourteen days. How are you?'

'Well. And you?'

'Yes, yes.' Bride waved the question aside. 'And before you ask, Gorri's still in the lower stud field with the mares. Listen, I tried to tell you earlier. Carvin knows.'

'Knows what?'

'Everything.' Bride started hammering violently. 'Everything about you. Carvin has his ways.'

Sarmatia remembered some of them with a shudder. She started walking again, whispering back, 'Keep safe!' It was a long trail to the hill fort.

She heard the screams when she was halfway up the slope, the steepest rise still before her. For an instant the old Sarmatia stirred and quickened her step but then she faltered. What was the use? Her head was bursting and her arms were numb. She was unarmed. She could do nothing.

It's the other girl, Sarmatia thought dully, as she slopped the biggest cauldron across a ditch and heard the wild sobbing. *Mother let it be over—*

The final shriek fell like a blow and after it silence. Sarmatia labored past the gate and into the muddy yard. As she passed Carvin's hut, its door flap was lifted and a young woman the same age as herself came out. The girl was dark and slender, smaller and finer-boned than she was. She was weeping and scarcely able to walk. She passed Sarmatia without seeing her and disappeared through the open gateway.

Sarmatia watched till the hill cut her from view, her face burning with grief and shame. How can these people bear it, she thought, dragging the big cauldron over to the stone fire pit and resting her head against its cool metal surface? Fourteen days, and each day Carvin had raped this young woman. He'd other women too, gorging an appetite that was never satisfied. And one day, perhaps today, it would be her turn. One day Carvin would make her say yes.

'God, god, god.' Sarmatia picked up a fire-cracked pebble and beat it along the edge of the stone pit.

Time passed. How long, Sarmatia could not say, but she remained where she was until a shadow falling across her arm made her look round.

'Come on.' The guard whirled her to her feet. 'Carvin wants you.' Sarmatia was thrust into the hut and left. Carvin was behind the blue hanging. She could hear his shallow breathing. A gray hand crept round the curtain and beckoned. Rebelliously slow, Sarmatia edged forward, keeping her eyes upon the chalk floor she had swept that morning.

This time at least he was dressed. He had another man with him too, a stranger who smelt like a rider, someone who must have entered the fort after she had done, and whose presence was a relief to Sarmatia.

'This is the girl.' Carvin flicked a finger at Sarmatia and settled back on his bed, draping a pelt about his calves to cut out the draught from the door.

'Pretty,' remarked the standing rider, looking Sarmatia up and down.

'Yes, a good bed-piece.' Carvin jerked his head towards a pitcher and cups just a hand's-length from his reach. 'That can be part of your message.'

Sarmatia poured the frothy beer from the jug, an evil suspicion growing in her mind. She did not look at Carvin as she handed him the first beaker.

'When can you leave?'

'Today, Lord, if you wish.'

'You know what to say?'

'I remember.'

'Tell me again, to be sure.' Carvin sucked in a mouthful of beer, motioned for more.

Sarmatia refilled his beaker, slopping the dark liquid into the cup as she heard her own name. The rider was quickly-spoken and his speech was formal, but the phrases that she did catch increased her alarm. For something to do, she started to pour the rider a beer, dashing the lip of the jug onto the tall drinking vessel with a clash.

Carvin smiled. 'Let us drink now to a fruitful conclusion of our work. And to your safe journey. It's a long ride to the Atterians!'

Sarmatia clenched her teeth, willing herself to be silent. Pleading would do no good here. Better to remain quiet and try to remember that the rider was taking nothing north but words. No proof. She moved and steadily filled the second beaker to its brim, but when she offered the rider the cup Carvin grabbed her wrist, pulling her down onto her knees.

'Give that shepherd-boy king back his trash, too,' he said harshly. 'No bitch of mine wears another man's token!' And though Sarmatia tried to stop him, Carvin ripped the leather thong from her throat in one searing tear, tossing Fearn's ring to the booted messenger. 'Here.'

Sarmatia started up, but the rider had been waved away and Carvin had his hands in her hair. 'I'll take these, too!' He wrenched the seal stone which had belonged to Sarmatia's mother from her wrist and dragged the Egyptian crocodile torc from her neck. 'No—' Carvin laughed as Sarmatia grabbed for the seal stone and struck her across the face with the torc. 'You have them back only when you've pleased me.'

Sarmatia fell against the bed, clutching her bloodied mouth. Carvin's face hung above hers. 'You're mine! I spun your shepherd-boy a pretty tale: said you'd fallen into my bed for the price of an earring. What do you think he'll make of that?

'That foul ring would convince any man,' he muttered tonelessly, lashless eyes widening, 'And even if the fool guesses you're my slave, what can he do? There are more sheep than men in his patch of dirt!' Carvin's voice grew shrill. 'His kind were eating grass when mine were ruling!'

Carvin rasped on and Sarmatia buried her head in the bearskin covering the bed and tried to shut him out. This was the end. Fearn would see the ring and perhaps even believe the messenger's story. He would despise and then forget her—forever. She would grow old as the slave of Carvin.

Sarmatia choked and pushed away from the bed, but as she tried to rise, Carvin caught her hair again. 'No tears?' He yanked her cold face into the light from the door. 'No touching scene? Don't you want me to recall that rider? No, it's too late now!' The man laughed and stifled Sarmatia's plea with a perfumed hand. 'Guard!'

A bronze-covered soldier strode into the hut and stopped at the other side of the hanging, staining the cloth black with his shadow.

'Lift back the covering!' Carvin ordered.

Momentarily, Sarmatia was aware of daylight again, but then was blinded by cold, green sparks of fresh pain when Carvin's fingers slithered round her jaw and squeezed. He spoke to the guard without taking his eyes from her.

'I wish to prepare for the feast, tonight,' he said. 'This piece can earn her bread by cooking it. See to it!' Carvin released Sarmatia with a spiteful push that sent her skidding along the chalk floor. Then, as though he had forgotten her existence with his dismissal, the man absently thrust out his tongue and licked the blood from his fingers. Her blood.

Revolted, Sarmatia found she could not stop looking until he had swallowed, then she lurched to her feet and stumbled outside with the guard.

Gradually, the relief of her temporary escape pared some of Carvin's misery away, and Sarmatia became aware of a world outside herself. This older guard, Riard, was one of the better ones. He might even allow her to visit Bride.

'Riard, I'll need some rowan berries for the sauce.' This was a lie. She would do no more than was demanded of her, but rowan trees grew close to the lean-to forge.

'Right. Let's get off this hill then.'

Relieved it had been so easy, Sarmatia picked up an earthen crock. Clutching it close, she drew a comforting warmth from its sun-glazed sides. Whether Riard saw the gesture or whether he too breathed freer away from Carvin, Sarmatia never knew, but the guard began to talk to her as they tramped away from the hill-fort.

'People might call me daft, but I always think this place is the oldest in the whole of the world.' Pointing out across the open countryside, Riard traced the long line of the horizon with his spear. 'Everywhere you look is holy. The Hill of Earth and the Hag Mound and the Making Way, where my wife and I walked to get our second child.'

Where Fearn and I will never walk, thought Sarmatia, her eyes picking out the granite sarsens of the Making Way that ran through the small oak wood of the valley and up and over the gently sloping meadows. She sighed and rubbed as much of her arms as she could without dropping the basin. Whenever she had dealings with Carvin, it set her skin on edge. Taking a chance on the guard's good humor, she asked, 'Where's the stud field, Riard? Can we go there?' It was important that she see Gorri, make certain the horse was safe. Up in the hill fort with Carvin, there was not so much as a shrew. Carvin kept no pets. Except her.

'It wouldn't take long, no one would miss us,' Sarmatia added, but Riard hurried on, his head bent close upon his chest. Halfway down the long tack to the village he came to a halt, swinging his empty water skin from his shoulder. 'Let's rest here, while the old sun's warm.' Riard prodded the rim of a chalky hollow with his boot.

Sarmatia watched the man settle back, her heart beating queerly when he put aside his spear and bow. One thrust and the guard would be dead, she'd be free to run—where? She did nothing.

'Here, eat.' Riard tossed her two crab apples and loosened the chin-strap of the leather helmet, allowing a knot of brown-gray hair to uncoil itself briskly out of his headgear.

'Thanks.' The thought of food, with her throat stiff and grief-tight, revolted Sarmatia, but there was no reason to antagonize the guard. Squatting with the basin protectively before her, Sarmatia chewed on an apple which felt like seal-blubber in her mouth. Thinking of escape for Bride and herself—where to, if she and Fearn were finished?—Sarmatia looked about, staring out over the landscape and wondering at the difference between Carvin's kingdom and Krete.

Here was a land full of people, ditches and boundaries everywhere. She could see men gossiping in the village and, farther off, men were hoeing in a field and others repairing a tumbled-down wall. There seemed to be no wild animals, only the fox. Not a chaffinch, or a weasel. Nothing that could help her fight Carvin, or escape from him. Was this due to the approaching winter, or was her power to sense the lives of other creatures beginning to fade, perhaps as part of a greater pining-away? Sarmatia did not know, but Riard's simple voice came as a welcome intrusion. He was speaking about the feast.

'That big stag was brought down in lands more than a day's ride from here, in the country of Carvin's Uncle. So cook it well, Sarmatia, else Carvin will be angry. His kinsman expects a gift for that meat as it is.' Riard brought out another apple to soften his warning and handed it to Sarmatia. 'This time, don't gulp the core.'

'I won't.' Sarmatia took the apple, her mind racing. It was all one, the lack of game and these tiny apples, no bigger than her thumb. Carvin was evil. His country was not fertile.

But she was his slave. Knowing that she would have to go back, Sarmatia shivered and thought once more of Gorri. She had always felt safe with the horse. 'Is the stud field far from here?'

This time Riard answered her. 'Far? It's way over the other side of the hill, up near the start of the Winter Born. That's why we can't see it. It's a good walk on any day, but I can't take you. Carvin won't have it.'

The thread of resentment prickled Sarmatia. 'What would happen if you disobeyed?' she asked, swallowing the last of her apple. 'You're a free man.'

'Maybe, but he's king. He lives in the hill fort. There's always another who'll obey him.' Riard tightened his helmet again and stood up to prevent further talk. 'Best we walk on.'

Down in the forge, Bride was shocked when she saw Sarmatia. 'Gods! What's happened to your face?' Bride tossed aside her tools and lurched to the end of her chain. 'From this morning to now you've grown into an old woman, bowed back and all!'

Sarmatia flushed, catching a note of fear in Bride's anger. 'It's nothing.' She smiled, making light of her bruised jawbone where Carvin had slashed her with the torc. 'Carvin's feasting tonight, so I'll be left in peace.' She hoped.

Bride made a dark sound and gave Riard a look that sent him scurrying on alone to the rowan trees. 'That pissbag.' She added a string of Tartessian curses. 'Where's that ring of yours?'

'Carvin has it.' No point in saying more. Bride had her own griefs. Sarmatia returned to something she could do to help. 'I'm roasting the deer tonight. Do you want leg-meat or offal?'

'Both. A piece from the rump would be good, too. That ox meat you gave me last was so stringy I spent the next day picking it from my teeth!'

Sarmatia gave a laugh which changed to a dry cough. She pressed her arms against her body as pictures of food set her insides grinding. 'I'll see what I can do,' she replied, glancing over Bride's hollowed-out face. Fourteen days of scraps had stripped off Bride's curves. she was all bone and angular planes. Sarmatia knew she looked the same.

'Sarmatia?' Bride's anxious voice.

Sarmatia clasped Bride's thin arm. 'I'll get you that meat.'

Bride put her hand over Sarmatia's. 'Be careful. No, I mean it! Carvin's more than cruel. He never gives up. Why do you think we were captured like that, miles out of his territory? He's had spies waiting for me on the ridgeway for six years.'

'That was what you were going to tell me, the reason we were traveling at night.'

'Yes, that trick worked for me when I last trekked these high plains, but not this time, I fear. It's my fault we're captives.' Bride frowned. 'I should have listened to you at the river ford. If something like that ever happens again and I'm my own mistress, I shall.'

'And if I hadn't wanted to travel north, we wouldn't have been on the ridgeway at all. Don't blame yourself, Bride, it's fate.' For Bride, rather than herself, Sarmatia tried to sound hopeful. 'We'll escape. Carvin's not liked so much that men'll stir to catch two runaways.' She faltered. Six years were almost half her own lifetime. What had happened?

'I punctured that enormous pride of his,' Bride went on, acknowledging Sarmatia's unspoken question with a grim look. 'Carvin asked me to captain his guards and I refused. And I rode out that night. I don't take orders from a ruler who rapes his own people. Didn't care for his guards, either. Bullies.'

'Riard isn't,' said Sarmatia, recalling the three crab apples.

'No, he's new to me. But the rest are exactly as I remember, poor copies of Carvin.'

Sarmatia looked aside, fingering one of the links of Bride's thick chain. 'How does a man become what he is?'

'Who cares?' Bride motioned with her head towards Riard, who had reappeared with sprays of rowan branches and berries. 'Just watch yourself round him, Sarmatia.'

Despite Bride's warning, the rest of the day—her preparation and roasting of the venison—passed in a strange procession. At twilight she stole meat for Bride and tried to show her gratitude to the graybeard Riard by serving him a choice cut, yet she remained as unconscious of the feast and her part in it as her own breathing. The day's events—the malicious message to Fearn, the return of his love-token, Carvin's vicious bruising of her face—had left her incapable of feeling. Close to midnight, Sarmatia crept from the feast. Oblivious to the drunken violence and tumult of Carvin's men, she curled up on the warm ashes of the fire pit and slept.

She dreamed of her spirit animal. It came limping out of the dark, its lion-like body covered in sores. Only the amber eyes were unchanged. The great beast walked by softly, without looking at her. The tip of its long tail brushed gently along her side, a valediction. She woke, cold, alone.

Chapter 24

Isle of Stones, 1561 BC. Fall.

Here they were—the boars, the stoats and the hares. Exercising, Bride lifted a length of chain over her head and counted the number of village elders stealing out to her lean-to forge. Four more: the force for a rebellion was shaping.

That night, the third day of the twelfth month, nineteen days before the solstice, the moon was in its middle phase, round and bright like a split apple. It gave good light. Staring up at the hill fort, Bride could see the single guard on the catwalk of the palisade. She spat, not caring to dwell on how Sarmatia was faring. Another week of Carvin and she'd be dead.

'Gods! What a mess!' The exclamation burst from the smith and the elders within earshot ducked behind the massive square sarsen that marked the northern entrance to the Making Way. Bride sighed. It would take some clever rallying to set them on. Frightened people, just as she had been, when Carvin had come to the forge and shown her the tools of torture he would use if she did not tell him about Sarmatia. Carvin had recognized Fearn's name and envied him. Fearn had been a noted healer once, and had traveled widely.

Bride returned to the approaching villagers. They had walked by her lean-to for a week, avoiding her eye, until one had come up with a blunted flint and asked how he should make it sharp. More knives had followed and a glint or two of metal, poor stuff and all of it copper. There was nothing in the village that would sever her chain, but now she was bringing them together.

Bride wound the bronze links around her arm and leaned back against the boulder to which she was fastened. The villagers crept by her and squatted beside the long wall of the forge. The last man gave her the ox-bone speaking mace.

'Have you found me bronze yet?' she asked. 'Do you think I can strike off this chain by magic?'

'We can't get bronze for ourselves,' muttered an ox-driver, who reddened when Bride stared. No one else would look at her.

A fellow Bride always thought of as Pig-Man had his hand extended for the mace. Bride handed it to him gratefully. This one was keener than most. He spoke of open attack.

'Carvin must go. We're agreed on that, right? And for that we need to gather our people one dark night, right?' He glanced nearsightedly around the group for confirmation. 'What next? Dig up the weapons that Bride has been making and charge up the hill fort to batter in the gate?'

'You'd better help me first,' Bride reminded him. Not only did she want to be free, she didn't trust any of these elders to run one step in front of the other, much less mount a successful attack. The Pig-Man's speech, though, had done the trick and talk was under way. The ox-bone passed to and fro.

'We could pick off the guards one by one, if we go softly,' said the woman whose eyes shone like a stoat's in the moonlight.

Bride could see the sense of that. She grinned at the woman. 'Let's say, then, that before moonrise on the evening of the attack, you take your family and deal with any straggling guard. That will be a few less.'

'But the dogs?' broke in another villager.

'The dogs are never used at the hill fort, only on the ridges,' replied the stoat-woman, her hard face glinting like crystal in the moonlight.

The old villager, however, was determined to have her say. 'Why are we even thinking of attacking at night? Do any of us know what might be waiting for us in the fort in the dark?'

Half as many guards as there would be during the day, thought Bride. She turned her back on the woman and spoke to the Pig-Man. 'Go over the defenses of the hill fort again. It's been six years since I've been up there.

The Pig-Man drew on the ground, in a moonlit patch of dirt. 'There are three circular banks and ditches, four clear entrances through to the fort itself.' He scraped the mace along the hard-packed earth. 'The two outer ditches are as shallow as dewponds. Carvin's men use them as middens.'

'What kind of refuse?'

'Bones, food, potsherds—'

'Nothing to slow us down?'

The man shook his head and Bride smiled at him, thinking of how they had concluded their meeting after the gathering last night. The villager hid the lower front of his tunic with a hairy arm and cleared his throat. Bride noted the jealous looks, then returned to the Pig-Man's rough drawing.

'The ditch beneath the palisade, is it too wide to throw planks across?'

Three hands came forward for the mace and one man answered without it. 'Yes, and it's steep-sided. Carvin sets the villagers to clear it out every winter.'

Bride closed her eyes, picturing the fort. 'And there are two gates? What are the entrances like?' She reopened her eyes. 'How are they guarded?'

The Pig-Man glared at the others, reminding them that he held the mace. 'The main gate is wider than a chariot. There are two oak doors.'

'Oak doors will be hard to move. It's a heavy wood.'

'Yes, so in the day the gate's open.'

'And at night?'

'Probably the same.' He avoided looking at her. 'The second, smaller gate leads down to the guards' camp. By day it's guarded, but not at night. Still,' he added warily, 'the watchman on the walkway is armed with a bow and the walkway passes over both gates.'

'So.' Bride thought for a moment. 'Carvin has a score of men,' she said to herself, 'and at night some must guard the ridgeway...' Then, in a louder voice: 'Where is this guardsman's camp?' As she remembered, it had been near the river, a mean place, since the soldiers were no farmers.

Nothing had changed. Yes, Carvin's men still had their settlement there, close to the stud field. Their wives were the offspring of the camp followers of those warriors who had conquered the land for Carvin's father. Such people had held themselves apart from the natives, and only Riard had married a local woman. There was no other liking between the two camps and the villagers began to talk boldly, working off their fear.

'Set their Long House alight, let them burn.'

'Win back the land that was taken from us.'

'Cut them down with their own spears!'

Bride clapped her hands to regain their attention. 'How many times must I say this? You need to free me, find something that will cut this bronze then we need to take the hill fort and have its walls to protect us. These are soldiers, trained for nothing else. Put a warrior in his own territory, with weapons to hand, and what chance has a shepherd?' She paused, then added, 'Tell me more of this Plains-King.' She had not stayed long enough the first time, to know much of Carvin's neighbors.

A generation ago two kings had invaded the rich chalk lands. The elder brother took the land around the Great Stone Circle, the younger— Carvin's father— the lands of the people by the Winter Born. The villagers were a subject race.

'And are the present rulers allies?' asked Bride, heart sinking. Even if she and Sarmatia escaped Carvin, it seemed they would hardly receive a welcome from the King of the Plains.

The villagers were irritatingly vague. It was said that the kings were close, but there had been rumors of a rift between them. Bride realized that she could make no more plans without further knowledge. She spoke to the keenest looking of the women. 'Find out what you can. We need to know our enemies and their weaknesses.'

'Or strengths,' came the answer, but Bride let it pass. She took the ox-bone and beat it against the boulder. 'Some things need more thought, but let us fix the night of the attack. The weapons are ready and our plans are forming. A time must be decided. All those who believe that we should strike on the first night after the moon turns from the full, now say yes.'

There were five ringing shouts of 'Yes' and general sounds of agreement. Bride glanced at the old woman, who had not spoken, then dismissed her. Speaking aloud, she praised the villagers' good sense and courage, exhorted them to find, steal or otherwise procure bronze and tools that she could use against her chain, and warned them against spreading word of the attack too soon. They agreed to meet the next night.

'We should make our final plans,' said Bride. 'Remember, we must know if Carvin and his uncle are friends or enemies.'

'That may take time,' said the Pig-Man, who looked both eager and anxious, now that the gathering was breaking up.

'Only to someone who doesn't know who to ask,' said another villager. He smiled at Bride, showing long canine teeth. 'I can answer all your questions.'

'Make it soon.' Wanting to keep these men keen, Bride glanced at the five who were lingering and thought, why not? Lust is a kind of loyalty.

Tugging at the drawstring round her neck, she said, 'It's hard to undress one-handed. I'll be so pleased when you've found a way to free me.'

Halfway through the five, while the Pig-Man sweated above her, Bride was again disgusted with herself. Why did she no longer enjoy this rasping flesh on flesh? Sarmatia, dressed as a boy, had been, ironically, the first for months who had deeply stirred her. Was it variety she craved? The last man slumped against her, leaving Bride still unsatisfied.

Chapter 25

Isle of Stones, 1561 BC. Fall.

Hunger had woken Sarmatia the morning after the deer-feast, eighteen days before the solstice. Stumbling over a broken pitcher in the dark, she sullenly collected two wooden buckets and began the long journey from hill fort to Winter Born. This would be the first of many trips for water through the day.

In the lean-to Bride was snoring, rolled up tight against the sarsen boulder. Sarmatia dropped the cooked venison beside the woman's fist and wandered on, leaving Bride to sleep. Her body ached as she walked jerkily past the thatched huts of the village, dragging her buckets in the dirt track. A child called out to her from the black inside of a hut, but Sarmatia did not understand what was said. Before she could reply there was the sound of a blow, a thin crying. She shivered in the raw morning.

At the river she hoped to meet the fox but the shallow banks were deserted. She filled the buckets. Today the Winter Born was gray. Drops of water smeared its surface when, without a change in the windless morning, it began to rain.

Sarmatia did not hurry. She let the rain soak her clothes and flatten her hair to her arms. Seams of mud drew brackish splashes on her calves. A rowan twig scratched her eye and whirled before her face, then was whipped away in the rain. She walked on, catching the two buckets against her legs.

She heard the horse and rider long before she saw them, weaving quickly in and out between the boulders of the Making Way. The rider was driving the dun-colored pony hard and the beast stumbled, almost skidding into the giant blocks. Sarmatia sensed its fear and was angry. She would not look at the guard when he hailed her.

'Girl!' Carvin's second in command reined in his mount in the gray dawn and Sarmatia grimaced, feeling the pain of the horse-bit as a twist of agony in her own bruised mouth. She stopped to save the mare.

'You've been missed.' The captain prodded her with his spear. 'Get back to the forge, or Carvin'll have plans for you, too.'

Sarmatia started forward, finally meeting those dead-alive eyes. 'What's happened to Bride?'

The rider made an evil face behind the bronze cheek-pieces of his helmet. 'Better run and see.' Abruptly he noticed that Sarmatia was attempting to comfort the shivering pony, stretching out her hands to touch its skinny flanks. The gesture seemed to enrage him. He struck at her with his fist and wrenched the pony round, snarling, 'Keep your paws off! Save that for your master!'

Stabbing his heels into the mare's belly and aiming one last punch at Sarmatia's head, the rider melted back behind the wall of rain. Sarmatia dropped her load and tried to run. Fear made her slower and short-winded. She reached the village and there was a pain in her side. Her limbs were like strands of wool. Yet the forge was ahead. She could see Bride through the crowd -

Two guards caught her before she fell and dumped her in the mud at Carvin's feet. Settled comfortably on a stool, Carvin leaned forward from a makeshift awning of skins to laugh at her. 'So, we can still run, eh, clod-lover, despite those lash-marks on your back? I'll remember that, the next time you keep me waiting. For anything.' His voice tightened another notch. 'Try my patience far enough, girl, and I might forget how useful Bride is to me as a smith.'

'No!' Heart bursting with fear and humiliation, Sarmatia forced herself to touch Carvin, clasp the muddy flesh of his knees. 'Please, don't hurt her.' About to appeal to Carvin's self-interest—Bride was, after all, the finest goldsmith in the world—Sarmatia heard a second, welcome voice speak over her head.

'Let the girl alone, Carvin.'

'Why, Bride? That's not part of our agreement. You alone go free if you complete the work to my satisfaction.'

Bride was still safe! Lightheaded with gratitude, Sarmatia almost forgot to release her grip on Carvin's body. What did he mean about her going free? Could his word be trusted? Might her friend at least escape?

Praying that Bride would, Sarmatia largely ignored Carvin as he turned his head and conversed with the figure seated beside him under the awning. This was a thin, pox-marked youth dressed in yellow and black, a messenger, it seemed, from Carvin's uncle, the King of the Plains. 'The gifts will be ready in seven days,' Carvin was saying. He seemed nervous. Overwhelmed by a mixture of relief for Bride and fear for herself, Sarmatia was almost too tired to wonder why.

The meeting seemed to be at an end. Guards were wielding their whips to break up the knot of villagers who had warily gathered to see their king.

But then Bride rose to her feet. To Sarmatia she looked like a bird of prey with her brilliant eyes and hunger-sharpened face. 'Wait, Carvin. I'll make what you want: metalwork, gold, mace. But I need a helper.' Bride pointed at Carvin's feet. 'She'll do. Sarmatia has some skill.'

It was a door and light, breaking in on her prison. Sarmatia hid her flushed face. If Carvin saw her hope, he'd deny it.

Yet the goddess had not forgotten her. Carvin was nodding his agreement, posting a guard. The awning was taken down and Carvin and the messenger stepped into the chariot that would take them back to the hill fort.

Sarmatia was seized by a fit of coughing. Bride dragged her to the lean-to, thrusting their guard out into the rain. 'You're worn out. Sleep now, there won't be time later.' Her hand brushed the matted strands from Sarmatia's forehead. 'Go on!'

Already the ground was drawing Sarmatia into itself. Bride's voice ebbed. She was arguing, dimly, with the guard. A jumble of images flickered though Sarmatia's mind. Tazaros with red rather than black hair. Pergia holding a perfume bottle which transformed into a knife. Fearn taking a ring from his hand and smiling because the band was too large even for her thumb. He was trying to tell her something—

'Sarmatia!'

Her eyes shot open, but it was Bride.

'We need to talk.' Bride propped her against the sarsen. It was still very dark: Sarmatia could scarcely see her face. She could smell her breath. Bride had eaten the venison. She was offering something in a bowl. Sarmatia tried to eat but her lower jaw seemed to be in the wrong place and most of the gruel ran down her hands. She persisted doggedly, straining to catch Bride's whispered conversation.

'We've less than seven days to plan this. I know Carvin. As soon as I've finished his metalwork—' Bride snapped her fingers. 'But I'll be ready. I've made enough weapons. People want him dead. Five nights from now, when the moon turns, that's when we'll strike. Hurry with that food! If the guard finds the bowl he'll want to know which house supplied it and it'll mean the lash for all of them!' Bride broke off as a huddled shape stepped out of the darkness, yet this wasn't the guard but a child, silently collecting the bowl. Glancing round to ensure no one was watching, the girl tossed the smith a bundle of fur then raced away.

'Good! They've remembered the lamp!' Bride set a roughly-fashioned lump of chalk at Sarmatia's feet and started the wick of the crude lamp burning with a spark from a scrap of copper. 'Let's have a look at you today!' She thrust the smoky flame towards Sarmatia.

After a moment she spoke. 'I'll tell the guard you're sick. That'll give you a day, at least.' Bride stuck out a flat disc of copper. 'Don't argue. Look at yourself!'

It was the face of a toad. Even her eyebrows had disappeared under a mass of purple-black bruising. Her jaw—Sarmatia brought her hand up to try to discover the jawbone—was twice its normal size. 'I look like a frog.' She made a joke of it. 'But I can still use a hammer.'

'Don't be so noble. The scars on your back are as bad. Has Carvin been lashing you every night?'

Not now anyway, thought Sarmatia grimly, but she didn't want to admit something that would only cause Bride to worry. She jerked her head at the rest of the contents of the fur parcel. 'What's that?'

As she hoped, Bride was diverted by the change of subject. 'Shards of copper and flint to make new slingshot.' Bride scrambled forward and began burying the parcel under a mound of dung. 'The guards never think of looking here. I've six hoards of arrowheads under this.' She glanced again at Sarmatia. 'You really want to work today?'

'I want to help.'

'You would, you stubborn... though when I think of it, there are things you can do. Only be slow.' Bride tapped the bronze chain. As yet, the guards had not thought it worth their while to place a similar fetter on Sarmatia.

'I don't think I could be anything else.' Sarmatia raised her eyes to the hill fort. 'Here's the guard.' It could be no one else: a solitary soldier walking down the slope with the bandy-legged gait of one of Carvin's riders.

'Peket,' commented Bride, as a ribbon of sunlight flashed over Carvin's captain. 'Carvin must be anxious to send him down with my tools.'

'He's eager with his fists.'

'That little grub? I doubt he'll try anything. Until this treasure's finished, even Carvin won't cross me.' Bride gave Peket a second stare, then pulled Sarmatia to her feet, holding onto the girl until she was steady. 'You're a different matter.'

'He'll be in earshot.' Sarmatia could hear the metal-working tools clashing together in the leather bag Peket had slung about his shoulders. Her throat was parched at the thought of another meeting with him.

'Don't fret. You're off to the river. I want a good load of sand and twenty, thirty handfuls of clay.' Bride's eyes flashed, quick as a kingfisher, from Sarmatia to Peket. She lapsed into a jumble of Kretan and the common speech, talking slowly as if she was only using Kretan where the common tongue escaped her.

'There's a flower called aconite.' Here Bride used the Kretan name, though the uses of the plant escaped Sarmatia. 'In summer it grows a blue flower and leaves like parsley. Even without the flower, you'll know it. Go by the river and dig for its root under the trees. Put the root in this fur and tie it. Then wash your hands. Touch nothing else until you've done that. Wait. You need something to carry it in!'

'No, I left two buckets somewhere.' Sarmatia stumbled from the lean-to, setting out for the river. She was outside. She could feel the sun pricking her aching back. Such moments were to be relished.

Chapter 26

Since Fearn returned from the east no one has known quiet.

First Fearn. He lurched into Orm's house a month back, bleeding from wrists and feet, bruised across ribs and back and with a tear in his side that made him short-breathed and flint-tempered. He is healed but restless, never more so than these last sixteen days, since he emerged from that strange trance.

Then there are Laerimmer and the council of the high born. They started by scolding Fearn and finished by excusing themselves. I know that Fearn holds it against Laerimmer for not allowing that foolish war band to venture outside the kingdom while he was missing. Laerimmer, reasonably enough, points out that Fearn created the war band to defend our homeland, but the King will not see it. Oh, he listens and nods and then says the quiet word, 'But'.

But the King needed the war band to look for him, when he disappeared—no one knew where—for four days. But the war band wanted to look for their king, when he vanished.

Fearn wants his young rams to feel so guilty and ashamed that they defy custom. Then he will use them to rescue Sarmatia.

Sarmatia. I have her name now. For a long time Fearn hoarded it to himself, like precious gold. The southerner.

One can work magic with a name. I curse you, Sarmatia. You and Fearn together will be in my way.

I did not know that Fearn had given her a ring until the herald came.

Fearn received him at Orm's house. That morning, he had cleared the dais of its usual clutter and sent the family away, as though he had foreknowledge of the man's arrival. And who knows where Fearn goes to, as he strides, staring into the sky? He and Orm were waiting, seated on chairs side by side on the dais. A bench had been drawn up to the fire. I was at the back of the hall, with beer and a platter of bread and cheese, ready to furnish refreshment to the herald. Fearn had sent for me specially to do this. He wanted to show off another member of the royal family, I think.

So I met the herald. He was tall and bow-legged, as is common among riders. He carried the short staff of the messenger with great self-possession and spoke to me as though I was a common servant. He did not thank me when I poured him beer. I hid in the shadows of the house to listen.

I knew already that Fearn had made a mistake in having Orm at the audience, although we were in his house. Orm's lameness made a bad impression. I wasn't surprised when the herald was coarse.

He began in the usual way, stating his master's lineage and naming the boundaries of his kingdom. Fearn sat quietly through that, although he stiffened at the king's name and repeated it, adding mysteriously in our own tongue, 'So that's what you're called! And now I know where to find you, Carvin.' He then nodded for the herald to continue.

The man came brusquely to the point. 'I return you this, which Lord Carvin has no use for, having gold in abundance.' Something bright flashed in his hand.

Not even trying to hide his feelings, Fearn started forward to the edge of his seat. 'Give it to me.' In one movement he left his chair and jumped from the dais. 'Hand it over, now.'

The herald looked ready to toss the thing on the floor between them, then thought better of it and dropped a bronze ring into Fearn's hand. Fearn stood turning it over. 'How did you come by this?' he asked.

The herald stroked the speaking staff lying across his knees. 'You admit it's yours, then?' he asked, rudely.

Fearn slipped the band onto his finger and held out his hand. 'This is my ring. How did you come by it?'

'Lord Carvin gave it me.' The herald looked up into Fearn's face and laughed. 'He had it from his harlot.'

Fearn seized the man's arm. 'Drink more beer, herald, your tongue's too dry.' He forced the wooden beaker to the messenger's lips. When the man gagged, he released his grip. 'Describe this girl,' he commanded.

Cowed, the herald mumbled and I strained to catch the words. Slender, handsome, brown hair, dark brows. It might have been a youth. I thought of witchcraft and wondered.

Fearn asked for a name. The herald answered. 'Say the rest of your message,' said Fearn.

Out it came: this Sarmatia, seeing the beauty and greatness of King Carvin, showered by his gifts, had chosen to remain in the kingdom of the Winter Born and so returned Fearn's ring.

'My lord Carvin says he has had great pleasure from the girl, and that for only a grain or two of gold,' added the herald.

'Has he indeed?' said Fearn, blushing like a boy. I thought he understood then, how ill-conceived his marriage plans had been.

'Only the ignorant think that a woman cannot be bought,' said the herald.

'Carvin had better watch his sisters,' said Fearn.

The herald bridled. 'If my lord had sisters, no uncouth northerner would touch them. A girl that is fit to marry in this kind of kingdom is only fitted to be Carvin's slave.'

I drew in my breath at that effrontery, ready for the storm. I didn't have long to wait. Fearn stalked to the door of the house and back.

'Take the cup you're holding and get out. If I see your face again outside this hall, I'll brain you with your own staff.' And, as the herald gawped at him, 'You can tell Carvin that I received his message and that soon he'll have my answer.'

My heart dropped when Fearn said this. It will not help my plans if he goes from the country.

Later, riding through the kingdom, I sought out members of the war band myself. 'We must keep Fearn in the kingdom. It's unlucky for a king to leave his homeland, especially so close to the winter solstice. And it will do him no good to look on the southerner who betrayed him.' I said this to the softhearted. To three who loved gold I gave presents—bribes—to make them stay. The last youth took the largest gift, but then Dill, although innocent in many ways, has at least some sense.

It may be that I'll find Dill very useful one day.

Despite these precautions, I could not stop Fearn from summoning the Council, nor from gathering an assembly of the people on the Sacred Hill that same night, only seventeen days before the winter solstice. There, by the light of their flickering torches, he told the people of the abusive herald and his uncivil message. Fearn can be cunning when he wants, and he had Orm witness all that he said. A lame man, whether he wishes it or not, invokes sympathy. By the time he had finished speaking the crowd was fairly boiling.

So Kingmaker and council had to address a hostile assembly. Laerimmer was untroubled, but several of the other speakers stammered and were hissed until Fearn put a stop to it. As king he could speak last. Now one of the royal twins, Gygest, was talking.

'We know that Fearn wants to avenge the insult done to him. That's fine and good. But the female who has caused this strife, shouldn't she stay with Carvin?'

I wondered how Fearn would answer that. From the ranks of the royal women I could hear Chalda saying that only a harlot would take pleasure from being bedded. Chalda's hypocrisy makes me smile. It's so unknowing. Fearn then spoke.

'If Wenna was taken by the Cattle People and you went into their lands, Gygest, and found her a slave, would you leave her with them?' Wenna was Gygest's wife. Driving home his answer, Fearn mentioned others. 'If Kere was taken... If Anoi was kidnapped, would you call her a harlot?' There were gasps, for everyone knows that Anoi is beyond reproach. 'Don't be so hasty to call Sarmatia a whore. Carvin is my enemy. Why should he not lie to me?'

Fearn dropped his voice. 'There was blood on my ring. Sarmatia did not give it up without a struggle. She suffers as I know too well!' Leaving the assembly as discomforted as he doubtless felt himself, Fearn gave way to Laerimmer.

The Kingmaker did not waste the chance. 'If Fearn believes that his former betrothed is a slave and not a courtesan, as the message clearly states, he has a perfect right to do so. However,' Laerimmer wagged a finger at the assembly, 'we should be at fault if we did not advise caution. Slaves bear children.'

He went on to develop this idea, the dangers of the cuckoo in the nest. When he'd done I thought Fearn would have no answer.

He was in fact quite brief. 'Can anyone name a girl who, taken at eighteen, bred a child in the first year of marriage?'

People glanced at each other but no one would look at Chalda and her first child. At nineteen, Chalda was the youngest mother of the Atterian women.

'Harlots breed like bitches,' said Goar, 'and that's what this girl is.' Stripped of its usual banter, his voice was almost shrill.

'You s-s-should know about harlots!' shouted Sowter, a youth from the war band whom I'd not bothered to approach, knowing his dog-like loyalty to the king. I wondered actually if Fearn had planted him there and coached him. Such a timely, clearly-spoken joke seemed far beyond his wit. Whether Fearn had or not, Sowter's answer did its work and people laughed. I laughed. You should always join in, even against yourself.

Chalda, though moved by vanity, was very pertinent. She returned to the pure bloodline of the royal kindred. 'Our children are all Atterian, and surely the heir of the king must be the same.' She appealed to Fearn. 'We don't want strangers to rule after you, my lord.' What lovely malice, in those last two words!

'See Sarmatia for yourselves,' said the King. 'I promise she has the makings of a queen.'

'If so, she would need to take the test,' said Laerimmer. Fearn was silent then.

It was close to midnight and though the moon was full and lit the scene, the night was cold. Looking about, I saw that people were becoming restive. It was time for Fearn to speak last and for the Atterians to vote. I thought of the custom that forbade the king to leave his kingdom. I thought of the feast of the winter solstice, which Waroch had always attended. Last, I thought of the three clear votes I had bought.

Besides, what kind of people would let a war band with a woman in it go anywhere?

Chapter 27

Isle of Stones, 1561 BC. Fall.

Sarmatia reached the Winter Born and found the little river crowded with women and children washing clothes. The children gathered round to point and whisper. At first Sarmatia was ashamed, thinking they stared at her bruised face, but no. Their mothers often looked as she did. The children wanted to know why she picked sand from the water.

'Bride needs it to grind and polish,' Sarmatia replied, shy amidst these bright faces. The children helped, made a game of it and filled the two buckets far faster than she could have done herself. Only the dark, slender young woman, whom Sarmatia had seen at the hill fort, stayed away from her. When Sarmatia smiled, she scowled, staring her dislike.

Ashamed that she had escaped what this young woman had been forced to endure, Sarmatia left to collect the clay, and Bride's mysterious aconite, before a guard came looking for her and made trouble for the women and children. The young ones waved, which made her laugh, but the dark young woman did nothing. She was on the far bank of the river when Sarmatia looked back, already apart from the others. How many women had Carvin done this to? 'Four days, he'll pay,' Sarmatia muttered, but the buckets were heavy in her hands as she wandered slowly away.

* * * *

That night there was a full moon. Sarmatia watched it rise, casting phosphorescence on the silver-gray boulders of the Making Way. One after another the tall sarsens turned black in silhouette, piercing the whiteness of the moon, then changed to deep azure as its brilliant sphere glided above them. At first she did not see the scurryings underneath, ghostly figures flitting between the stones. She clutched at Bride and pointed.

'Yes, I've seen them. Those farmers are our allies.' Bride raised an arm and waved. 'It's good you're to meet tonight. You slept through the last gathering.'

The dark figures squeezed inside the lean-to and squatted in a tight circle. Sarmatia counted fifteen men and five women, to judge by their rounded limbs all heads of families. The entire village seemed involved in the revolt. But what of Riard's wife and children, who also lived in the village? She listened in vain for their names.

'What news of Carvin's uncle?' Bride asked.

A thick-jowled farmer, the Pig-Man, leaned forward. 'Peket rides daily between the two lands. The King of the Plains is angry with Carvin's demands to take his country's deer and boar. Twice Carvin has ignored warnings. Now his riders hunt even where they have been forbidden.'

Bride held out her fist for the ox-bone they were using as a mace. 'So my work is a peace-gift. I suspected as much.' She laughed, and a muted echo of it went round the circle before her voice hardened. 'I'll see that the Plains-King doesn't enjoy it.'

The Pig-Man broke wind and asked what charms she would use.

'Ones that kill. Carvin's uncle will be buried with a black tongue. Perhaps his sons will die, too.' Bride shrugged. 'Death's the sure way. We don't want to fight Carvin's guards then have to battle with the Plainsmen.'

There was some debate then about when to free Bride. The Pig-Man had smuggled a bronze saw from the second settlement and wanted to use it that night, but Bride said that was foolish. 'Tomorrow, Peket is bringing gold for me to begin the Plains-King's richest gifts.'

'I can't see Peket leaving gold without a guard,' said Sarmatia.

'You're right.' Bride flicked her bronze chain. 'We must wait for the night of the attack, dispose of guard and chain together.' The Pig-Man looked disappointed, but agreed.

Talk changed to the unknown after Carvin's downfall and Sarmatia fell asleep. When she woke it was full day. Now, as she had guessed, there was a guard on them day and night, for Bride had started to work with gold.

After noon, the guard was Riard. Knowing the villagers' plans, Sarmatia found it hard to look at his grizzled face and retreated into her work, concentrating on gouging out a circular socket in a polished stone. It was to be the head of a wooden mace. There was a fashion for such things. Sarmatia had seen the mace, tucked in its bed of straw, and thought it handsome enough, its five bone mounts carved in a zigzag like the lightning flash of the Sky God. Now though she was glad to equip the staff with its extra head-ornament.

The chance to speak her mind came when Riard slipped off to the village for more beer. Instantly, Sarmatia was on her feet. 'We must warn him.' She seized a hammer Bride was looking for, forcing the smith to listen. 'Riard's been good to me.'

'Would you sleep any sounder if we told Riard of the revolt and saved him, and next day Carvin's men burned the village? I've seen what warriors on horseback can do to a few huts!'

Sarmatia cursed then thought. To watch a man walk to his death and do nothing. After Kerewos, she could do not that again. 'There are ways to keep a man from battle, without speaking.'

'Give him the bed that Carvin's missed, Sarmatia?'

'Why not?' It would be another, more personal vengeance on Carvin. 'While Riard's asleep I'll join the attack.'

Bride was shaking her head. 'Can't be, Bull Rider,' she said softly. 'Look at the back of your shift.'

Sarmatia twisted round. Blood. For the first time in six months, her course had started again. Bride threw her a bundle of rags. 'It's only nature. Don't look so stricken!'

With her gold and her promise of freedom, it seemed so easy for Bride to forget Riard. Sarmatia bit down on the bitter answer rising in her throat and attended to herself. After that, conversation was prevented by Riard's reappearance, and by dusk Sarmatia had her hands full helping Bride.

Bride had hammered the gold into a flat, thin sheet that she cut into an elegant lozenge, a metal breastplate fit for a king. Now she cleaned a small metal punch on her tunic and stood by the anvil, looking down at her work. 'Riard, be ready to bring a torch.' She glanced up into Sarmatia's face. 'Hold it steady.'

Her mallet tapped on the metal with a chock! and Sarmatia felt the bite and drag of the punch as the graver ploughed across the gold. The sensation shimmered up her fingers, blending into a continuous strum as the mallet rose and fell. In front of her a thin line was folding open in the gold, like a bud coming into flower.

It was painstaking art. Moving by minute degrees, Bride decorated the breastplate with fine chasing. Once, the moon was lost behind a cloud and Riard commanded to bring fire and stand with it by the anvil. The torch smoked, drawing tears to Sarmatia's eyes that she could only blink away. Under her fingers the gold was warmed by working and full of tricks. Sometimes it clung to her flesh as she tried to move her hands from the path of the graver.

At last there was only the central decoration to complete. Bride straightened, mopped her face and cracked her fingers, throwing a glance at the moon's position. 'Now it starts.' Again, she took up the graver. Sarmatia wondered why this looked strange then realized that Bride was gripping the tool in the wrong hand. Bride set the punch down on the gold and readied the mallet.

As she struck, the metal cried out, a high, thin note which seemed an echo of some other sound. Sarmatia felt a prickling down her back, a spark of lightning through her nerves. Her mouth was dry, a pulse turning in her head like a drill.

The note ended and Sarmatia was alone again. She opened her eyes and saw Riard, casually leaning against the sarsen. How can he not feel it? she thought, as the punch jerked forward and the gold sang its eerie echo. The forces of the spirit-world were closing in. Glancing up, Sarmatia saw Bride position herself for the final blow of the mallet. The moon at her shoulder draped a silver ribbon down her arm. Her black hair was bleached white.

The mallet fell, striking the graver. A bony finger of light trailed across the anvil and seemed to lift itself to touch Sarmatia's face. A spirit had come. Sarmatia recognized her by her cold and heavy breath. The Moon-Elder, hag-goddess of the sky. Her touch was clammy, like the air before a thunderstorm, and the breastplate which reflected her features had a sprinkling of hoar across its surface. The face of the goddess was white, even in the yellow of the gold, and her eyes and mouth were black.

'Chant,' whispered the Moon-Elder, making her voice like Bride's. 'Chant your curse and it will fuse with this metal.'

Her face dimmed in the gold and Sarmatia spoke of her anger and hate for Carvin, her voice pushing the graver along the gold. The line joined with itself and then the spirit was gone.

Bride looked up. 'It's done.' She looked finished, slowly straightening away from the anvil. Suddenly her eyes widened. 'You'd better catch the torch,' she whispered, caught between awe and laughter, 'Riard's asleep!'

An hour before daylight Sarmatia was awakened by a man's cloak brushing her arm. She guessed that Riard was creeping off to his wife in the village, though he'd need to return at dawn when another guard took his place. Sarmatia woke Bride when he'd gone. 'Can we use the time?'

'Is that clay still damp?' Bride thrust a hand into the bucket, testing for herself. 'Yes, that's workable. I'll make the dagger-moulds when it's light.' She felt about again and brought out the fur parcel, unwrapping it on the anvil beside the gold breastplate. She turned the long, tuberous root over with the bronze punch. The aconite was dirty, but Bride made no attempt to shake off the loose earth. She beckoned.

'Looks harmless. Yet one tiny piece, one seed, will kill a man in hours. First he grows sick, then hoarse-voiced then his breath fails. When I told the villagers that Carvin's Uncle would die with a black tongue, that wasn't a lie.'

'Would a metal-curse do this, too?' asked Sarmatia.

'The curse is worse,' replied Bride. 'Aconite takes only a few hours, whereas a strong spell can give weeks of agony. But the plant is surer. A curse works best on a man you know.'

The curse we made tonight will work on any man, known or not. Sarmatia stared at the breastplate and quelled the thought. To talk too freely of magic can destroy it. She leaned forward, drawn by the excellence of Bride's art. 'Don't touch,' said Bride, a mixture of pride and genuine warning. Reluctantly, Sarmatia drew back.

'Each engraved line is an hour,' Bride whispered. 'The number of hours that the man who wears this gift will live.'

Sarmatia began to count the lines, but Bride turned the gold onto a piece of linen, binding the two in the hood of her cloak. 'Now, the aconite. Let's have that root prepared. Hurry. Riard and the new guard can see the morning star, the same as us!'

Sarmatia did hurry, strewing tools in her haste to find grinding pebbles. She dismissed the quern that Riard had used to make their barley flour as too risky to use. A trace of the deadly aconite might be left behind. Two uneven stones made a poor substitute, but, with Bride helping, the fibrous tuber began to break down into long slivers that might be fixed onto the metalwork. The tip of the root wept a trickle of juice onto her fingers and encouraged by this, Sarmatia pounded faster. A yank of her hair made her glance up. Bride gestured towards her hand.

'Keep that juice off yourself. The poison seeps into skin.' Bride made to mop her own face with her hands, then smeared an arm across her brow.

Sarmatia snatched a rag, rubbed her fingers and had started again when Bride's sharp intake of breath warned of a new danger. The silhouette of two new guards on the horizon, marching from the hill fort. Already, Sarmatia knew one would be Peket, Carvin's captain. She scanned the path leading from the village. No Riard, only the curl of a breeze.

'Forget him, we've no time!' A hand yanked her round, shoved Sarmatia at the leather tool-bag. 'Hold that open!' Bride shoveled the flat base of granite and matted scraps of aconite into the bottom of the bag. Sarmatia scooped up the grindstones and threw those in. Inspiration struck and she tossed in her own bloodied rags. She slipped the drawstring knot, dropping the whole behind her.

Peket was on the last part of the track, quickening his step. Sarmatia darted to the tree-stump and, using her cloak, rubbed out the telltale mud stains where the aconite had lain. The bronze punch was stained by the poison, but there was no time to clean it. Peket was only a sword's distance from her. Sarmatia slipped the tool into her robe, where it fell inside the cloth to the rough cord belt at her waist. Meeting Peket's lifeless eyes, she was certain he'd spotted her sleight of hand.

'Where's Riard?' he demanded, but Sarmatia was ready.

'In those bushes,' she lied, hoping to win them all more time. 'His guts plague him. He has his bow. We couldn't escape.'

'Fetch him, whether the old fool's finished or not.'

The young guard saluted, starting off at a jog that set the bronze arrowheads ringing against each other within his quiver. Peket spun about, positioning himself so he could watch Sarmatia and Bride. When the guard and Riard, who must have reached the elder scrub in the same moment as the guard, appeared on the track, Peket shouted, 'Where in god's name have you been? Get these women searched and then the forge. There's something about this I don't like.' He assigned Riard to Bride, the younger guard to Sarmatia then settled on the anvil, nodding for the men to begin.

Firmly, the guard's hands felt over Sarmatia. They swept once over the metal punch, feeling its hardness as the knot on her waistcord. Head high, Sarmatia felt the graver shift a hundred times and knew it had not moved once. The moments dragged on, leaden-breathed, and the youth was almost there, within a fingertip of finding the metal. Sarmatia smelt the strong grease of his pigskin helmet and sneezed. Instinctively, her hands clutched over her middle and the guard backed away.

'Nothing.' He addressed Peket. 'She has the bloody flux, but that's all.'

'How long before she's clean?' asked Peket, speaking to the guard.

The guard shrugged. 'Maybe tomorrow?'

'That's not so!' protested Sarmatia, guessing where Peket's questions might lead, but Carvin's captain merely barked at her to get out of the way while his men searched the forge.

By this time Sarmatia was past alarm. She had been wary and relieved so many times in the short space of a sunrise that the roots of feeling were drained. The aconite was at the bottom of the leather tool bag, and if the young guard found it then that was their fate. Now he had the drawstring open and his hand was going deep inside. She stifled a yawn, reflecting that it was likely that the youth would be sick from the aconite's poison.

'Ah!' The young guard's mouth was frozen in an expression of agony. His hand whipped from the bag as though it had been burnt, the handful of bloodstained rags falling from his fingers like scorched flesh.

'You put that filth there, explain it!' Peket was shrill.

Sarmatia looked on his sharp-featured stump of a face with disgust. 'In my country, a woman must keep her bloodstained linen and burn it later as a sacrifice to the Moon Elder.'

The lie worked. Peket drew back. Hasty orders sent Riard off to the hill fort and the young guard to the Winter Born to wash. Peket waited restively till the youth could be seen returning on the track, then set out for the hill fort. As soon as he was out of earshot, the women looked at each other and began to laugh.

'You put your cloths in that bag on purpose!' Bride was laughing so much it hurt her sides. 'You saw his face? When he put his hand in—'

'Took it out—' Sarmatia was laughing even harder, giddy with the abrupt withdrawal of danger.

'Peket staring as though you'd offered him a turd!' Bride was weeping.

'Where's that graver now? Let's have it safe.'

'Before "young blood" sees what we're about.' Sarmatia pointed to the returning soldier, toiling up the track, and choked again.

As she finally drew the metal punch into the daylight, Bride asked, 'It hasn't lain against your skin, has it?'

'No.' Suddenly solemn again, Sarmatia rubbed where the graver had rested against her. It had just begun stinging. Had there been time for the poison to work into her? She dropped the punch into the gaping mouth of the tool-bag, staring into its black hole. How long had Bride said aconite would take to kill? A few hours? No great while to wait, then.

Chapter 28

Isle of Stones, fall, 1561 BC

Sarmatia swallowed. It was midday and her stomach was pinched. Hunger or poison? Preoccupied, her grip on the crucible slipped and drops of molten bronze spattered onto the rim of the dagger mould. Without raising her eyes from her work, Bride said, 'If you can't do better than that, fetch the water. I'm thirsty.'

At once Sarmatia picked up a water pot. Bride's final words were a signal for her to go to the village to ensure all was well. Sarmatia wished she could do the same for Gorri. The cord of life between them was so stretched and faint that she did not know how he lived.

In the village, children were hoeing their family herb plots. They smiled at Sarmatia as she passed. The women were in the fields, so she looked in vain for the dark slender woman.

Jumping across a gully of rubbish, she reached the edge of the village, where there was only a single house. An old woman dragged herself outside to prod a dying fire. Sarmatia shrugged off a strange feeling of bad luck and stepped closer. 'How are you? Remember me? Sarmatia, the one with the smith?'

'Get away.' A skinny arm thrust at her.

'I can fetch you water. That's always needed.'

'You'll fetch me nothing.' The widow was rubbing one withered hand against the other. It was clear her shove against Sarmatia had hurt her. 'You've done enough already.' She began sniveling. 'Carvin will break us.' She glared. 'One smith and a swarthy girl who think they'll change what we can't!'

Sarmatia gently caught hold of the widow before she could hobble indoors. 'Have you said this in the village?'

'Why should I? Look at you, scarred by Carvin's lash and the fear of Carvin in your eyes! Men take lessons from these.'

'At the forge the men were planning to fight.'

But the widow wanted no reminders of that. Her eyes furrowed into angry slits, red as a moorhen's eye. 'And what do you think they'll do two nights from now?' She lurched away.

* * * *

The morning of the rebellion followed, cornflower bright. Everything was ready, weapons and metalwork. Bride's last act with the gold was to fix some strands of aconite about the hilt of a golden dagger meant for the King of the Plains. 'No one will notice them, except Carvin's uncle, and he's a warrior. He'll not have other men tend his weapons,' Bride told Sarmatia.

'He'll take off the aconite.' Sarmatia also understood that his death would keep the Plainsmen busy and away from the ridgeway, along which she and Bride would make their escape.

Everything seemed easy, and when the black and yellow suited herald of the Plains-King came with two guards to the forge, it appeared that their plans were falling into place. Carvin was to send the metalwork to his uncle with the messenger.

Sarmatia unwrapped the gold breastplate and belt clasp for him on the anvil. 'Here are two of the gifts for your King.'

The messenger touched the breastplate, glancing at Bride. 'These are by her?'

Sarmatia nodded. 'Bride is the finest goldsmith in the world. Even the Tartessians acknowledge her as such.'

The messenger scratched at a red scar on his neck. 'Bring it all.' He moved from the anvil, glancing here and there. 'Lord Carvin spoke of a scepter and an axe. Where are they?'

Numbly, Sarmatia put the stone mace and copper axe with the rest and took up the bundle. She was to be a slave again. By moonrise, when the rebellion started, she might be dead.

Bride heard the scepter ring against the breastplate and turned. 'What's wrong, Sarmatia?' Her face became grim as she understood. 'The girl stays with me, herald.'

'These are Carvin's orders. See? His token.' The man produced a heavy gold ring.

The messenger was leaving. Ignoring the guards, Sarmatia seized Bride's hand. 'Good luck. Take care!' The soldiers wrenched them apart.

* * * *

Bearing the gifts, Sarmatia entered Carvin's hut alongside the messenger, her heart empty as she crossed that threshold.

Carvin was waiting on the high oak throne. He wore a black tunic that yellowed his features to the color of sand. A bronze sword lay across his knees. Sarmatia took her place behind the herald and bent her head, though not before she had seen the crocodile torc coiled about Carvin's neck.

It was a tense meeting, with many shadows. The gold work was displayed and given formally by Carvin to the herald, Sarmatia not daring to watch. She sensed the pause as Carvin's fingers lingered on the golden dagger hilt, close to the strands of aconite. Her heart began to pound but it was a false scare. The messenger took the dagger and Carvin continued speaking calmly of other tribute gifts to follow.

The messenger spoke, praising Carvin's generosity, thanking him for the soldiers' escort. He left at once, making excuses against staying for the customary beer and bread offered to guests. Beneath the seeming alliance, the rift between the two downland rulers was slow to close. Half a day longer and it never would, thought Sarmatia.

Hearing her name she glanced up. Carvin was frowning, his face seeming to grow and widen like yeast. Suddenly he cast the sword down and lumbered towards her. 'Do you know what day this is?' He slapped her, hard. 'Answer me! What day is it?'

Someone in the village had talked. The widow had been right. 'It's the ninth day of the twelfth month.'

'What else?' Another blow.

Did Carvin know everything already? Sarmatia flung her arms before her face. Let him think she was afraid. 'Is it the winter solstice? A holy day?' A quick glance to the door showed the sun past its meridian, there should be less than two hours of daylight. If she could throw him off the scent till then... Sarmatia started as a cold finger tapped her cheek.

'Perhaps it is. But then we know that the truth is much closer. How you shiver!' Carvin swung an arm about her.

Shivering, Sarmatia allowed herself to be steered to the fire pit. Standing side by side, it was easy to believe that it was not Carvin who was with her, but someone else. There was a gleam at the center of the pit, red as a man's hair. She wished she could see Fearn again, just once.

'Never a more quiet one than you. What would it take for you to tell me all your story?' Carvin turned to the sword.

'Is silence not good for me?'

Carvin stared into her face and laughed. 'How so, slave?'

'To listen, my lord.' Hiding anger, Sarmatia lowered her eyes. 'Will you not tell me, my lord?'

'What? Ah, the day!' His fingers tightened on her shoulder as Carvin called for the guard. It was Peket, sharp face glowering in the firelight. He gave a salute and shot Sarmatia a look, half-leer, half-triumph. The expression faded when Carvin asked him the significance of the day.

'Your birthday, Sir.'

Sarmatia closed her lips on the escaping sigh. Was this the heart of the matter? Why was Peket standing guard tonight, of all nights? She looked at Carvin under her lashes. The man's face was slack. Yet there was this sense of missing threads.

A finger flicked her breast. 'What gift have you for me?'

Carvin's hand slipped onto her waist and the threads came together. Sarmatia felt herself blush, though not from shyness. It was the same demand, questions or no questions. Peket was openly grinning, no doubt anticipating her refusal and Carvin's order to bring him the whip.

Loosely, one hand after the other, Carvin laid his hands around her throat. 'I like your hair unbound like that, thick and bright.' He swung her round and released her with a push into the center of the hut. 'Fetch me some beer.'

Outside, the sun was still too high. It winked at her over the jutting timbers of the palisade. Sarmatia scowled at its light and set out across the turf to the cooking area, going the long way round past the scrub-covered grave mounds of Carvin's parents. The guard on the catwalk laughed when he saw her, laughed again as she struggled with the heavy leather covering of one of the storage pits. Sarmatia did not care. A little more time had been spent in her struggle. She put her hand into the cold darkness of the pit, feeling for the rim of the beer-jar, and it was then that the sun finally dipped beneath the top of the palisade.

Carvin made no remark on her long absence. He took a beaker of beer and jerked his head. 'In there, on my bed.'

Sarmatia set the basin carefully on the floor. He wanted something, there was no need to fear. She stepped behind the blue hanging. A clothes chest yawned open, its contents untied, but the deerskin cover of the bed was empty.

'Almost, my blackberry, but that's not close enough.'

Sarmatia spun about. They were so close that she could feel that Carvin had no dagger, nothing she could use to kill him. An arm thrust her back onto the straw mattress and she was trapped, pinned at arms and feet.

'Best not squirm, ah, you can feel why! From the day I left you at the forge I've been saving you up. Stop that, or this time it will be more than the lash! You'll not refuse me again!'

Sarmatia dug her fingers deeper into the deer hide, praying that darkness come soon. Around her, the hut sides were dropping away into twilight, the edges of the blue hanging deepening to purple. She could hear the guards outside muttering against the cold. She started when one guard dropped his spear, and Carvin giggled. 'Stop shaking!' He struck her face. Finding she did not cry out, he hit her again.

Sarmatia bit hard on her tongue, though she could not stop trembling. Her loathing went deeper than fear. She lay under Carvin's dead weight, trying to devise a means to stop him. Even if she could kill him, there was no means to disguise the murder. At sunset, the night watch entered the hut and Carvin always spoke to them. If she said he was sleeping, they might try to rouse him. She would then be speared, the gates of the palisade shut and more soldiers summoned. Into that trap, all unsuspecting, would come Bride and the villagers.

Angry, afraid and frustrated, Sarmatia clutched at the bed. Her slight movement brought Carvin's head up and his lashless eyes stared at her lips and cheeks, both reddened by his fist. He slithered from her and rose, the stench of wanting reeking through his sickly perfume. 'Put yourself by the fire,' he commanded. 'I want to watch your face.'

Sarmatia heaped the skins by the ember-filled fire pit and, stealing the chance, prowled to the threshold. Despite every tactic of delay, the sun was not yet down. The increasing darkness was due to rising cloud. She leaned farther into the wan evening and the guard on the doorway shouted and thrust at her with his shield. Stumbling back, a hand raised to her shoulder where the bronze shield-mounting had drawn blood, Sarmatia fell against Carvin. He was naked.

'Careful!' He heaved her about. 'Much more clumsiness and I'll have you tied up... Or you can please me as you should. You could have new clothes and your old jewels.' Carvin fingered one curling lock of her hair and then tightened his grip. 'The choice is yours, make it quickly.'

Sarmatia wavered, glancing past Carvin to the blue patch of sky. There was so little time. Perhaps it was best not to arouse suspicion, not to weaken herself in what would be a futile struggle. Or she could tell him the truth: that they could not join. After Riard had returned to the hill fort, Bride had told her that there were ways to keep a man amused without mating, if Sarmatia really wanted to save the old guard. Now, reflected Sarmatia wryly, she could use some of those tricks to save not poor Riard but perhaps herself.

Sarmatia passed her tongue across her dry lips. If she gave in to Carvin, what would be left that was worth saving? He would probably kill her afterwards anyway. Her old will asserted itself. 'I'd rather bed a pig than you!'

A fist hit her and she folded without a sigh.

When pain and consciousness returned there were ropes around her neck and arms. Her legs were splayed and pinned by ropes, a gag was in her mouth. The guards filed out, though one returned with an armload of firewood and a lamp. Cloud or sunset, the daylight was gone. She lay on her back at the edge of the re-filled fire pit, heat searing her side, and Carvin stood over her. She yelled futile warnings and protests into the gag as he yanked back her robe, tearing a seam. A hand toying with himself, Carvin ripped aside the last tattered fragment of clothing and entered her. He did not notice the cord about her hips and thrust in deeply. It was as though a knife had been rammed into her. Despite the gag, Sarmatia screamed.

Carvin gave a grunt of surprise. He withdrew and a clot of rags came with him, spilling out of their twine cradle. He wrenched that away and a thin trickle of blood wept over his hand. The lust in his face flamed into hatred.

'You knew!' he shrieked, shaking Sarmatia. He called her a witch who had polluted him with menstrual blood. Releasing Sarmatia, he roared for the guard. She tried to move back from the fire, but at once Carvin was on her again, forcing her face closer to the heat. 'I'll burn you now!' His eyes slithered up, but before his gaze met hers Sarmatia escaped into unconsciousness.

She heard Carvin cursing. Then came feeling, the sensation of a fist pushing under her breast for a heartbeat, of the gag being clawed from her mouth. Yet she wanted to be dead.

It was clear that Carvin and the guard thought her so. Carvin whined, complaining. He hit her face and the pain was remote, an echo whispering up from a deep cave. Her eyes did not open.

The guard untied her and dragged Sarmatia outside, past Peket who kicked at her. He dumped her by the inner wall of the palisade and left her burial to go and feed himself. Head down, Sarmatia slid into the shallow ditch, coming to rest on her back with her face turned up to the sky. The old moon was rising and she wanted to watch it come.

As her eyes opened, pain returned, her ribs aching and her neck raw where the ropes had rubbed off flesh. In her legs, both legs, there was a terrible burning. Sarmatia was afraid to look down. An attempt to move sent fire all over her body. Something scorched her eyes, a piece of chalk lying near her head, incandescent by moonlight.

Chapter 29

Isle of Stones, 1561 BC. Fall.

The Atterian assembly, whether through greed, or fear of their king's anger, had disregarded tradition and the approaching solstice and had voted to let the war band go. Now, although the moon was no longer full, it was still very bright. Fearn and his men were moving quickly.

For three days and three nights they had been traveling, running for three hours, resting for one, repeating that pattern until most ran in a dreaming state, sleeping the moment they stopped. Fearn was grateful that his war band was so young, grateful too that they were with him.

Two of the band and another five, chosen by lot, had stayed to guard his kingdom. Anoi had been one of the five, and though she had pleaded to go with the main force, Fearn had not been sorry to leave her behind. Atterians would not have forgiven him, if Anoi had died abroad.

At the column head, Dill took over the lead from Sowter, running nimbly across the rutted tracks of the ridgeway. From the middle of the group, Fearn saw the youth's face as Dill checked that the others followed, his flushed cheeks looking black in the moonlight. Dill's eyes had glowed like that at the assembly, Fearn recalled, when as king, speaking last, he had talked of the riches of these southern kingdoms. In the end only two of the war band had not wished to leave the kingdom, and both had been mocked by the assembly. Fearn had not spoken up for them. A desperate man is rarely fair.

Exhausted after taking the brunt of the wind, Dill dropped back for Aren to take his place and the band moved up one. Speed was vital. On the second night out, in the border lands of the Otawe, six horsemen had almost run them down. The troop had sprinted to a nearby death-camp beside the ridgeway, a holy place of sanctuary where the Otawe laid out their dead.

Cursing, the Otawe riders had rattled their spears and bows and had to let the strangers go. After they had galloped away in standing clouds of dirt and frost, Fearn and his lads stepped carefully between the rotting corpses of the death-camp and set off again. Since then, they'd met no more hostile forces and no other travelers, except one.

Running at the head of the troop, Fearn laughed aloud when he thought of Carvin's herald. The fellow had been so shocked to find them encircling his campfire. Since it was time for his troop to be blooded, Fearn had let them kill the herald by whatever means they saw fit. They now felt they were warriors, and should fight well when they came to it.

Fearn ran at his limit, guessing he might be pushing some of the group into throwing up the instant that they stopped. He had little choice: speed was vital. Sarmatia was suffering. Her pain made it impossible for him to see or speak to her. Since the morning when he had woken with the certainty that today he would hear something, and had then received the bronze ring from the arrogant fingers of Carvin's herald, Fearn was no longer sure if Sarmatia was alive.

If she is not, he thought, *I can blame no one but myself, for setting her on this journey.*

He was coming to a crossroads which seemed familiar, where a track peeled down from the hilltops and ran away into a valley. Between the woods and fields of the valley floor, a huge circular bank and ditch, dwarfing and obscuring the villages set outside its boundaries, threw a black shadow across the country. As Fearn caught the gleams of moonlight on the standing stones, he understood. Here must be another part of the Making Way, which he'd seen first through the Sky God's eye.

'Down!' He flattened himself on the grass.

His warning was almost too late. Five of Carvin's soldiers leapt from the shallow ditches on either side of the ridgeway and shot off a volley of arrows before setting on their dogs. One lad fell down, another screamed as a hound worried him, but the rest tugged weapons and shields from their backs and, battering down the dogs, went into battle. Following Fearn, they pounded down on the guards, severing wrists and bow-arms and canine jaws, killing all but one.

'Get that man before he raises the alarm!' bellowed Fearn, stoving-in the last dog's chest with his boot as it bounded for his groin. The war band flew off in pursuit, howling. Wild-eyed, they stampeded along the ridgeway, unaware that one of their number was down, killed by an arrow. Even the boy who had screamed was rushing forward, blood spurting from the dog-bite in his thigh as he practiced with his new bronze sword.

Fearn spun back to speak a quick prayer for his young fallen warrior and to make certain that Nertez was dead. Closing the boy's eyes with a bloodstained thumb, Fearn heaped the dead hounds by his feet then rose to run on. Nertez would wait to be burned. In life the lad had been patient.

Ahead, the troop chased their hare, yelling encouragement to each other. The guard was running for his skin, dropping shield and spear, tearing off his armlets and wristguard in the vain hope that his hunters might stop to gather them up. There was to be no escape. Tired by the long run from their Atterian homeland, the youths had found new heart. In a blur of skidding limbs, they dragged the man into their midst. He never had time to cry out.

This one they stripped completely and then gathered up what he had flung down, each claiming a trophy. Proud winners, they carried the body with them while they approached the massive ramparts of the Making Way's circular bank and ditch.

Fearing that this section of the Making Way might also be a vast hill fort, Fearn had his war band weave between the trees and crawl the final stretch. The earth rampart towered over their heads, reminding Fearn for an instant of the first part of his kingship test then they were safely in its shelter.

Crouching to catch their breath, the youths looked at Fearn. 'What now?' hissed Dill, face half-covered by the deerskin cap he had taken from Carvin's guard. Fearn signaled Dill to wait while he counted the band.

'Drink your water, eat,' Fearn whispered. 'Check your weapons. Aren, if you want to wear that wristguard, tie it securely. You don't want it flapping while you use your bow.' Draining off his own water, Fearn rose. 'I'll see what's at the top of this bank. Stay here. Catch your breaths.'

The bank was steep and hard to climb. The shallow-rooted grass came away once in Fearn's hand and he slipped and slid back on his belly. Cursing, he let anger carry him, reaching the top while his men were still eating.

Discovering that there was nothing inside this enormous enclosure except more circles and avenues of standing stones, Fearn called up the rest of the troop. They ran along the flat top of the bank. From there they could see the two separate settlements and, rising between them, the long hill where Carvin lived. In the night, Fearn had not spotted the small fort from the distant road and, had it not been for the huge bank of the Making Way, they might have run straight into Carvin's guards. Dumping the body of the last guard into the sheer drop of the Making Way's inner ditch, the war band moved off along the bank top towards the nearest village.

Wading the shallow river in front of the settlement, Fearn untied the helmet from his belt and jammed it on his head so that he would be clearly seen and known. The bronze helm, which Laerimmer had brought out from some secret place, sparkled in the moonlight. His lads cheered. The sound was good to hear after they'd lost one of their number, thought Fearn. Yet, as they darted between scrub and reached the beast-pens where a dozen scrawny pigs squeaked and a mange-eaten dog bayed at the moon—these careless, cruel people didn't even keep their animals indoors in winter— Fearn felt a growing sense of dread. He must find Sarmatia, though he had few hopes that she would be here. His trance-memories six days ago, before his Bull Head's own hurt and grief had severed their bond, were of a lashless-eyed man and a fort, a tall, strong woman and a forge, a fox with glowing yellow eyes, a dark skinny woman with sad bright eyes. Still this settlement must be subdued and searched, and without raising the alarm to the fort on the horizon above.

The two shock-haired youths who did everything together crawled up to Fearn out of the gloom where they'd been looking over the rest of the buildings. From their whispered report, Fearn realized that these villagers lived together in a single dwelling. The other huts were outbuildings. Their long house stood at the center of the settlement. It had only one entrance.

Hearing that Fearn grinned and, in whispers, began relaying a battle-plan to his men.

They cut the pigs' throats, hoping to draw any loose dog there, and Fearn rushed a carcass to the long house. His lads raced up and stood behind their home-made wicker shields at either side of the barred wooden door as, alerted by the hogs' squealing death-throes, the long house door exploded open. Five dogs shot out like missiles from a sling and Fearn rammed the pig's carcass at their gaping jaws. Frenzied and badly trained, the threat of their presence having been enough, the dogs were distracted by the bloody meat, and the warriors running out after them had no clear passage.

The first three of Carvin's men were finished by the sweeping arcs of Fearn's axe. They slithered on pig-blood and fell amongst their dogs and the stabbing spears of the war band. The next, scrambling over their own dead, lost their footing and once down did not get up again. A guardsman inside the threshold of the long house tried a paean to marshal their forces and alert the hill fort, but the tall youth Sowter, stepping before the lines of shields, hurled a spear into the man's chest.

'Get back!' Fearn dragged Sowter towards cover. Sowter swayed and Fearn caught him, carrying him behind a shield-wall. It was too dim to see where the lad had been hit but he was fading. As Fearn laid him down, Sowter said, without stammering, 'Burn this place for me.' Then he died.

Silently, using all his strength for killing, Fearn leaped into the sweaty mass of fighting. The bronze rim of his helmet bit into his forehead as it turned a glancing sword-thrust. Then, as his axe smashed off the sword blade at its tang, he was over the threshold.

Inside the house, every man was an enemy and there was freedom to move. Carvin's men were in panic. They were beaten back by Fearn and his war band and the door slammed to on the screams of their dying and guarded against their escaping. The last man tried to hide amongst the shrieking women and children at the back of the long house, but Fearn hauled him out and chopped him down like a young tree.

His war band, realizing they had won, broke into a chorus of delight.

Fearn let them go on a moment, then beat on the beams of the long house with his fist until the tumult subsided to the children's high keening. As he'd feared, Sarmatia was not here and they must move quickly. 'Dill, Aren, keep these women inside. One of you bring Sowter's body here and guard it. You,' Fearn pointed to a youth who had hung back in the fighting, 'go back to the ridgeway, find Nertez's body, burn it and bring his bones back here - No argument! The lad there needs his last rites as much as Sowter.'

Fearn turned back to Aren and Dill. 'When the moon sets, take the captives to the animal pens and then burn the long house. This will be Sowter's funeral pyre.'

'And the spoil?' asked Dill eagerly.

'Strip all corpses but Sowter's and drag their bodies outside.' Sowter would have wanted no foreign ashes to mingle with his own. 'Don't touch the women, or their children.' He would not have his lads do to these poor wretches what Carvin must have done to Sarmatia. Fearn glared at Aren and Dill in turn. 'Harm them and I'll kill you both.'

Enough of his anger remained for the youths to heed that threat, and the spoil would keep them busy, reflected Fearn grimly, well-aware of Dill's and Aren's love of loot. Quite content now, they saluted, and Dill reopened the door of the long house to allow Fearn and the eight remaining members of the war band to run out into the still night air.

Chapter 30

Isle of Stones, 1561 BC. Fall.

At her forge beyond the native village Bride had run out of distractions for the guard and lain down as if to sleep. No one had come to free her, and the villagers had not even mounted their own attack. Frustrated, she stared at the sarsen boulder to which her chain was wrapped and waited for daylight. Was this the end, like a pig in a stall? Bride thought of the aconite she still had hidden then dismissed it. Suicide by poison was no proper way out. She would wait for Sarmatia to die first and then follow, taking as many of the guards with her as she could. Not the villagers. It wasn't their fault they were only farmers. She should have guessed what to expect after their idle lovemaking, Unless she herself was losing her touch.

The guard sighed. His spear-head sparked off her chain as he tumbled against her, legs jerking as he died. As Bride tried to thrust off his dead weight, his guts slithered out of the arrow wound in a hot mass across her face. Startled, she screamed.

Suddenly something lifted the foul mass from her and Bride stared up into a pair of keen, clear eyes. The face behind the old bronze helm was blunt, the body beneath was strong. No spirit: a solid human rescuer, who had his people turn out the forge for something for her to drink. The way he patiently held her and the cup while her teeth chattered against it made Bride think of a name. Ironically, it was from Carvin that she had learned what this man had once been.

'Healer? You're Fearn?' A nod. 'I am Bride. Bride the smith and warrior.' Speaking in the common tongue, she drew into the moonlight.

Another youth standing beside the crouching king said something and laughed. Fearn answered sharply in the Atterian tongue and Bride, despite her age and warrior status, blushed. She had forgotten her birthmark. Even so, she was surprised when Fearn bent forward and kissed her on the mouth, as friends do in the north when they meet.

'We must get you a sword.' Fearn spoke the common tongue more rapidly than she did. 'Does that village have such things? We saw your guard and did not stop to search.' Fearn had not dared to pass straight to the fort in case by some chance Sarmatia had been here, at this forge.

Bride shook her head. 'No, those villagers have nothing. They're Carvin's captives the same as me.' Her voice faded, yet it had to be said: 'Sarmatia's with Carvin at the fort. The villagers and I were due to attack there tonight.' She thumbed at the silent, darkened huts. 'They never came.'

Fearn had a king's unreadable face when he needed it. 'Let's get you free.' He spread a length of her chain across the boulder and drew a bloody axe from his belt.

'Wait. Sever the link here at the back and the whole thing will drop off.' She did not add, *I trust you.*

'Mind your eyes.' Fearn's tense voice reminded Bride of the need to hurry. She knelt, turning her head. A warm hand grasped the collar so it would not move or cut her. There was a rush of air, a blow that made her head ring, as though she was under a thunderclap, and the weight around her neck fell away. She rubbed her hands thankfully about her naked throat.

'Well done.' Bride wondered how she could be so easy with a man she had never met before. It was as if they already knew each other. But then they had Sarmatia in common.

As they set off together at the head of Fearn's young war band, Bride had been given a sword from one of the two shock-haired youths and was busy explaining the layout of Carvin's homestead to the Atterian king.

* * * *

At the fort, there was shouting close to Sarmatia and a frantic rush to shut the gates of the palisade. Ignoring pain and the breath which twisted in her lungs like a gouge, Sarmatia raised herself on one elbow. The man on the catwalk was dead, an arrow in his chest. Peket and another guard were struggling with the oak gates that had never been closed in memory, pushing desperately against the groaning timbers. As they sweated, a man without helmet leaped through the narrowing gap and began climbing one-handed up the steep ladder to the catwalk. Sheltering by the highest timbers of the palisade, he rolled the dead guard over and tore the horn from his belt. Still in shadow, the man lifted the curving aurochs' horn and a high, thin alarm wailed out over the hill fort.

The note wavered and was then cut short, the guard toppling to the ground. Riard fell in the ditch beside Sarmatia, his eyes open, a flint arrow lodged in the back of his skull.

Sarmatia tried crawling to Riard on her good leg, but found that her arms would not support her. She tried again, tears bursting in her eyes, and her reaching fingers had almost closed the wrinkled eyes when a battle paean sounded. The attackers had breached the gates.

Sarmatia saw Peket and the second guard turn and try to escape, only to be brought down by the screaming mob. She looked for Bride in the front ranks but did not see her, only distinguishing the bronze-helmed leader, bigger than the others and carrying no shield or weapon but an axe, bloodied from shaft to blade. He was shouting and the clash of metal took his words, but gestures told men to close the gates and man the catwalk, the rest to follow. At the head of his warriors, the leader rushed into Carvin's hut. In a moment he was outside, calling to his followers on the catwalk. Hidden at the rim of the action, Sarmatia could not understand until a shadow fell nearby.

Somehow, Carvin had escaped his hut and reached here. He was creeping round the edge of the palisade towards the rear gate. Dressed in black, he was almost invisible. He moved like a spider, softly shifting his weight along. His eyes were fixed on the tall battle leader, now turning his head to catch some message from the hut. As the man gave answer, Carvin giggled and moved faster.

The giggle she could not bear. Without thought for herself—what was she now?—Sarmatia raised the alarm, speaking automatically in Kretan: 'Here, Carvin's here. Over here!'

The leader spun round and Carvin dropped from the wall and tried to run along the ditch to the rear gate. He had not gone above five paces when there came a new bellow and Bride was there barring the way, a sword in her fist. Bride advanced and Carvin retreated, making a dash for the main gate.

As he passed her, Sarmatia grabbed his arm and clung on.

Cursing, Carvin threw her down. His sword slashed by her head and struck the ditch. The battle leader, coming at a run, threw back his arm.

There was a streak of light and Carvin tumbled into the ditch, his chest split by the battle axe. In shadow, the battle leader knelt by Sarmatia, unfastening his cloak. She spoke to him. 'I'm dying, save your cloak.'

But the man shook his head. As he leaned across and his hands wrapped her gently in warmth, Sarmatia felt the touch of water on her face. It surprised her, a bearded man weeping, until he spoke. 'You'll live, Bull Head. Though we must have a plank to lay you on.' The leader took off the helm which had hidden his eyes and most of his face and she knew him at once.

Chapter 31

Who would have thought it? The Atterian war band leaving the kingdom! For people to lose sight of their best interests, to applaud the war band for setting out on a foreign adventure! For Dill to betray me and vote with Sowter and those other fools.

I'm so angry I could kill.

Not yet, though. My mistake before, with the bribes and earlier, with joining the war band to tell its secrets to Laerimmer, was to be too hasty. Now I must plan more carefully.

The royal family dislike the idea of Fearn breeding outside his kin. Chalda is furious. She has her own child to think of and fears its birthright could be stolen. I can use Chalda.

Goar is jealous, envious of Fearn. Goar shall be my willing tool. He might even strike the final blow, rid me forever of Sar-ma-tia. Let Atterians be ruled by their own, by me. If Goar can't help, there are other expedients. Poison. A dagger.

Of Laerimmer's support I'm less sure. Our Kingmaker, like Fearn and the good Anoi, is more subtle; difficult to control. Yet I can't think that he is overjoyed by Fearn's leaving.

And finally the girl herself. Sarmatia, whom Anoi wants to meet, whom Fearn wants to marry, whom Chalda wants to hate, whom Goar thinks is every man's mate.

What a welcome for her.

Chapter 32

Isle of Stones, 1561 BC. Fall.

On the twelfth day after the attack, Sarmatia witnessed the funeral of the King of the Plains. From Gorri's back she watched the shaman cleanse the newly built charnel house, a shelter of skin and hides. It was a still day and the man sweated as he spun about, dashing salt across the hut sides and entrance. His invocation to the Goddess ended in a scream and Gorri snickered, one ear flattening against his blond mane. Fearn put a hand up to the stallion's neck, his voice just loud enough to be heard.

'Let's walk about. They'll not bring the body till noon.' Fearn glanced up to Sarmatia, his weather-reddened face showing dark through the chalk which the shaman had daubed on each comer, Gorri included, as a sign of grief. Sarmatia nodded and with Fearn leading, they made for an area of grazing pasture enclosed by hurdles.

'Only a moment, Gorri,' Fearn was saying. Sarmatia felt the stallion's response surge through her fingertips and loins. A press of her hand warned her not to forget herself. They were taking a risk in witnessing this burial. The black and yellow clothed herald might appear through the massing crowds and denounce Bride and herself as runaway slaves, or worse, if news of Carvin's death had reached here.

Sarmatia twisted round to look back and Fearn tightened his grip on her hand. 'Bride's safe with my men.'

Five of Fearn's war band had chosen to watch the funeral. The rest of the battle host, with the women and children, were camped safely on the ridgeway outside the Plainsmen's territory.

Fearn nodded towards the front of the crowd and Sarmatia saw the metal smith sidelong, topping the Plains-people by half a head, her facial birthmark looking like a bruise with its covering of chalk. It had been

Bride's wish to see the burial, to make certain that the Plains-King was dead.

'Now she'll be satisfied.' Fearn echoed Sarmatia's unspoken thought. 'Are you, Sarmatia?' His green eyes searched her face. 'It's good for both of us that we came, I think. Just to know the evil's finished.

'Look over there, Sarmatia,' he went on, without giving her time to answer, 'Do you see what it is? We arrived from the south, where it was hidden from us by the forest. When we were together on Krete you asked me if it had been built by giants.'

Following the line of Fearn's pointing finger, Sarmatia raised herself from Gorri's back. The plain dipped slightly before her, allowing a clear view of the stone circle. A shaft of sunlight illuminated the gray stone uprights of smoothly finished sarsen and Sarmatia understood. Here at last was the Great Stone Circle, famous even on Krete as one of the holiest of shrines. Once, in a dream, she had come to this sanctuary. The vision had partly inspired her to leave Krete. Now she was seeing the circle and it stirred nothing in her. 'The Great Circle. Why is it called that when it's so small?' At only a furrow's length the ring of stones was tiny, like a child's toy.

'If we could go among the stones you would not think them small,' answered Fearn grimly. 'But now the Plainsmen allow no one to approach the circle but members of the ruling clan. They've forgotten how the circle came to be built. Their magic is guessing. They never touch the power.'

'The wind will howl here, when it rises,' Sarmatia muttered, staring at the bare plain with the Great Circle settled on it like a jagged tooth in an empty jawbone. Nothing was how she had foreseen it. She shivered, and Fearn wheeled the horse around.

'Hold tight, Sarmatia. Gorri needs to run now and so do I.'

They raced round the grazing field three or four times, Fearn running alongside the stallion and letting Gorri guide him. The canter left his breathing ragged, though he was as pleased as a boy for keeping pace with the horse.

'Man has fire, but when the horse has flight then who'd be a man?' he asked, after a brisk slap of the stallion's neck and a brief mop of his own face, good temper restored. 'Gorri's wounds are healing well now, without poultices.' He lifted his hands to help Sarmatia from the chestnut horse.

'His pain has lessened, too.' Sarmatia hoped that Fearn would not see her trembling. He gave no sign of it, nor of having felt her instinctive stiffening as he caught her up under the arms.

'Soon you will not need to have a pad between your thighs.' Fearn set her gently on her feet. 'Though you'll be easier walking than standing for a while yet.'

Walking took all Sarmatia's energies, even with Fearn's arm as support. It required an effort of will to move, stretch the healing bruises and bear down on her legs.

'Not far, Sarmatia,' Fearn was saying. 'A few more steps and we'll rest. Good! Three more steps and we're there.'

They slumped to the ground, leaning back to back against each other. Fearn caught a breath and at once began moving again. 'What are you doing?' Sarmatia asked, annoyed because she could not see.

'I'm fetching out my knife.' The calm reply resonated through her own chest. 'There's a carving to finish. Do you want to see it?'

A tiny piece of oak-wood, the size of a man's thumb, was passed over Fearn's shoulder. A lapwing had been roughly blocked out, the crested head just emerging from the pale wood. The carving was already a pleasure to hold and Sarmatia gave it back with reluctance. 'I never knew you worked wood.' There was so much about this man that she did not know.

Fearn laughed. He still had good teeth, Sarmatia noticed, as he twisted his head round to look at her. 'No, it's a new skill. Some way to use my hands. The people would not have me as their healer as well as their king.' Fearn twisted the lapwing between finger and thumb, his body suddenly tense against Sarmatia's. 'Such toys are good for law gatherings and round the camp fire at night,' he continued, after a moment. 'I work and listen.'

'We had no chance, Bride and I,' Sarmatia murmured. 'Traveling and sleeping where we could. And then at home with farming and the Bull Rite—no time.' She was vaguely ashamed that she had no similar skills to display. Fearn though seemed not to have noticed the lack.

'You know, Sarmatia, that I've not yet explained how it is I'm here?' he began, quietly intense on a matter which had clearly occupied his thoughts. His head was so close to hers that Sarmatia could see the scattering of freckles by his browline and the thick red-gold eyebrows, so light beside her own. His beard was a dull russet through the smearing of chalk. Sarmatia could not meet his eyes.

'You came. The rest isn't important.'

'But you know it is, Sarmatia. I sent word to you in Krete that I couldn't leave my kingdom.' Fearn twisted round, placing his knee against Sarmatia's back as support. 'Since then we've been through strange times.' He looked within a breath of admitting something, but then his eye caught a movement outside Sarmatia's vision.

'There are children watching.' Fearn plucked a pebble from the ground and flicked it at the gaggle of youngsters who had left their places at the funeral and crept to within earshot of where he and Sarmatia were sitting. The group retreated a few paces, giggling softly with hands over their mouths.

Sarmatia rested her head against the man's shoulder. Fearn was good. He was disappointed that the children were close, but he had checked his anger. One day she would feel for him again as she had before. One day she would feel alive again. One day Carvin's ruthless cruelty would be a fading nightmare.

Now Fearn was trying to explain how he had found her.

'Carvin's herald returned my bronze ring, the keepsake I'd given you. I'll not tell you what the fellow said, but it was fortunate for him that he carried the herald's staff: he tempted my anger more than once.' Here Fearn paused, as though considering whether to tell her something. 'I dismissed him without any kind of gift and called a council.

'The old men wouldn't have me leave. They said no king ever left the homelands, even in war. I said that my going wouldn't matter. It was winter and the land slept. I told them my honor was at stake, that the herald had insulted me. I tempted them with the riches my war band would win as booty. I didn't ask the impossible—two or three months say, the length of a journey to the amber northlands or Egypt.'

Fearn did not have to add that the journey to Krete was even longer. He looked her straight in the eyes. 'I asked for fifteen days, swore to return seven days after the winter solstice.'

'And if you had not won the vote?'

'But I did, Sarmatia.' Tentatively, the knife and carving forgotten in his lap, Fearn brought a hand up to Sarmatia's hair. When she did not pull away he touched her cheek. 'I still can't quite believe it. You've traveled so far, for so long.'

Again, words brimmed on his tongue. Sarmatia wondered why he stopped. Two summers past he had not been so cautious. Where too, the bronze betrothal ring? He wore it neither on his hands nor round his throat.

And yet in many ways Fearn was the man she remembered: his blunt features pleasing rather than handsome and his smile still warm, if less ready than it had been when he was twenty. In the first days after the attack on Carvin's hill fort, when the hours had been snatches of light and shade to her, Fearn had tended Sarmatia and the other battle-wounded, moving from pallet to pallet in the rough tent where she had lain for four nights, hearing the groans of the injured. Despite his healing skills Fearn had lost two of his war band, though he saved one youth who had been brought to him as dead, stunned by slingshot, and he'd stanched wounds and reset dislocated bones. Exactly as the widow had predicted, the villagers had taken no part in the attack, but they'd joined in the looting, and several had been injured trying to carry off too great a load.

Fearn had spared their village, but the settlement of Carvin's soldiers had been sacked, the wives and children herded from the blazing wreckage and kept under guard. Bride thought them fortunate as captives, for Fearn made certain that no mother was taken from her children, and for their part his men married the women who came to them as spoil.

'Very good,' Sarmatia had said when Bride told her, whispering, for her chest was a mass of bruising where Peket had kicked her. 'Those women must be blessing their luck.' At that point Fearn entered the tent.

'The women will not be slaves, Sarmatia,' he told her then. 'The lads I brought with me were unwed, and their wives shall have the same rights as Atterian women. There are no slaves in my kingdom.' He knew this was important to her.

Sarmatia sighed and yawned, surprised that she was lying on the ground with a cloak tucked round her. 'I was just about to wake you,' said Fearn. 'If you want to see the burial we should go back.'

They left Gorri in the field and Fearn pushed a way through the crowd for them. Sarmatia found herself back beside Bride.

'Look at him!' Bride hissed at her.

The dead King had Carvin's features. His head had been daubed with chalk, but this could not disguise the color of his face, which was almost black. He wore the gold breastplate and belt clasp: scepter and axe were by his side. Sarmatia watched people kissing the dead man. Bride was grimly satisfied, Fearn wary and watchful. Only she, it seemed, was unmoved.

There was a barrier between herself and her deeper feelings. It had risen on the night she had been raped and had stayed there since. Even when the villagers rid themselves of Carvin, hurling his body and those of his followers into the Hag Mound, Sarmatia had not cared that she was injured and could not help. 'Let the ghosts keep them,' Fearn had said, as the capstone to the long burial chamber was hauled away. The people had wanted no trace to be left. It was the dark slender young woman, her fine black hair shorn close to her head and her manner still stiff and suspicious, who had thrown the last thing of Carvin's into the mound: the whip. 'He's dead forever!' the woman shrieked as Fearn and his men struggled to reseal the mound. Bursting into tears she had run off and Sarmatia had not seen her again.

Rubbing her eyes, Sarmatia forced her attention back to the shaman, who had finished anointing the corpse. The Plainsmen began the ritual mourning cries as the body was carried into the charnel house, and again Sarmatia let her mind wander. She could not prevent it. Gorri was grazing in the paddock with the mounts of the noblemen, the finest horse there, despite the wounds which marred his flank. Fearn's men reported them to be self-inflicted, the stallion rubbing himself against a boulder in the stud field until he had drawn blood. 'Then Sarmatia and Gorri must meet,' Fearn said. 'For if one is anxious for the other, my healing will cure neither.' And he brought Gorri from the stud field himself.

Theirs was a quiet reunion, for Gorri had fretted since the night of her being raped, knowing something was wrong, and Sarmatia had never known his grief, being too weak and ill to sense it. Now it was good to see that his coat was healthy and that the self-sustained hurt had faded to a few long scars. He was a hand's span taller than the other grazing horses and cropped the best turf steadily.

Sarmatia swayed and Fearn caught her. 'You're weary.' He touched Bride's arm. 'Seen enough? I think we should move on, before the burial feast, where we might meet the Plains-King's herald.' A smile tugged at Fearn's mouth. 'Sarmatia he may not recognize, but you I think he would.'

'I've made sure of the killing I wanted.' Bride grinned, tossing her hair plait over one shoulder in her old way.

* * * *

Taking their new horses from the stud field, Fearn and the war band rode home. They were all mounted now, having helped themselves to the ponies that had belonged to Carvin's warriors. Sarmatia's inner barrier meantime started to crack on the final day of the journey to his kingdom, five days after the winter solstice. There had been a freezing fog that morning and progress was slow until the air cleared, when Fearn's men realized that they were in foothills bordering their lands. They urged Fearn to press on through the swift winter sunset and the young king agreed, recalling his vow to return to the homelands by seven days after the solstice. When the force stopped again the children were hard asleep, hanging like rags across the horses. The women swayed in their seats, scarcely aware that their mounts had halted.

Dimly Sarmatia felt the toddler who had ridden with her that day being lifted down from her arms. She opened half-closed eyes and saw a man hoisting a pannier from the back of a colt onto his own shoulders and watched him lead his pony towards a narrow barn attached to a timber house. They were in the yard of a farmstead and the door had opened in the long wooden dwelling, the mother of the house running out without a coat to embrace her son. The new wife and children were shown off, Fearn and his men pressed to stay for the night, hospitality politely refused, and then the reduced host was traveling again.

Sarmatia counted a dozen homesteads visited, the last two a sad homecoming where Fearn brought news of the death of a son or brother and the ashes and bones in an urn for burial.

Finally, there were three: Fearn, Bride and herself. Rime coated Fearn's beard and the horses' manes and Sarmatia's fingers were bloodless. Bride huddled over her horse, breathing in its warmth. A wild cat wailed in the trees, a cry like a baby's, lugubrious and unending, and the three rode in silence, feeling the frost grind in their necks.

Later—how long after Sarmatia could not tell—they reached another farm where Fearn dismounted and unhooked the wattle gate, leading their mounts into the yard. Here there was no rush of feet to greet them. The central shelter remained dark and still. Fearn put his shoulder to the warped door and pushed it inward, returning to Bride and Sarmatia to help them from their horses.

'Go in and get yourselves warm, there's wood and kindling inside the door. I'll stable Gorri and the ponies, and bring the baggage.' Taking the ponies' reins and grabbing Gorri's mane, Fearn left the women and disappeared around the rear of the dwelling.

Bride looked at Sarmatia, sighed when there was no reaction. 'Shall we go in?'

The stink of sheep grease caught in the back of Sarmatia's throat and it was impossible for her to see. She waited until her eyes adjusted and then gathered an armload of firewood from the logs stacked neatly inside the entrance. There was little free space: a small triangle beside a puddle of ashes where a fire had been laid. A stack of tools was piled against the sides and eaves of the building. Reaching out, Sarmatia touched an apron. It was stiff and needed oiling. She rubbed the leather between finger and thumb. Deep within her head a new thought had begun to shape, the first chink in the barrier, though as yet she was unaware of it.

Fearn reappeared, carrying the panniers and a torch he had found and already lit. He set the torch upon the newly kindled fire and at once the logs burned up, throwing off a blessed heat. Warming his haunches, the young king looked at the women and spoke.

'I wish I'd a better place to bring you for your first night in my country, but my house will be bursting with royal cousins awaiting my homecoming and there we'd have no peace. There'll be time enough for their greetings when I give them their presents and send them on their way.'

Fearn paused, his face reddened, perhaps by the fire. After a breath he went on. 'I remembered this summer station and knew it would be empty. It's only used in the longest days, when cheeses are made here. Yet it's warm and snug, and when the sun rises, the land lies handsomely under your eye.'

'It serves.' Bride kicked a crock to one side and stretched out. 'Just roll me in a ball and let me sleep.' Bride covered her face with her cloak. Almost at once her breathing slowed.

Sarmatia envied her. For herself, her whole body was aching too much.

'Walk about, you'll not wake her,' Fearn said, again divining her thoughts. 'I'm sorry we rode so hard today, but there'll be no more journeys after this, unless you wish it.'

No more journeys. Of course! She was in the kingdom of the Atterians and had reached her goal. But the thought was too great, and Sarmatia fled from it into sleep.

Stirring late next day she found herself alone with Bride, who told her that Fearn had fetched fodder and clothes from another farm and then ridden on to his own winter home, bearing his share of the battle spoil: 'Like a goshawk about to share with crows.'

Sarmatia muttered a reply and crawled towards the door.

'Where are you going now?'

Sarmatia yanked the door open, meeting a sheet of water. 'Outside.' She had never thought much of houses. A house was to sleep in and your life was outside, under sky and sun. After Carvin, indifference had been replaced by fear. Men could be cruel in houses, private murder, secret rape. She crouched in the rain, teeth chattering, the hard drops of water pricking her skin like fistfuls of thrown sand. I feel cleaner here, she thought, and the crack in the inner barrier shivered open.

She lifted her robe and tugged at the bindings on her thighs, letting rain pour over her. Too long, it seemed now, she had thought of her hurts as Carvin's mark: it was time to make her body hers again. Slowly, Sarmatia touched herself. She could feel her fingers through the bruises.

'What are you doing?' demanded Bride, and Sarmatia raised her head and smiled. 'Healing.' The new thought of the night before had borne fruit.

'I like it here.' Sarmatia threw her head back to drink the rain. 'Do you, Bride?' Concern for others was a part of this growing well-being.

'Come in and get some breakfast, I'm not bringing it out to you in this. And you can make yourself useful by combing my hair.'

The food was simple, but Sarmatia ate as much as Bride. Sitting with her back to the threshold, comb in hand, she listened for the first time to a full account of the attack on Carvin's fort. Fearn had never spoken of it to her. To her surprise, she was intrigued by the tale, savoring the moment when Fearn smashed through the metal smith's fetters with his battle axe. '...I liked him from the first, that man of yours: a good pair of shoulders...'

'Bride, your hair needs washing. It's full of burrs.'

'Well, you smell like an old cheese. Speaking of which, do you want another cheese ball? It's the only food with any taste.' Two gray spheres rolled across the floor and Sarmatia took them one in each hand, eating from both until Bride had resettled.

'Are you wearing another tunic?' she asked, as she picked up the comb again. Bride turned, met Sarmatia's bulging cheek, full of cheese, and started to laugh.

'Do that at Fearn and he'll run away!' Bride stood a second time and paraded round the fire. 'You like them, my new clothes? What are you thinking, staring into the air like that?'

'A necklace of lapis lazuli. And earrings for your ears.' Sarmatia wished she could snap her fingers and have these things for the metal smith.

'Where on earth did you see lapis? But never mind that, these are men's clothes I'm wearing, so jewelery can wait. Atterian women are much smaller than either of us.' Bride's smile dimpled into a grin. 'There are men's clothes laid by for you too, Bull Rider.'

'They can wait,' Sarmatia said quickly.

'Oh, we'll paint your face, plait your hair—'

Because Bride was trying to be kind and had already forgone the rich gold of the west to come north with her and Fearn, Sarmatia admitted the truth. 'I feel safer as I am.' She touched the dull, ill-fitting shift she was wearing and covered her mouth with a hand, afraid of what other words might come out. Bride had gone through worse, fettered to a rock. 'I'm ashamed.'

'Sarmatia, look at me.' Bride squatted before her. 'Look and never mind those tears, it's only water. We've traveled together and I've come to know you and I'm glad our paths have run the same way. And here I'll be the best smith they've seen, whereas in the west I'd be one among many.'

Bride flicked her hair over her shoulder and laughed, the moment of self-reflection put firmly behind her. 'So to keep me pleased you're going to put on these fine clothes. If you drench them, that's your concern. Fearn says you're strangers to each other, but I tell you it's not like a stranger that he watches you.' She drew back. 'Which way then, self-pity and guilt? Are you going to let Carvin win in the end?'

No, thought Sarmatia. She rose. 'Where are these clothes?'

Under Bride's care Sarmatia stripped off her cloak and shift, using the shift to scour the marks of dirt and travel from her body before flinging it out of doors, the last link with Carvin finally broken. The rain washed her hair and Bride combed and plaited it while wet, winding the ends around her fingers to encourage the curl. She painted Sarmatia's eyelids with a mixture of fire ash and water, mixed to a smooth, sticky paste. The gray tunic she declared to be too loose fitting and proceeded to bind the long sash tightly around Sarmatia's waist and crosswise over her breasts.

'So there!' Bride concluded, knotting the belt behind Sarmatia's back and spinning her around and around. 'Go drape yourself by the door post, you're pretty now. Well, go on. Wait for Fearn's return!'

Chapter 33

Kingdom of the Atterians, 1561 BC. Fall.

Bride was leaving the summer house. She wanted to stay with the Atterian metal smiths to test out their skills. 'You need this time together, you and Fearn,' she told Sarmatia, as they walked outside in the rain. It was their third day in the northern kingdom.

Sarmatia put her arms about Bride, pressing her face against her cheek. 'Good luck!' She tried to sound cheerful. 'I'm sure I'll thank you later,' she added, prizing her hold off Bride, a finger at a time.

She waved until Bride and her pony disappeared into the gray rain then dived back into the hut. Fearn found her there later, staring at the fire. They warmed themselves in silence.

'I rode with Bride partway, but she insists on going to the smiths' settlement alone,' Fearn began. 'It's a clear track and an easy ride. She'll be there in half a day.'

'She'll be safe, too. No animals will want to hunt in this weather.'

Again there was silence.

'Bride's a rare woman, isn't she?' Fearn said suddenly.

'Yes.'

'Striking, too. The fire-mark simply adds to her looks.'

'That's right.' Fool, help him, thought Sarmatia savagely. 'Should we stay here while Bride is away?' She wondered how she would feel if Fearn answered that they would ride to meet his family.

'It's best, at least at night. Or Bride won't know where we are.' At last he shot her a quick look. 'Do you mind, Sarmatia?'

Did she mind? Sarmatia could not answer that question, although two seasons ago, at the start of her travels, she would have answered at once. The way had been straight: she was running north to Fearn. On Krete, Fearn had been a magnanimous golden hero. Since then she had seen him lessened: tired, preoccupied, no longer sure in his dealings with her. She recalled her old certainty, her stubborn declaration in Pergia's garden that love never changed. How childish! Feelings, she'd learned, changed continuously; ebbing or growing, taking on new shades of meaning and depth. The gods of her youth—Tazaros, Pergia, her father—had withered back inside her to a root that might never regrow. And Fearn?

But the hut was stifling. She had to get out. Why were the dealings of men and women so difficult, each way a new way? Sarmatia glanced up at Fearn, waiting patiently for her reply. They ought to be more like animals, she thought, with a single memory of a breeding place and ancient, laid-down ways of conduct. She swallowed. After Carvin, she was still not used to voicing her wishes. 'This smoke stings. Might we go out?'

Fearn dropped a cloak onto her shoulders, turning her to tie the throat-strings, as though she was a child. 'I'll come with you.' He spoke firmly, but his fingers fumbled with the drawstrings. Recalling how he'd dressed her bruises with such deft hands, Sarmatia felt for him.

Outside, where they could walk and watch, the two felt easier together. Fearn was tireless in pointing out the landmarks of his kingdom, speaking in their old mixture of Kretan and the common tongue. In the days that followed he took Sarmatia wherever she wanted to go. Into wooded valleys and small, bank-enclosed meadows, to rivers to count the beaver dams and ponds. Every night they returned to the summer house to see if Bride had come back, but they slept out in the yard and rose before dawn next morning to set off again. Fearn did not mention his family or the kingship. He seemed glad to be free of both, more interested in her journey.

Sarmatia talked of Tazaros and she talked of her travels. Later, she touched on the death of Kerewos and even revealed that she had been tempted to stay on in Egypt. She never spoke of Carvin. Fearn never asked.

This was a time of deception for Fearn. Not wishing to cause Sarmatia grief, he said nothing of the royal family's hostility to her. He glossed over the four days he'd spent in the Cattle Men's kingdom, saying only that he'd been a guest. In speaking of his past, Fearn did not want to admit he had been captured. He hid, too, the way he'd been made king, fearing that, if she knew of the test, his Bull Head might demand to endure it.

Here Sarmatia's flute, a gift Fearn had made her by firelight while she

was sleeping, became a way of filling any awkward silences. Sarmatia
played the flute each evening. It was a way of both sharing and purging.
Grief that could not be expressed in words could be made into music. Only
once, after a haunting, sad melody that had come to Sarmatia all of a piece,
did Fearn leap up and leave his place by the fire. Her next lament he praised,
so that Sarmatia knew for certain he was not angry with her.

'Here's a skill I didn't know I had,' Sarmatia said a night or two later, and
Fearn laughed, for that evening her music sparkled and sang.

By then, Sarmatia had regained the weight she had lost as a slave. Fearn
made her armlets of oak-wood: pale, to show off her dark coloring. Sarmatia
was delighted with them and wanted to give Fearn something in return.

To this end, she watched him. In her previous dealings with men,
Sarmatia had avoided staring. Now she took pleasure in it. Fearn was like
her spirit animal, beautiful and strange.

The strength of her spirit animal had returned, as Sarmatia discovered to
her cost. This was revealed when Fearn discovered a sickly roe deer from
the woods.

'I've healed wild things before,' he told her. 'You needn't fear that it will
suffer.'

But Sarmatia looked at the doe, so small and already thickening with
pregnancy, and she took its narrow throat in her hands. 'Kill it.' Even as
spoke, her spirit-predator moved her and the doe was dead.

Fearn seemed shaken rather than angry. He laid the dead meat on the
grass away from her. 'What a fierce thing you are, Sarmatia. I thought you
cared for all your fellow-creatures.'

Sarmatia laughed. Her spirit animal made her laugh. She licked her lips.
'Only the strong ones.' Which was true for times like these, when hunger
drove the pity from her heart. She fell at once to the skinning of the meat.
After a while Fearn knelt to help her, as she had sensed he would.

'There's no kindness, is there, in the wilds?' he said.

If Fearn was disappointed in her, Sarmatia was angry that he should be.
That night there was no music or talk. In the morning she was red-eyed
through lack of sleep and Fearn the same. They broke camp, careful not to
brush against each other.

The weather at least had changed for the better. Hanging a water flask
about her neck, Sarmatia walked to the edge of the yard and leaned against

the gate to look out. With the rain finished she could see past the bank meadows of the summer house and up to the rounded sweep of the hills.

These hills were higher than the wide ridges of Carvin's kingdom. Their sides were mottled patches of forest and field, while here and there a gray patch standing out from the landscape revealed a farmstead.

One hill was separate from the rest. It rose out of a wooded valley and lay like a curved shield upon the land, with no tree or bush growing on its sides to mar its smoothness. Sarmatia was looking at the hill sidelong. The view pleased her. The hill was so open. Mist and rain had obscured it before, but now she could see far in this amber-colored air. 'What's that hill called? I'd like to go there.'

Without a glance, Fearn did not look up. 'You can't. We're going to the Mushroom Wood today.' He finished tying the leather thongs of his shoes and rose, turning to damp down the fire embers.

Sarmatia was annoyed. Fearn did not usually stamp out the fire but let it die naturally. Then there was his refusal to take her where she had asked to go, his curt response to her questions. She drummed on the hurdle gate with her fingers. 'But I'd like to go. Why not?'

'We need more food. I know where there's plenty in the wood.' He would not have spoken so to one of his warriors, thought Sarmatia.

'We can do both: search the wood this morning and climb the hill at noon.' Sarmatia stepped away from the gate to open it.

Fearn whipped round and reached her in a few strides. He threw the gate shut, standing before it. 'Remember, Sarmatia, that I'm no more your slave than you're mine. The hill is sacred. We can't go there for your pleasure.'

Sarmatia sank back against the sharp hurdles. She had not seen Fearn like this, harsh, like a king, like Carvin. Despising her own fear, she spat back, 'Fine. You should have told me at once!'

Fearn gave a bark of laughter, the hard planes of his face dissolving. 'You're right, that was unfair. It's just—' He stopped, coloring up slightly.

Moved by his shyness, understanding now why he was on edge, Sarmatia put her hands up towards him. 'Fearn?'

She could ask no more. He drew her close, lifting and sitting her on top of the gate post. 'Shall we begin again? Now that you've said my name, which you speak so rarely and I listen for so hard.'

As though it had never been, his ill humor had vanished. Fearn held her lightly, one hand at each side of her waist, and from being afraid, Sarmatia felt she was floating. Impulsively, feeling like a bubble, she leaned forward to kiss Fearn. She missed and bumped noses, her lips resting on his moustache. She could feel his heart quickening, his fingers tightening round her middle. 'You'll not span my waist with your hands.' Her face pressed hotly against his cheek. She had tried to kiss him! And he was not moving or speaking. Was she wrong? Did he feel only pity for her?

'No, Sarmatia!' Fearn rebutted her thoughts. 'No, Sarmatia.' His beard pricked and tickled against her mouth and then his lips, gentle at first and fumbling. They told her she was beautiful to him. Sarmatia closed her eyes and gave herself to the kiss, winding her arms around Fearn's neck.

When they broke apart both were shivering. 'We'd best stop.' Fearn spoke in Atterian, his voice furred, but Sarmatia understood. She too, was ready to stop, a little nervous, though she put her lips to him again, teasing him. His mouth was fresh. He hadn't kissed many women before her. She hadn't kissed many men. They would learn together.

'That's enough!' Laughing, Fearn lifted her from the post and set her down, turning then to make a dash for the summer house with a muttered excuse about forgetting something. Sarmatia was not displeased by this. She hung her flute across her back on its thong and pushed the four wooden armlets past her elbows to her wrists, so she might feel them rub together on her flesh. Then she went to fetch the horses.

* * * *

'Play for me,' Fearn said later, looking up from their evening fire. The Mushroom Wood had been too damp for mushrooms. They had not stayed there long. It had taken the rest of that day to search for food.

Sarmatia unslung the flute from her neck, placed it to her mouth. 'What shall I play?'

'A tune to make you smile.' Fearn stood up, held out his arms, and with a sigh Sarmatia rose and walked into them.

'You aren't angry with me now?' Fearn had been so quiet today that she still wasn't sure if she had been too bold in kissing him first.

'I wasn't angry before,' came back the answer, with a kiss. Fearn paused in his caress. 'Yet you must teach your spirit animal,' he added, growing thoughtful. 'That roe-deer yesterday, the one you slaughtered with your hands...' He shook his head. 'You're not an animal, Sarmatia, nor should you wish to be.'

'So I must give you half my life.' What Fearn asked was impossible. She would not relinquish her creature-calling. But Fearn shook his head and smoothed her hair with his hand, turning the stab of anger in her face into a stab of fire. 'Ah!' she cried, as Fearn touched her again. When she reopened her eyes she was on his lap.

He kissed and tickled and caressed her to a pitch far greater than she had experienced in the spirit-skin of any creature, to an excitement greater than she had ever known. When Fearn laid her down upon her cloak and entered her, the sweetness was so intense it almost overcame her. Gasping, Sarmatia found the moment passed and her toes began to curl with the next warm surge. It scooped her up and carried her to the edge, where Fearn took her head between his hands and stopped.

'Is this better than animal-kinship, Sarmatia?'

'Yes!'

Fearn laughed and the wave spilled out across her thighs, the bright head marrying Sarmatia to the living heat of her companion. She moaned and threw back her head, giving herself up to the pleasure of their joining.

Sleep overcame them while fused as one and Sarmatia began to dream. At first the dreams were a mirror of herself, a warm jumble of images, but then they grew more solid and more real.

She was standing on the slope of a grassy hillside, the sun at her back. Her shadow stretched before her and, as Sarmatia watched, the head of her shadow grew bigger and the body longer. It dropped onto all fours and crouched at her feet, her spirit animal in silhouette. Sarmatia caressed its shadow head and ears, the spiky ruff at the back of its neck. A growling purred in her own breast. She and her animal were waiting for someone upon this hill, and soon he would come.

Her first awareness of his presence was not from sight but from a touch on her shoulder. *Your spirit animal is with us, then,* Fearn's voice was saying. The touch of his thumbs ran lightly down her arms. *Will it be revealed?*

Sarmatia looked down, but the silhouette had vanished. 'Now is clearly not the time,' she said, disappointed.

I would like to have seen more than a shadow.

'So would I. But I don't even know its name.' She leaned back. 'I've missed you.'

Yes, it's been a long time. This was the voice which Sarmatia had heard in the hall of Ramose and later, warningly, in the last moments before she and Bride had been captured and enslaved. Arms crossed over her middle, drawing her closer.

'But we were often separate,' Sarmatia found herself saying gently.

That was not my doing, Sarmatia. From the time of the letter and before, until the time I received back the ring, and after, my thoughts have been with you.

Sarmatia looked ahead at the blue sky, considering the bronze ring and why, if recovered, it had not been returned to her. The dream waited patiently. 'Is this how you could speak to me? Though earth and sea lay between us?' she asked, an uncounted time after, forgiving the long silences of the past; her long lonely month in the kingdom of Carvin.

I don't know. The need was there, the gods were kind. Perhaps we should not look too closely. He did not intend to reveal more: the Sky God's sight had never been an easy gift.

'Kiss me.'

You must wake first.

Still in Fearn's arms, Sarmatia awoke and he kissed her, his mouth lingering on hers. 'There are now other ways between us,' he murmured and Sarmatia laughed, letting the dream fade as other, earthier needs took its place.

* * * *

From then on, she and Fearn drew together like any man and woman, understanding each other through gestures and habit. The passing of thought from one to the other by means other than speech was less direct, although it grew subtler and more frequent. Sarmatia did not regret the change, nor she believed, did Fearn.

In the day: Fearn, kissing her neck in passing. 'Love you.'

'I love you.' Strange Atterian words, and yet how natural the feeling. 'I love you,' Sarmatia saying again as she lay with Fearn under the stars, tightening her arms possessively about her man's broad back. Her only fear now was that the nights might not be long enough for them to celebrate their vows in all the ways they were devising.

Chapter 34

There were three unmarried men and on alternate nights Bride lay with each. They were young, eager to please, but dull. As foot-warmers they were better. As smiths they were useless.

Bride had expected Fearn's smiths to be old-fashioned—the King, for all his youth, was old-fashioned—yet what she had found, riding into the smiths' homestead, beggared belief.

Once she had shown off the token Fearn had given her, the welcome had been warm. The smiths had been pleased when Bride told them she would stay, and no one stared at her birthmark. She retired in high hopes to the hut their chief had given her.

Disquieting revelations came next day. The smiths lived mainly by hunting. They had little metal, only a few trinkets.

A cloak pin was given to her, to show their craft, and Bride sat for a moment. Like Sarmatia, who had refused to take back the crocodile torc because it had been worn by Carvin, Bride had brought nothing out of that kingdom. She glanced round the Atterian faces. One or two men were trying to be clean-shaven. Her fingers closed on the thick bronze pin. 'With this I'll make you razors.'

They brought her tools, and from the pin Bride made six razors and gave them all away. One smith shaved off his beard and to him Bride granted her bed, followed quickly by two more newly-shaven males. Other smiths shaved moustaches. A look was emerging which rapidly became fashion. More bronze was brought to be turned into razors and Bride was in business.

Bride showed the way and the quicker-witted followed, bartering their hunting traps for metal. In the evenings talk was of alloys and moulds, and in the day the settlement rang with noise. More Atterians were taking time from their winter chores to ride to the homestead, and the chief smith spoke to her of gold. 'What's your favorite metal?' he asked, as they sat drinking heather ale during the quiet time of one morning.

'Gold. What's yours?'

'Gold, gold and gold.'

'You should get some.' Bride watched the smith's wife working at her loom, singing softly. She glanced at the chief, his boxer's nose, and wondered what their secret was.

'We do have gold here, but it's buried.'

Bride swiveled round on the bench. 'Gold's to be seen and touched. Dig it up!' Excitement made her brusque, but the chief was in his own reverie.

'Gold's dangerous to keep. When Waroch died in the fire, we thought it best to hide ours.' The chief slipped into a spate of Atterian that Bride could not follow.

'Who was Waroch?'

The chief's newly-shaven jaw set in a line. 'Ask any of the royal family. But don't say who told you.' He drained his cup.

'I'll get on.' Bride left her own drink. 'Think about what I said. Gold's meant to be worn.'

Walking back through the rain to her hut, Bride heard the rush, like the tide that pounds the Pillar Straits, and took no notice, being deep in thought.

The sea noise broke in her ears, a pony's head seemed to grow above her shoulder. Mud skidded up her leggings, and a hand tugged on her plait.

'You're the one!' The gray nag might have spoken, it was so close. A jerk of reins stopped the pony and Bride looked round.

The sun came out from behind the rain-clouds and sparkled. Smiling at her in the freshly-washed air was the most desirable young man she'd ever seen. He was as shapely as a young willow, his hair was like old silver, eyes green as malachite. Beardless, his mouth was perfect. He looked the kind who smile often, laugh more.

'My, my. Aren't you pretty?'

Bride might have said the same.

'Handsome as my boots.' The smile grew wider.

It was years since a man had called her ugly to her face. Too astonished to be angry, Bride listened to the light voice.

'You're the one who chaperoned our king's harlot.' The stranger's gaze danced. 'As men judge beauty, is she fair?'

'Can't say. I'm not a man.'

'As handsome as yourself, then?'

'Take care.'

'Perhaps I will. Fearn can't stay at the summer house forever.' The malachite of his eyes darkened. 'When he returns to his father's house, I'll be ready.'

He withdrew, drifting away with scarcely more sound than a rider in a dream, a lock of silver mane or hair floating into Bride's palm from where horse and man had been.

And I, thought Bride, shall be ready for you, when we next meet.

Chapter 35

Two days later Fearn and Sarmatia came down from the summer house. Bride had not returned from the smiths but they chose to wait no longer/ A message would be sent when they reached Fearn's homestead.

Once on their way, Fearn seemed sad. He kept looking back. Sarmatia, perversely, was lighter in spirits. The Atterians, she decided, were another challenge, much like the Bull Rite.

'Do you have embassies from other kingdoms?' she asked, showing that she knew play between them was finished for the moment. Fearn looked puzzled. She had spoken in Kretan. 'Many gatherings?' Sarmatia did not know the Atterian words. He grinned and answered slowly in his own tongue.

'The people meet four times each year on the Sacred Hill, and traders come then.' Fearn chuckled, as though a thought amused him. 'Here we're not like Krete, Sarmatia. If neighbors cross our borders it's usually for war.'

Sarmatia curled her fingers deeper into Gorri's mane. One can't demand of a king, What is it you do? even if he is your husband. 'Will I have work?'

'You can spin thread, or weave cloth. There's cooking and the making of pots, leather curing...'

Tasks around the home, indoor work. Sarmatia saw herself standing within a house at a loom, listening for Fearn's step on the threshold. The picture did not please her much.

'... or you could make rope for me, like Anoi.' Fearn was not teasing. She had asked and he was explaining. Among Atterians, the wife of a king is like the wives of other men.

'What is Anoi?' From the way Fearn spoke, Sarmatia could not tell if the word described a custom or a man.

'Just a girl, a cousin.'

Sarmatia noted the tense way Fearn spoke, but let that pass for now.

'Why does she make rope for you?'

"So that fences and gates can be lashed together. Bull Head, there's no mystery. I'm a hurdle-maker, sometimes a thatcher.'

His hands, curved lightly around the reins of his mount, were crosshatched by tiny white scars. Sarmatia thought of the way he could handle a knife. 'But you're Minos!'

'So I should do nothing?' Fearn was amused. 'Here, the king sets the land boundaries. For that he must first make fences. A wall made by a king is said to be lucky.'

'The thatching?' Sarmatia was trying to imagine Ramose repairing the roof of his palace himself.

'That's work for the summer.' Fearn talked of the harvesting of the heather. His plain face seemed to be lightening, as though lit from within. Here was her bed-mate, surely the rest was not important? Thrusting doubt aside, Sarmatia scratched at the paler chestnut space between Gorri's ears. She touched the stallion's flank with her heel. 'Let's race, Fearn.'

* * * *

They arrived at Fearn's house at midday, when the mist had cleared and Sarmatia could see the settlement from a distance. Of itself, the homestead was much like other Atterian farms—a windowless, rectangular barn, with a single door and a steep roof of heather thatch. It was set within a circular ditch and had before the door a fenced-off area of beaten earth. There were other buildings within the ditched enclosure whose use Sarmatia could not guess. She looked past the valley river, across meadows and forest, and felt her eyes widen. Rising on the horizon was the shield-like Sacred Hill. Now the shield was sideways in a long unbroken curve. She shouted to Fearn, but before he could speak the dogs were on them.

Barking, five hairy black and white hounds jumped the ditch. Sarmatia had to keep Gorri turning to prevent the stallion bolting, but Fearn slipped from his mount and ran amongst the dogs, roughing with the largest. Sarmatia grabbed the neglected pony's reins, dragging it away from the scrummage. There came a high-pitched whistle and the dogs whirled round and left them. Fearn ran up, panting.

'Sorry, I forgot.' He looked so excited that Sarmatia forgave him at once, recalling that her husband had little experience of dealing with a horse of Gorri's size and temper.

'No harm done.' Her eyes caught a bustle of movement by the farmstead door. Fearn's family would know now who was coming.

Sarmatia slithered from Gorri's back and tried to smooth out her tunic. She was conscious of her man's clothes, her dark skin. Fearn's hand found hers and she gripped it, clutching at Gorri's mane with her other fist. She walked up the slight slope that led to the farm and her heart was racing, though not from the climb.

The door to the house was open, pushed against the timbers of the walls, but no one had come out to greet them.

'They'll not wish to get wet. It can take days to dry clothes in winter,' was all Fearn said. Sarmatia understood, but she would have liked someone, even the dogs again.

To one corner, in the lee of the house, were four pens, the two closest heaving with sheep. Fearn saw the flock. 'Setir's home from pasturing. It must be time for the midday meal.' He squeezed her hand. 'It'll be easier for you to meet my people if we eat with them.'

Sarmatia doubted that. Table customs differed. 'Is there food for these?' She indicated the horses. For a moment, the penning and feeding of Gorri and the pony took her mind away from the silent doorway. As she carried hay to the horses and cleaned out their hooves and patted and settled them, Sarmatia felt eyes watching from within the house, eyes that moved with her.

At last she and Fearn were finished. Fearn wiped his hands on a rag from the barn, handing it to Sarmatia, who did the same. He looked at her, winked then walked to the door, ducking beneath the lintel. 'Come in, Sarmatia.' She lowered her head and entered the dark interior.

Within, the house seemed bigger than from outside, perhaps because of the tall roof, its apex hidden in smoke and the mutton and hams hanging in it for curing. Immediately inside the door sprawled the dogs, growling and showing their teeth. Sarmatia flashed a silent order to the pack to be still then in the quiet that followed became aware of over a dozen pairs of eyes.

These people had been at their midday meal, seated on two long benches round a trestle table, eating a porridgy mess with their fingers. An old woman had just finished laying two more places at the table end and now Fearn asked that the group be seated again. He took his place, smiled and beckoned. 'Come. You're safe here, in the house of my father's family.'

'Shy lass,' said one of the men, a redhead like Fearn with a homely face full of freckles. Leaving his wooden bowl on the table, the man rose, using another kinsman's shoulder as support. He limped towards her, dragging slightly on a withered foot. 'I'm Orm, Fearn's uncle, and head of this house with him. Be welcome!'

Sarmatia felt herself blush and saw the men round the table smile, although the women watched her carefully, their faces impassive. 'Thank you,' she said in Atterian. She clasped the lame man's gnarled hand in hers.

Orm kissed her lightly on the mouth. 'Come and eat.'

Sarmatia was led to the table, given a bowlful of food. Slowly, she dug her fingers into the gruel and began to eat the milky, faintly sweet food. Beside her, Fearn was answering questions about the Mushroom Wood. Across from her two children were kicking each other under cover of the trestle. The meeting had been easier than she had expected.

Never before had Sarmatia seen so many blond and redheaded people. Only the shepherd Setir and his eldest daughter had dark hair like hers. Amongst this tribe of auburn and gold Fearn's coloring, which she had thought so striking, was quite ordinary, although he was the tallest of the family even when seated. Compared to the others, with their narrow faces and slightly tip-tilted noses, Fearn's features were coarse. Sarmatia thought how strange she must look here: dark brown hair, black brows, brown skin. She was the largest woman there, the broadest-backed and the heaviest. Had Bride been with her...but Sarmatia dismissed that thought as unworthy.

She glanced about, wondering where she and Fearn would sleep. There were a number of alcoves at the back of the house where perhaps they could bed down. Already, she did not think the lack of a royal guard unusual. In a house such as this a ruler would live plainly.

In the center of the house, on a large, flat stone, burned a fire tended by children. There were bake-stones by the fire, and greenwood spits, but no bronze vessels, only those of earthenware or wood. The walls of the house were draped with animal skins. Sarmatia saw that the ground close to the door was churned with sheep tracks. The flock was brought in on rainy nights and kept from the fire and living quarters by hazel-wood fencing. Where the trestle was set the floor was dry, strewn with dried meadowsweet.

Near the trestle was a raised wooden platform where the family had their clothes-chests, away from damp and vermin. Here too was a tall wooden dresser, open-fronted, with spaces for keepsakes. Sarmatia noticed that as he talked Fearn would glance at this dresser, as though it contained a favorite trinket. She was puzzling what this might be, hoping it was her own bronze betrothal ring, when she felt a light touch on her shoulder. Sarmatia turned on the bench.

There, her blue eyes almost level with Sarmatia's amber eyes, stood a slim young woman. Her hair, unbound and straight, flowed in a golden fall down either side of her face and brushed at her knees. She was dressed in the way of these women in a long sleeveless gown of brown wool, worked over at breast and armholes with black wool stitching. She had many thin bangles of copper on each wrist that jangled softly as she ran her fingers along Sarmatia's shoulder to her elbow. An odd gesture, and Sarmatia felt the hairs of her arm prickle. She looked for Fearn, but the King was in a whispered conversation with a youth, who left the house soon after. The female stranger spoke.

'You're here, at last! My kinsman told me that you were weakened by your travels and must rest a time in quiet at the summer house, but I must speak truly. I was beginning to doubt your coming! I am Anoi. Fearn is my third cousin.'

Sarmatia gripped the girl's outstretched hand and rose, feeling very clumsy beside the tiny Anoi. 'I greet you,' she said formally, flushing hot red. So this was what Fearn had told his family! She flashed him a glance as he turned, hearing her slow speech, but Fearn's green eyes rested first on Anoi.

'You're not with our other relatives today,' he said.

The golden-haired girl smiled. 'The day's too wet.' Anoi turned her smile upon Sarmatia. 'How dark she is, Fearn!'

She spoke with such appealing innocence that Sarmatia laughed outright at Anoi's honesty, dismissing her recollection of Fearn's tense manner when he'd told her about his cousin. Drink had begun to circulate with the end of the meal and the jug and cups had come to her. Sarmatia held up two beakers to Anoi and Fearn. 'Have beer with me.'

Anoi at once settled on the bench, smoothing out her gown with a faint ringing of her bracelets. 'What did you do, in the south?' she asked, while

Sarmatia poured three measures of the honey-sweetened beer. 'Do women there make cloth and felt, and learn the cures of sheep scab and ticks?'

Poor child, if that had been the whole of her life so far. Sarmatia glanced at her husband. 'With joy!' She gave a Kretan toast. She, Fearn and Anoi touched cups and drank. 'Has Fearn told you that I was once a Bull Rider and Mistress of the Rite of Passage?'

Fearn spoke quietly in Kretan. 'There are no words for Bull Rider in our language, Sarmatia. Anoi won't understand you.'

And Sarmatia saw that this was true. Anoi was clearly bewildered. Here was the reward for her boastful beginning. 'No matter. It was long ago,' she said. The beer jug had come round again and Sarmatia poured herself another drink. 'Will you have more?'

Anoi put her hand across the cup. 'I have to work, later. Will you tell me what Bull Rider means?' She heard out Sarmatia's account, politely waiting until the Kretan had finished. 'Can southern women own flocks of sheep?'

'Some own a great number.' Sarmatia wondered at these questions. Was Anoi trying to tell her what to expect as Fearn's wife?

Anoi brought her palms together, opening her fingers like a flower. 'Sarmatia is a pretty name. What meaning does it have?'

'None that I know of.'

'Oh? I thought all names had a meaning. Mine means Golden Shadow.'

Sarmatia smiled. 'Suits you.'

'Oh, this!' Anoi shook her head. 'For beauty of hair you should have seen Fearn's mother. It's such a pity!'

Fearn drained his cup and snapped it onto the table. 'Anoi, don't start that now.'

'But why not, cousin? The lady's not offended, and consider your mother's family. What claims they have been making.' Anoi plucked at Sarmatia's cloak. 'Forgive me,' she said, 'but I don't like secrets, and harsh words are usually better out in the sunlight. Fearn should have warned you.'

Suddenly they were no longer speaking of Fearn's mother, but of her role in the royal family, reflected Sarmatia, wary of the seemingly simple manner in which Anoi had introduced the subject. She turned to Fearn, but his attention was still claimed by Anoi, who had risen nimbly to her feet.

'Don't scold me, cousin. I've a gift for you and your wife. Wait.' Anoi pressed Sarmatia back onto the bench with surprising force. 'I'll fetch it.'

Anoi returned, bearing a gray sheepskin parcel which she gave to Fearn. Fearn dropped it into Sarmatia's lap.

'Go on, open it,' he urged. Anoi was silent, smiling.

Sarmatia undid the parcel, her breath checked for a moment as her fingers closed on a rich mesh of fabric. One after another, she held up two cloaks for Fearn to see. 'Beautiful.' She ran her hands over the smooth, even wool. How had Anoi got the weave so close?

Fearn stepped forward to claim the larger garment, stripping off his white wool cloak. He tossed the wide scarlet about his shoulders. The vivid red clashed with his hair, but Fearn was pleased. He swept up Anoi and whirled her about, his earlier sharpness forgotten.

'Don't you remember, Fearn? I promised I'd give you this,' said Anoi, when he set her down. 'I always keep my word, though it's only a cloak.'

'Ah, but the color! No one has woven me a scarlet cloak.'

'Didn't you know that Fearn dotes on anything red?' Anoi asked, catching Sarmatia staring. 'Wait until the fall of the year when the trees change.'

'No one would make me a scarlet cloak.' Fearn was an echo of himself. He seemed much taken by the thought. Looking up at him, Sarmatia felt it a pity that the color should suit him so little. The King grinned at her, drew her up from the bench. 'Let's see your gift, Sarmatia.'

Her cloak was short, stopping before her knees, much to the appalled astonishment of Anoi. 'Oh!' She bobbed down to check if the hemline could be changed: 'Fearn told us you were tall. I used Harr as my guide. She's the tallest woman among us.'

It seemed she was unfeminine, thought Sarmatia, caught between humor and irritation. 'I'll use it as a summer cloak,' she told Anoi soothingly, then recollected her manners. 'Yours is a kind gift.' It was, after all, the first present she had received from any Atterian except Fearn.

'The color looks well on you,' added Fearn, which made Sarmatia chuckle. She didn't trust his opinion, not with his own face looking so hectic.

'You like it?' Anoi asked shyly, sighing when Sarmatia nodded. There was silence between them and Anoi motioned to the threshold. 'I must go.'

'Not yet, Anoi.'

'The meal's over, Fearn, and there's work.'

'I said not yet. Please—' Fearn was interrupted, not by Anoi, but by the harsh blare of a horn.

'By the Mother, couldn't they have waited?' Cursing, Fearn vaulted onto the raised platform. Sprinting to the dresser, he hauled out his axe and a small, gray package that he tossed to Sarmatia. 'Both have been through fire and water and made right for your hands. Take them, they're yours!'

With no more time for explanations, the young king shot through the door. Sarmatia heard the thunder of hooves as he rode away and glanced helplessly at Anoi. 'What's happening? Is there a war?'

Anoi looked at her through her veil of hair. 'Oh, it's nothing, only a raid. The neighboring kings have a fancy for Fearn's cattle, but he'll deal with them.' When Sarmatia would have started after him, Anoi caught her arm. 'Aren't you going to open that?'

Sarmatia considered Fearn's safety more vital than the package, but Anoi clearly wasn't going to let go until she opened the thing. She ripped into it, finding her mother's seal stone and also the bronze ring, the plain, heavy hoop of metal Fearn had given her on Krete.

Tears sprang into Sarmatia's eyes, happy, grateful tears that she hastily blinked away. There was no time, not when her husband was riding into danger. And yet she could not resist wearing Fearn's ring properly on her finger, not after so many years of carrying it around her neck. Quickly, Sarmatia tied the seal stone onto her wrist and slid the bronze band onto her finger, smiling at its gleaming snugness. Again, she tried to go after Fearn, but Anoi exclaimed, 'Look, Fearn's ring fits her!' and Sarmatia was surrounded by women.

'Fearn wanted to give you these later, but with the raid there's no knowing when he'll be back,' said one, snatching her hand to admire the ring.

'Isn't it lovely?' shouted another.

Sarmatia felt engulfed by this tide of faces. She had to leave. Fearn was going to fight and he was her husband. Whatever the custom for Atterian wives, she couldn't stand idly by and do nothing. 'Let me go!'

Startled by her vehemence, the women drew back and Sarmatia darted for the door, ignoring the alarms:

'Wait, you mustn't leave—'

'Orm, stop her!'

Setir the shepherd, whom Sarmatia recognized by his dark hair, ran towards her, but Sarmatia deftly side-stepped his pursuit and shouted to Gorri. She heard the man's yell of surprise as the huge chestnut smashed down the side of his pen and chased after her, hooves drumming on the wooden bridge at the farmstead's entrance. Gorri caught up and Sarmatia seized his mane and jumped onto his back. Encouraging the stallion into a gallop, she set off after Fearn.

Chapter 36

At that moment, in the settlement of the smiths, the boy whom Bride had paid to watch out for strangers rushed into her hut, gabbling news of a silver-haired man coming down from the horizon on a gray horse.

'Indeed?' said Bride, without looking up from her lunch, 'and does this vision have a name?

'Goar. It'll be Goar,' the boy panted.

Bride already knew that. After their first explosive encounter, she had lost no time in questioning the chief smith and his wife about the man and had been rewarded with a rich seam of gossip. Goar, it turned out, was a woman-lover, a pursuer of unmarried girls, but none of those had snared him yet.

They were using the wrong traps, Bride thought, pushing aside her empty bowl of porridge and flipping the boy his wages. 'Find me my three bachelors, will you? Tell them to come to my hut at once.'

The boy grinned, saluted and ran out again. Bride was smiling herself. Taking her advice, the smiths had dug up their buried metal hoard. Since discovering their fatal weakness for gambling, she had trebled her supply of metal and was well prepared for Master Goar's reappearance.

Whistling softly to herself, she washed her lunch pots, tidied her bed-space, looked over more plates and cups. She knew she would have time. Goar would have to pass the chief smith's house first and speak to him. Her companions arrived and Bride greeted them with kisses.

'Sit beside me on my couch. You on my left, you on my right. You, my dear, behind.' Bride arranged them to her liking, saw them supplied with bread and cheese and ale. She heard the horse outside and lifted her own beaker. 'A toast!'

A tall shadow fell across her door, followed by the man. 'Greetings, Lady. I bring word from the King. His messenger's horse went lame at our house, so I've come in his place.'

Interrupted in her feast, Bride lowered her cup. Curse the boy, she thought, ignoring the ear-nibbling of one lover. He'd been careless in his report. Yet it wasn't surprising.

'Please sit down.' To humble Goar, no bench had been ready. The young man squatted on the floor. 'Let me offer you refreshment,' said Bride.

For this silver-haired royal, she went through the forms of courtesy. The time came for Fearn's message. It contained both a question and a request, and parts were meant not only for Bride but for all the smiths. Bride thought carefully.

'For my answer, it's yes. But you must speak to the chief and his men, before you ride to the King.'

The messenger bowed his curly head, rising to leave.

'You're not Goar. Are you his brother?'

The perfect mouth smiled. 'I'm Gygest, his twin.' Gygest met her eyes. 'Few can tell us apart.'

'Your manners are better.' Bride walked Gygest to the door.

Chapter 37

Watching the ground race beneath Gorri, the sound of his pounding hooves booming like a metal torrent, Sarmatia soon spotted the tracks. Following them, it was only moments before she saw Fearn riding ahead. Even at a canter, Gorri could outpace a pony. Flat out, the chestnut ate up the distance between them. Fearn did not need to pull up or look back, as several more strides brought Sarmatia level with him.

'Leave your pony, Fearn, and come up with me!' You can tell me where Gorri must go.'

To her relief, Fearn did not waste time arguing. Only when he was sitting behind her on Gorri did the young king tap her lightly on the thigh with his axe. 'You shouldn't be here.'

'Scold me later. First, let's save your cows.'

'Ride for the forest then,' said Fearn, 'and don't leave Gorri's back.' His arms tightened around her. Mischievous, he added, 'Or after this is finished I'll beat you.'

'Like a slave?' answered Sarmatia promptly. 'But you told me Atterians have no slaves.'

Her jibe had found its target. They rode in silence to the edge of the forest. Fearn directed her to a wooden track way and they pounded along it, ducking under the hanging branches. Water spurted into their faces as Gorri forded a stream. From deeper within the wood they heard a frenzied lowing.

'They've caught one!' Fearn's curse was bitten off in a sharp intake of breath and he wrapped his arms even tighter round Sarmatia, clinging on as Gorri stretched his stride and raced off the track through the trees. Used to Gorri's speed, Sarmatia was only worried that the stallion might injure himself, though even she instinctively shut her eyes for an instant when a vast holly tree blocked their way. She gasped as spurs of holly bit into their legs and then Gorri streaked through a narrow gap between evergreen and oaks and the way was open before them.

In that clearing they found the cattle raiders, three shaggy-haired men riding ponies and a fourth on foot, beating the scrub to keep a mooing white cow and calf from charging back into the forest. The fourth saw them first and shouted, pointing with his stave, and the three on horseback wheeled round. Responding to Sarmatia, Gorri shortened his gait and pranced skittishly forward. Fearn slid from his back.

'Stay on Gorri. The raiders won't touch you,' he said urgently. 'The rule of this game is single combat.' Fearn's green eyes caught the glint of bronze on Sarmatia's finger and he laughed, dragging her half from the horse, putting a kiss on her mouth.

'Obey me in this too, eh, Sarmatia?' He smacked Gorri's rump. The stallion kicked into the trees and, by the time Sarmatia had calmed him, Fearn had already run into the middle of the clearing.

News traveled fast in these northern kingdoms, to judge from the opening remark. 'Tired of your marriage?' shouted the man with the stave.

Fearn did not answer, but threw his axe to pin both stave and raider to a tree. The three on horseback put themselves between Fearn and the cow and calf, fingering the hilts of their long swords, but they didn't rush Fearn, as Sarmatia feared they would. Instead, Fearn strode calmly up to the raider fastened to the tree. 'How's your lad?'

Sarmatia recalled how Fearn had told her that he'd once been a guest in the Cattle Men's kingdom.

'Thriving.'

Fearn nodded. He yanked his axe from the man's stave and cloak. 'That's you out, Narr.'

To Sarmatia's relief, Narr nodded and sat down, one less at least.

In casually dismissing the cattle raid, Anoi had only repeated the little Fearn had told the royal family after dragging himself back from the Cattle Men's country. Fearing that Laerimmer would suggest using the war band against his fellow kings, Fearn had played down certain aspects of their 'invasion'. Yet, as promised, they came ready to do battle.

Sarmatia saw it all. One after another, Fearn challenged the stocky, dun-haired raiders to single combat and each man swung down from his pony and came at the Atterian king. It was conflict without blood, for they used only the blunt edge of their swords and Fearn the back of the sarsen axe head, stunning and bruising but not killing. Sarmatia relaxed on Gorri's back and admired her mate's neat footwork. Bride would have enjoyed this, she thought. She hoped Bride was happy in the settlement of the smiths.

Two had been sent by Fearn to sit beside Narr when the third raider tried to best him. Unlike the others, this one was a talker. 'Will your wife fight too?' he asked, swinging his sword. 'Shall we take the calf, since we blew our horn and gave you warning?' When he said, 'Is she as pretty out of those clothes as in them?' Fearn tripped the raider with the head of the axe and the man sprawled full length on the grass. Fearn planted his boot across the fellow's neck.

'Take the calf, Ivak, if the cow will let you, and be off.' Fearn spoke in that same joking yet serious voice he'd used to Sarmatia, so that the raider was uncertain what he intended and flinched. Fearn drew the back of his axe along the raider's spine then let him up. 'Next time, I'll look at your cows.'

'They'll take no more than the calf?' Sarmatia asked, as Fearn mounted behind her.

'No more: or they'd have broken their word and could lose their kingship.' Fearn waved at the raiders, who waved back. 'They're brothers and share their royal herd between them.'

'Only kings have cattle here?' asked Sarmatia, watching as the four kings now attempted to separate calf from mother without being impaled on the cow's horns. The cow butted one raider, who yelped. Behind her, Sarmatia sensed Fearn grinning.

'They'll have a tussle on their hands. That mother never lets go. She's hard enough just to milk.' He chuckled a moment. 'Yes, only kings keep cattle, as a mark of standing. That's why we raid each other's herds. It's a game, but it's also serious.'

And that's why butter is so special, thought Sarmatia, recalling what Bride had told her about that rare northern delicacy. 'You care for them yourself?'

'Yes, though there's little care needed, except when they calve. Most of the year they roam freely in the forest. Wolves take some, but not many, only the weak—'

Fearn broke off, laughing. Curses filled the clearing as the white cow shoved one of the raider-kings into brambles and sent another climbing desperately up a tree. The cow broke across the clearing, long tail whipping, her black ears and nose working as she disappeared into the forest, her calf trotting mildly beside her. Sarmatia laughed herself. Despite their bravado, the Cattle Men had gained nothing.

As though embarrassed, the four kings now vanished quietly into the forest, heading east to their own lands. Only she and Fearn remained at the edge of the clearing.

Fearn glanced at the sky. 'We should go back. It'll be dark soon.' He touched her cheek gently with his free hand. 'Thank you. Without your help, I'd not have reached here in time, and they'd have taken calf and mother.'

Sarmatia twisted round to face him. 'So no beating?' she teased, watching a satisfying blush steal across Fearn's forehead. Reflected in his eyes, she saw a gleam like gold, possibly the setting sun.

'It's allowed by custom,' he teased back, and Sarmatia hit him. Her fist smacked into his cheek, almost knocking him off Gorri, and the horse shied, bucking its back legs. Gorri cantered a long way into the trees, with Sarmatia hanging on his mane and Fearn's hands gripped like fetters round her middle. Even before the horse stopped and began browsing the few green shoots of a hawthorn bush, Fearn had jumped down and pitched Sarmatia into the bracken. Ignoring her half-whispered explanations, he pulled her onto her stomach and crushed her right arm to the ground with his knee.

But he did not hit her. Sarmatia stopped struggling when his weight shifted off her and his head came down by her face. 'You're bleeding.'

Sarmatia felt at the oozing graze on her temple. 'Someone shot at you. I saw the sun catch on the arrowhead. That's why I struck at you.'

Fearn groaned at that and would have gathered her into his arms, but Sarmatia stopped him. 'We need to go on, into cover.'

They crawled through a tunnel of undergrowth, stopping only when they lost sight of Gorri. Sarmatia was unhappy at leaving the horse then reasoned that Fearn's attacker had not aimed at Gorri before, even though the stallion would have been a far easier target than the man. Reassured a little by that thought, she allowed Fearn to make a nest of bracken round them and then tend her wound, wiping the blood from her eye and forehead.

'It's not deep. A honey dressing will see that it heals cleanly.' Fearn took her hands in his. 'You saved my life.' He spoke in a quiet, wondering way that pleased Sarmatia more than any thanks.

'I still owe you one life,' she said laughing, suddenly shivering. 'Was it the raiders, do you think?'

'No, they bring only swords.' Fearn embraced her. 'We must wait till dusk then move. No archer can bend his bow at night.'

If the raiders had not shot at Fearn, then who had? thought Sarmatia, but Fearn said nothing more, despite her questions. Weary with shock and her wound, Sarmatia allowed herself to drift into sleep, safe in Fearn's arms in their bed of bracken.

* * * *

She woke in the clammy chill of dusk. Fearn had found Gorri and they rode back to his house. Riding into the farmstead, Sarmatia saw with relief that Fearn's horse had also returned.

After bedding down the horses, Sarmatia was first into the house. She found an old woman waiting just inside the door, shivering in a blanket. The old woman held out her thin arms.

'Come in quickly, child, and tidy yourself.' She cast a frightened glance at the center of the hut, dark except for the fire and fire-glow reflected in the faces of the company. 'One of the king's family has come to take a look at you.'

The family were so quiet that Sarmatia could hear the rustle of mice as they scavenged scraps from the straw. She finished cleaning the mud from her shoes, her mouth dry with excitement. 'Who?'

'Laerimmer, our Kingmaker.' The old woman put her hands up to her mouth. 'Where's Fearn? I wish he'd hurry!'

'Don't fear, Gei, I'm back.' Fearn replaced the hurdle door and clasped the old woman gently in his arms. 'What's wrong?'

'It's the Kingmaker,' Gei whimpered. Though in shadow, Sarmatia saw Fearn frown. He looked at her and she jerked her head at the center of the hut. 'I'll look after Gei. Go and greet your kinsman.' Sarmatia swept the cloak from her back, to wrap round Gei and lead her to the fire.

'It's you Laerimmer's come to see,' replied Fearn, and now Sarmatia stared at him, wondering at his grim face. She finished wrapping Gei in the cloak and coaxed the old woman forward.

Let's see this Kingmaker, she thought, as a figure rose from the prime place by the fire, standing to greet her.

Chapter 38

After Gygest had left, Bride set to pleasing her bachelors. They had parted from her in smug humor, oblivious to the knowing looks that greeted their disheveled state. Bride had chosen to be discreet, keeping within her hut to wash her clothes and hair.

Several hours later, waiting for her tunic to dry, Bride checked her new work, particularly the weapons. For herself, she'd made a long dagger, a rapier, and a round shield with five bronze mountings. She stroked the leather of the shield. It needed a further polish. Spreading a fur on the floor, Bride sat naked by her fire and, with cloth and rendered fat, set to work.

She was hard at it and did not hear the horse, or hear or see its rider sweep back the hanging to the door and dip under the crossbeam. She saw him first through the veil of her loosened hair and gasped, dragging the shield up from her thighs to cover her lap. Why had he strutted in now, bow and quiver hung across his back, game-bag full, bronze on his arms and bright gold in his ear? She had no face with which to meet him and her sword was out of reach.

Bride lifted her head. She had planned that Goar should see her as a woman desired; a woman lacking nothing. Instead, she was alone, naked, working. There was nothing about her body, her discolored features, that would excite an arrogant princeling.

Bride was wrong. By the light of her fire and the last gleams of dusk, Goar saw a woman in full flowering, luxurious and strong, every way his equal. Her pink-nippled, heavy breasts were as white and unblemished as a yearling lamb. Hidden only partly by the shield, glistening and streaked by streams of rendered fat, the sight of her thighs made his groin ache. Beside her, the Atterian girls were stiff and skinny. Here was the embodiment of plenty.

Confused, Goar flipped the door-hanging down behind him and sought her face. At their first meeting, he had noted her birthmark. Now he saw her eyes, the color of twilight.

'Goar, I presume: your twin was more courteous.' Bride broke their silence. 'Well, you can sit if you want, but fetch your own beer.' She carried on polishing her shield.

Another had dismissed him so, by lowering her blue eyes. Angry, Goar turned his temper on the one he blamed for everything these days. 'I thought I saw Fearn's harlot in the forest, late this afternoon, but it was only one of our local kind, serving another client.' He shrugged, before curiosity overcame him. 'What did Gygest have to do with you?'

'He came as a herald.' Bride said no more, for Gygest's message had concerned Sarmatia. Silently, she resumed her task.

Goar was disconcerted by the rush of pressure in his loins when Bride bent forward to polish the base of her shield. 'She's not royal,' he muttered, making that excuse stand for his own envy. He was royal, yet not king.

'If by she, you mean Sarmatia, then she's more famous and honored than you. As a Bull Rider, Sarmatia was without equal.'

'Oh, that!' Goar felt easier, having often heard Laerimmer making light of the mysterious ritual on those rare occasions when Fearn attempted to speak of it. 'Nothing of real power.'

'She's very beautiful.'

Goar rose to the bait. 'I've heard she's lumbering.'

'I dare say, to a midget.' Bride was surprised, after that mild remark, when Goar colored up. Fingers scratched at the door-hanging and the chief smith entered her hut. 'Gods, is my house a crossroads?' exclaimed Bride.

The chief made his excuses while he stretched his eyes over her body. He spoke, too. 'The King's messenger,- the real one this time, has returned with terms we find favorable. Will you hear them?'

'Might I have a moment to collect myself?'

The chief lifted the door-hanging to withdraw. He and the messenger collided in the doorway. Bride, who had hoped that Goar would take the hint and leave, now had to watch him burst into laughter. 'Come in!' she snapped. 'What's one more? Let the whole tribe in, why not? You, Aren,' she recognized the youth from the war band, 'speak!'

Aren obeyed, rushing through Fearn's latest message and blurting out the very thing which Bride had hoped to keep from the royal family. 'Fearn says it's for his wife, and he'll be very pleased if you can honor it.'

Goar roared with laughter. He jumped to his feet, twanging his bow-string as though it were a lyre's. 'Listen to the tale of peerless Sarmatia, queen of bull-crap!'

Ignoring Aren and smith, Bride dropped the shield and rose. 'Enough! Say more and it's battle between us!'

'It's that already, Lady.' Their eyes were level, but Goar allowed his eyes the luxury of sweeping Bride up and down. 'It's no use your hoping. I swear you'll never get me into your bed.' Goar brushed her scarlet cheek with his fingers. 'What a pity.' He dismissed himself from her presence.

Not caring that she was naked, Bride strode after him as Goar drifted through the deepening twilight to his horse. 'When I see you again, you're dead!' she yelled at his retreating back. *Or in my arms,* the thought came, and lingered.

Chapter 39

Sarmatia was glad she was prepared for her meeting with the Kingmaker. The round face, black hair and flickering eyes fitted her memories of the snake priestess of her childhood. She had left Pergia in Tartessus. It was the past that had returned.

'Pick up a torch, Fearn. Let me see the beauty that has cost the lives of two of our young men.'

By speaking, the mask revealed itself as a man. Beside Sarmatia, Gei was trembling, Fearn cold and taut. Someone moved. A torch illuminated her face. Sarmatia did not lower her eyes.

'Pretty enough,' said the Kingmaker.

Faced with the mask of Pergia, Sarmatia felt his mockery of her dark skin and man's clothes. The torch wavered between them. The family remained silent.

'Give me your hand. I might tell you your fortune.'

Sarmatia did not trust the mask. 'I make my own fortune.'

'You would be queen? Here we test our queens.'

'I'm not afraid.'

'Sarmatia will not take the test. I'll not lose her again, because of you.'

'The choice isn't mine or yours, Fearn, but the gods'.'

'She's my wife, Laerimmer. She will not take the test.'

Fearn spoke from love, for her protection, so Sarmatia was silent, though determined to find out more when they were alone.

She had a long wait, through the evening meal and bedding down of Laerimmer, who as a guest had a bed made up for him by the fire. The moon was on its descent when she and Fearn hung a bearskin between the posts of the smallest alcove and wormed into the jumble of furs and cloaks Sarmatia had heaped together as a bed. Cold and need drew them close and it was only later, in the warm glow of contentment, that Sarmatia remembered to ask. Her new husband was sleepy and disliked being roused but her persistence paid off when Fearn sighed and admitted he was fully awake. The thing he'd feared had come and he must face it.

'Please tell me, then. What is this test?'

Fearn leaned up on an elbow, rubbing his eyes. 'That's not so easy to say, Sarmatia. The test is different for each person who undergoes it. For me, it was a test of patience.' He stared at the smoke-filled roof. 'Had I failed, my head would have been shattered by an axe, my blood kept to scatter over the sheep to increase their fertility.' His eyes slipped from the roof to her face. 'Do you see why I couldn't bear you to take the test?'

His features told Sarmatia what he shrank from saying; that as king it would be his hand that would send her into the dark if she failed. At nineteen, Sarmatia did not appreciate what this knowledge meant to her husband. She saw it as an unlikely risk. 'You took the test and lived. Am I less?'

Fearn laid a hand over hers. 'Don't joke, Sarmatia. Please.'

His gentleness was worse than if he had been brisk. Sarmatia felt her face burn up. Rolling away from Fearn onto her side, she wondered again who had fired the arrow at him. Speaking to the wall, she asked if he had any ideas.

Fearn had none. It seemed he had no one he called enemy. To probe more would only be unkind, Sarmatia thought, so instead she changed the subject, asking why the royal family, Fearn's mother-kin, were so set against their marriage.

Relieved at Sarmatia not pursuing one mystery, Fearn ran a finger up her spine—they were naked in bed—and brushed her shoulder with his beard. 'They're an old family, set in their ways. They dislike the change you bring with you.' Mellowed by their earlier lovemaking, Fearn curled up against her.

Sarmatia fought off the lethargy of contentment she knew in his embrace: with Laerimmer here, she had to know everything she could about this royal family. 'Did they have a marriage in mind for you?'

Fearn's neck drew back from her neck. 'There was a girl, but they couldn't make me marry her.'

Sarmatia turned in his arms to face him. 'How did they make you king?' Fearn had never really explained.

In the dim light she saw her husband rub at his beard. 'That was none of my choosing.'

'I know.'

At Sarmatia's answer, Fearn relaxed against her. 'You wish to know the whole tale? As you like. Warm your feet on mine.'

Settling on his back, Fearn drew her closer. 'When I returned from Krete, I started training Jart, the youth who'd take my place as the main healer. My heart was full of plans for the future and our lives together.' He stroked her cheek with his thumb, remembering. 'Then, five seasons after I left you, in midwinter, there was a fire at the house of my mother's family. King Waroch died. My people were left without a ruler, and they looked about for scapegoat or savior.'

Even after a full year, there was an echo of bitter sadness.

'Our Kingmaker, Laerimmer, marked a pebble for each of my mother's kin and stirred them up in a crock until stones were flung from it. One of the pebbles was mine.

'When Laerimmer held it up, I thought of you on Krete and told the royal family I had no wish to rule. They mocked me, Sarmatia, called me bewitched by a southern peasant girl. Laerimmer even said it was the test I feared, that he would go before the people and proclaim me coward.'

Fearn's voice had not changed, but the downy hair on his arms pricked up as though charged and when he moved Sarmatia felt a shock jolt down her back. It was too dark for her to see his face easily, yet for the second time that night she sensed an iron-willed restraint. After a moment, Fearn continued.

'I thought that even if I fled the kingdom and came to Krete this fate would follow at my heels. Neither you nor I would ever be sure that I'd returned to you in good faith. That it wasn't fear that had driven me south, into your arms.'

Sarmatia stroked his hair. 'I should have known.'

Fearn shook his head. 'So you say now, but think how the tale would have sounded to you or to your brother Tazaros on Krete. Perhaps at first you would have believed, but little by little, with each quarrel between us, doubt would have grown.

'So I stayed, my heart bitter. Death did not find me and I learned another had survived and we were to fight for the kingdom. I wondered if I should let him cut me down, that you might dream of this in Krete.'

'I'm glad you didn't let him murder you!' Reflecting on this and on her homeland, Sarmatia added, 'Your Laerimmer is the twin of the snake priestess. Did you know Pergia?'

'Yes, I knew her, although I can't see her in Laerimmer.' Fearn returned to his own memories. 'It took a battle wound to wake me, make me realize that the world was good and there were ways we might be joined in it, but only if I stayed alive.'

A flicker of laughter in his face then made Sarmatia smile. 'So you won then wrote me the letter.'

'Ah, my letter. I spoke with a trader's wife and found she'd traveled safely even to Krete. Ell knew the Palace of Phaistos. I gave her a gold armlet before she left me.' Suddenly, Fearn returned to the present. 'You didn't travel with Loge and Ell, did you?'

'Loge died in Tartessus. I had the letter through other hands.' Sarmatia laughed softly. '"If you would send a message or a thing of yours to keep safe, entrust yourself to him."' She repeated part of his letter. 'I knew from that you wanted me here.'

Fearn's smile filtered through the semi-darkness. 'I prayed those words would tempt you to come. I knew even as I wrote them that I should let you go, but I had to leave hope, a spark for myself.'

As though he'd admitted something shameful, Fearn turned quickly away. After a moment he seemed to be genuinely settling for sleep. Sarmatia tucked the furs about him and lay back. The picture of the royal family that was forming in her mind was not pleasant. She understood now Fearn's reluctance to speak of them. Another reason, quite apart from his looks, for her to dislike Laerimmer. He was the one who'd called her man a coward. Yet had he lost anything, or anyone, in the fire or its aftermath?

'Tell me this last thing,' she begged Fearn. 'Who was the man you killed for the kingship?'

'It was Tanek, the half-brother of Anoi.' Fearn buried his face in the furs away from her.

* * * *

Fearn woke Sarmatia before dawn to smear honey on the wound on her forehead. It was healing well, he said. Any other thoughts he had concerning the incident Fearn kept to himself. Indeed, it seemed far from his mind.

'Forgive me for leaving you, one day after you've come to my house,' he mumbled, mouth full of a hastily devoured breakfast. 'I must check my trees in this mild spell of weather. You'll be able to make friends with the women. I've told them to be sure you're not lonely. Can you ask Orm's wife to send a child to the hazel wood at midday, with food?'

Sarmatia knelt up on their bed, catching her hair against the wattle walls of the alcove. Fearn had drawn back the bearskin separating their space from the rest of the hut. Over his shoulder, she could see men moving about and one man, an orange shadow in the lowering fire, waved in their direction. For her to ask to go with Fearn might show him up before these men, Sarmatia realized, with a sinking heart.

'I must go.' Fearn's kiss was meant for her forehead but brushed only the top of one curl. 'The men are waiting. Please remember the midday food, Sarmatia, eh? Enough for four.'

'I'll bring it myself. Fearn? You'll be careful, won't you? Watch out—'

'For archers? Yes, I know.'

'Fearn?'

'Please, Sarmatia, I have to go.'

'Is it—is it still raining?'

Fearn answered that it was, wished her a glad day, and left, leaving Sarmatia lost. Fearn knew what he was doing, collecting the axes and tools from the store, walking with the other men to the hazel woods. She had no work. She did not know her place within the family.

Shivering, Sarmatia lay back on the bed and threw Fearn's scarlet cloak over her shoulders and head. Pressing her fingers into the sheepskins, she prayed: 'Give me a place within this house of strangers. Let me belong here.' It was the first time she had asked to be part of any human settlement.

She dressed quickly in the gray dawn. Anoi and the other women had bare feet within the hut so she did likewise. Head high—no one must know she was nervous—Sarmatia stepped out of the alcove. The hangings had not been lifted down from the other sleeping chambers. Women were dressing themselves and their children. Their voices paused long enough for Sarmatia to know she had been heard.

Alone by the fire, Laerimmer rolled onto his back, opening his black eyes. 'You're early. Here in winter people keep warm in bed. We don't waste fuel.'

'I'm not cold.'

Laerimmer rested his hands on his chest, looking like a man laid out for burial. 'Tell me about yourself. Are you royal?'

'No.'

Laerimmer turned his head. 'Is that why you've no dowry?'

Sarmatia briefly wished him dead, but her guilt in the death of Kerewos—the likeness of Laerimmer to Pergia reminded her—lay upon her tongue. She did not speak of the spoils that Fearn and his war band had won in Carvin's kingdom. She was aware of the knot of women gathering with water pitchers. If Laerimmer wanted them to hear him, they should hear her, too.

'A dowry isn't always paid in gold,' she said.

'No, you may have other gifts. Fearn boasts that you've a marvelous way with wild animals. Or is he mistaken?'

'Can the King be wrong?'

Laerimmer rolled onto his side, knelt then was on his feet by her. 'And how do you master these forest beasts? Why do they approach you? Do you bend their wills to yours by thought?'

Sarmatia was revolted at the idea. If animals found her, they did so as friends. Her close understanding with Gorri, and before him with the bulls of the Rite of Passage, was a sacred trust, not to be exposed to the mockery of this fat Kingmaker. 'I don't master other living things,' she answered, bluntly. 'They're my equals.'

Laerimmer bent his face into the fire-glow so that Sarmatia could see the crown of his head. 'If you won't or can't talk, can you at least prove Fearn's ridiculous claims? Can you take these from me?'

Even in that poor light it was plain that his hair was riddled with lice. Parts of his scalp seemed to move with their numbers. Sarmatia willed herself to touch his greasy hair, disgusted not by the lice but by the conceit of this man who was so proud that he did not care. She released the sticky lock of hair. She didn't want to invoke her creature-calling for such a circumstance. 'I could rid you of them. Clean water would do just as well.'

An odd look of recognition slid across Laerimmer's face. He threw the hood of his cloak over his head. 'The creatures can bite, they do me no harm.

Away!' He clapped his hands and the knot of gawping women drifted off.

The draperies of the final alcove parted and Anoi came into the living quarters. She had one arm round Gei, supporting her as they walked carefully to the fire.

Now that Sarmatia knew that Tanek had been Anoi's half-brother, she was shyer of the girl. Putting off a meeting with her, Sarmatia decided to join the other women. Laerimmer caught her back.

'What a quick thing you are. I've not finished half my questions. How many living children did your mother bear?'

Sarmatia stared down at the hand round her arm, but she didn't want to throw Laerimmer off with Anoi and Gei watching. She answered without looking at him. 'My mother had three children.'

'Well, what else? How many were sons?'

'Two. One died in infancy.'

'Why was that? Did your mother leave him out in the cold? We've heard of your southern custom of baby killing.'

The words were evil, and Sarmatia furious. 'Believe what you will!' Whatever else she said, Laerimmer was sure to twist it. Besides, why should she justify herself to him? More words would suggest she was having to apologize for her own mother.

At her answer, Sarmatia heard Anoi, who had been building up the fire, catch in her breath. Her anger turned against the blonde girl, too. On Krete we don't leave our mothers to watch by the threshold at night, she thought, and then was ashamed, for Anoi raised her head and smiled at her.

'If your people do expose your children,' said Laerimmer, 'no doubt those who are crippled or diseased are discarded at once. By that fair reckoning, Fearn's uncle Orm wouldn't have survived. Maewe would never have married him, nor suckled Ormson. Does that thought please you, Sarmatia?'

Sarmatia started at her name. Careless of appearances, she whipped her arm free of Laerimmer and stalked out of the house.

* * * *

His words twisted in her thoughts through the morning and were still in her mind when Sarmatia set off before midday with a basket of food for

Fearn and his men.

The hazel wood was south of the house. Its man-made banks, dug out to protect the growing trees from grazing wild cattle or deer, could be seen from the settlement, so she needed no guide. Once inside the grass bank, she found Ormson and his two eldest sons at the wood edge, trimming hazel. When Ormson saw Sarmatia he buried his axe into a fresh stump and pointed. 'Fearn's over there, beyond that ash. You can leave the food with me.'

Guided by the rhythmic thud of a single axe, Sarmatia pressed on through the wood. Fearn she found at a small clearing. She had a good view before a carelessly snapped twig made him twist round. Despite the rain, he was stripped to the waist. The flesh across his back and shoulder blades was red. Water spat and bounced from the stone head of the axe as he raised it—

Then suddenly spun about, axe at the ready for enemies.

Sarmatia ran to him as he flicked a twig from his beard.

'Is this not the best?' he asked her, patting the tree.

Sarmatia nodded, glad to see him glad.

'This is good wood for a cradle,' he went on, 'but what now, Sarmatia? All at once, you seem as glum as the rain.'

He had playfully cupped her breast, causing a brief light-headed burst of lust in her, but she answered clearly.

'I do not mind the rain, but I was thinking then of Laerimmer.' She thought it best Fearn should know, in case he heard a distorted version from someone else.

Fearn withdrew his hand. 'What's he been saying?'

They were close to the wood-edge by now, and tow-headed Ormson was watching, mouth open as he chewed. Sarmatia turned her back to the stocky Atterian and mouthed, 'Ormson's curious.'

Fearn sighed and walked on. 'Tell me tonight, Sarmatia.' Then in an undertone, 'If Laerimmer worries her, I'll test the thickness of his neck.' He swung the stone axe head up in an arc, his hands lingering on the blade.

Chapter 40

In bed, it was Fearn who brought up Laerimmer. When Sarmatia told him the tale though, he surprised her by his answer.

'Laerimmer has forgotten that you're not Atterian. I'll talk to him, and if he speaks in this way to you again, then you must tell me. But it's a hard thing for us to understand,' he added thoughtfully. 'How you races of the south can leave your children to the wilderness.'

In the warmth of his arms Sarmatia felt a stab of cold between her breasts, as though she had been spat on. 'So you think his words to me don't matter?'

Fearn laughed at her softly. 'What should I say to you? How can I explain? Laerimmer is a guest in my house. Should I drag him now from his bed?' He ran a fingertip along her flanks. 'Here it's the custom for the Kingmaker to pry to the marrow, to question all our actions and beliefs. As I said, I'll speak to him. Then, if he plagues you again, I'll certainly trim his tongue.'

'I don't need your help for that.' Sarmatia stopped Fearn's finger with her hand. 'But do you think he's right?'

A breathing silence. 'In some ways perhaps, I think Laerimmer is right,' Fearn began fair-mindedly, but now Sarmatia would not listen. She was instantly angry with her husband for taking any of the Kingmaker's part.

'Kretans never desert their children!' she hissed. 'In famine years, mothers have starved themselves to put bread into their babies' mouths. Yet for a new-born that is sickly, that will know pain all its life, then an early death is the kindest thing.'

Fearn stiffened against her. 'I remember your kindness in the Mushroom Wood, when you butchered that yearling doe. Or was that your hallowed Kretan rite put into practice?'

Sarmatia ripped off the bed furs and began to tug on her clothes without any clear idea of what she was doing. Laerimmer had angered her, but Fearn's accusations hurt and she wanted to escape. She thrust off his hands, blundering into the middle of the house.

Laerimmer was awake of course, sitting comfortably beside the low fire, hands clasped round his knees. He gave a loose-lipped grin as Sarmatia stalked from the hut a second time.

She had planned to spend the rest of the night with Gorri, but Fearn came naked out of the house and plucked her from the newly-repaired animal pen. 'You want to make me a fool before my people?' He gave Sarmatia a shake as he carried her back indoors. He slept quickly, sprawled over her, but Sarmatia was awake until the early hours.

Towards day-break, Fearn stirred and rolled off her. He opened his eyes and looked into her face. 'Good day.' He smiled.

Sarmatia's heart jumped but she kept still. She wanted Fearn to confess that he was sorry, not shuffle off their quarrel as though it was forgotten. She decided to attack. 'It's wrong to keep Gorri penned.'

'Oh?' Fearn had not expected her to start again. He lay on his stomach, chin resting on his fists. 'We can't let the ponies roam freely in winter.' He yawned and reached for her. 'Too many hungry wolf packs at night.'

'Then let the horses roam in the day and pen them at night,' argued Sarmatia. She felt Fearn's body grow hot.

'We don't have the men to spare for such a task,' he flashed back.

Sarmatia wanted to shake him, to tip him out of bed. Then, realizing she must do the task herself, she began to smile. 'Very well.'

Putting that from her for the moment, Sarmatia untied the drawstring of her tunic. She thought of Fearn chopping wood, his feet braced between the tree roots, his strong body moving with the motion of the axe, and held out her arms.

They parted friends and Sarmatia, though she knew it was unwise, could not resist making a scene of their affection. She kissed Fearn and said goodbye to him by the door of the house, in clear view of the fire, and laughed when Ormson grumbled about the late start into the woods that day. She watched Fearn walk through the yard, agile and light on his feet for all that he was the tallest of the men, and let some of her smile remain for Laerimmer, who called out.

'Pity you didn't kiss like that last night. The rest of us could have slept in peace, then, and this morning I wouldn't have had an earful of scolding about you from Fearn, before I was half awake.'

'You seem fresh enough now,' Sarmatia called back. She was easier dealing with Laerimmer when she could not see his face. There was a pause, as if the man had to bite back a chuckle.

'You look like a wench that's planning more mischief. Be careful, then, of Fearn.'

'More likely the other way about.' From the gasps that issued from the hidden alcoves, Sarmatia realized that her jesting answer was amiss.

Laerimmer didn't let the opportunity slip. 'Whatever happens in the south, here we expect modesty from our womenfolk.'

Sarmatia shrugged, still amused. 'Such things are between husband and wife.'

For a plump man, Laerimmer was quick. He had crossed from the fire to her side in an instant. 'You're not going to help prepare the acorn-bread?' he asked, seeing her tying on her shoes to go outside.

'I did that yesterday.' Sarmatia wanted to look at the grazing for Gorri and the other ponies.

'The women will expect you to work with them. It'll cause bad feeling if you don't.' Laerimmer had sloughed off his carping like an old skin. Sarmatia closed her eyes against this twin of Pergia, and slowly nodded her head.

* * * *

She found Laerimmer's advice timely, for that day there was to be a feast, with Fearn's entire family coming together under one roof. There were many things to do, and Sarmatia guessed that had she left the women, it would have caused trouble.

Late in the afternoon there came a shout from the children: 'Here they are!' The women echoed the cry, darting about the food-laden trestle.

Sarmatia dragged her white cloak about her shoulders. Fearn, who had returned early from the woods with his men, was calling orders. She stood alone at the back of the house, close to the wooden dresser.

A man entered the house. Sarmatia stiffened, but it was Orm, limping quickly to the head of the table. Behind him, sweeping into the hut with the assurance of royalty, were Fearn's second family. The men stacked bows and spears by the door, nodded to Orm and sat on the bench at one side of the table. Fearn and the other men of his father's family then re-entered the house, the men going to the table, while Fearn approached Sarmatia.

'Are you well?' He put his arms about her. 'You look like a ghost!'

In his embrace, Sarmatia felt her anxiety flow away. 'I'm hungry, that's all.' She smiled to reassure him.

'Then come, eat.' Fearn tried to draw her out of the corner, to seat her beside him at the second head of the table, but Sarmatia resisted.

'No, Fearn. I should wait at table with the other wives.' She had learned this was the custom of feasts. The women of the house would wait on the men and guests, and eat only when these had finished.

Fearn bent his head closer, trying to read her face. 'I know you're shy, my Sarmatia, but there's nothing to fear. You needn't talk if you don't want to. Come, eat and be merry! This is also our wedding feast.'

Still Sarmatia hung back, aware that the women of the royal family had filled the last spaces on the benches and that the whole group was waiting for Fearn. 'I'm your wife. I should be like the other wives. Otherwise, they'll feel slighted.'

'You think so? Well, if you're sure that's what you want.' Fearn remained standing, his back to his family and guests, his thoughtful green eyes fixed on her. Laerimmer gave a dry cough. It was time for the feast to begin. Sarmatia thought of a way to reassure her sometimes overprotective husband.

'Serving at table is not strange to me. I'll serve you, as I once served my brother.'

That touched Fearn, as she guessed it would. He kissed her hard then straightened. 'As you wish, Bull Head!' Though obviously still surprised and puzzled, he let her join the women and at last took his seat.

The feast began. Sarmatia was pleased to wait upon it. Serving gave her the chance to observe the royal family without being noticed herself. The group had walked from their homestead and they fell on the food. There was no talk. Dainty feeding, Sarmatia noted, but no manners, no thanks as she refilled plates with hot boiled meat, turnip, parsnip and silverweed roots. Except once. A girl in a leather cloak with a hood covering her hair lifted her cup and, as Sarmatia filled it, she turned and thanked her.

Astonished, Sarmatia drew back, but there was no doubt that it was Anoi whose cup she had replenished. The girl wore a golden collar shaped like a crescent moon. Her mother Gei was behind her in the shadows.

Sarmatia jumped as Ormson's wife nudged her. 'There's our Anoi, looking like a princess among them. Her father was of the blood, so she can wear the royal token by right.'

Sarmatia now realized why Gei wasn't also seated at the feast, wearing gold. She scanned the faces round the table. Five other people were wearing such collars. Fearn apparently did not possess one. Perhaps as king he didn't need it but Laerimmer had a burnished disc about his throat. The sign of royal blood. It flowed in Anoi's and Laerimmer's veins but not in Gei's.

Looking under her eyelids, Sarmatia studied the five. Two were twins, men of similar age to Fearn and as tall but more slender in build. They had silver-blond hair, narrow, brooding faces and green eyes. There was an older woman, dark and heavy as Laerimmer, possibly his sister. Beside her a slim girl with short curly hair and a pretty laugh. She dangled a baby on her lap and had a breast bared to suckle it. The child—Sarmatia stepped forward to be sure—also wore the golden token, in a tiny, exact copy of the mother's.

Six royal family, seven with Anoi, and breeding, not marriage, was what counted. Will these proud people think me less than them? thought Sarmatia, before she reminded herself that she was trying to be a good wife, nothing more. Now she saw Fearn looking for her, his broad features frowning with concern. She grinned, teasingly holding up a beer jug, and he saw the joke, chuckled and lifted his cup.

As she passed Laerimmer, the man put out a paw to stop her. 'Here is the bed-mate of our kinsman. Sarmatia, will you give me beer also?' he asked, so that she was obliged to face him and the guests.

The youth opposite Laerimmer—a sinewy, clean-shaven boy with stained hands and the pouch and charms of a healer slung over one shoulder—gave Sarmatia a frank yet friendly stare. The royal kin reacted differently.

Goar ignored her. He would have liked to make a more pointed snub, and had bragged to Bride of some direct threat, but now he hesitated. Faced with the certainty of Fearn's anger, he was already wary, yet there were ways of standing up to a king and coming off best. Fearn had to hold his temper on a taut rein tonight, sitting at his own feast. Goar comforted himself that he would have smacked the wench's rump and made a joke, had it just been a case of riding out Fearn's temper.

Only there was more to the southerner than a pleasing form. It was true that in this alone, although dark to Goar's eyes, she was astonishingly lovely: silken-skinned, slender, yet shapely. She moved with a fluid grace that outstripped all other women and hinted at nimble, taxing times in bed, yet she was no harlot. Goar tried to think of the insult he had applied so readily to Sarmatia in her absence and found it was impossible. The truth was he did not dare. Her eyes were dangerous: brilliant, amber and fixed.

Instead of open scorn, Goar made the most of what he would get away with. 'Gygest, will you lend me your spears? Tomorrow, I'm going to hunt.'

As Goar hoped, Gygest backed him by his answer. 'I'll come with you.' United in their mutual support, if not by a single intent, the twins began to talk of hunting.

But Goar had underestimated Sarmatia and Fearn. Sarmatia knew an insult when she saw one, and the King knew his family.

'Cousins, didn't you hear Laerimmer?' Fearn asked softly. 'Here is my wife. And let me remind you, all of you, that I don't need your approval for my choice, but by god you'll need mine, if any of you show her disrespect.' A broad arm wound possessively about Sarmatia. In Fearn's touch she felt the burn of his anger.

Realizing they had gone too far, the twins looked first at each other and then appealingly at Fearn. 'We meant no insult.' 'We meant nothing.' Their excuses stammered away as Fearn glared at them.

The woman with the baby looked up from her plate. 'A wife isn't a queen, Fearn, as well you know. The girl has brought no dowry or honor to our house.' She spoke as though Sarmatia was not present and pointed, as though Sarmatia could not see. 'Look, she's almost as black as charcoal!' She lifted a strand of her baby's flaxen hair and ran it through her fingers. 'The family shouldn't take her brats for the kingship.'

Sarmatia by now was simmering—she, who had been Mistress of the Rite of Passage, abused by these petty chieftains! Curses almost burst from her but she choked them down for Fearn's sake, checking the spirit animal that was on the prowl within her.

In any case, Fearn was speaking. 'Master Healer, get your woman's tongue within bounds. Chalda does you little favor in this house, although you're my guest.'

The woman Chalda paled and said no more, but now another woman rapped her knuckles on the table. 'You can't silence us forever, Fearn,' said Kere, in the same reasonable tones that her brother often used. 'And you must grant that she's strange to our eyes, and unattractive.'

As you are to me, old woman. The sound of it in Sarmatia's mind was a deep growl. Silently she moved towards Kere, gathering herself for a springing leap at those round, shocked eyes.

Another moment and Sarmatia would be gone, thought Fearn, and what would be found in her place? He wanted to rage at the family, seeing them wither down in their seats, but there was no time. He caught his young partner, feeling the spirit animal stretching within her, and pulled her firmly onto his lap. Grabbing the beer jug that she would have battered over Kere's head, Fearn found Sarmatia's mouth and locked her into a long, passionate kiss.

Desire blunted the attack of her spirit animal and Sarmatia came back to herself, embracing Fearn with a greedy vigor that set both their pulses spinning. Hearing laughter, Sarmatia broke away first, her body still stiff despite Fearn's urgent loving. Now you shall be introduced, his eyes told her, but, disliking being on view any longer, Sarmatia tore away. Ignoring Fearn's whispered pleas for her to stay, she returned to Ormson's wife and broke sticks to burn on the fire. She was still angry for both herself and Fearn at the arrogance of the royal family. Behind her eyes, in her head, her spirit animal clawed at her injured pride, turning like a beast in a cage.

Sarmatia ate when the last guest had risen from the table. The delicacies were gone. She and the women and children dined on the scraps of the feast which they'd been so long in preparing. When the food was finished, she would not settle even then beside Fearn, but helped Orm's wife Maewe clear plates.

It was a time when in Krete guests exchanged presents with their hosts, but the royal family had brought nothing with them. In their midst, Fearn was stiffer than with his father's family. A log flared at his feet, showing him with a knife and a new carving in his fists. Fearn did not need such a pastime with her, Sarmatia thought. She grinned, but it promised to be a dull evening: no stories, no music, no gifts.

A gush of air swirled the fire. The pelts covering the door were first swung inwards and then dragged back. A dark figure dipped under the entrance and replaced the stiff door-hangings. The shadow came in a crouch to the center of the house, straightened, and wound a cloth from its face.

'It's pitiless outside, Fearn. Can I stay?'

Chapter 41

Fearn looked up at the visitor, smiling. 'Yes, Bride, and welcome!' Life and energy flushed back into him. He darted up and was at Bride's side in a few strides, clasping her gloved hand. 'By the Mother, you're ice! Come close to the fire.' Fearn looked round for Sarmatia, but failed to see her in the shadows. 'Have you eaten?' he asked, then in a louder voice, 'Bring ale and food for my guest!'

Now that Bride was claimed by Fearn, the group by the fire stirred, several men rising to their feet. The King led his guest to the heap of skins that served him for a seat and sat her on it, then stripped off her mittens and raked embers by her feet. A long puddle of fire lit Bride's face and Sarmatia heard the hiss as Fearn's kin saw her birthmark.

Bride made the most of the moment. She gave one of the twins standing by her a long look, then reached up and patted his arm. 'Can I have this warrior tonight, Fearn?'

'Certainly,' replied Fearn, who had not forgotten Goar's bad manners at the feast. He knew the twin's liking for young girls and thought a night with Bride a neat revenge.

Delighted, Bride licked her lips. 'I've left my gifts outside.' She smiled. 'What's your name, my silver-and-white?'

'My name's Goar.' He bowed, playing up to the lie that they had not met before. Fearn and Bride had him trapped and squirming.

'Beautifully done,' said Bride. 'You may kiss my hand.'

Goar crouched and lifted her fist to his lips. 'Tonight, I'm your servant.'

'Of course you are. And one day I hope to return the favor.' She brushed his hair and tweaked one curl.

'No need, my lady.' Unbidden, Goar rose and was off to the door. No one else had moved or spoken.

'Bride, if you charm all my followers so, I'll soon have no people to lead.' Still standing, Fearn took bread and a filled beaker from Maewe and, with another glance about for Sarmatia, handed both to the smith. People leaned forward to see if her teeth were like other women's, or of iron.

Bride winked up at Fearn. She was enjoying herself. 'Where's my beer-pourer?' Her eyes raked the families, lingering on the young men. 'Why isn't Sarmatia at your side, Fearn?'

'I've asked her repeatedly, but my wife will not come. You should call her, Bride. You may be more successful.' He and Bride stared out into the greater darkness of the house.

Sarmatia stepped into the firelight, clutching the largest of the beer jugs. She felt shy. She could not even say, Welcome to my house, for this was not her home. 'I'm glad you're here.'

'You're very stiff, Bull Rider,' replied Bride in Kretan. 'Are these sheep-stares grinding you down?' She nodded at the silent faces and clapped her hands. 'The ring is prettier on your finger than round your neck,' she said in Atterian, winning laughter. 'Have you grown taller since I left you?'

'Why don't you measure against each other and find out?' suggested Laerimmer, silky-smooth. Bride though took him at his word.

'Hold these then.' She thrust her beer jug and Sarmatia's at the Kingmaker and rose to her feet. 'Stand by me, Sarmatia. Fearn, you are lord here, you decide.'

A gasp went round the family, for Sarmatia was the tallest woman they had seen, yet Bride was taller. It was Fearn who was of a height with the smith. He walked round the two women. 'Thanks, Bride,' he said softly, in passing, and smiled at his wife. 'You're right. One of you has grown a finger-width in recent days.' This time the laughter was general.

'There are compensations in being tall,' said Bride, her eyes on Goar, who had returned with an armload of bundles.

'I'm looking at two,' came Ormson's voice from the dark.

'In quarrels now, a long arm is useful,' went on Bride, indicating that Goar should collect the remaining packages. She stuffed bread into her mouth, licking her fingers. 'That was good. Have you any more?'

'Not without baking.' Fearn stood on tiptoe and cut down a haunch suspended from the roof. 'I hope this will do instead.' Quickly he spitted the smoked meat. Bride would have more than the family had at the feast, but no one dared protest. Laerimmer tried his dry cough, which Fearn ignored.

He beckoned two grandchildren of Maewe, whispered and let each go with a ribbon of meat. The children scampered round the fire and disappeared.

Fearn squatted in the ashes. 'What are the other advantages for a tall woman?' he asked, placing the spits over the fire.

Bride answered strength and grace. She swayed her hips, turned her hands and the Atterians watched. She had them all now, including Laerimmer. Watching her, Sarmatia tipped up her chin, realizing that she'd been slightly stooped over. Goar brought in the last bundle and Bride had him throw it over the heads of the family. The noblewoman Chalda shrieked and cracked heads with her husband. Sarmatia hid a smile. Now the woman would not be so haughty.

Bride tapped her booted heel for silence. The grandchildren pelted back, tunics bulged out with whatever they'd been sent for, and Fearn drew them down beside him, cautioning them gently to be still. Sarmatia scented the roasting meat and prayed that no one could hear her stomach rumble. She watched Bride untie the final knotted cloth, heard the jangle of metal and would have moved, had not the smith whispered that she must stay put.

'In my lands, it's custom to bring gold into the house that offers food and shelter,' Bride began, so softly that the families became still to hear her. 'Perhaps there's a gift here for everyone. We shall see.'

Bride laid the opened bundle on the floor, holding up a long neck-ring made of leather covered in gold wire. She threw it over Sarmatia's head and made a circular motion with her finger. Sarmatia spun about slowly, displaying the first gift.

Bracelets of electrum were fastened on her wrists. Six bronze bracelets came next, three on each arm. A head-ornament was bound to her temples.

'Amber from the north,' said Bride.

Sarmatia turned, sensing the ripening interest amongst even the royal family.

'Jet from the Otawe.' Bride's voice flowed, dreamlike, and a necklace of this black amber was arranged against Sarmatia's white cloak. 'See the pale jewels in this hair-comb? They are the tears of the Moon-goddess, won from the ocean.'

Another comb, of pure silver, was fastened in Sarmatia's dark brown hair. The second package was raided and more wonders revealed. At a word from Bride, Sarmatia stood motionless, and bolts of linen were draped over her outstretched arms. Yet from where had Bride obtained these riches?

'Did you kill for this?' hissed Sarmatia, as the smith pinned another treasure on her. Bride smirked.

'All fairly won, as gift or gamble,' she whispered, and, under the pretence of fastening a clasp, added, 'The smiths buried a mort of treasure for safekeeping, when King Waroch was burned to death. I had them dig it up again.'

That explained the bounty, thought Sarmatia, but not the precise timing. It was clear to her that Fearn and Bride had somehow engineered this show. 'How and when did you speak to Fearn?'

'His messenger came to me yesterday.'

Sarmatia took a deep breath. It was hard to keep her arms straight under the weight of linen cloth. Bride was ready with the final pieces. She bent Sarmatia's arms at the elbows, level with her breast, closing her hands over a bronze halberd and axe.

'Last a mirror, clear as a summer lake.' Bride raised a silver hand mirror so that Sarmatia could see herself. 'The sword I stand at Sarmatia's feet is her own, and no general gift.'

Bride drove a blade point first into the earth floor, where it remained, swaying from front to back. Sarmatia felt the breeze it made. The sword was a copy of the one Bride had given her in Tartessus. She had lost it through her enslavement. Sarmatia contemplated it in silence, until Bride snapped her fingers. 'Look at yourself!'

The mirror confirmed the weight of jewelery. Sarmatia glanced at Fearn, laid back upon his elbows and staring up at her, leaving the meat to burn upon the fire. Tears sprang to her eyes. 'It's perfect.' She stepped closer to the sword.

Bride accepted the tribute as no more than natural. She smiled at Sarmatia then gave her attention to the families. 'These are the gifts. I hope that not only Sarmatia will be pleased by them.'

'Why have you loaded these treasures on Fearn's wife?' asked Laerimmer, a malicious stress on the word wife.

'Isn't it clear to you yet? These gifts are also Sarmatia's. Some are part of her dowry.'

'That girl's too laden-down to hand out presents,' grumbled fat-cheeked Ormson, the first to speak after these revelations.

'So approach, my man, and take one,' answered Sarmatia, recovering first. Her own wonder at this change must wait.

Not one of the family stirred. Bride glanced at Fearn, testing the meat with his knife. 'Will the King take the lead?'

'It will be an honor.' Fearn handed Bride her meat and walked to Sarmatia, who dared not move now in case she disturb metal or cloth. He lifted the silver comb from her hair. 'This I'll take, as a gift of Sarmatia's, from her dowry.'

Fearn kissed Sarmatia on the mouth and Bride, who was eating, on her cheek. 'It shall pass to my children, and those who use and wear this comb, delighting in beauty and excellence, will remember the woman who made it, and she who gave it to me.' He bowed to Bride and then Sarmatia. 'I give you both my thanks.'

Fearn stepped back and a grandchild of Maewe tugged at his cloak. He crouched, listened, and raised his head. 'The children ask—do you want your fruit, Bride, now that you've finished the meat?'

Again, the family laughed, and Bride answered why not, lifting both children up to ride on each hip, where they fed her alternately with crab apples.

Laerimmer, trying to look bored, wandered within reach of Sarmatia.

'I see southerners have generous natures.' He addressed her in tones of deep suspicion, as though he guessed the entire occasion was fixed. Laerimmer took the amber pendant, nodding curtly to Sarmatia, then Bride.

Thereafter, the family crowded about, removing gifts. Chalda, Sarmatia noted, took the other hair comb set with pearls. Anoi, more modest, removed only one of the six slender bangles.

At last, with the family showing off their presents to each other, Sarmatia could lower her arms and shake her hair. Still astonished, deeply touched, by the effort of planning and skill which Fearn and Bride must have spent between them for her, she wandered forward in a daze, brushing the pommel of her own gift.

Gently, Sarmatia grasped this new, marvelous sword around the tang and eased it from the earth. It was heavier than her first blade and balanced well. The tip was wickedly sharp. Exhilarated, she brandished the sword aloft. 'Look, Fearn!'

'I couldn't avoid doing so, my Sarmatia,' said her husband, laughing and placing an arm about her shoulders, pleased as she was pleased. 'It's a handsome thing, though deadly.'

'In fact, isn't a sword a strange gift for a wife?' said Laerimmer, twisting Fearn's remark. The kin paused to look.

'Sarmatia's sword is quite beautiful,' said Anoi gently, 'and cunningly wrought.'

'Yes, very cunning.' Ormson made a different meaning, at which Sarmatia laughed, although she could sense the new, dangerous mood. Her spirit animal was intrigued by it.

'What does our king say?' Laerimmer goaded.

'A sword is a beautiful weapon for a woman,' said Fearn. 'Yet as I'm a man, give me an axe in battle.'

'I might match your axe to my sword one day,' said Bride, swinging the children down off her hip. 'Then we could settle the matter of which is the greater weapon, in friendly contest.'

'A contest!' laughed the children, glutted with food and presents. A featureless hum started within the hut.

'Why not now?' called a woman.

'Let's see this battle of woman and man!' cried another.

Sarmatia knew that Fearn and Bride would not want this. They had spoken of a private skirmish, where neither would lose face. Forced to fight now and blood might easily be spilt.

Before Fearn could respond, Sarmatia issued a challenge of her own. 'To the man who can beat me with an axe, who can make the first cut, I'll give up this sword.'

'No!' cried Fearn. 'If there is any fight, it's with me.'

'The challenge is made, husband,' said Sarmatia mildly. 'It's only to the first cut.' Amongst warriors, such a fight was scarcely a fight at all. She appealed to Fearn's honor. 'Would you shame me by refusing my right to carry arms?'

Fearn's face contorted. 'You know I wouldn't, Sarmatia.'

'Say what you please, Fearn, your woman made the challenge!' bawled a man, to loud agreement.

Fearn shouted that they were drunk, but the family had scented blood and the hunt was on. Sarmatia caught it herself. When Fearn bellowed, 'This is my wife!' she yelled back fiercely, 'Can a wife not fight? Can't I try my new sword?'

And at that moment, Laerimmer rolled himself to his feet. 'I accept the challenge,' he said.

Chapter 42

Fearn sprang at Laerimmer. 'If you do more than scratch her, man, I'll break your back!' As the family, unhearing, broke into applause, Fearn straight-armed the man right off his feet. Shrugging off the Kingmaker's attempts to resist, he drove his knees into Laerimmer's spine and bent the man back like a curving bow.

In the distance overhead Sarmatia heard a roll of thunder. The crowd's breath caught and they stopped applauding, faces blank then concerned.

Fearn bent his head to Laerimmer. 'Once too often you'll try me.' To the gasps and protests of the family he jerked the man even farther back.

'No, Fearn!' shouted Sarmatia, appalled, but now Laerimmer, face scarlet, cried out, 'I swear I'll not harm her!'

That promise extracted, Fearn abruptly let him go. He lurched away, sitting amongst the women by the table. 'Go on, then. It's what Sarmatia wants.' He turned his face aside, indicating royal displeasure.

The crowd were not to be cheated of their contest. A space was cleared between the keeping platform and fire, and men positioned to light the area with torches. Bride would referee. She helped Sarmatia scrape her hair into a cap.

'I'm sorry for this, Bull Rider. Things haven't happened as we planned. The gifts were Fearn's idea.' Bride tucked more loose hairs under the felt bonnet. 'He thought it would increase your status if we could provide you with a dowry. I've done well myself out of the arrangement. Fearn's paying for all the metal I want when the traders come in the summer.'

Too keyed-up to remark or reflect on Fearn's generosity, Sarmatia interrupted. 'Honor is won, not bought,' she said, knowing even as she spoke that was unfair and ungracious.

'Spare the fighting talk for Laerimmer. Your man did his best, and his best's very good.' Bride's eyes flicked across to where Fearn was seated, watching the preparations with an intensity which warned that he would be intervening the first moment Sarmatia faltered. 'He's tough once he's roused.'

Bride smeared soot onto Sarmatia's palm to improve her grip. 'Watch that Kingmaker, he'll fight low.' Bride kissed her and stepped back. 'Cut his face, then it'll be clear who's won. Gods! You look like a youth with your hair back and the cloak. I think the Atterians have forgotten you're a girl.'

'I'll keep the cloak.' Sarmatia didn't want any favors in this fight.

'Good. The cloak should remind you that this is a friendly contest.'

'Shall we begin?' called Laerimmer, subdued after his rough handling. Sarmatia nodded.

Bride walked to the middle of the lighted corridor. 'This is a friendly contest to the first cut. There'll be no insults, gouging, kicking or biting. Begin.'

At the signal, Sarmatia ran forward, the silence of the kin replaced by a roar within her own head. To outsiders, this was like a drinking bout, entertaining but not to be taken seriously. To her, and also she sensed, to Laerimmer, it was more. Not quite a battle and yet...

Laerimmer had not moved. The wood axe they had brought him hung loosely in his hand. He looked like Pergia again, his black eyes glinting in the torchlight. Sarmatia pitched her sword towards those eyes. The axe scraped off the earth. Laerimmer ducked under her blow and swept back with the axe. Over the shouts of the family, Sarmatia heard Fearn cursing and, mindful of what he might do to the Kingmaker if she closed too often with the man, she dived neatly away from danger.

The family were cheering. Anoi screamed, 'Go on!'

This time Sarmatia waited for Laerimmer to attack. The axe slid round her feet, then haft first, shot up and struck her in the gut. She doubled over, but kept her grip on the sword. The blunt edge of the blade hissed on Laerimmer's tunic. He knocked it away with his free arm. Caught off balance, Sarmatia staggered then tucked in her head and rolled. When she gained her feet her cap had come off and her hair was loose but she still had the sword and now she cut with it, flicking her wrist like a whip.

Laerimmer jerked back his head. The bronze missed him by only a hair. As Sarmatia swirled in for a second strike he grabbed her cloak and tugged, dragging them both into an untidy scrummage on the floor.

For Sarmatia it was like struggling with Carvin again. She heard a sobbing breath, knew it was hers, and shouted, thrusting the man's hands from her shoulder. Laerimmer tried to catch her fast. She felt the scrape of the axe, twisted her head and the blow spent itself in her hair.

Laerimmer thought she was pinned and dropped his axe to take her sword. It was a mistake. Rearing up, Sarmatia punched into his side. As her grasp on her sword-arm slackened, she flashed the blade close to Laerimmer's head. It nicked his ear, but then Sarmatia felt warmth seeping from her arm and knew she had been cut.

The Kingmaker rolled onto his back, chest heaving with effort. The sword lay against his throat. His face was the living image of Pergia. If she struck now it would be like killing the woman herself. Some part of her nature urged her now. Do it and free yourself forever of the past. It wasn't as though she liked or trusted Laerimmer. Suppose he was the one—or more likely behind the one—who had fired that arrow at Fearn in the wood?

Thinking of these things, Sarmatia grasped the sword pommel firmly, lifted the blade and raised herself to her knees.

She smiled at Fearn, who had rushed to her side and, recalling his threat to Laerimmer, turned quickly so that her hurt was hidden from him. The Kingmaker was still gasping on his back. Strangely, he looked satisfied. Sarmatia stood the sword in the earth and leaned her head against it. Murder wasn't for her, whatever Laerimmer was, or resembled, or had done.

'Who won?' she asked Bride.

'It was an equal match. Both drew blood together. Sarmatia will keep her sword and Laerimmer his honor. Should any wish to dispute this,' the smith let her features mould into a smile, 'they must contest with me.'

A hot wave of relief passed over Sarmatia. She lifted her head, startled to see that Anoi was weeping. The girl had plucked a bronze meat hook from the cooking area and was clasping it between her breasts, perhaps afraid that the fighting would break out more widely. Clearly frightened, Anoi gazed at Sarmatia, her face wet with tears.

Ashamed to be the cause of such alarm, Sarmatia felt her earlier jubilation drain off. She rocked forward slightly and at once Fearn had his arms about her, half-carrying her to the fire. 'Where are you cut? Did Laerimmer harm you?'

Sarmatia put a hand on his chest. 'I'm not hurt. Look at Laerimmer, his ear bleeds. I must pass water.'

Fearn let her go at that. Sarmatia walked to the door, moving slowly because astonishingly her excuse was true. Suddenly her bladder felt full.

* * * *

The night was star-filled but cold and Sarmatia had no plans to stay by the midden. Then, as she let down her tunic, she heard voices: the royal twins, then Ormson, with a woman. Gygest and Goar were discussing a hunt again while they relieved themselves, and Sarmatia marveled at the way they continuously spoke across each other without ever losing track of their conversation. She did not mean to eavesdrop, only wonder at this closeness of twins, until Gygest asked casually, 'Will you take your bow to the wood?'

Sarmatia drew back into the shadows, her breath stopped in her throat. Goar, an archer! And did he often hunt in the woods? Had he been there, that day of the cattle raid? A royal kinsman, entitled to wear the golden disc.

Straining to hear she listened, yet it wasn't Goar's answer she heard next but Ormson's, and to a different question. 'Yes, she looks like a she-bear and fights like one, too. A bear with a sword and a cloak.'

Sarmatia was never closer to breaking the narrow tang of her sword than then. Anger rose in her like a blister near to bursting. It betrayed her presence as her hand tightened dangerously on her sword and the blade scraped along the frozen ground. Instantly, two sets of shadows became aware that they were not alone and the groups broke up, disappearing back into the house. Sarmatia stayed where she was, trying to think clearly. She must follow Gygest and Goar when they hunted. No, she must confront Goar, confront that fat-cheeked Ormson.

Behind her, she could smell animal fat, stale cooking, human and animal dung. A smell of fresh animal fat was growing stronger and she turned, expecting Bride.

Two bright blue eyes and a very sharp meat hook flashed in her face. Sarmatia caught the hook as Anoi gave a little scream, the Atterian even more startled and upset than she was. 'Anoi! You steal around like a kitten!'

The tiny girl looked so frightened that it was cruel to laugh and Sarmatia bit hard on her lips to still a mischievous impulse to say Boo! Instead, she took the meat hook from the frozen-faced Anoi, heart stampeding with pity when she considered the fright that must have inspired the girl to take up such a tool.

'There, it's all right. We just gave each other a shock in the dark. Don't cry.'

But Anoi began to tremble and when Sarmatia put an arm about her shoulders she gave way completely. 'I might have killed you!'

Sarmatia trembled herself, perhaps with cold, and awkwardly patted the girl's arm. 'Steady,' she murmured, much as she might have said to Gorri. 'No harm done. We'll go in now.'

Anoi's hands gripped over one of Sarmatia's wrists. 'What is it, Sarmatia?' she cried, blue eyes clouding with fresh tears. 'Why do you avoid me now? Don't you like me?'

'I—' Sarmatia was caught. She had been avoiding Anoi, ever since learning that Tanek had been her half-brother. Bride's curse sounded strange on her lips, but she used it anyway. 'Gods, I like you, Anoi.'

The girl's fingers warmed as Sarmatia said this. She seemed to open somehow, like a flower filled with sunlight. Anoi had forgiven Fearn for her brother's death. She seemed to bear his present happiness or his marriage no grudge. Here was a lesson she should learn, thought Sarmatia. Forget the past, be less proud.

'I wish I was half as good as you, Anoi.' Sarmatia embraced the Atterian. Anoi's lips lay against her cheek for a moment, very cold. The two young women turned to the house.

'You will be my friend, Sarmatia,' said Anoi solemnly. She held out her hand. 'I should carry the meat hook. You cannot manage that and your sword.' She stepped aside for Sarmatia to lead the way back.

Sarmatia smiled and moved forward. Anoi was well-named, she reflected, a golden shadow flitting on her heels.

'Gods, watch where you're going, fool, you'll spike someone!' Bride loomed out of the black night like a tall ship in the sea. She grabbed for Sarmatia's arm and turned her back on Anoi. 'Come on for a walk. Fearn's busy finding beds for his family. We won't be missed.'

'What about Goar?' At the thought of the royal twin, Sarmatia was suddenly alarmed, but then she decided that he could not commit murder in the house. Too many witnesses.

Bride at least had no fear of Goar. 'He can warm my place. Wait.' There was a trickling sound as Bride passed water. The women felt their way from the settlement, going towards the river.

'Are you happy at the smiths?' Sarmatia asked Bride.

'Ah, yes. They have gold enough, even though they don't know how to work it. More satisfied, I'd say, than happy.' Bride stared up at the faint stars. 'Is it hard here, Bull Rider?'

'I'm happy.' Happy, but anxious.

'But not satisfied. You're as stiff amongst these Atterians as you began with me, in Tartessus.'

Sarmatia threw the hood of her cloak over her head to shut out these discomforting ideas. Bride though did not allow a few threads of cloth to deter her. 'You're content to be the house-wife?' she goaded.

Sarmatia clenched her teeth. 'If that's my place.' Despite the cold, she felt stifled and cast off her hood. 'What else can I do? Everyone expects this of me.' She thought of the fragile Anoi and of Ormson's blunt comments, and was ashamed. Fearn deserved a wife, not a she-bear.

'Everyone, you say?' Bride stopped Sarmatia with a hand. 'Put down your sword. I'll take a look at that axe wound. I'm no healer, but I know a good cut from a bad.'

She scooped the cloak away and peered at Sarmatia's upper arm. 'I'm glad you made no fuss over this in the house. Laerimmer would be nursing a battered head now, or worse.'

Bride began deftly cutting the tunic sleeve. 'Your thinking's wrong.' She peeled the cloth back from the wound. 'If Fearn had wanted an Atterian housewife he would have picked a girl from his own country. If he's overprotective of you now, it's only after Carvin: give him time. Um, it seems clean, no tearing anywhere.'

Sarmatia watched Bride sniff the long thin gash. 'Leave it, Bride, it's nothing. I want to be good, to be accepted by people.'

'Open your eyes, Sarmatia. The women here are more than you think. I saw their faces as you fought.'

'Did you like the fight?'

'Humph!' Bride jabbed a finger into Sarmatia's arm, grinning as the girl flinched. 'Good. Now move your arm for me. Let's make sure no tendons are severed. That's it, round in a circle and then the other way. Pity I'm returning to the smiths. I'd like to see the explosion when this goodness of yours comes to a head.'

'You've spent too long in the wilderness. I'm content within the house.'

'Well, we'll see, Bull Rider.'

Bride turned back to the black bulk of the house with a spring in her step. Sarmatia had done well tonight in the fight, and now it was her own turn with Goar.

Revenge was certainly sweet.

Chapter 43

Bride entered the house first and heard Fearn behind her draw Sarmatia into a dark corner. 'Goar's in our chamber. Tonight it's yours,' he whispered. He and Sarmatia disappeared.

Bride picked her way round the sleeping royal family and banked-down fire. She could see that the smallest room—really no more than an alcove— was open. A tall figure lurked beside the bed, dressed in loin cloth and jet necklace.

'I'm glad you chose the black amber.' Bride closed the hangings behind her.

'Anything to please. Will you bury me in it?'

So Goar thought he knew her mind. Bride unsheathed her sword, floated its point up to his left shoulder. 'There. The bead was wrong.' She arranged it with the blade tip. 'Now you've seen her, do you think Sarmatia beautiful?' The lethal point trailed down his chest.

'For a woman in man's clothes she's outstanding.'

The fool was brave. The point had reached his lights. The blade side twanged, a gentle reprimand, against the hard flatness of his stomach, and jagged along the top of the loin cloth. Goar hadn't the length of arm to retaliate as the sword stroked along his flanks. Involuntarily, his hips moved.

'Just like a man. Fickle.'

There was no mistaking the satisfaction in Bride's voice. Goar was resentful. The hesitant caresses of his Atterian girls had been nothing as deadly-sensuous as this.

Warmed by his body, the blunter sides of the rapier scraped on Goar's dark-blond leg hairs and glided upwards. Resentment sharpened as the sword mesmerized him. The point touched him intimately, through the cloth. Goar began to sweat. His breathing was like that of one of his girls, in their moment of yielding. He hated the humiliation.

'Hate? You'd kill me if you could.' Bride goaded him.

Goar began to pant. The blunt part of the blade alternated with the narrower tip in a killing parody of a woman's mouth and tongue. Abruptly, both were withdrawn. Goar swayed slightly.

'Here I am—the woman you swore you'd never bed.' Bride's mouth was dry as she dropped sword and tunic by her heels.

Goar forgot danger and his years of turning aside. He stepped forward.

'Wait!'

His potent picture of himself shattered, but Bride wasn't teasing. Frowning, she picked up the sword and flicked back one of the bed furs. A long black shape struck at her and she recoiled.

The adder spilled over the bed, fell writhing on the alcove floor, followed by a spider. Another dozen huge spiders scrambled over the furs in every direction. Goar caught the adder's tail, whipped it onto the bed, bundled snake and spiders' nest into the biggest fur and carried it to the midden.

Returning, he found Bride almost as he'd left her, except that she'd been sick in the waste bucket. When he touched it, her hand was clammy.

'I didn't put them there.' Goar didn't insult her by suggesting that the adder and spiders had found their own way into the alcove. 'Did the snake bite you?'

'No. We'd better find Fearn.' Bride choked, her shoulders heaving. This time, she managed to keep the sickness down. 'I don't think that gift was meant for us.' She tried to laugh. 'Unless Sarmatia brought the adder here.'

Neither idea seemed likely to Goar. 'Forget it. A bad joke.' The families had drunk a skinful tonight. Anyone could have dumped their bedfellows into the alcove while he was out at the midden. Goar squeezed Bride's chilly fingers. 'The snake's gone. You can sit down.'

She stared at him with the round eyes of a child. Men or snakes were one thing, but everyone has a weakness. Goar gave his light laugh, suddenly understanding.

'Let's make sure we've no other bedtime visitors.'

Hand in hand they scoured the tiny chamber and shook the remaining furs. Two spiders dropped to the floor and Goar pushed at Bride before she stiffened. 'Into bed with you. I'll get rid of these.'

He didn't kill them. The spiders had made a peace between him and Bride.

* * * *

Bride felt like a woman with a spirit lover. There was a quality of a dream about Goar, about the way he seemed to know her body better than she did. Bride pictured herself as a shining fortress. When she opened her citadel, it wasn't to an attacker, but to an ally.

He was within. The gates closed round snugly. A yell of triumph broke from Bride's lips.

* * * *

Goar said he would tell Fearn about the adders and spiders, but later confessed that he forgot to do so. Often he was frivolous, which charmed Bride. He teased her in ways none of her previous lovers would have dared.

The day after the feast, when they'd left the house within a few moments of each other and traveled together to the settlement of the smiths, Goar had put a spider on Bride's bed. She caught him in her hut with it. 'It worked so well by accident, I was hoping to use it by design.' He grinned.

Unlike Sarmatia and Fearn, there were no arguments or principles between them. Goar was proud of his older woman. Yet he was still shy. He would not relieve or wash himself in her presence, and would gently lift away her hands if her fingers strayed too low.

So Goar was horrified when, taking him off-guard one evening, Bride reached over in bed and grasped him. 'Now, don't disappear,' she said, employing artful fingers.

'There's little enough to wither.' Goar tried to pull away.

'Gods, you men! So here's the reason for your young women! They talk. Didn't you know? Have you seen a lack of interest amongst the rest?' Bride teased him with her fingernails.

Goar shuddered and gasped, but at the moment of completion, the part which was most himself and over which he'd least control, faded and died. He struck the offending flesh and rolled away. Bride tried to touch him. He shook her off. She left the bed and returned.

'Beer won't work,' said Goar, hearing the gush of pouring liquid. 'I'll go soon. You won't have to look at me again.'

'Have you spoken to a healer?' Bride asked briskly.

'It'll make no difference now!'

Bride clasped his shoulder. This time, Goar did not flinch away but allowed Bride to draw him onto his back. He was still talking. The words pouring from him.

'My first girl - she wouldn't let me. Said I was too small, that I wasn't a real man. She said women would laugh at me.'

Goar's face tightened. Even in their lovemaking he had been light, thought Bride, but now he was in deadly earnest. 'You're the only experienced woman I've known, that I thought worth the risk. The rest—' He tired to smile. 'Oh, even a midget looks big to a beginner.' That explanation gave a crude twist to something Bride had said to him.

'And all women harlots to a man who can't please them,' Bride answered, now understanding that aspect of her lover.

Having confessed his obsession, Goar felt compelled to tell the rest. 'She said if a woman saw me, I'd fail, forever.' He was like a ghost, lying stretched out in the night. '"And when the sun rises next day, your manhood will be dead. Your seed will be useless."'

The mysteries surrounding their mating were laid bare, thought Bride. The darkness, his foiling of any intimate caress from her, the manner in which they joined. Goar had been hoping to hold off a magic curse. He had risked more than his pride to lie with her. Bride was staggered. 'You should have told me.'

'But my dear, you were worth it.'

The gallantry sounded glib, yet Goar had lived with her half a month already and had been faithful. Bride did not want to give up their nights. 'Who was this girl who mocked and cursed you?'

'She said I'd die if I named or accused her.'

Bride rolled onto her back, taking Goar's hand in hers. 'Tell me the whole, why this girl put a curse on you. Did you try to force her?'

'Of course not!' Goar glanced at the gray light creeping past the door hanging: soon it would be day. 'It was nearly two years ago. Fearn had just started south with Minos' herald.'

Bride was startled that Goar remembered the ruler's name in Krete.

'Fearn wasn't going to leave, but the herald told us Minos was dying, and Waroch said that Atterians would manage very well for healing from the midwives. Waroch was always jealous of Fearn.'

Waroch: the king who was burned to death. Bride resisted a desire to question Goar on that event. 'That's to no purpose here,' she said gently. 'Take my hands and look at me. It was two years ago. Begin from there.'

'Laerimmer sent the girl and me...' Goar's fingers broke from Bride's. 'Did you know our Kingmaker paid the war band not to leave the homeland?' he asked suddenly, in a different voice. 'I don't think Laerimmer cares for Sarmatia. I'm not sure he cares for Fearn. If I was Fearn, I'd be wary of the Kingmaker.'

Goar stretched like a green-eyed cat then gave a sudden start. 'I can't like Laerimmer,' he muttered. 'He stares at me.'

Listening, Bride felt a stillness descend around her, like the silence in country districts at midday, when panic is never far off. She understood now that the spell put on Goar protected itself by deception, forcing its victim to throw up false trails so that it might remain hidden, like poison in a wound.

'I don't believe you've mentioned Laerimmer before,' she said quietly. She didn't know if Goar's fears were true, or the workings of the spell.

In another unnatural change of mood, Goar was chuckling. 'I'm glad our Kingmaker's bribery didn't work.'

This was woman's magic, thought Bride. Magic to distract, to deceive a man, to make him forgetful, incapable of action or of coherent thought. To fight it, she must use her own wiles. Leaning up on her elbow, Bride unbraided her hair, which Goar loved to wind about his fingers and flicked it over him. 'Two years ago, Laerimmer sent the girl and you,' she coaxed.

Little by little, between many false starts, the story of the curse emerged. Goar and this girl had once been secretly betrothed, and he had tried to press his suit. It was his first time. The girl watched him strip, responded to his kisses, but then refused him. When he pleaded, she was scornful, then angry, and then she cursed him.

Hearing this, Bride shrugged. 'You should have killed her.'

Goar was shocked. 'That's forbidden by our goddess. Women are hers.'

Then I'm hers, thought Bride, and I may act.

Goar smoothed her hair then released it, moaning and covering his face with his hands. 'I'm a dead man.'

'Don't worry, now,' said Bride. 'I've charms, lots of charms.' Some were practical, some fanciful, some guesses. She would try them all, for one must work. Otherwise, it might have been better if she and this once lighthearted man had never met.

Chapter 44

Seventeen days of rain. Sarmatia sighed, drawing back from the door to her weaving. Bride had returned to the smiths' settlement, Gorri was now outside the farmstead in the day. The royal family had gone back home.

Sarmatia missed the company. She missed her quarrels with Laerimmer. Once she'd tried teasing Anoi, who had looked hurt. Perhaps I'm evil, perhaps I'll never be satisfied, she thought, miserable.

She pushed the heddle bar and stared at the brown weave. In this damp climate she'd developed chilblains, but not known what they were until Gei had complained of 'dreadful sores' and pulled off her shoes. Gei moaned and grumbled but the other women and Anoi merely advised her not to sit with her feet so close to the fire. Sarmatia's toes broke open in red welts, but these she hid from Fearn. He had enough problems.

To pay for her dowry, Fearn had promised to re-thatch the homestead of the smiths, six dwellings in all. Now he was at Rossfarm, preparing new land for harvest. That meant a long ride, both ways in darkness, and a day pushing an ard through untilled earth. Remembering the archer in the wood, Sarmatia hated him working alone, but Fearn said that the king always turned the furrows of virgin soil.

Sarmatia bent to tie another stone to the base of the warp threads. Her weaving was poor. 'She weaves like a cow,' Ormson remarked, and Sarmatia heard and hid her anger. She could have said that at an age when Atterian girls were learning to weave she was already trainer for the Bull Rite, but Ormson would not have understood. She stuck to the task Maewe had given her, this puckered cloth that she hated. Finish it, your next will be better, Sarmatia promised herself. She thought, with a pang, of the beautiful red cloaks that Anoi had woven for Fearn and herself. A gift for Fearn in his favorite color. It was a poor thing when a cousin knew her husband's wants and she did not.

Blushing, Sarmatia recalled an incident from the day of the midwinter feast, when Fearn and the men had returned early from the woods to relax while the wives prepared the meal. They had hindered and Fearn had been the worst, setting the place whirling by a request for hot water. 'Not boiling, but warm, to wash myself in comfort.'

Seeing Anoi reach for one of the pitchers hanging from the roof, Sarmatia bit down on her retort that Fearn would do well enough at the river. Schooling herself to be like other Atterian women, Sarmatia beat Anoi to a pail, collected water, heated it, and found comb and soap.

Fearn was happy to let her tend him. His forehead was as shiny as a boy's when she had scraped the muck off him, and his hair dried to the color of new copper.

Yet this service had not been sufficient for Atterian wives. Each had given her man a morsel to eat and beer to drink, combed his hair, washed his feet, piled beads and armlets upon his body. All with sly looks at her. Angry and bewildered—she had been trying to do the right thing— Sarmatia had bent over a quern, pounding the grain in it to powder. As a child she had not been troubled by censure, as Bull Rider she had been above it. In Fearn's country, she had found that she was subject to the same customs as other women, and that here the women seemed to resent her, being quick to point up her inadequacies.

'You at a loom, Sarmatia?'

Sarmatia laughed at Laerimmer. 'I didn't hear you enter.'

'Perhaps I should try again, but how will I be greeted? Not, I hope, with that object raised like a club.'

Laying aside her shuttle, Sarmatia meekly placed palms together. 'Is this sufficient?'

'You southern races have no true humility.'

'We've had no conquerors to teach us that lesson.'

'You're very trim with your answers.'

'Laerimmer, you inspire me.' He did too. They were flirting. Could one flirt with a man so old?

The Kingmaker craned his lousy head to her work. 'That's poor stuff.' At his words, Setir's and Ormson's wives, pounding flax seeds for oil, stopped their pestles, awaiting the reply. Sarmatia decided not to disappoint them.

'Could you do better?' She found herself staring at the place where her sword had cut his ear. There was only a tiny notch in the flesh.

'I heal well, as you see, and not just on the outside. I'm not one to bear a grudge.' Laerimmer paused after that reminder of Fearn's rough handling of himself, and then continued. 'You shall come to my house, Sarmatia, today. I met Fearn at Rossfarm and he agreed, albeit grudgingly.'

Despite his experience at the winter feast, it seemed that Laerimmer was still not afraid to press Fearn for what he wanted, but his invitation was unexpected. Sarmatia glanced at her weaving, at the other women. This was not Pergia, yet could she trust Laerimmer? Fearn had hurt and threatened the Kingmaker because of her. Still, whatever the risk, it might be useful to see the royal homestead. She'd be able to check for bronze arrows.

'What about the weaving?' Anoi's question returned Sarmatia abruptly to reality. However intrigued she was, however useful a visit might be, it was impossible. Not the custom.

Suppressing a sigh, Sarmatia spoke. 'Sorry. I can't leave.'

'I've spoken to Maewe and she sees no objection.'

'That's true, Sarmatia.' Maewe nodded to Anoi. 'We're ahead with our work.'

'Come, I want you to see my hawk,' said Laerimmer. 'You'll like her if you love gold, and jewels.'

Doubtless it was a model. Sarmatia grinned then strove to be more modest. 'I shall look forward to that.' She considered the request again, hesitating. The royal household. She might be trapped there.

Impatient, Laerimmer rapped Sarmatia's loom with her shuttle. 'Look, we shall ride together. Or don't you want to ride Gorri any more?'

'I'll fetch my cloak.'

As she ran to her chamber, she heard Laerimmer say, 'Forgive me, my dear, but you can't ride with us today. My pony went lame at Rossfarm and I had to walk the rest of the way. Now I'll have to ride behind Sarmatia.'

'Poor Laerimmer,' answered Anoi, with a gentle sigh. 'At least allow me to bathe your feet, they must be sore.'

'No, no. I'm not yet so broken down.'

'Then I wish you good speed, kinsman.'

* * * *

At Laerimmer's direction they rode south by the hazel wood, then followed the valley river to a basin, where its waters divided. They struck out beside the greater stream, tracing it to its source. After a second river, forded with the water butting Gorri's chest, Sarmatia realized that the day was waning. 'If I stay tonight, where will Gorri sleep?'

'There'll be a bed in the barn, another in the house. You may decide between yourselves which bed will be yours.'

They rode on, climbing for a high wooded knoll. The light scrambled ahead of them across a dense scrub that covered the lower slopes of the hill. Gorri approached this living wall at a canter, a trot then stopped. Laerimmer slipped from his back.

'From here I'll go ahead.' He brushed back gorse with his sleeve.

Sarmatia and Gorri did not stir. Sarmatia ran her eyes up the knoll. She could see no way forward. 'Gorri can't pass through,' she said flatly.

'No one does without a guide.'

A way seemed to open before the Kingmaker and close when they were past. The man wound and doubled back. He told them when to make haste, where to go carefully. 'My forefathers laid these paths in times that were wilder than today,' he explained, as they neared the tree line at the knoll's summit. 'Each family was a law unto itself then.'

Sarmatia stared at the furze and wondered how the family had avoided being burnt alive. She looked at the wood on the summit and saw the huge-girthed beeches, their bark green with mosses. Here was a natural fire break, and for added peace of mind the family had made a gap between gorse and trees by controlled burning. 'Are such defenses needed now?'

Laerimmer took Gorri's mane to guide the horse through the last thicket of briar. 'Well, the king before Fearn did not meet a peaceful end,' he murmured without looking at her.

On the south side of the knoll was Laerimmer's home. It was the oldest dwelling Sarmatia had ever seen. Unlike other northern houses it was built in a circle, the roof beams jutting out beyond the walls. The building bore signs of a massive fire. Its walls were blackened and the roof had been rebuilt. Standing before the house, as its guardian, was a rowan. Laerimmer bowed to the tree, and Sarmatia, swinging down from Gorri, did the same. She continued on foot to the largest outbuilding.

Gorri chose to remain in the barn, settling to the bowl of mash provided by Laerimmer. At the Kingmaker's suggestion, Sarmatia went on alone to the main house. For a proud family it was a filthy place, walls shiny with grease and soot. Everywhere told of idleness—rank meat, a barrel of beans tipped over and left to rot, a stack of kindling but a poor fire. Someone, doubtless Fearn, had built a new dresser, probably to replace furniture lost in the fire, but such clothes and possessions as there were scattered about the floor. Sarmatia wondered how the family lived. The barn was full of hay, but no beast to eat it except Gorri. There was no plough, sickles or spades.

'How did you come here?' Chalda: her voice distinct even if her poorly-lit features were not.

'I was invited by Laerimmer,' Sarmatia answered mildly. A quick head count showed that some of this family were missing. Were the ones left her enemies? Laerimmer had not entered behind her, and without taking her eyes from the troll-like shadows of the royal family, Sarmatia called out: 'Leave the door open. A draught will lift this fire.'

'I'm cold, Laerimmer, so close it,' said Chalda.

'Sarmatia is my guest. We'll respect her wishes.' Coming in, Laerimmer tipped Sarmatia a smile. 'Forgive me for leaving you to the welcome of the family. It was necessary for me to tend my hawk.'

Under cover of her cloak, Sarmatia's hand relaxed on her dagger. If these people had been intent on harm they would have attacked by now, before her eyes had fully adjusted to the indoor gloom. She allowed Laerimmer to remove her cloak.

He tossed the cloth from sight. 'What's for supper?'

Chalda snorted. 'It was to be porridge. I had to leave the stuff for my baby and it spoiled. If you wanted a rare meal, Laerimmer, you should have cooked.'

'Any meal's impossible in this house,' muttered Laerimmer.

Sarmatia laughed. She liked Chalda's spirit. 'Where's this porridge?'

Chalda threw her a sullen look then pointed to a heavy pot stranded sideways on the floor. 'That's where I threw it.' Her eyes glittered. 'Now it's only fit for pigs.'

Sarmatia shrugged off the jibe. She was hungry. She righted the crock, tasted the porridge. 'Is this the only vessel? Can you find another?' And, as Laerimmer stepped back, added, 'Spices too. Whatever you have.'

Soon the remains were bubbling in another pot over a brighter fire and Sarmatia was sifting through a hugger-mugger of spices to make the meal tasty. She stirred in the best, and while these cooked asked for plates. A quarrel broke out between Chalda and Gygest as to who should leave the warm fire and search. Seeing good food about to go to waste a second time, Sarmatia banged on the pot with her ladle.

'Have you no sense?' she said in the astonished silence. 'Gygest, please take a torch and search for platters and spoons. Chalda, you fetch water or beer, we'll need a drink with the food. Go!' Sarmatia had forgotten her aim to be mild.

Overnight however she decided that it would be bad manners to comment on any deficiencies of the household. She watched then as members of the family rose and tottered about, seeking their thrown-off clothes. The fire burned out as no one knew who should tend it. Breakfast was cold porridge, as the family couldn't decide whether Gygest or Jart was cook for that day. On the start of another wrangle, Sarmatia gave up trying to find her cloak and dashed out of doors. 'Do nothing,' she whispered to her spirit animal, but its blood was stirring none the less.

Her one consolation was that there were no bronze arrowheads to be found in all that muddle. Or perhaps the archer who'd shot at Fearn was even more cunning that she'd realized.

She fretted by the rowan until the babble lessened then risked a look into the house. Laerimmer greeted her at the door with her cloak and flute.

'We've a busy day ahead.' He handed Sarmatia her things. 'And you must see my hawk. She'll be irritable at this early hour, but we can take her with us, let her fly from the hilltops.'

He had a leather guard strapped to one forearm, Sarmatia noticed. She heard a twig snap, turned and saw the royal family a few paces behind, each bundled up in mittens and cloths against the raw cold.

Laerimmer tugged at her sleeve. 'We don't sit indoors, as some do,' he said, with a nasty smile. 'We seek our bread and fame outside.'

He brought Sarmatia, the family tagging on their heels, to a bird cote raised on stilts off the ground. The man put his mouth to a narrow crack in the wood, whistling softly. Sarmatia sensed the bird inside attending the gentle summons. She helped Laerimmer remove the cote front, revealing the falcon on its central perch.

She'd underrated the Kingmaker. Here was no toy. The bird was powerful, with short wings and tail. The white and gray barred underbelly, blue-gray wings, reminded Sarmatia of the sea, and this was plainly a falcon of open spaces, an aerial hunter relying on speed.

Laerimmer covered the bird's head in a soft leather hood, speaking to her in a continuous mewing whisper. With the bird standing proud on the leather guard, he walked from the settlement without looking back to see if Sarmatia and the rest were following.

Sarmatia fell in behind, matching her step to Laerimmer's. Glancing round, she saw a procession of figures emerge from the trees and disappear one by one into the gorse. She kept close to the Kingmaker, impatient for the bird to fly.

'Remove her hood,' ordered Laerimmer. They were on the steepest part of the knoll. Below was open moor. Standing to one side so the falcon wouldn't feel trapped, Sarmatia cupped the leather hood from the black head and the peregrine was revealed.

'Kri-kri-kri!' Making the high cry of the falcon, Laerimmer raised his arm and the bird launched herself, rising easily in the fine cold air. Up near the tree tops she found wind and whirled higher, like a leaf, circling the knoll.

On the fourth darted circuit, a pigeon broke cover from the trees. With a flash of silver underbelly, the falcon angled her body, bent wings towards tail like a drawn bow and stooped in a long breathless dive. There was a blur of feathers, both birds were down.

Watching the falcon begin to feed, beak glutted with feathers, Sarmatia went on one knee to the bird to clean its beak. The killing had been so swift that she'd felt nothing as the yellow talons ripped the young pigeon from the sky. Instead a rush of light, strength in her veins, the land spread out before her with the prey standing up in high relief. Sarmatia closed her eyes, dazzled. Hunger wove through her in the hunger of the peregrine, growing even as the appetite of the feeding falcon diminished. Her spirit animal was awake.

'Neatly done,' said Laerimmer, crouching before them. 'Have you dealt with hawks before?'

Her spirit animal wanted blood. Her throat was dry. Her head filled by the sun. A faint high chatter broke from Sarmatia's lips. She tried again to speak and the cry of the falcon rang out under the trees. Wordless as a bird, she stared at the Kingmaker. Laerimmer produced a water bag and held it before her face.

'Drink, and when you swallow, close your eyes.' He spoke in the same gentle way he had to the falcon. Sarmatia put the water to her mouth. When she opened her eyes, the bird was hooded and she could speak. 'What happened there?'

To her surprise, Laerimmer had an answer. 'Your spirit didn't want to leave the hawk. Such experiences are rare, I know, but they're dangerous. You must learn how to deal with your spirit-beast.' He finished securing the bird on his arm, rose and looked down to where Sarmatia still knelt on the grass. His black eyes were as bright as the falcon's.

It was like a sunburst within Sarmatia. She and Laerimmer. They weren't enemies, they were akin. Laerimmer was a creature-caller like herself as she could have recognized sooner, had she not allowed the past, a chance resemblance to Pergia, to influence her judgment. Their way was not of possession or force but of sympathy. The peregrine was wild and had come to Laerimmer for help, half-starved. In spring she would return to the marshes.

'Did you think you were alone in your power?' Laerimmer asked, as Sarmatia scrambled to her feet. 'The time for lies between us is over.' He raised his free hand in salute. 'Look round and see how you've surprised the family. Until today both they and I thought I was the only one with this skill.'

Sarmatia held his gaze. 'Are you sorry you're not?'

The man shook his dark head. 'To have power is often to be lonely. I'm glad we're alike.'

Watching, Sarmatia saw that he spoke the truth. Satisfied, she turned and walked free of the trees. The family were ranged about her in a circle. Sarmatia bound her cloak about her wrist, held out her arm and called softly. Laerimmer removed the falcon's hood and the peregrine cast herself off his arm, sweeping over the gorse. On she came, graceful and deadly, fixing herself onto Sarmatia in a grip that could crush a bird.

The family shied, then, seeing the girl had come to no harm, moved in quickly towards her. Sarmatia, falcon on wrist and keen as a whetstone, was pleased to see them wary.

Let one of these royal kin call her peasant now!

Chapter 45

It was clear as the family closed on her that, though they had been startled by her reaction to the hawk, they were rapidly accepting it. Sarmatia was addressed with no servility or fear. Chalda gave her a sideways look. Gygest grinned as he passed by her. This was not as Sarmatia expected, though she preferred their quiet acceptance of her animal-kinship to empty flattery. The family seemed at last to have gained a measure of her, and appeared satisfied rather than confounded. Silently they left her, going their ways down the secret paths of the gorse.

With no one left in the homestead, Laerimmer brought Gorri out of the barn. From the house he collected a perch that could be driven into the ground for the falcon.

The Kingmaker and Sarmatia set out. The sun was strong, too good to miss. By mutual consent they stopped at a high place called Wolfstones, where great moss-covered rocks rose up like the knuckles of a raised fist. Gorri was content to graze and the falcon bask upon her perch. Sarmatia, giving a shamefaced thought to Fearn breaking his back over a plough, climbed the widest knuckle. She watched Laerimmer scramble up the rock after her.

'You said you'd an explanation for me.'

'Wait till I've got my breath. I'm not built for climbing.' Laerimmer sat down, rubbing his grazed fingers. 'You haven't seemed so keen on talk.'

Sarmatia sat up quickly, counting the distant scatterings of sheep in the landscape of moor, woods and fields. She flipped a pebble on her fingers, deciding not to speak of the archer, not until she was surer of Laerimmer. 'I didn't think questions mattered, so long as I could make Fearn happy, do my work. But what is my work?' She sounded young, especially to herself.

'There are many ways open to women,' said Laerimmer, as she sighed. 'Did you think there was only the one?'

Sarmatia tossed the pebble away. 'You've a kinswoman, kind, gentle, beautiful, modest. Her weaving is perfect, her dyeing bright. She is well-loved, accepted. I tried to be like her.'

'If you succeed in mirroring Anoi, you'll no longer be yourself.'

'So it would seem,' replied Sarmatia wryly. She smiled. 'Your womenfolk seem different, but accepted.'

'There are reasons for that. You don't make a magic fire by a hearthstone.'

Laerimmer's black eyes held hers. The world was quiet, the dark gaze growing in her mind. It wished her to breathe more slowly and be still... A buzzard cried overhead and she started. 'What did you do to me?' Disconcerted, Sarmatia rubbed her eyes.

'A little charm to catch your breath. Chalda makes it to send her child to sleep, although her real skill is in searching. When farms have lost tools or treasure, they send for Chalda to find them.'

'What other skills does she have?' Sarmatia was still shaken. How easily Laerimmer had touched her inward self. 'And Anoi: she too is part of your family -'

'Those of indifferent cooking, but I'll say no more about Chalda. Anoi, sadly, has no magic, but Gygest is good for weather. And Goar can charm a stone to its target.'

'You don't need magic for an ordered house,' snapped Sarmatia, alarmed at what Laerimmer had said about Goar. She frowned. 'Sorry. I should be the last to find fault. As Ormson would be delighted to tell you, I weave badly.'

'We're not as idle as we look,' remarked Laerimmer, a gleam in his eye. 'Magic is our work.'

Sarmatia propped her chin on her hand. Laerimmer's words made sense. She'd eaten bread made by others and repaid the debt in the Bull Rite. She bathed in the warm sun, wondering whether to ask more about Goar's stone charms. Would they also work for copper, an arrow, say?

Goar wasn't the only royal member who might hanker after the kingship. 'There's a woman who looks like you, Laerimmer...'

'My elder sister. If a spring goes dry, Kere will set it right. Although it's Fearn who's the rainmaker.'

'Yes, on Krete, Minos is rainmaker. Is that Fearn's magic?'

A rare look of awe crossed Laerimmer's round face. 'The true power of a king is peculiar to himself, though the magic may have been inside him already, waiting to reveal itself.'

'Then what is Fearn's power? What buried seed blossomed in my husband, Laerimmer, when you crowned him?'

'That's for Fearn to answer. Please, ask no more of me.'

His fear brought out the hunter in Sarmatia again. 'It'll be pleasant for me to watch you squirm, Kingmaker. It was your mockery that forced Fearn to take the test of kingship.' She gripped his arm. 'Fearn was a good healer. Why did you make him king?' In a sudden rush of anger she gave the man a shake. 'Why did you choose Fearn?'

'It was the test. I'd no choice in the final outcome. It's true Fearn was a good healer. By eleven years old he knew more healing than his mother, and at thirteen he was a wonder. But we needed him as King. You don't know what it was like, Sarmatia, when Waroch died.'

Remembering herself at thirteen, when she'd been a wonder in the Bull Rite, Sarmatia's anger faded. She released Laerimmer. 'Tell me what it was like.'

'People were terrified. No one could be sure that the next ruler might not also be a murderer. The land then would turn barren, the people perish.

'Fearn I knew to be guiltless. On the night of the fire he was at Rossfarm with Jart, the boy who's now healer in his place. They were tending a cow in calf. He didn't want to rule. He was preparing to leave.'

Laerimmer extended his hands to her, as though pleading in council. 'Sarmatia, I swear I didn't tamper in the choice of the three to take the test. Yet, when I held Fearn's token aloft, I knew it must be him. The applause of the family was like an acclamation, as though he was already king.'

'Has it been proved that Waroch was murdered?'

Laerimmer actually blushed. 'No one knows for certain, but the fire which killed Waroch started in the roof. Goar told me later he'd smelt sheep fat roasting.' He wagged a finger. 'We keep no sheep on our homestead.'

Sarmatia's breath hissed. Goar again! 'Who was first out of the house?'

Laerimmer gave a queer dry cough. 'My sister, Kere.'

'And Chalda? And Goar?' Those proud heads would suit a diadem.

'Chalda was at Rossfarm with Fearn and me.'

Pretty auburn curls and Fearn's voice: 'There was a girl, but they couldn't make me marry.' Sarmatia closed her eyes. 'So, you were trying to tempt Fearn to stay even then.'

'Yes, and you may laugh. Yet Chalda waited in vain for Fearn to see her.'

'Then married the new healer.' Sarmatia whipped to her feet. 'Who was the last man out of the house that night?' Impatient, she snapped her fingers. 'The last man, Laerimmer, who might have risked staying to make sure the King would die!'

'It was Goar, but it can't be him!'

Sarmatia was astonished at how both Laerimmer and Bride seemed to have lost their wits over this beautiful young man. She was less impressed. 'Why not Goar? Indeed, why not any man?'

'You've forgotten the defenses of our homestead,' replied Laerimmer, obviously relieved to change the subject. 'Only the family know the paths of the gorse hillside.' He paused. 'You should be our queen, Sarmatia.'

Sarmatia allowed herself to be distracted. 'Fearn says not.' She gave the Kingmaker a smile that made the man go pale. 'Or do you hope to kill me in the test?'

'If you think that, there's no dealing with you.'

Laerimmer's anger convinced Sarmatia that he was honest, and calmed her, as another show of fear could not have done. She cut through further exclamation with a motion of her hand. 'I believe you. Though it's hard for me to trust you, Laerimmer, even with what we share in common.'

'Ah, certainly you resent me, and have a dangerous temper, but then those keep you clear-headed. One thing I've noticed in you, Sarmatia, above others, is that often you're too quick to trust. A bad practice for a queen.'

'I, dangerous?' Sarmatia picked up on that.

Laerimmer gave a humorless laugh. 'You don't know how murderous you can look, my queen-to-be.'

Sarmatia thought of that moment in the fight between them, when his throat had been naked to her sword. A louse lighted on the stone between them and she pursed her lips, blowing it back to Laerimmer. 'Was the challenge another of your tests?'

'If it was, you succeeded. A queen must sometimes be merciful even when tempted to be otherwise. I knew by the end of our fight that you're not one to abuse power.'

Laerimmer placed his hand on the rock and Sarmatia watched the louse climb up the long dark hairs of his arm.

'Why do you want me as queen? You called me a southern peasant.'

The Kingmaker had the manners to look embarrassed. He scratched his head, fingers finding a scab at which to pick. 'I was wrong. So was the royal family. Yet they'll see. We'll all see.' Laerimmer spoke almost to himself. 'A born leader. No Atterian, entering the royal domain last night, would have dared to command the family as you did. I knew I'd made a mistake about you from the instant we met, the way that you answered me, your boldness. Look at yourself, snapping your fingers at me! Can you deny it?'

Sarmatia could not. Instead, she looked back over her life since leaving Krete and found that she had changed not merely in height. From the taciturn girl at home she had become, if not talkative, then far more open and able to express herself. She had taken command last night quite naturally. There were other changes too: a greater liking for people, a growing self-knowledge that she must deal with men and women as naturally as she did with animals. She smiled, shaking her hair luxuriously in the warm air. 'I've missed this! It's so dark in your land.'

Laerimmer walked cautiously up to her. 'A child might make you less homesick.'

'Babies! Man's answer to a woman's every grief.' Sarmatia paced the rock, thinking again of the lone bowman in the forest. 'Why not make magic? Show me the evil doer, and I'll kill him.'

'I've no magic for that.' Laerimmer closed a fist upon her cloak. 'You think I find this easy? For a year I've doubted my own kin. Goar I love as my son. It must be as a son.' He gave her cloak a vicious pull. 'Get back from there. You're no good to me with a broken neck!'

Sarmatia flicked round. 'Will Fearn be safer if I'm queen?'

'Safer still if you bear him an heir.'

'Chalda said you'd not choose my "brats".'

'Chalda speaks as the only woman of my kin who has borne a child that still lives. Do you see how I need you as queen?'

Sarmatia folded her arms across her breast. 'I might have guessed you'd have a use for my offspring.'

'But you will be queen?' This time an anxious question.

He was the living mirror of Pergia. It was perhaps fitting, Sarmatia thought, that she should now accept the will of Laerimmer, as once the snake priestess had acceded to hers. 'I'll consider it. First, you must do something for me.'

'You give orders easily for one not yet royal.'

'As you've noticed. Now, your test,' Sarmatia laughed as he stiffened. 'You remind me of someone I would rather forget, so you'll grow a beard. A new start for my new life.'

'I'll do it.' Laerimmer lifted his hand, pinching her cheek. Their eyes met in a rare moment of total accord.

Chapter 46

When Laerimmer's beard was as thick as a bear's pelt, and the spring sun brought flowers to the early heather, Sarmatia spoke to Fearn. 'Work grows slack in the house. Can I come with you?' She hoped to go with him to the woods, where they'd be alone and she could speak of becoming queen.

Her hand paused in its combing of her husband's hair. They were in bed in their tiny sleeping chamber.

Before answering, Fearn kissed a patch of moonlight on Sarmatia's elbow, then on her shoulder. He pushed her gently back on the sheepskins.

Sarmatia flicked at his beard with the silver comb. 'Let me cover you!' She rolled him off her. Fearn remained on his back and Sarmatia straddled him. As she placed her hands in the curve of his ribs and began a caress, Fearn spoke.

'It's the last pig-killing before summer.' The words spurted from him like slingshot. 'Would you wish to join me in that?'

Sarmatia shuddered and stopped. 'Fearn, what a time! Can't we talk later?'

'I don't like to refuse you after. And pig-killing... I thought of your animal-kinship.' He also remembered the roe deer Sarmatia had killed, though he did not say so.

On Krete, Fearn had seen only her friendship with animals. He had watched, in genuine admiration and delight, Sarmatia's handling of Nestor, the old beast of the Rite of Passage, while she was still injured from the Bull Rite. He had thought her sympathy a gift. The full truth, he was finding, was not so simple. The spirit animal within Sarmatia was becoming so strong, so persistent, that it colored her actions.

Fearn stifled a cry. She had bitten him in the neck. As Sarmatia drew back, her hips still grinding against his, he saw blood on her lips.

'Sarmatia—'

She moaned, collapsing forward onto his chest. 'My arms won't hold me up any more,' she gasped.

Still joined, Fearn put her onto her back. She cried out strongly, like a warrior, and her nails raked into his sides. The long shuddering moment passed, leaving her spent. Careless of his need, Sarmatia slept.

Seeing her at peace, Fearn did not wake her. Trying to ignore his own desire, he held his wife closely in his arms. Though she never grumbled, he knew Sarmatia was not content. Although Anoi had tried to be friendly, his Bull Head seemed uneasy of the Atterian women. Her flute lay unplayed in their chamber for days at a time as she tussled with a scrap of weaving or worked so hard at a skin that she tore through it with the scraper. Gladly he would have taken her with him, had it not been for the mockery of his men, or the danger.

Looking at Sarmatia in the moonlight, Fearn kissed the tiny scar on her forehead where the arrow had nicked her. He hoped that she had forgotten the archer. He could not. His plowing alone at Rossfarm had not drawn his enemy into a second attempt, so he must continue to watch his back.

His back was aching, as it often did these days. Fearn tried to rub at the spot while not disturbing his mate. Sarmatia looked so calm, it was hard to think of her being angry. Had Laerimmer been filling her head with his nonsense about Waroch's death? He had agreed to Sarmatia's trip with the Kingmaker in the hope that a change of place would work some charm for her. On her return, however, it seemed nothing had been gained. Sarmatia remained tense and unhappy.

I must do more, he thought. Perhaps if I speak to Maewe.

Drifting into sleep, Fearn smiled. He had an answer.

* * * *

He woke from a lascivious dream, starting as a hand pawed at his crutch. A dark head moved there, a mouth opened. Moonlight flashed on white teeth.

Fearn caught her hair and tipped Sarmatia off. 'Wait. We must talk.' He gave her head a playful shake. 'Tomorrow, you can go to Setir. He's busy with lambing time so close and would welcome help. What do you say?' He tugged at her fringe. 'Do you think you have the skill to manage a flock?'

'Of course.' Thwarted in her desire, Sarmatia was sulky. She knew about Setir, a shepherd with no children old enough to help him. Helping Setir was no hard task for her, to be out of doors and with animals, to be active, running and climbing, not standing by a loom all day. Later, Sarmatia would bless the perception of her husband. Tonight, the heat was bursting in her thighs. Suddenly furious at his checking her, she slapped him, not caring where she hit.

She was beyond reason. He could only restrain her until the tumult of blows had stopped. Finally, after several painful struggles, Fearn got her fast beneath him, one hand across her mouth. She bit him again and writhed, refusing to give in. 'Steady, Sarmatia,' he breathed in her ear.

She stiffened then was still. Under his hand, Fearn felt her mouth shape into a smile. Looking into her eyes, he glimpsed a dark, bristling shadow that was gone when she blinked. Her features softened, subtly. 'How strong you are,' she whispered, through his fingers.

Throughout the house men and women, roused by their struggle, were muttering and half-arguing themselves. Tired children, fractious at being woken, wailed and would not stay in their beds. A current of tension hummed through the homestead. A fist struck at their door-hanging as someone passed. Fearn and Sarmatia looked at each other.

He loved her, all of her, and could not deny himself the pleasure. He took her, fiercely, and she responded with passion.

Like a beautiful animal, Fearn thought, as he sank, satisfied, into sleep. He prayed that working with Setir would please Sarmatia, yet not take that kind of hunger from her.

* * * *

They slept until day-break, then rose and went their separate ways: Fearn to the woods and Sarmatia to the lambing fields. The brown-haired Setir was building a roof onto a lambing pen and he beckoned her.

'You know the hazel wood? Good, then take these baskets and get some ivy leaves. My ewes relish ivy before lambing...'

Without question or fuss, Sarmatia became a shepherd.

* * * *

Setir was quiet, more laconic than Sarmatia had ever been. She soon learned not to play her flute when he was near, but found him tireless in caring for the sheep.

They reached an understanding. Setir would stay with the ewes in the lambing field and let Sarmatia take the rams to pasture on her own. Sarmatia was happy to spend her days with these nimble, hardy creatures. Her own legs grew stronger walking the sheep-runs. She rubbed her feet with sheep's wool and her chilblains healed. The songs of her flute became lively.

Days and nights were spent without Fearn as she guarded the sheep on some distant pasture. In fields close to the homestead, Fearn would join her in keeping the flock. Then they had the privacy Sarmatia had craved. But she didn't speak of the archer, or the kingship.

'I am with child,' she said. 'Are you glad?'

For an answer he swept her up into his arms, rising and lifting her with him so her feet left the earth and she was spinning, whirled about by the young king.

'Our babe! Ours!' he was saying, half-shouting, causing the sheep to start and bleat in complaint.

'Ours,' Sarmatia agreed, relieved at his heart-felt joy.

* * * *

Laerimmer beamed, his teeth liked honed flints above the black curls of his beard. 'Excellent! An heir!' He knelt and kissed her hand. 'Now we can make you queen.'

Sarmatia tapped him with her shepherd's rod. 'Get up, Laerimmer. You're not a slave.' Her spirit animal was aware of the man at her feet, its hunting instincts aroused by his show of weakness. She resisted a sudden, frightening impulse to strike out at the man and at once a wave of sickness passed through her body. Fighting it, Sarmatia clutched at the wooden pole. 'Why do you look at me like that?'

'Because I've seen what your test will be. The goddess shows it in your face.'

Sarmatia opened her mouth, but Laerimmer held up his hand, and though he was still on his knees, she remained silent.

It's the art of the Kingmaker to persuade and counsel the King. A woman carrying a child may not be harmed, whatever crime she commits... whatever test she takes and fails.' Laerimmer climbed to his feet. 'Fearn will agree to your attempting the test for that reason. When will the baby be born?'

'Sometime in winter.'

'Then you'll be made queen at the late spring gathering, when the Atterians come together on the Sacred Hill.'

Chapter 47

The southerner has a charmed life. Twice by my own hand I have tried to kill her and yet she lives.

No other Atterian is her friend, only Fearn. Goar and Laerimmer seem to be leaning her way, but that's only expediency, I think. The Kingmaker isn't the kind to spread his wealth without return. He'll be calling in his bribes soon.

Goar's apparent change of heart is of no importance, seeing he's under a ban and keeps silent because of it. I met him, secretly, and promised to remove the curse if he'd help me. Strange, that he wouldn't wait to hear what I wanted from him. It was nothing much.

So. I can't rely on Chalda, who as a mother will risk nothing if it touches on her family. She talks, too, and I can't risk a breath of scandal.

I wait, spread rumors, and wait.

At last! One of my stray rams has returned, and with him he brings a key. Dill, greedy boy, has delivered Sarmatia into my hands— the means of her destruction. Oh, I knew he'd be useful some day!

I turn it in my hands, this precious matter that was once Sarmatia's. I know it will hurt her.

If the test does not kill, I'll still have two clear chances. Whether Sarmatia wears the diadem or not, she won't live. My plans are complete.

Chapter 48

One of the mysteries of the Sacred Hill was that when a man looked at its summit from its foot the hill was unbroken, but if he climbed the hill then the mound was seen to divide. It was as if a huge woman had knelt in the oak forest and bent forward. There was a flat spine, falling away in a curve, a dip for the neck and then the head of the hill, golden with flowers.

The Atterians had gathered on the long spine of the hill, carrying their armloads of firewood and the sheep that were to be culled from the flocks. These would be sacrificed throughout the day, then roasted and eaten. Fresh meat was a rarity, and a mood of gaiety and abandonment showed on people's faces.

The traders were now here, more cause for celebration. Sarmatia had decided that tomorrow, after her test, she would summon the chief trader and ask him to take a message to her brother Tazaros on Krete. She could pay the trader in gold, for after the test she would surely be rich.

Sarmatia was on the neck of the Sacred Hill, apart from the people. Somewhere on the body of the hill, Fearn waited for her. He had said goodbye the previous day, for on nights before an assembly the king lay with the goddess of the hill. He came to Sarmatia dressed in the gift of Anoi, his scarlet cloak. The stone battle axe that had killed Carvin was slung over one shoulder and a pot of woad hung from his belt. They had embraced, and afterwards Fearn had taken her head in his hands.

'I love you. The outcome of the test makes no difference to that. Remember, no harm will come to you, whatever happens.'

His fingers pressed on her skull as he blessed her, and Sarmatia heard the muted invocation, 'Let her win for the child.' As he released her head, Sarmatia felt her scalp tingle.

The next person to see her had been Laerimmer, who'd found her bent over the river, braiding back her hair. 'You'll have to wear women's clothes, tomorrow,' he'd said, as a greeting.

Sarmatia rubbed the gray tunic and gave the Kingmaker a sly look. 'I'll be different, tomorrow.'

'You have kept apart from other women? You have purified yourself?'

'Yes, and I'll sleep apart tonight.' Sarmatia combed her hair until it crackled. 'You told Fearn that our child would rule after him.'

'It was the lever by which to move him,' Laerimmer admitted, moving away to hide from Sarmatia on the head of the Sacred Hill. Later, by his questions, he would determine if she had succeeded or failed.

* * * *

A woman who undergoes a test is allowed two attendants on her journey to the foot of the Sacred Hill. Sarmatia had chosen Bride and Anoi as her companions: Bride her closest friend, Anoi her closest ally amongst the Atterian women. She spent the night before her test with Gorri in the open, and in the morning Bride came to meet her.

Bride whistled when she saw Sarmatia. 'You're going to your test like that? Does Laerimmer know?'

Sarmatia ran her fingers beneath the waist of the loin cloth that had taken her most of the night to stitch and grinned. 'Neither Fearn nor Laerimmer know anything yet.' She shook back her long, loose hair and stood up on her toes. 'How do I look?'

Bride looked her over from her bare feet and legs to her bare squared shoulders and breasts. 'Well, I think you could do with some more clothes on,' she said bluntly, 'but you look just like the frescos of Bull Riders, right down to the face-paint and the scars. But it's what you are, or were, and if it brings you ease...' The bigger woman shrugged.

Quickly, stopping herself in a new habit of holding a hand upon her belly, Sarmatia glanced down the field. 'Here's Anoi. I wonder what she'll think.'

'Yes, I wonder.'

'Don't frighten her.'

'Would I waste time on such a feeble thing? Though I bet Anoi doesn't like your costume.'

* * * *

Anoi stared at Sarmatia. 'You're very handsome, but I'd hoped... Fearn wears the gift I made him. I hoped, today at least, you would do likewise.' Delicately, she attempted a smile. 'Might this not have a bearing on your test?'

'And now we know.' Bride broke the sober mood with a wink over Anoi's blonde head. 'Let's have you walk in your finery, Sarmatia. You're not showing much, by the way, any more than I am myself.' Bride burst into a peal of laughter. 'You should see your faces!'

Sarmatia rushed at her, sweeping her arms about the older woman. She was giggling and weeping, standing on tiptoe to kiss Bride's cheek. The warrior was amused to find her friend just as fluttery as other women at this vital point in her life.

'We may be lying-in together!' she was saying. 'We can raise them as family. Fearn will make us their toys.'

'That's enough kisses, thank you.' Bride turned her head aside. Conscience pricked her, but she could see no other way than this. Anoi, she noted, had exhibited the proper responses of an Atterian woman to such news. No reckless embraces for her as she wished Bride a safe pregnancy and confinement.

'How far are you along?' Sarmatia interrupted Anoi not from rudeness but from sheer good-humored excitement.

'Gods, how do I know? A good month, I'd say.'

'Then your little one will be younger than mine. You'll be able to practice with my girl or boy!' In her delight, Sarmatia turned a cartwheel and darted in again to land another kiss. Pregnancy seemed to have made her even more open, and more openly affectionate. It will be a pity if she goes soft, thought Bride regretfully.

'Goar is very pleased,' she said aloud.

Instantly sobered, Sarmatia answered, 'So he should be.' The barbed reply was perhaps not intended, yet it showed Bride that for some reason her lover and Sarmatia were not friends. Caring for both, Bride was sorry.

'Come, we should be setting out,' she said gruffly.

Still Anoi made no move. Her mouth pouted. 'The test should not be mocked,' she began, but Bride answered, 'The battle's for Sarmatia, not for us.' She caught Anoi by the shoulder, whirling the girl along.

* * * *

Standing alone on the neck of the Sacred Hill, Sarmatia recalled her parting from Bride and Anoi. Bride had hugged her and wished her good luck. Anoi had taken her hand. 'Good fortune, Sarmatia.' She came close, perhaps because she was nervous of Bride. 'Here, you should take a drink before you leave us.'

Anoi removed a flask from her neck and would have touched it to Sarmatia's lips, except that Bride intercepted it, and, to Anoi's shocked disgust, drained off most. The foolish little scene made Sarmatia smile, as she waited in solitude.

There would be a sign, Laerimmer had told her. She would know the sign when she saw it. Follow it, Laerimmer said. Be vigilant, for the test begins with the sign.

* * * *

Sarmatia watched on the Sacred Hill. She saw Laerimmer's falcon, now set free, and started up, but the peregrine flew straight overhead. Her call was for her mate. Sarmatia settled again, narrowing her eyes up and down the smooth curves of the hill. Presently she saw the gleam and moved towards it.

The light was constant. It ran before Sarmatia as she scrambled onto the head of the hill. She climbed amongst cowslips, seeking gold in gold, and came upon a spring. Beside its clear waters was a goblet. A golden light flashed from the goblet rim as Sarmatia stretched out her hand.

The wine she drank was sweet, full-bodied. It warmed her and piled swathes of cowslips one on another, so that she walked in a golden cloud. Wrapped in light, Sarmatia plucked the flower stems of cowslip and wove them into a wreath for her head. She found a plate of gold and three narrow leaves of vervain, the plant of magic and divination, laid upon it. The scentless, tender leaves were swiftly swallowed.

The vervain seemed to have no effect on her. She saw the stranger beckon even without magic. Her feet were not winged, no fleeter, as she picked a way down the hill. She came within an arm's length of the man, who spoke without turning. 'What? Is a fisherman too poor for you now?'

Sarmatia sprang forward and was gathered into the firm arms she had never forgotten. With her head against his thick black hair, she smelt salt and harshness and felt living warmth. 'You're not dead!' she cried, in joy beyond laughter or tears.

'What's death?' Her father was as abrupt as in her childhood. He pulled back and Sarmatia looked into his face. His brows were heavy and dark, his features those of her brother, but his eyes were her own.

'I'm your ancestor-soul. In me is all your will and purpose.' The amber eyes looked deep into hers. 'Be wary of the end of will, Sarmatia. Remember how your father died, stubbornly putting to sea in poor weather.'

The arms released their grip, the sea scent drifted off with the wind. It was as though Sarmatia was staring at a deep lake and only her eyes were reflected. She might have watched forever, but a breeze blew dust into her face. She had to blink it away. Opening her eyes, she was alone.

No time for sorrow: another figure had appeared on the hill. Clutching her cowslip wreath, Sarmatia ran to meet it. Suddenly she stopped. The figure also stopped. Under long white robes covering even hands and feet there might be woman or man. The head was hidden by a dark blue veil. Sarmatia bowed her head. 'Who are you, please?'

The figure gave no sign of hearing. Sarmatia walked round it. She sensed its eyes seeking her through the dark veiling. 'Please, let me see your face.' She grasped the blue cloth and, meeting no resistance, lifted it.

The face was hers, as she would be in old age. The eyes were closed, for which small mercy Sarmatia was thankful, but for the rest— She brought her hands up to her own unwrinkled cheeks, afraid she would find them as ugly as the features shown before her. Every line and liver spot of age was on that face. The mouth, her mouth, drooled open to show the remaining teeth.

Sarmatia had always feared creeping old age, hid the fear in her heart and never looked too closely. Confronted by the certainty of all her beauty wasted, she was almost overwhelmed by self-pity. This was how she would be in later years, but how many? And how sad that at the end even laughter should wear out flesh.

With that second thought came compassion. Gently, though her fingers trembled, Sarmatia lifted a hand and closed the ancient mouth.

At her touch, the eyes of her future self opened and the wrinkled mouth spoke. 'I'm your self-soul. I'll always be with you.'

The face about the eyes grew younger and Sarmatia looked upon herself. Not as in a glass, which reverses left and right, but as Fearn could see her, as she was beyond the mirror. What she saw surprised her.

'Yes, you are softer than you think, Sarmatia. Whatever your hopes, you weren't meant to live alone, or with the animals you love so much. To every human being you met on your travels, you owe a part of your life.'

'Even Carvin?' asked Sarmatia, chilled to the marrow.

'Carvin sent the bronze ring north, didn't he?' Her self-soul smiled and there was solace for Sarmatia, though she knew it was her own lips that moved.

'Are you old or young?' she asked.

'Is forever old or young? I'm your self-soul that will be reborn. You and I are one.' The white-robed figure walked forward and Sarmatia experienced the deepest embrace she would ever know, spirit over flesh and flesh over spirit. It was sweeter than her animal-kinship, a light she could gather in her arms and keep. The white robes fell onto the earth, melted away.

She had faced her most hidden fear. The rest of the test might be harder but she would meet it gladly, eager for the lessons it would teach her. Sarmatia looked up at the sky.

It was still only noon. The sun seemed scarcely to have moved since her discovery of the golden cup. For the first time since moving on to the head of the hill, Sarmatia heard laughter and music and beneath these the featureless roar of people's movement and speech. She looked back and waved at the tiny crooked figures round the many campfires. Streams of sacrificial smoke drifted up to her. She could have no food until she had completed the test.

She had made a mistake in looking back. Her appetite alerted, other scents came crowding in: rich stews of cooking mutton, crushed spices, fresh baked bread. Yet she had to remain on the head of the hill. The goddess would know if she cheated. I would know, thought Sarmatia, running uphill, putting distance between herself and the cooking smells.

A stumble brought her to her knees, hair and hands dusted with flowers. Fascinated, Sarmatia saw how the pollen had been smeared on her in stripes, so that her hair was patterned in brown and orange. She lifted one hair plait and tried to shake off the clinging pollen when a shadow fell across her face.

Sarmatia raised her head, heart quickening as her eyes met the lounging shape of her spirit animal. It lay with its back to her, head at rest on the hidden paws. Like a beast on some fabulously woven cloth, the yellow stripes of its long body were the nodding cowslip flowers, the darker stripes of its coat was her hair. Now the narrow trumpets of the flower heads were thickening into fur. The brown hair blackened and the shape grew and took on the rounded contours of a living creature. Her spirit animal yawned, a red tongue rolling round its fangs like meat in a huge bronze cauldron, and a liquid eye, deeper than any sunset, slid round with the head to fall upon Sarmatia.

Both were still. Only the wind lifted Sarmatia's hair and stirred the shaggy facial whiskers of her animal's broad head. Then the great beast thrust its front paws forward, raised its rear haunches and described a graceful curve. Her spirit animal yawned a second time, rocked out of the curve and came to push its head under Sarmatia's hands.

A small, bear-like ear rasped against her lower ribs as she stroked the creature, feeling its purr warm her body. The white cheek fur tickled her stomach and the great golden feet, so graceful in running, clumsily trod over hers. Her spirit beast was larger than a lion, with a bigger jaw and gape, but Sarmatia was not afraid. Her spirit animal was herself. She was proud of the powerful limbs and gleaming fur, touched by the long tail with the tuft of springy black hairs at its tip, so incongruous when compared to the dignity of the rest. Like herself, her spirit animal had increased in size and stature. This pleased her, until she realized that her creature was continuing to grow.

Soon she had to release the head, stepping out from the shadow of the white underbelly. She smelt the rank breath of the meat eater and stepped back still farther. Her spirit animal was as tall as a young tree, each claw a curving sword-blade. They raked the earth and the air was full of torn flowers.

'Stop!' she shouted, but the claws dug deeper and dirt hailed round her shoulders. She ran at the big cat to stop it. A paw flattened her to the hillside. Broken-breathed, Sarmatia gained her feet and set off in pursuit.

It was making for the neck of the hill. The people on the body of the hill were blind to its coming, deaf to Sarmatia's warnings. Only Laerimmer's falcon, bending its flight through the air, set up an alarm. Her spirit animal fixed its sights on the bird and the peregrine shrieked.

'Stop it!' cried Sarmatia, but her animal would not leave the falcon. The bird was snatched in midair by the will of her spirit-beast. Terror stooped into her. Sarmatia struggled and screamed. Separate from her animal-kinship, a part of her mind tried to reach her spirit animal. She felt its resistance and then a force thrust her back, down into the life of the falcon.

The sky was rolling. She was slipping. The bird flapped her wings and struggled to gain more height, Sarmatia desperate that she would succeed.

Her spirit animal moved again. Before she could speak it lunged forward. Its killing ripped into Sarmatia as it lashed out at the flailing peregrine. Sarmatia closed her eyes but it made no difference to the end. The bird fell in a spatter of black and gray feathers: a life wasted, because of her.

She did not know how to control this monster. Ramose and Laerimmer had been right to warn her. She must find the means of its mastery. Again she shouted, but her spirit animal growled, the soil vibrating in a low shuddering note. Help me, Sarmatia prayed, feeling the strengths of her ancestor and self-soul well within her. She caught hold of the beast's tail that was as thick as a rope and tugged.

The creature shook the hill with its roar. It twisted back and struck, missing Sarmatia's face but rending her hair. Unable to loosen her grip, it ignored her and set off at a bound for the lower hill. Sarmatia screamed warnings at the crowds, but no one looked their way. Soon the beast would be across the narrow bridge that divided the two hills.

Sarmatia tried to dig her heels into the earth. Her feet skidded and she could find no purchase. She fell back and was dragged, slashed by stones, peppered by dirt. The neck of the hill came into view. On its far side, a group of children were playing with toy spears, oblivious to the beast. Her spirit animal quickened and Sarmatia missed her footing again, going down belly first. Like an empty sledge, she careered down the slope and her sight began to blacken.

Her ancestor-soul saved her. Slowly, arm after arm like a fisherman drawing in a net, the tail was pulled in. Link by link, Sarmatia rose up the striped fur, until, with a final leap, she could vault onto the creature's back.

Sarmatia locked her legs about her spirit animal's neck and seized a handful of white cheek fur in either hand. Their cries boomed across the hill, yet none of the people heard or saw their struggle. Sarmatia forgot them as she forged her will onto that of her creature's.

It was a hard battle and her only weapons were those of gentleness and patience, for even with the strength of her other spirits she could do no more than hold her own against the vigor of her spirit animal. Her limbs were numb but she continued to speak calmly, turning her spirit beast away from killing.

At last it heeded her and broke into a run, its feet crossing beneath its body as they zigzagged the hill. The ground passed under Sarmatia's feet as her spirit animal moved, its tail floating straight out behind, carried on the air of its passage. She felt the wind smack her cheeks. The land rushed beneath them. She was spinning, falling—

She touched earth, the flowers clasping her in a golden net. Seated, laughing, Sarmatia held out her hands. In the fall, her spirit animal had shrunk in age and size. She caught it easily.

Sarmatia lowered her head and with a weak, tired laugh, nuzzled the white underbelly of the mewing cub. She had not won easily over her spirit animal—it was too powerful for that—but she had checked its worst excesses. As a cub it would grow, but now she could teach it.

Tenderly, she watched it squirming in her lap. Her self-soul had her own name, her ancestor-soul she knew as her father, only this spirit remained unnamed. Sarmatia stroked its back and flanks. The cub quietened and raised its dandelion head to hers.

'You'll be bigger than a leopard, and stronger,' she whispered. 'You will be the ruler of the forest. That is the name I call you. Hail, Lord of the Forest!'

* * * *

Sarmatia settled to wait until the cub slept before she walked farther on the Sacred Hill and fell asleep herself.

She was woken by Laerimmer. Her spirit animal was gone, its presence locked deep within. Their struggle seemed to have occurred in some ancient time, and yet be more real than the cup of water that the Kingmaker offered her.

'Did you note the sign?' he asked.

Sarmatia smiled and tapped her empty cup.

'Tell me what other things you've seen.'

The words flooded out and Laerimmer sat by Sarmatia's feet and listened, his face mournful in repose and growing sadder when she spoke of the death of the falcon. At the end he scratched himself thoughtfully. 'You know that you've won your test.'

'Yes.' Sarmatia met Laerimmer's gaze, seeing him with the clear vision of the spirits. 'Why did you bribe the war band?' she asked, reading that guilt in the man's eyes.

The Kingmaker's face grew yet more mournful. He looked away and made no answer.

'Did you think that Fearn's choice would be so poor?'

'I did it so that Fearn would stay. I didn't want our king to leave his country.'

'And why should Fearn have what you could not?' said Sarmatia, thinking of the silver-haired Goar.

The man's eyes flashed. 'You're coming back.'

Sarmatia fingered the cup that the Kingmaker had given her, delighting in its coarse, grainy surface. In the last few moments, the world about her had grown more immediate. She nodded, 'Yes. I'm ready.' She laughed. 'What do you think of your bribery now?'

'That I've gained more than I've lost.' Laerimmer took her hand and kissed it. 'The queen of the Atterians is beyond all wealth. You're better than gold or bronze.'

'I'm glad to hear you say it.'

The man tweaked her hair, just as Pergia the Snake Priestess had done in her Kretan garden, when Sarmatia had been only a Bull Rider, famous, but facing an uncertain future.

'Let's get you crowned,' he said.

Chapter 49

Laerimmer would not have her move from the hill at once. He went off alone, a fat man making haste. Sarmatia savored her victory. She would send word to her brother on some of Fearn's hoarded papyrus: *I, Sarmatia, Queen of the Atterians*. Fearn need never be ashamed of her.

Sarmatia rested her hands on her body, interlocking fingers. So often she forgot the babe within her, and yet it grew. After this assembly she must take up needle and thread and make the child some clothes. She would work for Bride, too. It pleased her to think of Bride and herself as mothers. Though they wore men's clothes, they had proved their womanhood.

Pressing her thumbs against her greater roundness, Sarmatia sighed, a sound echoed from a lower slope of the hill as Kere and the women of the royal family approached. They were laden with baskets and Sarmatia ran to meet them, her flower wreath finally slipping, to land at the feet of Chalda.

Chalda's baby started at the pretty thing, hanging forward from her mother's arms. Sarmatia scooped up the wreath, setting it about the child's neck.

'We're here at Laerimmer's command to get you ready,' said Chalda. As though she could not bear it to touch her daughter, she seized the knot of flowers and cast it aside. The baby began to bawl, but when Sarmatia attempted to distract her, Chalda cried out, 'You've done enough by your witchery!' She clutched the child so closely to her bosom that it was frightened and started to scream.

'That woman annoys me,' said Sarmatia, as Chalda flounced off, her child's howls redoubling. 'Go after her, one of you, and see she comes to no other harm that she can cast at my feet.' She nodded as Anoi put down her pitcher and went after the woman, but a little of the pleasure was gone.

'Will it content you to be bathed and dressed by us, Lady?' whispered a woman, her eyes averted from Sarmatia's face. Remembering the lesson of her spirit animal, Sarmatia spoke gently and watched the narrow face rise up to hers. 'It pleases me,' she said, smiling.

They bathed Sarmatia in water from the spring, rinsing her hair in water steeped with herbs. There was a woman's gown, made specially long for her, and a golden ribbon for her hair. The women combed and smoothed, rubbed woad onto Sarmatia's cheeks and stepped back to admire their work.

A horn sounded from the body of the Sacred Hill.

'It's time,' said Kere. They fell back for Sarmatia to lead them.

On the body of the hill, men and women waited to join in her train. Amongst these, Sarmatia spotted a southern plainswoman who had been brought north as a captive-wife. She paused to speak with her. The woman was newly pregnant, even as she was.

'Do you hope for a son or daughter?' Sarmatia asked.

The woman blushed to be singled out. 'Either, Mistress, so long as the child is whole,' she said in Atterian. Glancing at her youthful husband, she added, 'There'll be others, I hope.'

Bystanders laughed, but touched by the woman's answer, Sarmatia bent and kissed her. There was a roar from the people, and for a moment she wondered if she had done right, but all was well. The crowd acclaimed her. Their shouts swept her forward.

Set in the middle of the hill top were two high backed chairs, painted blue and red. Fearn was seated on one, with Bride and Laerimmer standing close. His father's family were a little farther off and now they moved to fill the swollen ranks behind Sarmatia.

'Will you not raise your head to greet your fellow ruler?' asked Fearn, so softly that only she could hear. He was smiling. She could tell that from his voice.

Sarmatia looked up. Fearn was standing before her. The scarlet cloak which Anoi had given to him lay discarded over his chair. He still wore the gray woolen tunic of any farmer, plain and worn at the elbows. His forehead was dyed by a dark woad. His gaze was like fire. On his head was a bronze diadem: heavy and strong, and yet he bore it easily. Now he drew her onto the second painted throne.

Her eyes were as piercing as ever, Fearn noticed, like those of a beautiful animal. He recalled that Anoi's eyes were like flowers, large and blue, and was angry and confused that he should think of his gentle cousin now, and compare her to Sarmatia, to his Kretan's disadvantage. He puzzled briefly what Sarmatia's test might have been and then, as suddenly as they had formed, the disquieting thoughts were suppressed by a surge of pride and strong feeling.

'Fetch me a crown, Kingmaker!' he cried.

The heavy bronze was brought and Sarmatia whispered, 'I can't wear it, the weight will break my head.'

'The Queen can carry it,' answered Fearn. With his own hands he placed the polished diadem upon her brow.

Horns and drums sounded along the length of the Sacred Hill, men pounded the earth with their feet. Sarmatia felt her high throne shake, shuddering her backbone. The diadem pressed on her temples but she fixed her eye on the evening sun and lifted her head. There was another blast of horns. Crowds jostled and children sat high up on shoulders to see.

Fearn went down on one knee, his face level with hers. An expectant stillness fell over the people.

'You are the Queen,' he said. 'The goddess of this place has made you hers. From today, you are my right hand as I am your left.'

Sarmatia held up her hand, the bronze ring flashing on her finger. 'Come then,' she commanded softly. 'Let us begin our rule.'

Slowly, their two hands met and joined. Sarmatia looked amongst the Atterians for her friends. She smiled at Bride, who was talking to Goar and did not see her looking. She saw Chalda, who scolded her husband; Maewe, Orm and Laerimmer, proud, and Setir, laughing. She did not see Anoi.

Sarmatia looked again at Fearn. His nose and lips were chiseled in profile. She loved him, she carried his child. His head turned to her, the green eyes softening.

'You wear the diadem well.' He chuckled and bent his head to whisper, 'You and I should walk amongst the people, at least until sunset.'

'And after sunset?' murmured Sarmatia. The drums pulsed in her ears. Suddenly exultant, she rose from her seat and started towards Bride, managing her long woman's robe with one hand, keeping the diadem steady on her head.

* * * *

She and Fearn wandered about the hill top, admiring the goods of the traders. Tall as they were, both could see over most heads. One trader, spotting her as Fearn was called away, called out to her.

'Lady, for a queen, there is nothing more fitting than lapis-lazuli.' He rippled a necklace like sparkling blue rain through his hand.

Sarmatia thought of a wish made over a season before and moved in slowly through the crowd. Though she knew of no gift yet for Fearn, Bride would have this necklace.

About to barter for the gleaming lapis, Sarmatia heard Fearn ask, 'What, is my queen about to spend all our harvest?' She glanced up into Fearn's smirking face and laughed, but the trader, with the speed of his kind, spoke first. 'Permit me, Lord. I have something that will please you and your lady both. Please take it as a gift.'

A rummage in his packs produced the thing and, at the gasps of admiration, the trader was bold enough to slip up to Sarmatia and place it around her throat.

But Fearn grabbed the man and shook him. 'Who gave you this?'

Beside him Sarmatia moaned, trembling from head to foot.

'Take it off!' She tried to grip the torc. Sobbing, she dropped on her knees, the gold still round her throat. There was a burning pain that seemed to shrivel her insides. Warmth trickled between her legs.

'Look, she bleeds!' cried a woman. Children screamed.

Fearn kicked the trader in the groin.

Sarmatia tore the torc from her neck. Women closed on her, faces drawn in horror. She let herself be laid back on the ground. She could hear Fearn shouting, saw men and sheep scattering over the hill.

'Will I lose my baby?' she whispered, as a woman covered her with a cloak. The woman shook her head.

'Lady, you must rest. Think of nothing.' The words were lost in the unearthly wail of horns blowing an alarm.

Sarmatia rolled her head to one side. Close by, gemstones glittering, lay the discarded torc once given her by Ramose, all gold, in the shape of a curving crocodile. She had last seen it entombed, still about the neck of its final owner, Carvin.

Chapter 50

'Rumors are spreading,' said Laerimmer.

'When there's news, people will hear,' answered Fearn. 'Have you questioned the traders again?'

'The traders are preparing to leave.' Laerimmer stood back from the rush-strewn bed, grimacing at the stench. 'The spice-seller sticks to the same tale, that he received the torc from a boy with blue eyes. You shouldn't be here. Even the healer does not sit in at a birth.'

'This is my wife. I guard her as well as any woman.'

'It'll be sad if we lose our queen through your meddling.'

Sarmatia braced her fingers on Fearn's arm, pulling herself up from the rushes. 'You're a fool, Laerimmer,' she said harshly, before Fearn could be angry. 'Offer gloomy counsels to others, but not the King.'

'As you will, Madam.' Laerimmer lumbered from the alcove. Sarmatia flopped back on the bed.

'You must leave, too. You've shocked Maewe enough. No—' She raised her hand in a plea. 'Go see the traders. They must take a message to Tazaros that I'm safe.' Her pallor showed that this was false, but Fearn rose from the bed.

'I'll speak to the traders if you wish, Sarmatia.' He bent and kissed her forehead. 'And I'll pay for this message.' Fearn made to drag the blood-soaked rushes off the bed, but Sarmatia snatched at his hand.

'Fearn!' She crushed the cold palm against her own. 'Gorri and the horses, they know something's wrong.'

'As these know?' Fearn motioned to the rafters. In one night, five owls had gathered on the beams above her chamber. People said they were spirits. Sarmatia knew the birds for what they were: heralds of the forest. She commanded that the entrance to the house stay open.

Fearn stared up at the ghostly creatures, their eyes reflecting light like facets of crystal. The birds were oddly alert for the hours of daylight. He nodded to the five then returned his gaze to Sarmatia. 'When the traders have gone, I'll visit the horses.'

'Ask Laerimmer to ride Gorri. He needs a gallop.'

'Who, Laerimmer? No, Sarmatia, don't frown. I'm going.'

Sarmatia called him back a second time. 'Speak to the people, Fearn. They've waited all night for some word.'

Fearn disappeared through the door-hanging and her face crumpled. She could no longer hope that she would keep her baby. The pains had increased. She had been carried on a litter to Fearn's house, the Atterians following in silent procession. When she'd been taken inside, people had broken ranks and streamed into the yard. Several faces had been bloodied as tempers boiled in that confined space, but overnight the Atterians had settled to a brooding quiescence. They seemed to sense, like the animals, that she was almost spent.

Sarmatia rose on her elbow as Maewe and Kere swept into the chamber, but sank back when she saw they had only brought in more rushes to pack under her. They spoke in bright voices, saying the worst was past.

'Chalda and the others will come when they have eaten.' Maewe's faded chestnut hair swept against Sarmatia as she straightened up from the bed. 'Then we'll keep that husband of yours from worrying you again.'

'Fearn's no trouble.' Sarmatia's eye fell on the bloody rushes that Kere was taking out to burn. Maewe nodded.

'No, you don't want Fearn to see you so. Believe me, child, in some matters women do best without their men folk.' Maewe laid her hands upon Sarmatia. 'Are the pains strong? When they come closer together, cry out. We'll cry with you.'

It seemed the women would witness her struggle. Sarmatia's heart sank, but she found her voice. 'Has Bride been found? Might I see her?'

Kere sniffed. 'I can't see what you want with such a person. She can hardly help you now.'

Laerimmer's sister bustled from the chamber, leaving Sarmatia distraught. 'Where is Bride? Why will no one tell me anything?'

'Gently, child.' Maewe pressed her back onto the rushes. 'Kere meant no harm by her sharpness, it's simply that we're anxious for you.'

I grant that you are worried, but Kere and Chalda? No. She felt alone amongst these women. She kept still while a pain grew and receded within her. 'What is it? Has something happened?'

'Now, don't get yourself upset.' Maewe sat on the bed. 'Oh, you might as well learn now, as later. Bride has taken to bed. She could lose her own child, poor creature.'

The gifts of the dead, thought Sarmatia. It's because of the torc that Bride and I suffer. Carvin's spirit wants revenge, and the thing was his for a time. Or is it a sign that in some way this is Carvin's child? What if Carvin has taken over my baby?

Sarmatia started to scream.

* * * *

'Bride, this is madness . You can't go anywhere,' said Goar from the hut entrance.

'Where have you hidden my boots?' Bride pounded the bed then wished she hadn't.

Noting her sudden change of color, the desperate clutching at her stomach, Goar withdrew.

When the spate of sickness had run from her, Bride crawled between the furs. She dozed then made herself sit up and take some milk, even though she knew it would go straight through. When she had first fallen ill, soon after Sarmatia had collapsed and been carried off the Sacred Hill, Bride had thought her own sickness too much of a coincidence. Between bouts of fever, she observed its progress and now was certain of its cause.

'Just a little more milk, my lovely.' Goar encouraged her to eat from the doorway.

'Ach, I look a sight,' said Bride, catching sight of her reflection in the metal basin.

'Even uglier than when I first saw you,' Goar agreed. Yet he was still there. Bride had been surprised that he'd not returned to the royal home. She would have thought no less of him had he done so. It wasn't as though she had really been pregnant.

Bride grimaced as her guts went into another spasm. 'Go away!'

'Let me fetch Jart. Or some of the smiths' wives.'

'There must be no one! The healer's place is with Sarmatia.'

Everyone, including the smiths, had to believe that her illness was a threatened miscarriage, not so far along as Sarmatia's, where the help of other women might be required, but sufficient to keep Bride in bed.

'I hear Sarmatia's got the midwives with her,' said Goar. 'The baby's come too early.'

Bride closed her eyes. 'She's lucky to be alive.'

'That's a little unkind to a girl about to lose her first.' Goar had ventured inside the hut. Seeing Bride quiet, he came closer. 'Anything you want?'

Bride opened her eyes, smiling at him. She guessed he would be gone the moment her next crisis began, but then you don't ask a moth to stay out in a gale. He had done well this last month, rarely despairing even when their attempts to mate ended limply. A more serious-minded man than Goar might then have decided—with much sorrow and regret—to leave her. Goar had stayed. If it was because he believed she could shift the curse, Bride still preferred to pretend it was because he cared.

He could be surprisingly steadfast. 'Tell me the name,' she had said to him, more than once. 'I'll plead with the girl.'

'I can't.'

'Surely you don't believe this girl's lies about your dying if you name her?' said Bride, but she dared not press him. She was not sure herself.

'Point her out to me,' she begged him. 'I'll challenge her.'

'And you'd kill her. Then I'd be a man who slew a woman by a woman.'

'Go to her yourself. Speak to her.'

'I can't.' Goar had tried talking to the girl, but she had demanded too much for her removal of the curse.

In the end, Bride had pretended to be pregnant, telling Goar that it would weaken the spell if people thought he was potent. While such belief could do no harm, the real purpose of her false pregnancy had been to draw Goar's adversary out into the open. Now, with this sickness, she was almost sure.

Her color must have changed. Goar was retreating. He had brought the bucket up close and left her a pot of fresh water.

'Thank you,' called Bride, hastily swallowing.

'Please let me fetch Jart. Your illness may be catching.'

No more than my supposed bleeding, thought Bride, but she saw that her young man was at his limit. 'Alright,' she gasped. 'And take this message to Sarmatia. She's to taste no food put by for her. Go!'

Bride had her head over the bucket, and did not see Goar leave.

* * * *

As Maewe predicted, Sarmatia's pains drew together with no respite. The chamber was packed with the women of Fearn's two families, some crouching, some standing. Now they would have her walk in the house and, supported by Maewe, Sarmatia dragged herself from the bed. Maewe and Kere hooked their arms under hers and Sarmatia lifted her head.

'One of you, go to Fearn,' she pleaded. 'Stay with him.' She shuddered. Chalda climbed over the bed, pretty face drab.

'Sarmatia, Anoi has gone to Fearn. She will keep her kinsman company. Now you must let us help you, poor thing.'

She stretched her hand, and Sarmatia screamed. She did not trust Chalda. Yet, as the young woman's hands closed over her stomach, Sarmatia found her touch soothing, and when Kere grew weary of supporting half her weight, Chalda took her place, knotting her fingers into Maewe's.

'Rest,' whispered Sarmatia to the young mother, when Maewe finally sank onto the bed and Ormson's wife took her place.

Chalda shook her auburn curls. 'I'll rest with you. I know what it's like to be sleepless. I miscarried the winter before last.' She kissed Sarmatia's cheek. 'You'll have another, as I did. The birth pangs are far easier next time.'

Sarmatia knew she was dreaming. Chalda speaking kindly to her? Then pain swelled and a burning flow of blood spattered over her legs. She stopped walking, rigid with fright. Her guts seemed to be hanging by a thread and if the thread broke—

She sneezed. The thread snapped, the pain stopped. With a horrible sliding, a shuttering of matter fell onto the alcove floor. Sarmatia's knees gave way, but Ormson's wife caught her and Setir's wife stepped forward and they took the girl between them.

'Soon you can sleep,' Setir's wife told her. Chalda and Maewe were cleaning the mess into buckets, Kere and Harr changing the rushes. They seemed satisfied, as with a job well done, but Sarmatia sensed fondness, too. She had not realized that she was held in such affection. 'What a fool.'

'What's your name?' she asked Ormson's wife. 'I want to know all your names.'

Ormson's wife was called Janne.

Setir's wife was Thrif.

Chalda's baby was called Tatta, but that was only a first name. When the child lost her milk teeth she would be given a second, adult name.

Somewhere amongst the names, Sarmatia fell asleep.

Chapter 51

She came awake in the night. 'What is it?'

'People are dancing in the yard, celebrating your escape from death,' Chalda answered. 'Fearn is with them, dancing with Anoi. Shall I fetch him?'

'Please, let him dance.' Sarmatia snuggled back on the bedfurs, marvelously soft after the rushes. Someone had stripped off her brown woolen dress, taken her diadem. She was clean and comfortable.

Chalda bent over her, moonlight sparkling on the pearl comb set in her hair. 'Sarmatia, I must say something to you, and quickly, while we are alone. I'm sorry you lost your child, but keep this in mind: within a year you can get another.'

That would be Fearn's for certain, no taint of Carvin's, thought Sarmatia, but she said nothing.

'When you were in such pain,' Chalda said, 'It made me see you...you, and not some image I'd fashioned in my head. Oh, Goar was right when he said it was nothing but hurt pride that made me look on you as some foreign peasant.'

Sarmatia gave a dry little cough. 'I am a peasant by birth,' she said, amused. 'Goar scolded you, you say?'

'Yes, my elder cousin Goar. He came here, yesterday, with a message from Bride, though he could not deliver it to you.' Two pale, silver-gilded hands hovered like lacewings in the air between them, uncertain whether to settle or fly. 'From today I wish you nothing but good, Sarmatia.'

Sarmatia gripped a silver hand. 'It seems we've both been wrong.' The two were still a moment then Chalda left to find Tatta for her next feed.

* * * *

'Did you see Sarmatia?' Bride saw that Goar had brought the healer, but ignored Jart.

'The women wouldn't let me in for me to give her your message. She was far into labor when I reached the house.'

'She lost the child, but otherwise is doing well,' put in Jart.

Bride started up in bed. 'Fool, she's still in danger!' She gripped Goar's arm. 'This is the moment—meet it, be a man. Get back to her!' Her eyes rolled, limbs thrashing as she went into a convulsion.

'She's raving,' said Goar, backing away. 'It's the fever.'

Jart, trying to stop Bride injuring herself or biting her tongue, answered, without looking at him, 'No fever would cause these sweats and sickness. Your woman has been poisoned.'

Goar paled and ran out of the hut.

* * * *

Fearn spun Anoi in the dance, gave her a smacking kiss and moved on. He seized a beaker from a man, drained and then smashed it, kicking aside the pieces to the drunken cheers of his people. He was far gone himself.

'Swing me! Me first!' shouted the children, as Fearn danced with each, flinging them up, spinning them round. He whirled about for happiness and relief and life, and these children were alive.

And his own child was dead. 'Sarmatia will be weeping for days,' Anoi had said.

Fearn drank, celebrating to forget.

* * * *

Sarmatia woke to someone moving in her room. 'Maewe?'

'No, Kere.'

Sarmatia could just see her in the dawning light. From the yard came the beat of a single drum. Some revelers still continued. Kere put a basin of flowers by her bedside. 'Here, I gathered these for you.' She bent and placed a final posy by the girl's colorless cheek. Sarmatia breathed the perfume.

'If you need a waiting-woman, when you've recovered, that is, I shall be glad to serve you.'

The offer was the nearest Kere would come to an apology, but Sarmatia understood. One by one, the royal family were finally accepting her as their Queen.

She inclined her head. 'Thank you.'

* * * *

'You have to let me pass this time,' Goar said to Chalda, at the door of the house. 'I need to see Sarmatia alone.'

'Fearn, Anoi and Maewe are with her now.'

'I'll wait.' Goar took up a position by a doorpost. He was there when Fearn and Anoi emerged from the house.

'I've seen Sarmatia weep over a drowned kitten,' Fearn was saying to Anoi, 'But I've not seen her shed a single tear over her own dead baby.'

'Give her time, Fearn,' answered Anoi. Seeing Goar she halted a moment then came swiftly forward. 'Kinsman, how is it with Bride?'

'Not so good, the bleeding grows worse.' In Fearn's hearing Goar would not mention poison. The young King was already distracted.

'If there's anything I can do, anything she needs.'

Goar nodded and the two shook hands, united for once by their common concerns. 'How is it here?' Goar ventured. 'Can I see your wife?'

Anoi answered for Fearn. 'Sarmatia's sleeping. She needs to rest.'

Goar resumed his position by the doorpost. 'I'll wait.'

Fearn clapped him on the shoulder in thanks, and walked across the yard to Orm and Laerimmer, leaving Goar with Anoi.

'What about Bride?' Anoi asked. 'Are you deserting her?'

Goar paused until Fearn was well out of earshot before he answered. 'There's nothing I can do at the smith's. A miscarriage isn't men's business.'

Besides, Bride had told him to guard Sarmatia.

* * * *

Now that she, Chalda and Kere had become easier with each other, Sarmatia began to see other Atterian women in a different way. She had thought them soft, yet none had flinched at the sight of blood. These housewives were tough. More surprisingly, they seemed to like her.

'You were so docile,' said Sarmatia to the tall Harr. 'It nearly killed me, trying to follow your example. I remember that day of the winter feast, when I watched you all feed and groom your husbands. You kissed their hands!'

'Well, so we did.' Harr smiled as she recalled the feast day. 'But we'd just watched you wash Fearn's hair. We tried to match that service.'

Sarmatia's face puckered in amusement. She had not thought the wives might be nervous of her, nor seek to rival anything she did. 'My weaving will never equal yours,' she said, and was entirely satisfied by the reply.

'A queen that guards our sheep doesn't need weaving skills.'

* * * *

Maewe had told Sarmatia that the tiny, fish-like fetus and afterbirth had come away from her cleanly and that she would have no more bleeding than in a normal monthly course. Until her bleeding stopped, though, she should not step outside the house. A spirit might creep into her unprotected womb. In another month, Maewe said, she and Fearn could mate, but until then they were not even allowed to speak to each other alone. The women hovered, persistent as hedge sparrows. If they thought the King stayed by Sarmatia's bedside too long they drove him away.

For two days Sarmatia was forbidden to rise from her bed. She asked for her flute and was told that Setir had taken it to the high pastures. The sheep had become accustomed to the sound, and fretted if they did not hear the mellow call of the flute at least once in a day. So, although Sarmatia at first slept from exhaustion, later it was from boredom.

She was dozing when Fearn and Anoi entered the chamber to visit.

'Fast asleep. We'll wait a moment to see if she stirs.' Fearn crouched on his heels, scuffling in the dirt.

At the sound Sarmatia struggled to open her eyes. She felt the furs tighten around her legs as Anoi perched on the bed, then she slipped back into unconsciousness.

Their voices woke her next. Anoi's quiet whisper. 'I shall never be as beautiful as her. Look at those long dark lashes!'

'Yes, Sarmatia is lovely.' Fearn touched her eyelid. 'Still no tears.'

'Everywhere she goes, men smile at her.'

Untrue, thought Sarmatia, but her tongue would not work. Through the veil of her lashes she saw Fearn's fingers encircle Anoi's.

'You're also pretty, Anoi. Men smile at you. In fact there is one young man, whose name is Dill—'

Anoi snatched away her fingers. 'Dill is nothing to me.'

'You were dancing with him, the night before last,' teased Fearn.

'I don't remember,' said Anoi sulkily. 'It's not important.'

* * * *

Sarmatia needed to talk to Bride. Fearn had already summoned and questioned his warriors, but they denied stealing the torc from Carvin's burial mound. King and war band looked sidelong at each other and Sarmatia thought it wise to let Fearn be. She talked to him of other matters, of how the five owls had returned to the forest, of how she and Chalda were reconciled. Her thoughts on the torc she meant to share with Bride, except that the smith was also sick.

One day before her bleeding stopped, Sarmatia rose, put on a pad of felt and dressed in her clean brown robe. Looking down, she noticed that her breasts were still swollen, although her belly was empty. She could not weep for that, the doubt had waxed in her mind that the child could have been Carvin's spirit: part of Carvin's evil, growing in her.

Sarmatia turned back the hanging to her chamber and walked into the middle of the house. It was deserted, fireplace bare, children's toys left derelict by the wooden dresser. Sarmatia picked up a rag doll and was staring at it when Chalda came in.

'You have news,' said Sarmatia. As her grasp of Atterian had improved, she had become more adept at reading people's faces.

Chalda smiled, plaiting her fingers through an auburn curl. 'Have you seen Anoi today? Have you seen what she wears about her neck? Her necklace of copper?'

'A wedding gift?' asked Sarmatia.

'Just so. Our kinswoman is lately betrothed to Dill.'

Sarmatia swallowed the delighted shout, since to utter it would have been unqueenly, but she grinned. 'I knew it! She had that eager look when she spoke with Fearn. When will they marry?'

'After the solstice. Anoi's gathering her dowry. Gei's happy, and for once admits that she's healthy. As mother of the bride, she's the center of attention.' Chalda freed the curl.

'There's something else. Bride... She's alive and now looks to be thriving, but—'

'She has lost her child, too?'

Chalda took her hand. 'Goar's outside. He can explain everything. Will you see him?'

'Bring him in.'

Chalda freed her hand and disappeared through the door. Sarmatia sat on a bench by the dead fireplace, hugging herself. A tall, slim figure bent under the entrance beam and came quickly towards her.

'Watch the door,' Goar called behind him and to Sarmatia he said, 'Lady, I've watched these four days, waiting for a chance to speak with you alone.' He knelt in the ashes at Sarmatia's feet. 'This meeting must be secret between us. You must speak of it to no one, not even your husband.' Realizing he could not work alone, Goar had demanded the same vow of Chalda and Jart.

Goar not only treated with her differently from the first time they had met at the winter feast, Sarmatia thought, he also looked different. His mouth was firmer, his eyes guarded, less amused, and were there threads of gray in the silver-blond hair? Trusting her instincts, her newly tamed spirit animal, Sarmatia laid her fingers on his cheekbone. He had cut himself shaving.

'My hand is none too steady these days. Lady, your word. I beg you.'

'Forgive me.' Sarmatia removed her hand. 'I only hesitate because of Fearn.' She hated the idea of keeping secrets from him.

'One of his present company is dangerous,' replied Goar, 'and the one may have followers. Fearn in innocence might pass on word to a certain quarter that could result not only in my undoing but place Bride under threat while she is still weak. Yet even without that word, you may be in peril, Lady.'

'Sarmatia.'

'Sarmatia,' Goar repeated. He had been dazzled by the Kretan at her crowning: kneeling at her feet he felt ashamed of his long churlishness.

'It seems I've no choice, so I give my word. Nothing I hear from you shall pass my lips.' The promise made, she waited.

'There's no easy way to tell you. Bride has been poisoned. The healer says she's lucky to be alive.'

The shock was like having Gorri land a kick in her stomach. 'How? Why?'

'Only Bride knows for certain, and she's not saying.'

'Her baby?' Sarmatia asked.

Goar shook his head. To deny that Bride had ever been pregnant would take too long to explain, besides wounding his fragile vanity. He had failed, earlier, to give Sarmatia Bride's message, but he had guarded her since and could still warn her. 'You must take care yourself. Taste your meals carefully. Don't linger alone anywhere.'

Sarmatia started to laugh. Scarcely recovered from her miscarriage, she was easily overwrought.

'Go now,' said Chalda to Goar. 'You've stayed too long already.'

Sarmatia hiccoughed and rubbed at her nose. 'I knew you royal kin couldn't meet without having some quarrel between you. You're a quarrelsome family.' She burst into another bout of laughter, then, seeing Goar about to depart, she lurched after him.

Chalda pulled her back. 'Not until your bleeding stops!' she cried, and then, as Sarmatia stopped trying to get free and started weeping, she put her arms about the young queen.

'Bride is well attended,' she said softly. 'My man's with her, and Goar returns to her today. She's recovering fast.' Chalda stroked Sarmatia's hair. 'Truly, you can do nothing more for your friend than is being done.'

I pray you're right, thought Sarmatia, who was now ashamed of her tears and reproached herself because she had sent no message of sympathy to Bride, nor even questioned Goar properly about his suspicions.

She blotted her face dry with her fingers and reassured Chalda that she could be left. They parted, and Sarmatia watched the auburn haired woman wander off towards the garden, calling for her child.

She knelt in the suntrap of the doorway, considering events. From Goar's warning, and her own promise, she knew she could no longer discuss either the torc or the lone archer in the wood with her husband.

Not when one of Fearn's closest advisors might be the traitor.

Chapter 52

Midday came and Maewe and the other women returned from their gardens. They sat around Sarmatia in the doorway with a dish of wild strawberries at their feet, and talked.

Sarmatia learned that some of the family were to move to the summer homestead. The sheep were there already, grazing the uplands. When Fearn and the men folk had finished carrying tools and goods from the main house to the summer station, it would be time to begin the cheese-making.

'Are you coming to the summer house, Maewe?' asked Thrif.

'Only for a day or two. Orm and I like the comforts of the main house too much.'

Janne muttered that she too would be staying. Her young ones always ran wild at the summer house. For now they made do with crashing and squabbling like bear cubs in the hazel wood.

Lighter footsteps were approaching the palisade, and Sarmatia watched the entrance until Anoi came on through the open gate. Her pale blonde hair was rich in the sunlight. She wore the necklace of copper, and copper bangles on her arms. She had never looked more beautiful.

Sarmatia greeted her and, putting her own troubles and worries aside, waited to admire Anoi's betrothal gift.

'Is Dill not with you?' Chalda asked Anoi, when the exclamations over her gift had ceased. 'I wanted to congratulate this jewel of a man.'

Chalda was sharp even with her own family. She had a proud, jealous nature that disliked attention being heaped on another. From what she said and from the tone of her voice, Sarmatia guessed that the courtship of Anoi and Dill had not been slow. She opened her mouth to smooth over the moment, but Anoi drove her foot against Chalda's shin.

'You're a pig, Chalda!' As the baby Tatta gave a wail, Anoi came forward with a raised hand to strike her, too.

'If you want to squabble like children, get out into the meadow.' Sarmatia jumped to her feet. 'I take it, Chalda, that the sun has gone to your head this morning. Perhaps you should borrow Maewe's shawl. Anoi, you're not a mare, keep your legs for walking.'

There was an astonished silence, and certainly it was strange that Anoi should almost hit a baby. After some coaxing, Sarmatia persuaded her to sit down and talk about her dowry, although the girl's eyes kept wandering to where Chalda spoke loudly with Janne. It was a relief when Anoi said that she must leave. For courtesy's sake, Sarmatia asked why.

'Oh, I'm helping Fearn at the summer house.'

Sarmatia nodded and let her go. The other women were also returning to their work. When Anoi was out of earshot Sarmatia called Chalda back.

'Envy's a dangerous thing, Chalda.'

'It's not envy. The men leap like tumblers to do her bidding. Yes, including Fearn. Even our king.'

'When you told me of Anoi's betrothal, you seemed glad.'

Chalda blustered excuses. 'I feel happy for Anoi until I have to meet with her!' Sarmatia laughed. That she could understand, after her own tangled dealings with Laerimmer.

Chalda went off on and Sarmatia took care of Tatta, having begged Chalda to let the child stay with her for company. The baby twitched and snuffled in her arms, relaxed and trusting. Sarmatia gazed down at the flaxen head and thought of how the times had changed, if Chalda could leave her daughter with the woman she had once accused of sorcery.

Later she heard a low rumble of horses. Fearn, Ormson and Anoi dismounted at the gate of the palisade and led their ponies inside the ditched enclosure. Fearn was coming towards her. He crouched close and would have kissed her, but Sarmatia felt shy of him after so many nights of sleeping alone, and drew back.

* * * *

Fearn saw her withdraw and could not understand it: Sarmatia seemed so cold these days. She showed him, calmly, the child asleep in her lap, as though it meant nothing to her to hold another woman's baby so soon after losing her own.

Fearn did not want to think of it, and started to speak about the summer house. Anoi called him and he rose at once, relieved to get away.

Chapter 53

Time passed. Sarmatia could leave the house on the day chosen as the most auspicious for the move to the summer house. She went outside, hoping to meet Bride.

The yard of the main house was packed with people, summoned that morning to mark the departure for the summer house. They came to help, too, and had brought food and drink with them to mark the occasion.

Careless of her own safety, Sarmatia wove through these crowds, seeing neither Bride, Chalda nor Goar. After many fruitless searches she returned to the main house. Orm, from the height of the keeping platform, was overseeing the final gathering of goods. Fearn had risen at dawn and ridden to the summer house with the last of the heavy tools, so only the lighter things remained.

There were not enough horses in the kingdom for everyone to be mounted, and Sarmatia decided not to disturb Gorri from his summer grazing. A long procession of figures wound off into the distance and, following an Atterian with a bundle of clothes, she began to walk.

Sarmatia climbed on the path until the lime trees of the valley faded out and were replaced by oak, and then knew she must sit down. Falling behind, she cast aside the broom Orm had given her to carry and settled to one side of the track by a clump of sweet cicely.

She had intended to rest for only a moment, perhaps she dozed. A grip on her shoulder warned her that she had been found out.

Don't be alarmed, Lady. We're your people, too.

It was not a man who spoke, but the sound made words in her mind. Again her shoulder was nuzzled. Grey lips grinned in a gesture of friendship. Sarmatia sat up, her weariness gone.

Crouched belly-first on the damp earth, the two would not look at her directly, though she knew who they were—her first northern wolves.

Now the dog-wolf raised his brown and white muzzle and licked her face. Memory passed between them of a cold spring day, when Sarmatia had found a dead ram amongst her sheep. She'd cut the ram and removed its innards to prevent the flesh spoiling, then had gone out of her way to leave the bloody parcel in the forest. As she'd hoped, the wolves had found her gift.

'I am pleased you are mine,' the whisper purring deep in her throat. Her spirit animal was alert, but she kept it hidden, not wishing to frighten the wolves. Again the dog-wolf claimed her mind, not in sound this time, but scent. *You gave food to the pack. Our territories are shared.*

He and his mate melted into the forest. When they were gone Sarmatia looked down the path. An Atterian family were coming into view and she prepared to meet them.

* * * *

The wolves had promised friendship to Sarmatia, but it was through the wolves that trouble came. It happened that the family she fell in with were young, and they drank and chattered as they walked. Sarmatia was drawn along in their midst, a tall, brown-haired girl in a crowd of redheads. As the drink was passed between them, Sarmatia began to talk. The group was her own age and relished her traveler's tales.

The crocodile torc was much discussed. The family had seen the trader place it round Sarmatia's throat. They said there was a rumor that Carvin had been her lover. Sarmatia told them the truth and, though uneasy, tried to think nothing more of it.

She continued with the family up the steeply twisting track like a seed on the wind and so out of the forest. Three fields away she could see the roof of the summer house and the camp of hide tents, enclosed in hurdles of pale golden hazel, where Fearn's family would live out the summer. Rows of men and women were already there, pounding down a square of earth where the main fire would be made.

As she drew near, a man at the back of these rows came forward. It was Ormson. His round face was caked with dust, his lips showed purple through it.

'Put those things under cover.' He waved an arm at the summer house.

Sarmatia burst out laughing. 'A fine greeting! Sweeten your tongue, Ormson.' She held out the skin of mead the family had brought with them.

Her voice killed the pounding. Over Ormson's shoulder Sarmatia saw Fearn emerge from the summer house, puzzled by the sudden quiet. Ormson's wife, Janne, began to push her way through the rows of watchers. Ormson muttered under his breath. 'Take the drink,' Sarmatia commanded.

His hands closed on the skin. He scowled. 'This stinks of wolf.' Ormson poured the mead onto the ground.

There were gasps from the crowd. Sarmatia smelt the drink, heard the drone of bees settling on the dark liquid and was shocked.

'Why don't you run off with your friends, Sarmatia? You're half-wolf yourself. Any decent woman would be still in mourning, but we know southerners put their kids out on the midden without a care.'

Tears smeared Sarmatia's vision. Was this what people believed? 'I've paid in blood, Ormson. What else would you have me do?'

The man blushed to the roots of his red hair. Sarmatia wiped her face with her hand. The wolf scent was there, sure enough. Had she not turned aside Ormson's complaint... She shivered, thinking of what might happen if the crowd became a mob. Evil was at work here, the more cunning because it struck through others and would not face her directly.

She looked Ormson in the eye. 'Tell the King I'm here.'

Ormson stared, then saluted and moved to obey. A scatter of applause rippled through the people. Sarmatia smiled, fighting down fear. Never had her bull riding scars itched so intensely.

Fearn would not come to her, so Sarmatia went by the silent, still rows of people and walked into the yard of the summer house.

Despite the heat of the afternoon Fearn was wearing his scarlet cloak. In the sunlight his hair was a fiery copper. His face looked bloody, surrounded by blood. The back of Sarmatia's neck prickled. Conscious more than ever of the wolf scent on her skin, she looked down at the jutting twigs of the broom gripped in her hand. Momentarily her courage failed and she stopped.

Still Fearn would not look at her. He had his head bent to a weaving frame that he had dragged out of the summer house. Crouched at its foot was Anoi, her face hidden by her hair as she pegged the sled-rod into the wooden uprights. Sarmatia felt shut out by both of them.

'Your betrothed.' She forced herself to speak. 'I should like to meet him.'

Between the rapping of the stone she was using to hammer home the sled-rod, Anoi answered, 'Dill isn't here. Do you expect me to magic him out of the air for you?'

Her words were muffled, for she did not raise her head, and for an instant Sarmatia thought she had misheard. Fearn, who had not heeded or had chosen to ignore Anoi's answer, took up the weaving frame's crossbeam. He braced his feet and lifted the tall timber high over his head. With a graceful dip of her body Anoi rose to her feet.

'Let me help you, kinsman.' The uprights of the loom were taller than a man at full stretch. Fearn could just touch their tops. Anoi climbed up one side of the loom and stood with her feet balanced on the heddle bar. Together, she and Fearn fed the thick crossbeam between the two forked timbers of the main beams. When that was secure, Anoi climbed up again and sat on it. Her head was level with the roof thatch, but the height did not trouble her. She dangled her legs into the space where the warp threads would hang.

'Come down, Anoi,' Fearn insisted.

Anoi laughed, leaning forward on her high perch. 'You should catch me, Fearn.' She dipped her hands down to him.

Shut out a second time, indignant and not a little humiliated, Sarmatia decided to leave the two cousins.

She had taken the first backward step when Anoi stood upright on the crossbeam of the loom and ran along its length. Her bare feet hummed on the beam, copper sparkled and clashed as she darted to and fro, stopping and turning on the narrow frame as though it was as wide as a track way. Her hair streamed out against the sky, the ends spilling against the thatch of the summer house like sparks from a fire.

More images flashed in Sarmatia's mind. A blonde girl with a meat hook clutched in her hand like a dagger. A pretty girl kicking Chalda. A smile like a child's. 'How dark she is!' Anoi had said at their first meeting, marking Sarmatia at once as an outsider. Always Anoi's words and actions had carried an edge. She had given Sarmatia a cloak which was too short. She had given Fearn a cloak, a fine scarlet one—

Sarmatia stared up at the impudent white feet flashing over the beam. There was a swishing in her ears like the sea and, as she watched, a rope of golden hair coiled down from the loom and drifted about Fearn's throat. For a moment, Fearn was surrounded by the rippling tide and his hand came up as if through water to brush it away. Fearn swimming in a scarlet sea. It was a dream well known to Sarmatia. In it there was also a monster, a snake-like creature.

Anoi's soft voice whispered in her head: 'Isn't it strange that Sarmatia has never cried since the loss of her baby? Do you see how she can hold Chalda's child in her arms, Fearn? Isn't she brave?' Yes, it would be like this, a subtle, wheedling poison.

Sarmatia's knees buckled. She had to sit down on the sun browned grass. The images were falling into place and a picture was formed. Anoi might be betrothed to Dill, but it was the King she wanted. *She is my enemy, not my friend. And that rumor that Carvin was my lover... I am in danger here, not Fearn.*

She almost sprang at the loom, ready to tear it down, but mastered the anger. She needed proof of more than Anoi's envy.

Next day came the news that Dill had disappeared.

Chapter 54

As Orm had promised Sarmatia, he and Maewe had come to the summer house, and that night she slept in their tent. Where Fearn slept Sarmatia did not know, dared not guess. In the morning, still thinking of Anoi, she prowled the Atterian camp until she spotted the girl leaving one of the animal pens with a pail of ewe's milk. Then she shamelessly followed.

Anoi took the pail to the barn, though not to make cheese. She had used the tepid milk as a wash, patting it liberally over face and arms. Sarmatia watched from the shadowy recess of the porch—the porch where she and Fearn had once waited out a rainstorm—and heard the quick, firm tread of Fearn's approach. He had come in search of his queen, and once found, he had not looked inside the barn. Instead he broke the news. Dill was missing and no one knew where he might be.

'I must find Anoi, who knows nothing yet. Maewe and Orm are returning to the main house to tell Gei. It will be a long day for all.' Fearn stole a look at Sarmatia to note any reaction. A tremor passed through his rigid body. 'This summer has seen nothing but sorrow.' He was shocked, his face as white as Egyptian paper.

Sarmatia felt for him, where she could feel nothing for the youth, who had been only a name to her. She wrapped her arms about Fearn's body, hugging him fiercely. 'I'm truly sorry.'

Fearn stiffened then his arms locked around her back. His beard scratched her forehead, Sarmatia lifted up her chin and the two kissed.

Yet, as their kiss deepened, Sarmatia dared not forget that only a narrow recess separated them from Anoi. She tried to draw away, but now Fearn prevented it. Gripping her shoulders, he dragged Sarmatia with him to the floor of the barn. Once more his mouth came down on hers. His left hand moved under the skirt of her robe. Glancing up into his darkened eyes, Sarmatia was afraid that he had forgotten the taboo that forbade the act of love between them and meant to have her here, in the porch. She tried to twist her head away to speak. Failing, she nipped her teeth into his tongue.

Fearn laughed, the chuckle vibrating in Sarmatia's mouth. His head lifted only a fraction while he withdrew his hand from her body and spat upon his fingers, impatient to moisten her quickly. 'If not love, give me something.'

'Fearn, wait—'

'Enough teasing. I want our children, though you may not.'

'But we can't! Ah!' Sarmatia cried out as he rolled her onto her stomach. And now, at the worst moment, when her skirt was rucked around her waist and she was without dignity, she heard Anoi.

'Such a scuffle! Why do you trouble, Fearn?'

There she was, gliding into the shadows to join them, her blue eyes angry but also bright. She was stripped to the waist.

Fearn drew in a hissing breath and his hands slackened their hold. Seizing the chance, Sarmatia scrambled away. Stripped of any will to fight, she fled from the barn.

Fearn yanked himself up by means of the porch wall. He stared at Anoi's white skin and rose-colored nipples, watching in a haze of lust and incoherent, unfocussed anger. His wife remained an enigma to him, warm one moment, cool and withdrawn the next.

In his heart, Fearn had never believed that Sarmatia had deliberately aborted her pregnancy, but her seeming lack of grief had shocked him. Every Atterian woman he'd tended as healer after a miscarriage had been fretful, given to easy tears. Sarmatia seemed uncaring and whenever he'd tried to speak of their loss, she had somehow gone from him, not in her body, but in her spirit. He had felt as though he talked to himself, and wondered if the animal side of his Kretan's nature had swallowed her human feeling.

But an animal would not have cared about committing a taboo act, or hugged him because one of his war band, a stranger to her, had vanished. An animal would not have broken from him when Anoi appeared.

Anoi peeled off the rest of her long dress, revealing the short skirt of cords that she'd worn at the secret training meetings of the war band.

'I know you've always liked me in this, Fearn. I've seen you trying to steal a look. Now you can do that, and more.' Anoi giggled and parted the skirt cords.

The perfect Atterian maiden, his little cousin Anoi. She was putting on a show that made him blush, thought Fearn, stunned. The air between them, heavy with her rose perfume, seemed in a moment to be full of wing beats, stirring her long gold hair. The unexpected fullness of her figure pricked at Fearn's aching groin like the spines of some great fish. His salmon and eagle spirit animals—had they made themselves known as a sign of fortune, or in warning? Fearn had sensed neither for months, and certainly at no time when he and Sarmatia had mated.

'I'll let you. Dill won't mind.'

Her casual dismissal of her betrothed froze Fearn. He watched her eyes change, no longer dreaming but sharp, calculating, with the greed that some have for gold.

'Another awkward one, like Goar.' Her voice was lightly mocking, intending to tease. 'But I'll help you, Fearn. You'll know delight in my arms.'

He didn't want her to touch him. 'I can't. Dill... Sarmatia...' He was stammering like a boy: he'd never had to refuse a woman. 'I'm sorry.'

Then he fled the barn. Anoi remained behind.

* * * *

He is gone. I am nothing, rejected for a foreigner. How many years have I waited for Fearn, plotted for him, killed for him? I lost even my brother. My intended consort tramples me in the mud. I, Anoi, the rightful ruler of the Atterians, Queen to Fearn's King.

Do not hate me, Fearn, it was all for love. I could have had our cousin, Goar, but chose you, being the more fitted for the diadem. You I would never have cursed, as once I laid the spell of barren loins on Goar. Perhaps that was cruel, but then he'd made me angry pressing his suit, too sure of his charm. I gave him a 'charm' equal to his nature.

Yet for you, Fearn, anything. I have even tried, with that small part of myself which was timid and shy—the gentle Anoi, which you thought was all—to be kind to Sarmatia. How I hate that name!

Wait. 'I can't,' Fearn said, and why? Because of Dill and Sarmatia. Dispose of both, kindly, carefully, and he will come.

He will come to me for comfort and lay his head upon my breast. I shall feed him on roses and honey and keep his first wife's memory bright as our children grow and prepare for the kingship.

I killed your child, Sarmatia, and your best friend, who, even at this moment, sickens to death. Had I known Bride would snatch at my potion, I would have prepared more, but then perhaps the best way to be rid of you is the very first way I tried.

This time, Fearn won't be there as a distraction. I know where you're going, Sarmatia, and who you hope to see, but I'll be there before you.

Tonight, Sarmatia, you'll be dead.

Chapter 55

Recovered from the poison, Bride sat outside her hut arm in arm with Goar. Chalda, Jart, and Tatta were their guests. To any smith who passed, they seemed to be drinking and playing dice.

By a practiced flick of her wrist, Bride rolled the dice. Bending to see the result brought their heads together.

'You say hellebore might have caused my sickness?' Bride asked Jart. 'Could it also have brought on Sarmatia's miscarriage?'

The healer fingered the amulet round his neck. 'It's possible. Being foreign, she may have eaten part of the plant without realizing what its effects would be.'

'Sarmatia didn't eat it. The poison was given to her as a drink.' Bride glanced at each of her companions, even the baby, in triumph, pleased at her own cleverness.

'I know because I drank some of the stuff myself, most of it, actually. I happened to be thirsty.'

Jart whistled through the space between his teeth.

'Who gave Sarmatia the drink?' asked Chalda.

Bride gave Goar a look. 'Your royal cousin, Anoi. She offered Sarmatia a toast before she took her test. I can't say I really suspected Anoi then, but the drink tasted odd enough for me to get into some bushes and make myself sick.'

Jart, taking these announcements in his stride—Anoi was no kin of his—gave a grunt. 'You acted well. If the Queen had drunk it all, as must have been intended, we'd be burying her.'

From Goar and Chalda there was silence, but not only silence. Goar's features showed recognition and on Chalda's face there was growing realization. Her baby, feeling her Mother's arms relax about her, pushed herself out of their grip and crawled for the dice.

'That's why Anoi was always drawing me aside and whispering dark hints about witchcraft!' Chalda slapped her hands to her cheeks. 'What a fool I've been!'

'That's her skill, though, isn't it, dissembling?' muttered Goar, 'I think we've all believed what Anoi has told us, one time or another.'

'So what do we do?' asked Chalda.

Bride picked up Tatta and removed the dice from her mouth. 'What's the family busy with these days?'

'House moving.'

'Humph! Well, nothing should happen there. After it's done, you keep an eye over Fearn and Sarmatia. I'll deal with Anoi. I've the largest score to settle.' She bounced Tatta on her lap, smiling as the baby laughed.

Chapter 56

Outside the barn Sarmatia ran, trying to burn the shame from her body. There were voices shouting and fading. The camp of tents receded in a blur. Soon one of the high resting places of the dead came under her heels. She was running more slowly now, pacing herself so that she could breathe but not think. There was a rumble in her ears like thunder, but it was her spirit-beast, urging her to greater speed.

Sarmatia sprinted down a dry stream and then her feet bit into mud as she entered the dabbled twilight of a wooded valley.

She stopped at last by a small stream to drink. Suddenly she was weeping. That Anoi should have seen them! She was ashamed of Fearn. The love between them had been clouded by rumors, and the gods alone knew what lies from Anoi, and yet still he would have mated with her. Perhaps he was making love to Anoi at this moment, kissing Anoi as she smothered him with her blonde hair. Was it chance that had brought her bare-breasted to Fearn?

Sarmatia wiped her eyes as she considered the 'chance' disappearance of Dill. How much did the youth know about the crocodile torc? If she could find him, Dill might have some strange tales to tell of gentle Anoi.

She wanted proof. If she challenged Anoi now she might lose more than Fearn's trust. She was a queen and must be seen to act with justice.

'What should I do?' The water bubbled back to her like a baby and gave no help. Near the spring was a rowan tree, its branches bearing the green berries that would ripen in the fall. Sarmatia remembered the rowan by Laerimmer's homestead. It struck her that she had not seen the Kingmaker nor any of his family, except for Fearn and Anoi at the summer house. Where were they? Avoiding the work of house-moving?

Retracing her steps through the dry stream bed, Sarmatia climbed away from the wood to take a bearing from the sun. Laerimmer's homestead was some way off, but she should reach it before nightfall.

She meant to tell Laerimmer everything. He was Kingmaker, wise in the ways of the people. It would be a relief to have him listen. Of all the Atterians, he would know how to get proof of Anoi's treachery.

By late afternoon, Sarmatia was staring up at a knoll covered with briars and gorse. Through the trees at the knoll's summit there rose a thin smoke. Several of the royal family must be at home, yet she could not get to them.

Sarmatia snorted and crouched with her head in her insect-bitten hands. She had forgotten the briars of Laerimmer's home. The gorse had burst its yellow flowers and was going over. The wild roses were at their peak and the hill was scented by their fragrance. Sarmatia, not yet fully healed from her miscarriage and exhausted by her long run, looked now at the silky flowers on the impenetrable thicket of spurred branches and wondered what she should do.

She tried to find a path, each attempt ripping threads in her robe. She could avoid parts of the gorse by turning and lifting her arms, but every forward pace meant stepping on thorns.

Soon she was hemmed in on every side. There was a flat stone near one gorse bush and Sarmatia rested her feet on that. She was no more than a few strides into the gorse, but already it was impossible to tell the way that she had come. She stood still, a wild rose tangled in her hair and brambles pricking her stomach. Whichever way she moved some other spur would catch at her. Enough. The family might laugh when they saw her, but she needed help.

'Is anybody there?' Her calls seemed to fall short of the knoll top, muffled by the walls of furze. A golden-throated finch dropped from the sky onto the gorse to sing. She caught a flicker of movement, but no sound, from a higher ridge. 'Hello at the house! Can you hear?'

A sharp sting made her break off and clutch at her thigh.

The bowman.

Sarmatia ducked, and a second arrow hissed past the spot where she had been standing and spent itself in the gorse by her heel. A fierce tug freed her hair from the briar and she was off. There was no question of avoiding it. She must endure the gorse's caress or die.

She sped through the scrub, the wooden arrow shafts knocking on ancient tree stumps. As she climbed, the steep curves of the hillside shielded her from her attacker on the summit of the knoll. Sarmatia stumbled on a few more paces then was pitched onto hands and knees as she lost her footing. She took in four great gasps of air and was still. The arrows had stopped. The bowman did not know where she was. On a bush two ridges down, the finch was whistling alarms. Quiet, thought Sarmatia, and the bird choked off.

A snap of dead gorse spines, the faint slap of sandaled feet. Scraping her hair forward to veil eyes and face, Sarmatia risked raising her head. The gorse was rippling, its spent golden flowers gleaming like the scales of some legendary beast. There was one still point... then movement, as a figure came down the hill. The sun shone on braided blonde hair, lit a small, tip-tilted nose and one large blue eye.

Dressed as a boy, Anoi made a pretty youth. So she had been the bowman in the woods, and unlike Goar, she had no magic to charm her arrow to the right target... *All this time*, Sarmatia thought, *I've been seeing threats to Fearn where none existed, and so has Laerimmer.* She gave a hard, bitter laugh, and Anoi turned her head.

The distance between them was short, too short. Light glinted on the arrowhead and shimmered on the drawn bowstring. The bronze was level with her breast and at this range could not miss. Heat drummed in her ears as Sarmatia prepared to launch herself in a final life or death struggle.

Sunlight saved her. It was shining into Anoi's eyes and she went on down the hill without noticing the dun-colored robe in the brown-tipped furze. Sarmatia did not waste time. Keeping on hands and knees she wormed into the space Anoi had quit and found a path. It was a risk using the track, yet Sarmatia reckoned on reaching the house and rousing the family.

She came right to the firebreak when a pricking of her scars made her look back. Anoi had followed her. She stood in shadow, a small woman, the braids of her long hair tucked neatly into her boy's tunic. The sunlight was no longer in her eyes. She had notched an arrow and drawn back the string.

'If you shoot me here, I'll scream and the family will hear.' Sarmatia watched Anoi's bow arm waver, then the Atterian shook her head.

'Are you sure you can finish me with one arrow? If you fail I could hurt you badly. You've killed before, Anoi. You know how long it can take to die.'

Anoi motioned sideways with the bow. 'Get down the hill.'

Sarmatia had no choice but to obey. Each time she missed her footing on the narrow path, she heard the faint creak of the bow as Anoi tightened on the bowstring. They walked in silence to the foot of the knoll then Anoi told Sarmatia to stop.

'The family are still in earshot,' lied Sarmatia without looking round. She sensed Anoi smile. 'Do you mean to shoot me in the back?'

'Under those bushes there's something I want. Find it, Queen. Remember, my bow will be on you.'

The scrub was thicker on the lower slopes. Raising fresh wounds on her hands and arms, Sarmatia grubbed between the hard bracts of thorns, looking perhaps for a bronze hoard or gold—

Suddenly her outstretched hand touched on a cold, yielding mass. Her thumb slipped farther in, coming against thick slime. Sarmatia looked along the line of her arm and her stomach heaved. She had put her hand on to a dead man's face.

He was young and beardless and the wound where his throat had been cut showed on his white neck as a vivid red scar. His mouth was open and Sarmatia's thumb was inside it, resting on his tongue. She wiped her fingers on her robe and the feeling of sickness steadied, though did not recede.

'You wished to meet my betrothed,' came Anoi's lilting voice. 'This is Dill. You might have known him from the war band which brought you here. He had a fondness for gold, which put him at odds with the King. He stole the crocodile torc. Of course I put it to better use. Dill was a hoarder.'

'Please, no more,' said Sarmatia, thinking of the boy. Her words drew a sigh from the figure behind her.

'Dill was slow. That's why I chose him. He was easy to charm. After your miscarriage he panicked and that speeded up his thoughts. Two days ago we met here and he started to ask questions about what I'd done with the torc and why I'd been so interested in it, after I'd learnt that it was once yours, but that you'd rejected it in loathing.

'I was very understanding and told him all I knew. He didn't cry out when I cut him. I think he recognized that I was doing him a service. Fearn would never have forgiven him.'

The dreamy whisper stopped. Sarmatia reached down to scrape earth with her nails. The late afternoon sun shone on her head, but her limbs were clammy. Everything in the world seemed to have slowed, become less alive. The dead boy looked like a flaxen-haired doll. The blood that had pooled on his clothes was like paint. Slowly Sarmatia closed her fingers on a handful of dirt to sprinkle on the boy.

'No need to do that, Sarmatia. Dill is going to have a companion. Drag him out of there. I'll see if I can find a more appropriate resting place for two. With your own hand on the dagger, it'll look like a lover's pact.'

They must have made a strange procession, Sarmatia thought: the tall Kretan dragging the body; a trail of flattened grass and flecks of dried blood and then Anoi. Her features seemed serene, but her eyes held only a dreadful blankness.

'Where are we going?' asked Sarmatia, toiling with her burden. They had not reached the trees and the ground was beginning to rise.

'Where you will be discovered side by side. I meant to shoot you on the hill, Sarmatia, but this is so much better.' In the gap between the taut bowstring and the shaft of the arrow, Anoi threw her a sparkling glance. 'You can't delay me by talking.'

'You're evil, Anoi.'

'No, I take what's mine. I won't hurt you. That would be evil. But you're like a squealing animal in a trap, soon to be put out of its misery. You love Fearn, but he doesn't love you.'

Fighting off defeat, Sarmatia contrived to glance ahead. The long treeless slope was familiar, though its lack of cover would give her little protection should she try to escape.

Not that there was much likelihood of that. Dill was a small youth, but she was already wearied by her long walk and the humid afternoon. Her steps became smaller, her breathing more erratic. Her mouth was as dry as a withered leaf and there was a strange taste on her tongue. Sarmatia paused. 'Please, give me a drink, Anoi.'

Anoi had a flask of water hung around her neck, but she made no attempt to remove it. 'Walk. You don't have much farther to go.' Her eyes were wide, like a doe's, but blue and cold.

They plodded on a few more paces. Sarmatia caught a whiff of scent and the taste in her mouth grew stronger. Her eyes closed on the throbbing sunlight. A roll of thunder sounded.

'Leave him. Walk over there. Quickly now!' Suddenly Anoi seemed uneasy. She fumbled with the arrow and her aim faltered. Sarmatia leaped forward but was not quick enough. Anoi fired.

Sarmatia folded at the waist, though the arrow went wide over her head. Had she kept her footing she could have charged Anoi, but now the girl had time to draw another arrow. She stared at her fallen adversary and her lips curved into a mocking smile. 'Goodbye, Sarmatia.'

The taste within her mouth was overwhelming. For an instant Sarmatia thought it was fear then she recognized the high place to which they had come and understood the signal. 'I think not, Anoi,' she replied, rising unsteadily—but still rising—to her feet. 'This is a more ancient meeting place than you know. Others gathered here, before men, and the land is no less theirs than ours. The name should have warned you.'

Anoi screamed. Her bow fell onto the grass as long, lean bodies enclosed hers in a circle and the wolf-pack leader ran to Sarmatia, who put out her hands to him in greeting. 'I'll have that drink,' she said quietly, knowing that the girl could not refuse her.

They were at Wolfstones.

Chapter 57

'Shall we take a look at this house move?' asked Bride, when she and Goar were alone at the settlement of the smiths.

'If you like.' He grinned, running his eyes over this long-legged, broad-hipped woman. Bride did not have as much flesh on as when he'd first seen her, but she was still superb. And Anoi a cruel bitch.

Goar blushed at the thought of his youthful infatuation. Yet why had Anoi encouraged, then rejected him? 'You're a woman,' he said, catching Bride's eye.

'So it's been rumored.'

'Maybe you can give me a reason.' He told the sorry tale of his and Anoi's courtship.

Her young man wasn't in the foremost ranks of the wise, thought Bride, but then she could never have lived with a fellow who felt himself cleverer than she was.

'Why did she do it?' Goar was asking and Bride answered, 'I can tell you that in one word: Fearn.'

'The King? But he's never seemed interested in her.' Goar still shied at using Anoi's name because of the curse, itself now an open secret between Bride and him.

'None so blind as will not see, eh, lover? Do you think that would stop Anoi from hoping? Did it stop you?' Bride flicked at his silver curls. 'I'm still waiting for these to look untidy.'

'I don't understand.'

Bride pushed him down on the bench and sat beside him. 'It's easy. Fearn goes away on a long journey, from which he might not return. Anoi attaches herself to you. Fearn comes back, looks as though he'll be staying a while, and Anoi breaks off your betrothal so that she's free to pursue him.'

Bride gave Goar's knee a shake. 'The spell was to keep you quiet. Of course, had Fearn left a second time, Anoi would have lifted the charm and continued the courtship. You were her live prey for later, shall we say.'

Goar snorted and Bride chuckled. 'No wonder I've never liked her. Your Anoi weaves her plans on some long threads.'

'The fire. It was to keep Fearn here.' Goar had caught up with her thoughts. 'The fire that killed Waroch.'

'How did that happen?'

'It started in the roof above the loom. We woke, coughing our guts out, blundering in smoke. We had to save those we could, those we could find.'

'We?'

'Gygest and me.' Goar made a wry face. 'It was a mess, that night. We didn't even know how many people were in the house. Briht was panicking and Kere rushing about with jugs of water. Tanek was calling on his war-god. A mess.'

Goar scowled. 'Anoi, you may be sure, added to the confusion. We thought she was hysterical. Gygest and I tried to get her outside on three occasions, but each time she broke free and ran straight back into the thickest smoke. She kept screaming for Waroch—the old king—and said we must find him. It was queer, really, because it should have been easy to do that. Waroch always used to sleep in the same spot, except of course that night he hadn't.'

I'd have liked to have seen how Anoi moved him, thought Bride. She hated the girl, but conceded that Anoi had a strong stomach and wits. A dangerous opponent.

'Did you speak to Fearn or the Kingmaker about that night?'

Goar shook his head. 'Fearn was never interested. He'd always said there'd be an accident with the shiftless way the family lived. Laerimmer pestered me a bit, but then Laerimmer's always asking me about something. I wanted to forget the fire. Waroch was no great loss to me.'

Anoi had been fortunate, thought Bride. Waroch had died in a strange manner, yet no one had cared enough for the man to find out the truth.

She caught Goar's head between her hands. 'I think it's time that you talked to Fearn.'

A horn sounded dimly in the distance, answered almost at once by a second horn from the smiths' own settlement.

'What was that?' Bride drew back.

'It's the call to assembly.' Goar was as startled as she was. The Atterians had already had their spring gathering. Side by side, they listened intently to another exchange of sharp, falling horn notes. 'The people are to meet at Wolfstones,' Goar translated. 'Where are you going?'

'For weapons.' Bride ran back into her hut.

Chapter 58

Anoi spun about, doubling back as a gray or a brown wolf swung in towards her. Hunted by wolves, she ran to the tallest of the boulders of Wolfstones, fingers finding invisible ledges as she began to climb.

Escape was an illusion. A broad muzzle loomed over the summit of the flat topped boulder. Anoi screamed, lost her footing and fell. She landed on her feet like a cat and lashed out at the wolf prowling up to the rock face.

She was lucky. It was a youngster who at once gave ground, backing up with its tail between its legs. Anoi shot out from the shadow of the boulder, dashing in a quick springy run for the bridge of land that would take her off Wolfstones. Sarmatia started after her, but could not close the gap. Two wolves ran out in a long arc to cut off the Atterian's flight, but Anoi eluded their trap by a swerve in almost the opposite direction. Then she was running for the trees.

We'll lose her if she reaches cover, thought Sarmatia, but her limbs seemed weighted. She could not run. Then a horn sounded nearby and Anoi stopped as though struck.

'Where are you going, Anoi?' Laerimmer was standing in the shade of one of the stones. Again, he blew the bronze horn, and the wolf leader howled, then was quiet.

Sarmatia spoke at once. 'Anoi killed Dill, and Waroch.' She pointed to Anoi's bow and quiver of arrows in the grass. 'She was trying to kill me.'

Laerimmer said nothing to Sarmatia's accusations. He put the horn aside, settling himself comfortably on the grass. The wolf leader pushed his head into the Kingmaker's lap, a giant guard dog released from duty. The rest of the pack lay down in the shade of the stones. Only Anoi and Sarmatia remained standing.

'Didn't you hear me? It's Anoi who's our killer!'

'So you say. Where is your proof and your witnesses?'

'A boy's dead with his throat cut.'

The Kingmaker did not even glance in the direction of Dill. His eyes never left Sarmatia's face. 'That might have been done with your knife.'

'It was. I saw them together!' A tear ran down Anoi's face. She stifled a sob. 'Sarmatia murdered my betrothed.'

At her accusation, the wolf brought his head up from Laerimmer's lap, but Laerimmer pushed him back, smoothing his fur. 'These are serious matters that can't be settled in a moment.' Tension boomed as thunder in the distance.

Sarmatia shook herself in an attempt to ease her heavy limbs and head. 'I say again that Anoi tried to kill me.' She walked and picked up the bow. 'With this.'

'I've never seen it before this moment,' said Anoi quickly. 'Kinsman, you know I can't even shoot with a bow!'

She was clever, making such a direct appeal. Laerimmer had no choice but to answer. 'It's true that you don't possess a bow.'

Anoi sank onto the grass with such a look of satisfaction that Sarmatia wanted to hit her. She vented her anger on the bow instead, plucking the bowstring like a harp.

'See, the grip's too small for me. The arrows are too short.' She notched an arrow and pulled on the bowstring, but before Sarmatia had drawn her arm into line with her shoulder, the bronze arrow-head clashed onto the wood of the bow grip and the arrow fell out onto the grass. 'It's not mine.'

'I didn't say it was.' Again, Anoi was clever and did not counter-accuse Sarmatia.

'It's for the King to judge between you and decide your fates,' said Laerimmer. 'We must wait for Fearn.'

He looked at the wolf lying with its head in his lap. 'These were your heralds, today. They came through the gorse to guide me to you.' He began to stroke the wolf's head.

Had Fearn already been summoned? Sarmatia relinquished the bow and settled cross-legged on the brown-tipped grass of Wolfstones. The mate of the leader crawled out of the shade to come and put her head on Sarmatia's knee. She touched the heavy jaw with her fingers and blew gently on the half-closed eyes. She could feel the animal's steady heartbeat through her hands.

Laerimmer and Anoi were watching, the Kingmaker's round, bearded face expressionless, Anoi's features a mixture of scorn and fear. No member of the pack had approached her. She was alone.

Laerimmer drew attention to this. 'Come sit closer, little cousin. We should talk. Tell me what's happened today.'

Anoi did not need to be told twice. She slipped close to the Kingmaker and knelt back on her heels. She said that Sarmatia and Dill were lovers. She'd seen their last meeting. Sarmatia had demanded a necklace to match the one Dill had given to Anoi herself as a betrothal gift. When he had refused, the two had quarreled. Sarmatia had stabbed him and he'd died.

'She saw me hiding in the gorse when she came looking for a place to leave him, and pursued me to Wolfstones. I'd have been killed but for you, Laerimmer.'

'Dill was stabbed by the Queen?'

'She struck him in the throat.' Anoi's fist pounded the grass in mimicry of a fierce blow.

Laerimmer flinched. 'What have you to say?' he demanded Sarmatia.

'The boy was dead when I came here. Why should I murder for a trinket? Fearn's ring is the only jewel I want, and that I have.' She lifted her hand to show off the bronze ring.

Ugly blotches bloomed on Anoi's forehead and cheeks. 'The southerner lies to save herself. I saw her stand as close to Dill as she is now to that wolf, look down into his eyes,' Anoi could not resist a malicious reference to Sarmatia's height, 'and stab him.'

Laerimmer sighed at that. Gently, he pushed the wolf off his knees and walked to where Dill's body lay face upwards on the grass, dead eyes staring into the sun. Laerimmer crouched, touched the wound on Dill's neck then came back.

'Sarmatia, have you a knife and may I see it?'

Sarmatia felt about her waistband for her eating knife, then realized with a stab of shame that it had been lost in the barn that morning in her struggle with Fearn. 'I don't have it with me,' she said, aware of how the excuse must sound.

Laerimmer's black eyes widened a fraction then narrowed. 'We must wait for Fearn,' he said again.

The three sat, though scarcely at ease. Anoi watched Sarmatia and

Laerimmer, and the yellow eyes of the wolf pack flickered restlessly between them all.

Above their heads the air grew thicker, the sun heavy through a skein of clouds. Even for a northern summer, the day seemed long.

'Is this an afternoon without an evening?' Sarmatia asked Laerimmer. 'The sun's still high.'

'It's close to midsummer,' replied the Kingmaker. 'Soon, we'll celebrate the solstice on the Sacred Hill.'

'Not this year, thanks to Sarmatia,' put in Anoi spitefully.

There was a loud crack of thunder following her words and after that a heavy silence. Time stretched on. Finally, harsh as the call of a buzzard, came a horn blast, and from different directions, several answering notes.

'Fearn has reached the Beaver River,' said Laerimmer. 'Now the others will wait for him to lead them here.'

Sarmatia's heart quickened. She wet her lips, an act not missed by Anoi.

'Do you think that will help you?' she asked, scornfully. 'Fearn was with me this morning, as he should have been last year, when Waroch died.'

The she-wolf gave a snarl that went right through Sarmatia. She dug her fingers into the wolf's thick pelt and looked Anoi straight in the eyes. 'I know you murdered Waroch to keep Fearn in this kingdom,' she answered calmly. 'Three times, to my knowledge, you've tried to kill me, twice with arrows and once with that meat hook. Do you remember? What a pity that my man was never yours to keep.'

Anoi's blue eyes wavered.

Now, between the hills, Sarmatia could see clouds that were not clouds moving quickly to the high plateau of Wolfstones. Anoi, too, had seen them.

'Fearn will believe what I tell him,' she said fervently.

Sarmatia scratched at her bull riding scars, lifting her head to watch the Atterians come. They rode up and drew rein in a dusty, swirling mass: the war band and elders of the people. Sarmatia could see the smiths with their bright bronze swords; Kere of the royal kin and Ormson from Fearn's household. Most carried horns.

At their head were Fearn, Goar and Bride. Goar had a silver horn, which he set to his lips and sounded as the tribe swept towards the tall boulders of Wolfstones.

Fearn carried the stone battleaxe. He was mounted on Gorri. He pointed left and then right with the stone axe and the tribe divided, making a wide circle about Sarmatia and the others, moving slowly so as not to alarm the wolves. Fearn urged Gorri forward into the middle of the circle.

Warily, nostrils flaring at the wolf-stink, Gorri walked on. The she-wolf whined softly and backed away.

Sarmatia wiped her hands on her dress and rose. She had nothing to say to a man who could wear a scarlet cloak made for him by Anoi.

A figure ran into the closing gap between them, arms raised. 'Fearn, you've come for me! Why don't you look at me?'

But Fearn took no notice except to tear off his cloak and cast it at Anoi's feet. He nudged Gorri closer to Sarmatia and spoke to her softly in Kretan, so that only they would understand.

'Let me start by saying sorry, Sarmatia. You seemed so cold, so unmoved by the loss of our child ,as Anoi was swift to point out. I've dealt with you unfairly.'

This was part of what she wanted to hear, yet Sarmatia's old obstinacy surfaced. She tilted her chin proudly. Recalling Anoi's claim that Fearn had lain with her, she was determined not to forgive too quickly. 'Time will work for us, perhaps.'

Fearn's face blazed, but he would not give up yet. 'Can there be no peace between us, Sarmatia?'

Not if you mated with Anoi. Sarmatia would not speak and said nothing of Carvin, of the fear that her unborn child had been touched by Carvin's spirit. Thunder dinned in her ears. Fearn was off Gorri's back and holding her.

'Feel them, Sarmatia. These arms have known no other but you.' His grip was so fierce that it hurt her. The butt end of his axe drove against her shoulder blade. His whole body seemed to burn. 'Go, then,' he whispered, 'but only for now.'

Strong hands lifted her onto the stallion, and a slap on his withers sent Gorri amongst the people. The she-wolf followed and stretched out beneath the head of the horse, allowing Gorri's breath to stir the pale stripe of fur along her spine. Sarmatia looked sideways about the circle. Bride was easy to spot, but there were many men between them. She grinned at Sarmatia, raising her hand in a lazy salute.

'Just like the funeral of the Plains-King, eh, Bull Rider?' she called, clearly her old self again and no respecter of place or occasion.

The same circle, the same quiet rows of people, the same still heat and sense of death. Bride was right, yet here at Wolfstones there was an eerie difference. Sarmatia had no name for it: power, fate, spirit, the wolves—it was all of these and more. The hairs on the back of her neck lifted.

Laerimmer was accusing her and Anoi. 'There needs to be a judgment,' he finished. 'Perhaps even against your queen.'

Sarmatia flicked Gorri's sides with her heels to return to the circle, but at a sign from Fearn, two men on either side of the horse caught hold of his thick mane and kept him back.

'Let's hear first what Anoi has to say,' said Fearn.

Anoi took several swift steps closer to Fearn and picked up his discarded cloak. 'I'll keep this for you,' she said softly.

'As you wish.'

Anoi laughed as though his answer pleased her. She swept the cloak about her own shoulders and walked about, addressing the people.

'Warriors and tribesmen, I speak to you as one who is royal by birth. You all know me. I was born and bred in this country. Like you, I'm fair of hair and skin. Look upon me and upon the creature the Kingmaker has seen fit to crown. Ask yourselves who has been bewitched.'

There was a silence in which no man would look at his neighbor. Laerimmer drew in breath to speak, but again Fearn put up his hand.

'Go on, Anoi. Let the people judge. You must have been a long time waiting for this moment.'

The way he spoke then told Sarmatia that if Anoi had ever had Fearn, she had lost him now. Perhaps Anoi sensed this too. She shrugged off the cloak and ran towards the crowd.

'Give me a dagger and let me kill this evil! Look at her cohorts, the wolves that tear our sheep and destroy our livelihood! Look at her familiar, a giant who has made another of the royal family her slave. How could such a gross and ugly female charm any man, except by witchcraft?'

'I'll pay you for that, too, bitch!' muttered Bride, but her words went unheeded in the general din. Anoi had darted into the crowd and dragged Ormson out into the circle.

'Tell them how southerners deal with their children and leave them out in the wilderness to die.' She thrust the man forward with her hands. 'Speak!'

Ormson peered at Anoi through his shocks of ginger hair. 'Yes, I know,' he said thickly. 'I know what tale you made of it, too, Anoi, that time beside the midden heap, when the royal family were in our house and you told me what you'd heard. But I'll not be your mouth or your hands again. Who do you think it was that brought Laerimmer's message to Fearn?'

He flung off her placating hand and went to Sarmatia, going down on one knee to her. 'I've been following you,' he said, gruffly. 'I lost your trail at the river and wasted time. The excitement was over here, when I got out of the woods. Laerimmer saw me and waved me back. He didn't have to tell me to find a horse and make sure that word got to the King.'

Ormson's voice grew even thicker. 'It was me that put those things in your bed, but I swear I never meant to harm you. I can't say why I did it now, except that I've been a fool. I hope I've served you better now.'

Sarmatia smiled and leant down from Gorri, over the back of the she-wolf, and touched the man's ruddy forehead. She had not the slightest idea of what Ormson was talking about, but she knew what she should say. 'Indeed, Ormson, you've traveled far. As for your service, you've already helped me by your faithful serving of the King.'

At that reply, Fearn smiled, but Sarmatia herself did not know how greatly she had changed from the silent child he had first met on Krete. She was watching Ormson and listening to the crowd. When the man glanced up at her, and the circle of watchers did not laugh at the look of wonder on his face, she knew that it was time.

Motioning Ormson aside, Sarmatia spurred Gorri and the she-wolf forward. Ormson and the two Atterians who had grabbed at the stallion's mane walked on either side as her escorts. They went into the circle and Sarmatia spoke.

'Ormson has learned what you have not, Anoi. Though I'm dark and a stranger, I am Queen. I've been tested by your goddess on the Sacred Hill. Don't think that you're more worthy of the diadem!'

'Is a murderess worthy of the crown? Even the Kingmaker doubts you.' Anoi started towards Fearn, read the grim expression on his face and whipped back to Laerimmer. 'Kinsman, you know what you saw,' she said cajolingly. 'Tell the people. Tell the people how my betrothed—my poor Dill!—has been stabbed. Tell them how that woman has "lost" her dagger.'

'Not so, Anoi,' broke in Fearn. 'I have it here, with me.' He took

Sarmatia's dagger from his belt, holding it aloft. 'Do you recognize this, Kingmaker?'

Laerimmer looked long and hard at the dagger and then at the paling Anoi. 'I know it as Sarmatia's,' he answered slowly, 'and now I know nothing of what Anoi is saying.

'Tell me, Anoi,' he said in softer tones, 'Did you wear that boy's tunic when you spoke to the spice trader? "A youth with blue eyes". That's how the trader described the boy who bartered him the golden torc which has brought Sarmatia so much trouble. Dill's eyes are brown. I made sure of that when I looked at him first, but yours, my dear, are a deep, deep blue.'

'Kinsman, how can you say such things?'

'You've been found out, Anoi, by your own words,' continued the Kingmaker implacably. 'You said that Dill was stabbed by the Queen, and I thought that strange, for his wound is not a stab but a cut, which slopes downwards. That is because it was someone smaller than Dill who slashed open his throat.'

Suddenly, in a gesture of both anger and frustration, Laerimmer seized Anoi's shoulders and shook her. 'Tell the truth, woman, you've nothing to lose! You've already shamed our family!'

There was no sound from Anoi but quickened breathing. Her blue eyes scanned Laerimmer's face, traveled quickly to Fearn, back again to the Kingmaker. 'He tried to rape me. Dill was strong. I had to use my knife to defend myself.'

She began to cry. Laerimmer released his grip on her shoulders and Anoi wept softly into her hands.

'Rape is evil and the man who attempts it is vile,' said Laerimmer slowly, 'But your answer does not explain why you accused Sarmatia of your own deed.' He took hold of Anoi's hands and withdrew them from her face.

'I was ashamed,' the girl whispered. 'I feared you'd not believe me. I was mad with fear.' She slewed round to Sarmatia. 'I've not been myself these past days. Forgive me.'

Her blue eyes were desperate. She was like a bird beating its wings on the bars of a cage. Sarmatia looked at Anoi and forgot Waroch, the fire, the crocodile torc. She remembered Carvin, how he had raped her. No woman lies about rape. She leaned across the she-wolf's head a second time, stretching out her hands to Anoi.

* * * *

'They are bewitched. Gods, they must be!' Bride watched in disbelief. In another moment, Anoi would be in Sarmatia's arms, and it seemed everything would be forgiven and forgotten. Bride had a sudden, terrible vision of Dill meeting his end like this, going trusting into Anoi's embrace, not seeing the knife.

'Ours is a magic family,' said Goar. 'And as I've said, deception is Anoi's skill. She fooled us all for years, even Fearn and Laerimmer thought she had no power.' Anoi had fixed her enchantment on those within the circle, so Goar was free to swing down from his pony and interrupt the frozen tableau.

'Sarmatia!' he bawled. 'Anoi murdered Waroch!'

* * * *

Sarmatia started. The crowd gasped. The spell of Anoi's suffering vanished like a dream. Sarmatia saw the girl's eyes glitter and flinched, but the venom was not directed at her.

'Beware of what you say, Goar!' shrieked Anoi. 'You know the power I have.'

Goar made a courtly bow, making light of his danger. 'Thank you for that reminder, cousin. Are you quite sure that your power is what it once was?'

Anoi threw him a knowing look. 'Perhaps not,' She glanced at Bride, a look which said *you should be dead*. Her gaze swung back to Goar, a disappointment in many ways, and yet there was still this: 'But your whore didn't carry the thing to its birth, did she?' Bride and Goar had succeeded in deceiving her, but Anoi's faith in her curse remained strong.

In that belief at least she was not alone.

'Say no more!' Bride's voice cracked in the heavy air as she stumbled from her horse. 'Goar, don't speak!'

Goar shook his head. 'Do you remember, love, when you told me to be a man? That time has come. I can be a youth no longer.' He walked to her, touching her check. 'Don't cry, Bride. My time's here.'

Fearn looked from Goar to Bride. 'Have you proof for what you say?'

Goar colored under his steady gaze and said nothing.

'You know I can't condemn without proof,' Fearn continued, and, as Goar drew breath to make the ultimate confession—for which his own death would be the proof—Fearn's eyes flashed, and he said quickly, 'I'll take no more argument from you!'

Bride and Sarmatia groaned. Bride in relief, Sarmatia from despair. It seemed impossible to bring Anoi to justice.

Then Laerimmer stepped back, planting his hands upon his hips. 'Fearn!' he shouted, startling the wolves that milled about him. 'Let Anoi and myself endure the Sky God ritual. I accuse her of murder, sorcery, and of ill-wishing the Queen. Have the people see who is the first to run.'

At his words, a deep murmur ran round the circle of watchers. Anoi's face went white. 'If I submit to this, so must the southerner.'

'I'm willing,' said Sarmatia at once.

'So be it.' Fearn sighed.

By this time it was early evening. A pall of dark clouds had gathered over the Sacred Hill. The sun hung over the eastern hills like a bloodstained shield. Fearn looked up at the sky.

'The God will come here when I summon him and we must be ready. Each of you strip off your gold, your silver and bronze. The Sky God does not like the gleam of metal on others.'

He lifted the bronze diadem from his head and laid it on the grass. 'Pile your ornaments here together. Give it to the earth for safekeeping. Quickly!'

At his command, Atterians broke their circle and came to heap their metal broaches, swords, arrows, arm-rings and finger-rings upon the King's diadem. Sarmatia watched Laerimmer take off his golden throat disc and glanced down at her own bronze ring, reluctant to remove it. Looking up, she saw Fearn walking towards her.

'Must I take off my ring?' she asked in Kretan as he reached her. Fearn answered in the same tongue.

'I fear so, Sarmatia.' He looked at her. Men were still gathered about the growing heap of metal. He and Sarmatia had a moment together.

'What is this ritual?'

'Nothing you need fear, Sarmatia. The Sky God knows our hearts. He does not touch those who are innocent. Twice now as King I've been asked to do this rite. The God may take some of our metal as sacrifice and payment, but that's a small thing for the truth.'

Sarmatia took off her bronze ring and gave it to Fearn. 'You must put this with the rest, Fearn. I can't.' Then, although she already sensed the answer, she asked, 'Is the Sky God the same whose shrine is the Great Stone Circle?'

'It's the same God. And this is the rite the southern kingdoms have forgotten.' He turned and left her.

The last piece of metal was dropped onto the hoard and the people scattered over Wolfstones, some to the shelter of the stones themselves and others to patches of scabious or bracken.

Sarmatia slid from Gorri's back and saw the horse taken away from Wolfstones with the ponies. She scanned the seemingly deserted plateau, lingering briefly on a small crop of pink primroses where Bride and Goar crouched hand in hand. Bride had briskly wiped away her tears and recovered the bow that Anoi had dropped. She had her own bigger bow slung over one shoulder.

'Sarmatia?' Fearn's voice brought her gaze round to him. 'I promise that nothing shall touch you. Will you stay near me?'

It was a simple question, yet Sarmatia felt the stiffness leave her body and spirit. Suddenly she did not care what Fearn and Anoi might have done, because Fearn doubted her no more. Even before the ritual. She ran across the grass and went to him, lifting her head up to his broad face. There was no need for words.

Under Fearn's instructions, the two men and women that remained made a small circle round the hoard of gold and bronze and linked hands. Sarmatia stood between Fearn and Laerimmer. Anoi clutched Fearn's hand, but would not take the Kingmaker's. Fearn bent his head. His lips moved in prayer.

Clouds rolled towards Wolfstones and he opened his eyes.

'Move back to the distance of a spear-cast. The Sky God approaches. When he is here, stand in the light of the God, true as a pillar of stone. Release your hands.'

Fearn dragged on Sarmatia's fingers before he freed her so that she stood closer to him than the others. Sarmatia put her arms down by her sides. She was vaguely aware of Fearn and Laerimmer. Her mouth was dry, but she was not afraid.

The sky grew darker, a midsummer evening changed into midnight. A spot of water splashed down her cheek and then another. Fearn lifted the axe and smashed the stone head into the earth at his feet. He invoked the Sky God and thunder cracked. Wind flayed through Sarmatia's hair. The wolf pack howled as the axe fell again. A spill of lightning ran over Wolfstones, bathing the hill in a bluish glare. Fearn was singing, the song lost in the storm. His red hair streamed back, the muscles of his upper arms tightened as he raised the axe right over his head.

Lightning fell like a hammer blow into their circle. Sarmatia felt its scorching power rush up her body and the voice of the God boomed in her head. She covered her dazzled eyes and heard Fearn shout.

He stood in the lightning like a thing of fire himself, rain smoking off his axe and casting a flickering halo of silver about his limbs. Here was the hidden power of the Great Stone Circle, the mastery of lightning and storm. No wonder Laerimmer had been afraid to answer when she had asked him what magic Fearn possessed. No wonder that Fearn kept such rein on his anger, or that the trial for his kingship had been a test of patience.

Sarmatia took her hands away from her face. Earth and sky were a blaze of colors. Lightning forked twice over the gray forests. The place where the metal and her bronze ring had lain was a blackened hole. She stared at it in awe as Fearn called and the wind seemed to answer, whipping softly round her heels. The wolves crept back through the rain, eyes and teeth glittering in the semi-darkness. Thunder sounded, drawing closer, and Fearn braced his feet for another blow.

It never came. Anoi stumbled, ran, and cast herself at Fearn's feet. She was screaming and begging him to stop the storm. Even over the din of thunder she could clearly be heard. Her voice was shrill. Words tumbled from her lips, revealing a sad story of murder and grief.

To stop Fearn leaving the kingdom she had fired the royal homestead and killed Waroch. It had been easy, when the household slept, to drag the drugged king to a dark corner, to climb the loom—she could climb anything—and grease it and the roof with sheep fat. One touch of the flint-spark, and what a blaze!

The affair of the torc was even simpler. She'd had it from Dill, after she said she would marry him, and then bartered the torc to the trader. He had accomplished the rest, although the southerner ought to have perished already, through the arrow, or the meat-hook. Had she, Anoi, been allowed to leave with the war band, the matter could have been resolved last winter, but no matter. The miscarriage showed that Sarmatia was unfit to be queen. And yes, Dill had had to die: looting from the dead was a serious crime. Fearn should thank her, yes, he should!

Anoi's voice rose suddenly to a spine-chilling shriek. 'Are you all so perfect, my royal kinsmen? Laerimmer who bribes, Goar who despises, Chalda who flaunts? Are you so godlike, so very just? Is it you who can condemn me?'

She was silent. The only sound was the rain, relentlessly bombarding the earth. People who had been moving back to Wolfstones stopped, uneasily shifting their feet. Sarmatia looked at Anoi and tried to suppress a shiver. She knew, very well, what Anoi's 'resolution' would have meant for her, had the Atterian girl come south to Carvin's kingdom.

She looked at Fearn. Standing above the prostrate figure of Anoi, he seemed aged. He bent down and hauled his cousin to her feet.

'Did you hate Waroch so much that you could murder him in cold blood?' he demanded. 'And the lad, who loved you? Why?'

Anoi gave him her gentlest smile. 'Don't you know, Fearn, after this morning? Haven't you guessed, these long years? Oh, can't you see?' she cried impatiently. 'With Waroch gone you would be king. I knew you would be made king! I would be queen, as is my birthright. And I wanted you, I've always wanted you and never had you!'

Again Anoi screamed and Sarmatia shut her eyes, ashamed now that she had ever doubted Fearn. She felt for her young husband.

The color had drained from his face. He was as white as a drowned man. He passed a hand over his eyes and for the last time his thoughts went out to Sarmatia as they had done before, through the burning vision of the Sky God, reaching her as though he had spoken them aloud.

Some of the blame must be mine. I knew she had a fondness for me. I rejected her.

He had been attracted to Anoi, but that morning in the barn had finally settled Fearn's relationship to his little cousin. For years he had thought of her as being better than himself, almost better than Sarmatia. Now he knew that Anoi was worse than both of them. Anoi had ended so many lives. His own and Sarmatia's in Krete. Briht and Tanek, Dill and Waroch, all dead. It shamed him that he had never questioned the way in which Waroch had died, that he had never troubled to consider it. He remembered the night he had won his kingship, when he had been furious with the family for leaving Anoi to grieve Tanek's death alone. Had they sensed more of Anoi's true nature then than he had?

Fearn recalled how, as soon as Anoi had joined the war band, Laerimmer had learned of their secret meetings. When he thought of how Anoi had pleaded to go with them to rescue Sarmatia, he blushed.

It shamed Fearn too that the archer in the woods had been Anoi. He had thought that threat was directed at himself and had tried to expose it, working alone and seeking to draw the bow-man out. In this, as he now realized, he'd given himself too much importance. It was Sarmatia who had been in danger, and he had done nothing to protect her. Yet what could be done with Anoi?

It will kill her mother if I harm Anoi. What should I do?

* * * *

In the pouring rain the crowd stirred restlessly. The leader of the pack lifted up his head and howled again, the mournful sound echoing across the hilltop. The sky was dark, thunder still rolling and reverberating in the distance, although the storm was passing, the horizon lightening.

Sarmatia rubbed at her face, surprised to find it dried in the air. She felt drained, the elation of the storm giving way to weariness, but she must think. If Fearn was troubled at killing a woman, she need not be. She could even set the wolves on Anoi, have them tear her apart. Her spirit animal was ready. She need just let go.

But what then? What would follow the killing frenzy? And what would happen to her friendship with the wolves, after she had forced them to prey on another human being?

No, slaying Anoi would not bring Dill or Waroch back to life. The girl was already broken, half out of her mind. That, and Sarmatia's concern for Fearn, with hard choices to make and no one willing to counsel him, made her speak:

'Let it end here,' she said, still uncertain as to how it could finish. 'I thought Anoi was my friend. She was one of the first to bid me welcome. I was wrong, yet even so, I pity her.'

Anoi stiffened, her eyes suddenly refocusing. Back erect, head held high, she glared Sarmatia. 'Do you dare? You're not fit—'

Suddenly she lurched forward and buckled at the knees, her hair falling over her face in a golden shroud. Fearn shouted and went down on one knee, rolling Anoi over on the grass. Her eyes were open, brightly blue, staring and surprised. Her face was unmarked, beautiful as ever, but her body was bathed in blood. A bronze-tipped arrow, still quivering from its flight, was embedded in her throat.

Gasps broke from the people. Heads were turning, eyes searching for the bowman. Yet surely only one person could have fired that arrow, only one who served such justice without a qualm. It was with no sense of surprise that Sarmatia turned and saw Bride standing straight and tall on the plateau of Wolfstones. Motionless she waited, her bow already notched with another arrow. She looked exactly what she was: an experienced warrior, ready to attack or defend.

'Murderess!' cried Laerimmer, shocked that any commoner should strike at the royal family, 'It's forbidden by our goddess for us to kill a woman. Why have you done this?'

'By right.' Bride planted her feet more deeply into the soil, as though daring the goddess to do her worst. Her birthmark was livid, her eyes blazed.

'Anoi did not tell the half of it!' she cried, shaking the bow before her like a challenge. 'She'd have poisoned your queen before her test, had I not taken the flask from her hand. I drank it myself, as Sarmatia can witness, then I was sick.'

'Yes, and nearly died,' said Goar, glaring at the Kingmaker, 'and if that does not satisfy you or Fearn, and you have any further objections, Laerimmer, then address them to me.'

Goar stalked forward, pulling Bride behind him. The woman he was defending was as tall as he was and broader in the shoulders, but the crowd did not laugh. Bride was proud of him.

'Enough,' said Fearn wearily. 'There's nothing to be said.'

'Yet so violent an act!' protested Laerimmer.

Goar reached for Bride's hand and their fingers gripped in a living tie.

'You heard the King, Laerimmer, now hear me. Here is my woman and I'll keep her.'

He hadn't asked her, but that didn't matter. Bride was in full agreement. Anoi's curse was dead at their feet and she was eager to enjoy the fruits of victory. She squeezed Goar's hand and drew close to whisper. 'Let's make a real child this time, eh?'

They turned as one and left the hill.

* * * *

Slowly, after Bride and Goar, other men and women began to leave. The horses were brought, and Atterians made their way home without a backward glance. The wolves slipped between the boulders of Wolfstones and disappeared silently into the rain. In a few moments, all of the beasts and people were gone, leaving Laerimmer, Fearn and Sarmatia alone.

It was over.

Chapter 59

After Anoi and Dill were buried Fearn was quiet. When Laerimmer suggested that he and Sarmatia might stay at the royal house, Fearn had agreed without argument. It marked an end to the long dispute between the King and his royal cousins, although Sarmatia sensed that such thoughts were far from his mind. He was like a man stunned.: His spirits were subdued. He spent his time huddled by the fire, hands idle in his lap.

Remembering herself after Carvin's death, Sarmatia was gentle with him. A few days after the storm she came to the hearth and touched his wrists with her fingers. 'Gei has died.' An innocent victim, and in that the saddest death of all. She kissed his cheek and went on with her work. She was bringing order to the house and so had a great many tasks.

Three days later, she ran to the hearth. 'Bride is to remake my Bull Riding things! She likes her lapis jewelery, too. Says the workmanship's superb.'

Fearn smiled at her excitement. 'So Goar has told me.' There was a look upon his face that made Sarmatia softly laugh.

That night marked the end of the time that she and Fearn must sleep apart, and Sarmatia persuaded the young king to go outside. They walked hand in hand round the wooded summit of Laerimmer's home, watching the moonlight.

'I'm sorry for these last days,' Fearn told her. 'The Sky God rite drains me, but never so much as this time. It was the shock of Anoi.'

Sarmatia brought his hand up to her lips and kissed it. Here, then, she thought, was the reason the Atterians had not wished Fearn to be both healer and king. The ritual of summoning the storm took so much power.

'I knew Anoi had an affection for me,' Fearn was saying, and then he rubbed at his beard. 'I always tried to be gentle with her. I did not know she was so obsessed, that she would do what she did.' He stopped walking and looked down at Sarmatia, his face grave in the moonlight. 'I'll never forgive myself. It's my fault you were put in danger from her. After that meeting in the barn, when you'd broken from me, Anoi came. She offered herself. I refused her. Perhaps if I hadn't, she would not have gone mad. Dill might be alive.'

'Dill was already dead,' answered Sarmatia bluntly, impatient at all these doubts. 'A king must live with the threat of assassins and so must a queen. And I am queen of the Atterians.'

She felt Fearn's hand tighten in hers, then, with a sudden rough urgency, he pulled her into his arms and kissed her.

'This last month I've almost gone mad, seeing you and never able to touch,' he said, after a long embrace. 'And you seemed so cold, so shy.'

Despite her best intentions, Sarmatia stiffened. But it was time for the truth. 'My miscarriage—Ormson was right, I didn't grieve long. I feared the child was somehow touched by Carvin's spirit.'

There, it was said. Sarmatia shut her eyes, but Fearn did not draw back. He took her chin gently in his hand.

'Don't be afraid, Sarmatia. For certain the next one will be ours: totally.' Suddenly, the moment was too much and he laughed. 'You've some very strange ideas of childbearing, Bull Head. Some very strange ideas. Did your mother never speak to you about these things?'

'You've forgotten, Fearn. My mother died when I was a baby.'

'Then perhaps you'd better talk to Maewe.' Fearn was still chuckling when they returned indoors.

That following morning, Sarmatia rode out to see Gei buried. Returning to the royal homestead, she went first to Wolfstones. There at the bottom of the blackened pool left by the lightning bolt, she discovered Fearn's diadem and her own bronze ring. The diadem had buckled and fused with the gold breastplate of the Kingmaker, but the ring was unharmed. Sarmatia placed it on her finger and left the rest of the metal. She would give Fearn her diadem, at last a gift from her to him.

Halfway up the knoll to Laerimmer's house, Sarmatia found that she had lost the path and neither she nor Gorri could remember the Kingmaker's directions. She cupped her hands to shout up to the house when Fearn came dashing through the gorse. He leapt onto the stallion behind Sarmatia and put his lips to her ear.

'Come on!' He was as excited as a boy.

'Where are we going?' asked Sarmatia, as Fearn deftly guided Gorri back down the gorse pathways.

But she knew it really didn't matter. They were as they had been so long before on Krete, with no shadows or fear between them. In the years ahead, whatever troubles were before them, Sarmatia knew that she and Fearn would meet them united, as equal partners: King and Queen.

Together.

THE END

http://lindsaysbookchat.blogspot.com

ABOUT THE AUTHOR

Lindsay lives in Yorkshire, England, where she was born, and started writing stories at an early age. Always a voracious reader, she took a degree in medieval history and worked in a library for a while, then began to write full-time after marriage.

Her first unpublished historical found her an agent and the second got a publisher in London interested. They wanted her to write with a modern setting, which she did – several romantic thrillers set in Greece, Italy or on Dartmoor in the English West Country - and enjoyed it, but historicals are really her first love. For Bookstrand, Lindsay has written books mostly set in the ancient world, especially Rome, Egypt and the Bronze Age, which have always fascinated her.

When not writing or researching her books, she enjoys walking, reading, cooking, music, going out with friends and long languid baths with scented candles (and perhaps chocolate).

Her other historical titles with Bookstrand are:

FLAVIA'S SECRET - sensual historical romance set in Roman Britain. 4.5 Red Roses and Blue Ribbons. 4 Books. Book of the Week at LASR 4 Stars.

A SECRET TREASURE - romantic suspense set on Rhodes. The perfect holiday read. 5 Stars. 5 Angels. 4.5 Red Roses. 4Cups. 4 Books. 4 Bookmarks.

BLUE GOLD – historical adventure romance set in ancient Egypt.

Lindsay's website is http://www.lindsaytownsend.com.
and her blog is http://lindsaysbookchat.blogspot.com.

BookStrand

www.BookStrand.com

Lightning Source UK Ltd.
Milton Keynes UK
172509UK00008B/91/P